. . . I know nothing but this body, nothing
But that old vehement, bewildering kiss.

—W. B. YEATS

DANIEL EASTERMAN

BROTHERHOOD
OF THE TOMB

DOUBLEDAY

NEW YORK LONDON TORONTO SYDNEY AUCKLAND

PUBLISHED BY DOUBLEDAY
a division of Bantam Doubleday Dell Publishing Group, Inc.
666 Fifth Avenue, New York, New York 10103

DOUBLEDAY and the portrayal of an anchor
with a dolphin are trademarks of Doubleday,
a division of Bantam Doubleday Dell
Publishing Group, Inc.

Library of Congress Cataloging-in-Publication Data

Easterman, Daniel.
Brotherhood of the tomb/by Daniel Easterman.—1st ed.
p.   cm.
I. Title.
PS3555.A697B7   1990
813'.54—dc20   89-49463
CIP

ISBN 0-385-24178-x

For my parents, David and Isobel, for forty years of patience.
And for Beth: don't give up, I may have another forty in me yet!

And a special dedication for Sammy, who tried to sabotage discs,
papers, and author in a manner best known to himself and other cats.

ACKNOWLEDGMENTS

Several people have helped enormously with this book. As always, I want to thank my agent, Jeffrey Simmons, for his encouragement, suggestions, and unfailing good humor. Patricia Parkin at Grafton contributed several excellent ideas. Jeremy and Nicoletta Johns were indefatigable sources of information, humor, and good Italian. Dr. John Healey of Durham University did wonders with Aramaic. Damien O'Muiri improved on my Irish. Eveleen Coyle enlivened my stay in Dublin and did some formidable checking of facts afterward. My wife Beth read the manuscript innumerable times with a keen eye and a keener intelligence. To everyone, many, many thanks.

GHOSTS

PROLOGUE

Giv'at ha-Mivtar, North Jerusalem
October 1968

The tombs had always been there. Aloof at first, then hidden, then lost entirely—a secret place where death went about his business unseen and uninterrupted. For centuries, the city had been remote, almost irrelevant. The living had become the dead, their mourners had in turn been mourned, and always the fields of death had been left strictly to themselves. No one had built his house over them or set his plow to their earth or put his sheep to graze among them.

In the city, there had been fire and famine. Armies had passed by. High towers had fallen, the sun had turned to blood, ashes had drifted on the wind like black snow at the end of winter. And new gods had come to dwell on the ruins of the Temple.

A year ago, the old God had returned in battle. Israeli armies had taken East Jerusalem, hurling their Arab opponents back across the Jordan. The *shofar* had been blown beside the Temple Mount once more. Now bulldozers were nuzzling the ancient hills, digging out roads, clearing the ground to make way for houses and schools and hospitals. The descendants of the dead had come to claim their heritage.

In the previous month, a bulldozer had been nibbling its way into a hill called Giv'at ha-Mivtar, just to the west of the Nablus Road, when one of the workmen saw the first tomb. There were three in all, grouped together on separate levels. One was accessible only from the roof, its entrance having already been covered by the new road that was being laid. A fourth tomb had come to light later, far to the west of the others.

A team of archaeologists from the Department of Museums and Antiquities had been given a month in which to examine the tombs and their contents. At the end of that period, in a few days' time in fact, the bones were to be returned to their sarcophagi and reburied. Then the bulldozers and rollers would return, tar and concrete would be poured in molten streams, and the dead would sleep again, while all round them the living scurried about in a sleepless and inarticulate dream.

Gershon Aharoni stumbled, swore beneath his breath, and turned to the man behind him.

"Be careful, there's a bit of a step here," he said, forcing a smile, holding a helping hand toward the Italian. He had to bite back his annoyance, his irritation at being here at all. There was urgent work to do back at the museum, and little enough time to do it in. He could thump Kaplan for having given him this assignment.

"Do your best, Gershon. Show him round. Get him interested. Let him poke about a bit, get his hands dirty, find an artifact. Plant something where he can stumble over it, make him feel involved. But for God's sake, soften him up. If you need to, tell him we expect to find the remains of Jesus, the Virgin Mary, and all twelve apostles any day now. And John the Baptist's head and Salome's tits if he looks gullible enough.

"But get him in the mood to spend some money. Big money: enough for a research foundation, a new museum. Let him use his imagination, if he's got one. The Bishop Migliau Trust for Biblical Archaeology—let him try that on for size. He can have it in ten-foot-high letters if it turns him on. Just get him to my office tomorrow morning looking like a man who signs checks for a living."

"Thank you. It is darker here than I thought it would be," said the bishop, resting momentarily on Aharoni's hand, like a reluctant dancer being led to the floor.

Aharoni swung the lamp high, shedding a sulphurous light across the loculi, long, narrow shafts cut deep into the walls of the chamber to serve as burial niches, some for whole bodies, others for limestone ossuaries that sometimes held the bones of an entire family.

"We'll have the generator working again in the morning. If you prefer, we can come back then." *And let me get back to my pots for the rest of this evening.*

It was dark outside. The workmen across the road had gone home. No one had been on the dig since four o'clock, when the generator that powered the lamps had packed up. Since there was in any case plenty of work to do back at the institute, recording and measuring finds, photographing artifacts, and reconstructing pots, everyone had gone back there. A technician would be sent out early next morning to get the lights working again. In the meantime, Aharoni used a hurricane lamp to show their guest round the empty tombs.

"No, I am very happy. I think perhaps it is more exciting like this, more . . . authentic."

Bishop Giancarlo Migliau was a big man, over six feet tall, and all in all he made a presence in the tomb. He was in his mid-forties, a lean, sublimated man, all flesh without substance, heavy boned but light in his bearing, as though his body did not belong entirely in the space it occupied. He hung in the chamber, as it were, filling it, not by bulk but by the simple fact of his being there. And he awoke memories in Aharoni of a scarecrow standing in a field after a storm, its black arm casting a ragged shadow on rows of sodden corn.

He was a rich man, descended from a family of Venetian aristocrats, one of the few that had not faded into obscurity or died off entirely in the eighteenth century. His distant ancestors had been Jews, but from the time of their first ennoblement they had given offspring to the Church. Giancarlo's brothers followed in that other family tradition of banking, dealing no longer from trestle tables on the Rialto but out of astonishing marble office blocks in Mestre, Rome, and Milan.

Giancarlo had for years now been a passionate amateur of biblical archaeology. He attended conferences whenever he was able, contributed occasional papers to the more popular Catholic journals, and gave liberally from his personal fortune to endow research fellowships in the field. At least one month of every year he spent in Israel, visiting archaeological sites, touring museums, and meeting scholars at the Franciscan Institute of Archaeology in Jerusalem.

On several occasions, he had helped out at digs, wielding a trowel and soft-bristled brush, uncovering fragments of pots and lamps to be handed over to the experts for cleaning and assessment. They had been in the main sites dating from New Testament times, places where he could lay his hands on an artifact as it came up out of the clay and think to himself: *This pot was here when Jesus lived on earth,* or put his feet on a stretch of pavement and whisper: "Perhaps Jesus walked here, on these very stones."

His imagination had been stirred by the discovery of the tombs at Giv'at ha-Mivtar. As far as could be ascertained, they contained burials dating from between the first century B.C. and the destruction of the Second Temple in A.D. 70. The work of clearing them had been too specialized and urgent to let amateur diggers take part, but he had received permission to pay this visit and to see the contents of the tombs currently being examined at the Israel Museum.

"Is this where you found the bones of the man you think was crucified? The ones I saw back at the museum?"

They were in Tomb I, the largest of the four, in the lower burial chamber, a rectangular space off which radiated a total of eight loculi.

"In here." Aharoni lifted the lamp toward a shaft on the right. "The bones were in an ossuary along with those of a child."

Migliau remembered the bones: two heels transfixed by a large nail, shins that had been shattered by a heavy blow. They had made him giddy with a sort of recognition. The man might very well have been one of the two thieves crucified with Jesus, might have hung on the Mount of Golgotha inches away from the Son of God and the world's redemption. He was close. He felt it in his bones.

"What was he called? Was there a name?"

"Jehohannon. The name was written on the side of the ossuary in Aramaic."

The bishop had touched the bone gently with a finger. There had been a fragment of wood between it and the head of the nail. Roman wood and Roman metal, God's bane. It felt warm in the tomb and close, as though the air had not been changed in centuries.

"And the child. Was it his child?"

Aharoni shook his head. The lamp flickered. Shadows wormed their way across the roughly hewn rock walls.

"No. The child was named Jehohannon as well. But his inscription reads: "Jehohannon, the son of Hagaqul." At least, that's as far as I've been able to decipher it."

Bishop Migliau sighed. The low-ceilinged chamber seemed to press down on him. He had never been able to bear the thought of death, the knowledge of decay.

"What's over here?" he asked, moving across to the southern wall. "They seem to have left a large space without any niches."

"Yes, we thought that was a little odd. But you have to remember that the tomb was far from full. They weren't obliged to cut more niches. The limestone's very hard in places. When we get to the fourth tomb, you'll see that someone made a start on shafts but gave up."

Migliau ran a hand along the wall.

"I think someone was working here as well," he said. The wall was rough, and sharp in places, as though an adze or a chisel had been used on it. He let his fingers wander over the limestone.

Aharoni came across and swung the lamp upward, shining its light on the wall.

"Yes, I think you're right," he said. It was peculiar. He had not noticed it before, in the harsher light supplied by the generator. But in the muted glow of the hurricane lamp the signs of rough work could be seen quite clearly across a section of wall.

Working together now, the two men traced the lines along which the tool had been worked.

"The marks seem to stop about here," said the bishop, running his fingers along a narrow fissure at about waist level.

"I'd say the cutting was confined to this central section," Aharoni added, marking out an area about three feet square. He ran a finger along the sides, first the left, then the right, on down to the floor. A few pieces of limestone fell to the ground. Bending down, he traced the bottom of the square, then straightened up and stepped away from the wall.

Migliau turned and looked at him. His face was in shadow, his eyes invisible.

"This isn't part of the wall at all," he said. His voice sounded hollow, insubstantial. The thick walls buried it like flesh and bones.

"What do you mean?" The Israeli felt a prickle of excitement stab at his spine.

"It's a block that's been cut out and reinserted, then worked over to conceal the joins. I do not understand. Why have you not seen this before?"

Aharoni knew the answer to that. They had been under so much pressure, rushing against time to do all the obvious jobs: measure the chambers, remove the ossuaries from the loculi, gather up the pieces of lamps and pyriform pots that littered the floor. There had been no time for subtleties.

"We'd better get back to the museum, let the director know. There's maybe just enough time to see what's behind the block, if anything, and if necessary ask for an extension. We could start work on it in the morning."

"But we are here now. You have already told me time is pressing. I think we should at least look at it tonight."

Migliau had never been this close to a discovery before. The digs he had assisted at had all been relatively mundane affairs, the main work already finished by the time he became involved. Now he had a chance to see a new find at first hand, even to rank as its discoverer. Who could tell what might lie behind the block? It might even be what he was looking for. He placed both hands against one edge of the block and began to push.

"I don't think we should . . ." Aharoni fell silent as the sound of stone grating against stone echoed through the chamber.

"Please help me," Migliau called. "The stone is very heavy."

"Let him poke about a bit, get his hands dirty, find an artifact." What the hell. The excitement of discovery was everything. Aharoni was an archaeologist, after all. Such moments came rarely, if at all, in a lifetime. He put the lamp down carefully and stepped to Migliau's side, laying his hands on the heavy stone.

They pushed together, straining their arms and backs, feeling the stone's weight in their legs, a dense, trembling weight that belonged somehow to this place, beneath the earth. The stone moved, a little at first, then, as they got the measure of it, several inches at once. Suddenly, they felt it rock—a fraction only, but enough to show that it was beginning to come free. They pushed harder, veins standing out on their necks, muscles knotting with the strain.

Without warning, the rock flew from their hands and fell back into blackness. A split second later, there was a loud crash, followed by the most absolute of silences. Neither man breathed. A stale smell of long-untasted air crept through the opening into the chamber where they stood. And deep beneath the surface flatness of the stagnant air there lay another smell, an odor of spices, elusive, intangible, mournful. It seemed to touch them for a moment, then it was gone.

Aharoni lifted the lamp and held it into the dark aperture. A million shadows seemed to crowd round it. He leaned forward into the opening, squinting into the darkness. When he spoke at last, his voice was muffled and tense.

"I think we've found another tomb."

II

Aharoni was the first to enter. He trod carefully, holding the lamp nervously in front, anxious lest he disturb or break anything that might chance to be lying on the floor. The tomb was tiny—smaller than any of the others. But it seemed better finished and tidier. Parts of the walls had been plastered, and the floor had been carefully swept. There were no loculi, just three large limestone sarcophagi in the center of the domed chamber. They were much longer and sturdier than any of the ossuaries found in the other tombs.

Migliau took longer to work his way through the narrow opening. His greater bulk made it a much tighter squeeze, but he made it in the end, very dusty, scraped raw in places, and breathing heavily. At once he sensed it: this was no ordinary tomb that they had stumbled upon. Correction, he thought: that he had stumbled upon.

He stood tensely by the entrance, watching the Israeli as he moved between the coffins, bending to read an inscription, then straightening again, the soft yellow light transforming the harsh limestone to the texture of butter. The bishop wanted to speak, but his mouth felt dry and his tongue would not move.

Finally, Aharoni stood and turned to face the other man.

"I think you should come here," he said. His voice was shaking, and Migliau noticed that the hand in which he held the lamp was also unsteady. The bishop felt something clutch at his heart and squeeze it like a wet sponge. This was no ordinary tomb, these were no ordinary coffins, they contained no ordinary bones. He was certain of it. And his certainty frightened him to the marrow. Something told him that he had found what he had been looking for.

It seemed to him that the distance between the wall and the sarcophagi was the longest he had ever traversed, that it was not mere feet and inches, and not even centuries, but something more tremendous and more internal than any of those.

"What's wrong?" he asked. "Is something wrong?"

Aharoni's face was pale in spite of the yellow light. Migliau wanted to laugh, to cry out, to strike something. His mood was fluctuating wildly. He felt confined in the tiny chamber.

The Israeli licked his lips. He could hear the faint hissing of the lamp. He could hear his own breathing, in and out. The rest was silence. He had not wanted this.

"Can you read Aramaic?" he asked.

"A little . . . Enough to get by on. I'm no scholar, I . . ."

"No matter. I just want you to help me examine these inscriptions, that's all."

"But you've examined them. What do they say?"

Aharoni did not answer. He looked at the Italian enigmatically.

"I think you should take a look at them," he whispered.

The first sarcophagus was a long box with a gabled lid, ornamented with rosettes and incised lines. It was about six feet long and rather over two feet wide. A typical Jewish sarcophagus of the period. An inscription in Hebraic characters ran down one of the long sides.

"Can you read it?" asked Aharoni.

Migliau shook his head. It was nothing more than a box full of bones, he told himself. The flesh had been allowed to rot away, then the bones had been gathered together in a heap and placed in this box. Why should the sight of it disturb him so?

"I'll read it for you. Tell me if you think I'm wrong."

Aharoni bent closer to the inscription, bringing the lamp nearer.

"הדא קבורתא די יעקב בר יוספ רבגא ורעא' *hd' qbwrt' dy y'qb br ywsp rbn' wr'' '* . . . Then there's a couple of words I can't make out, then מן טעם חנניה כהנא רבא ביומיא די באתר מות פהסטס הגמון' הבורתא די בירשלם קטיל *hbwrt' dy byršlm qtyl mn ṭ'm ḥnnyh khn' rb' bywmy' dy b'tr mwt phsṭs hgmwn.'* As far as I can interpret it, it reads: 'The body of James, son of Joseph, guide and shepherd of *something something* flock in Jerusalem. Killed on the orders of the High Priest Ananus in the days after the death of the Procurator Festus.' "

Migliau said nothing. His breath caught tightly in his chest, but he was unable to breathe out. He was no scholar, but he knew enough to understand just what the inscription was about, whose bones it referred to. James, the brother of Jesus, first head of the Christian community in Jerusalem, had been stoned to death with some others in A.D. 62. By decree of the Sanhedrin. On the orders of Ananus.

The bishop did not know what to do. He wanted to weep or shout or find some other means of giving voice to the emotion he felt, but all he could manage was to stare at the stone as though the very sight had struck him dumb. He breathed out at last and reached for Aharoni, grabbing him hard by the upper arm.

"Are you certain?" he demanded.

The Israeli placed a hand on his, dislodging his fingers.

"That hurt," he said. He paused. "No, I'm not certain. The lettering's poor, this light is terrible. But I think I'm right. When you see the other two, you'll understand."

"Understand? Understand what?"

"You'll see." The Israeli stood and went across to the second ossuary. It was simpler than the first, but otherwise of the same design and quality. The outline of a tree had been carved on the lid, but the sides bore no pattern, only a brief inscription. Migliau knew how it would read. He had known for years.

"גרמי מרים אתת יוסף ואם ישוע ואם יעקב שלמא עליה" *grmy mrym 'tt ywsp w'm yšw' w'm y' qb šlm 'lyh*," read Aharoni awkwardly, as though the words refused to surrender themselves to him. " 'The bones of Maryam, wife of Joseph, mother of Jesus and James. Peace be upon her.' "

The light made ghastly shadows all across the walls and ceiling. Migliau thought he could hear them as they moved, like vast black wings flapping in the enclosed space, the wings of blind, outraged birds. He raised a hand as though to ward them off, but they grew still and left him in a vast silence.

"There's one more," said Aharoni, and to Migliau the voice seemed to come from the other end of the universe.

Together, they walked the last few paces to the third and final sarcophagus. It was a thing drained of color, white and delicately carved, yet very solid, as though it was not hollow at all but a single block hewn from living stone. Migliau watched as Aharoni ran a hand lightly along the lid. A row of sharply cut characters struggled for expression in the light.

He read in a slow voice, meticulously pronouncing each word, not with the awkwardness of uncertainty, but with the precision of one who knows exactly what it is he is reading and what it signifies:

"והוא קבור בהדן אתרא למליות כולא ביומינא שלמא עלוהב בשנת ארבע להגומנותה והוא דבחא די יבלא קורבנא די היכלא

יוסף בר מרים די אצטלב מן טעם פנטיום פילטום הגמונא ביהודה
שמי ישוע בר

tmy yšwʿ br ywsp br mrym dy ʾstlb mn ṭʿm pntyws pyltws hgmwnʾ byhwdh bsnt
ʾrbʿ lhgwmnwth whwʾ dbhʾ dy ymlʾ qwrbnʾ dy hyklʾ whwʾ qbwr bhdn ʾtrʾ
lmlywt kwlʾ bywmynʾ slmʾ lwhy.ʾ

He fell silent. Migliau had understood. Not every word, not every syllable, perhaps, but as much as was needful. Aharoni could not bear to look
up, to see him watching him. There was nothing he could do, nothing. He
had read the inscription. It only remained to translate it.

" 'The body of Yeshu, son of Joseph and Maryam, crucified on the
orders of Pontius Pilatus, *praefectus* of Judea, in the fourth year of his
prefectship. He has been made a sacrifice in completion of the Temple
offering. We have laid him in this place at last, in order to give him safe
burial with those of his mother and brother, and with others of his family,
if the Lord grant us the means of their discovery. Peace be upon him.' "

For a long time, neither man spoke. Words were inappropriate, dangerous. Neither man could bear to look the other in the eye, Jew and Gentile,
believer and unbeliever. Two thousand years of misunderstandings stood
between them.

Once, Migliau almost giggled out loud. A terrible tension had taken hold
of him. He felt simultaneously euphoric and appalled, like a child brought
suddenly into the presence of adult matters. In an instant, a lifetime's
doubts had been resolved and transformed to certainty. What had been
mere belief had become knowledge. His search was over. And his mission
was about to begin.

Time passed as though it no longer had any meaning. Finally, Aharoni
broke the silence.

"Bishop Migliau," he whispered, "I think we should go. There may still
be someone working late at the museum. This will have to be reported.
Arrangements will have to be made. You understand that this is . . .
monumental. We must take steps to ensure that news of this discovery is
not leaked prematurely. You do understand? If word got out before there
was time for a proper investigation . . . I think there might be trouble.
Newspapers, television—every newspaper, every television company in the
world! We couldn't cope with that, not without help.

"And there may be political dimensions—do you understand me? Your
Church will naturally demand a say in what happens. No doubt it is excep-
tionally fortunate for them that you are here. But the Orthodox churches
will want their say too. Then the Anglicans. The other Protestants. But
look at the inscriptions, look at the sarcophagi: this is a Jewish tomb.
Doesn't it seem that way to you? You do understand, don't you?"

Aharoni knew that a Catholic bishop was as big a complication as anyone in his position could possibly have feared. Another archaeologist would have appreciated the need for caution, for tact. But Migliau would want to milk this for all it was worth. Aharoni had heard that the bishop was ambitious, that he had expectations of being made a cardinal. To be associated with a discovery of this order would no doubt secure all that and more for him. And he would, of course, want to be sure that his own church had total control over the tombs: they would not want another Holy Sepulchre on their hands.

"No, Dr. Aharoni," said the Italian. He looked up. All his diffidence had evaporated. He was coming to terms with their discovery at a rapid pace. "I don't understand you. I don't see what you're driving at. What you think and what you want are unimportant. I don't think you so much as have a right to be here, let alone to pass opinion about what should or should not be done."

The big man took a step toward Aharoni. In the confined space, he seemed to tower over him. His tension was becoming anger. The Israeli could not understand it.

"Do you want to know what I think?" he went on. "You are a God-hating Jew, that is what I think. You and your kind chose to wander the face of the earth sooner than recognize that your Messiah had come and had been sacrificed for you." He turned and pointed. "There, there in that tomb. The world's sacrifice. But I do not expect you to understand. You stand there and talk of 'political dimensions.' That has always been your way. You would turn God into a plaything."

Migliau's voice was growing guttural and menacing. He felt hemmed in by the walls, and as much threatened as uplifted by what he had found. More than anything, he felt an obscure resentment against Aharoni building in him like a tide. It was irrational, he hardly knew the man, had no reason to fear or hate him, yet it rankled to have him here.

"I think you should leave."

"What . . . ?"

"I think you should get out of here. This is a holy place. I don't expect you to understand that. But I do. You've no right to be here. No right at all."

But that was no good. If the Jew left, he would only bring more back with him. They ran this city now. They would just march into God's inner sanctum with their foul bodies and their foul breath. He hated them for their self-righteousness, for their sanctimonious possession of the land where his Savior had walked. A stiff-necked people, that's what God had called them. *Ye stiffnecked and uncircumcised in heart and ears, ye do always resist the Holy Ghost: as your fathers did, so do ye*—so Stephen had cried out before they stoned him. And now, here they were, about to lay godless hands on the mortal remains of God's son.

"I think we should both leave," said Aharoni. The Italian was overreacting to their discovery. It was understandable. Aharoni, who wasn't even a practicing Jew, let alone a Christian, had been deeply moved by what they had found. He appreciated its emotional charge. That was why he wanted the whole thing handled properly, before the wreckers and sloganizers and opportunists had a chance to move in. With a shudder, he remembered how an American company had offered to market pieces from the wreck of the *Titanic* as paperweights. What would Jesus's bones fetch on the stock exchange?

He took a step forward and put a hand on the big man's arm. Migliau grabbed his wrist and pulled him toward himself.

He knew what he had to do. What God wanted him to do. It was God's will. The Jew wanted to tell the unbelieving world of this place. He could not be allowed to do that. God would not let him.

Migliau looked once into Aharoni's eyes.

"Forgive me," he whispered. But he knew that God had already forgiven him.

He pushed the Israeli hard. Aharoni stumbled backward, losing his balance. He tripped on a hard object and fell, striking his head hard on the sharp corner of the middle sarcophagus. He did not even cry out. There was no time between push and crushing blow, between fall and final agony. Death was instantaneous. Blood streamed across the white stone, bright and gleaming.

Migliau watched the red stain spread and listened to his heart beating in the stillness. He felt the weight of the sepulcher all about him, and the air moving heavily through it without sound. Aharoni lay slumped where he had fallen, a scarlet pool forming beneath him among shadows on the floor.

He lifted the lamp and shone it on the coffins. Aharoni lay unmoving at the Savior's feet. The blood had stopped flowing. Migliau turned and looked at the little opening through which they had entered. There was plenty of time. It would not be too difficult to put the entrance slab back as it had been. He could push it along the floor, up into the first tomb, then tilt it back into the opening.

The generators would provide their harsh lighting again in the morning. No one would ever find the break in the wall. No one would ever know that another tomb existed. It had remained hidden all these years, it would remain hidden now.

In three days, they would rebury the bones of the dead and seal the tomb again. The bulldozers and cement mixers would return to work. Houses would be built, and shops, and car parks. Next year, he would buy the entire development through one of his family's holding companies. He had come into his true inheritance at last.

III

Trinity College, Dublin
October 1968

Her name was Francesca. His friend Liam had told him during Commons one evening. Francesca Contarini, an Italian. Her family lived in Venice, in a golden palace, so Liam said. With servants and painted rooms and a private gondola to go to mass in. She had been sent to Dublin to improve her English, which was already fluent, and to study English and Italian literature. He had been madly in love with her for over two weeks now.

Patrick Canavan had arrived in Dublin five months earlier. He was eighteen, American, and in search of a heritage. Twenty years before, almost to the day, in the summer of 1948, his parents had said goodbye to the city and set off for a new life in America. They had sent him back alone, a sort of ambassador to the past.

He had found its frontiers and outposts everywhere: in the names of streets and theaters; in the river by night, ripening and spreading like a long, thin stain through the heart of the sleeping city; in the voices of beggars on O'Connell Bridge, young pale-faced women with paler babies wrapped in shawls, selling their poverty for the price of a wheaten farl.

The summer had passed like a dream. He had stayed and got drunk on Guinness and cheap red wine, and late one night in August found himself on the beach at Dalkey, kissing his first girl and dreaming that he had found his roots. At eighteen the Celtic twilight seemed full of promise.

The girl had left two weeks later. Kissing on a beach and holding hands while the moon swept over a white sea had been fine enough for the time of year, she said. But those other things he was suggesting would only lead them both as sure as crikey to the fires of hell. He had yet to learn that virgins are Ireland's oldest, largest, and best-organized professional group.

In spite of his disappointment—perhaps even because of it—he decided to stay. The city spoke to him in whispers of things he barely understood. It revealed itself to him slowly, nervously, in quiet, distracted gestures, in unexpected moments of intimacy. Suddenly Brooklyn seemed a universe away, a noisy place full of noisy people.

Once, on a long afternoon as summer drew to its close, he lay on the cricket pitch at the back of Trinity and watched a student fly a red kite against a pale blue sky. The moment entranced him: at eighteen a kite in the wind can seem as substantial as a kiss. At the beginning of September, he enrolled at the College to study Semitic languages.

Autumn was turning to winter now, and an elaborate stillness lay across the gray expanse of Trinity's inner courts. Inside the 1937 Reading Room, a dim, academic light fell across endless rows of books. He sat two tables away from her, glancing up from time to time to catch a furtive glimpse of her face. Even when he looked away again, pretending to read, her image swam across the page: long, dark hair falling in a stream against her shoulder, gray eyes opening in the book-warm half-light, small white teeth pressed against her lower lip, the slope of tiny breasts against thin fabric.

Strictly speaking, he should not have been here, but in the main library. The Reading Room was reserved for literature students, and it had no books on his own subject. But a large part of Ireland's attraction for him lay in the country's literature, which he had begun to discover. He had already become a regular theatergoer, attending performances at the Abbey, the Peacock, and the Gate. On one occasion he'd traveled up to Belfast to see a trilogy of plays by Yeats, directed by Mary O'Malley at the tiny Lyric Theater.

Now he was reading Yeats's collected poems, partly because they matched his romantic mood, but mainly because they gave him an excuse to sit in the 1937 Reading Room stealing glances at a girl he might never meet. He looked at the page.

> O cloud-pale eyelids, dream-dimmed eyes
> The poets labouring all their days
> To build a perfect beauty in rhyme
> Are overthrown by a woman's gaze.

There was a play at the Abbey tonight, Yeats's *Deirdre*. He had bought two tickets with the intention of asking her if she would like to come; but the longer he sat and watched her, intently reading in the pale green light, the more his resolution faltered.

Suddenly she closed her book and stood up. She had not been in the library more than half an hour—surely she could not be leaving already. He watched her guardedly, knowing he could never summon the courage to ask her out. She went upstairs to the balcony and began looking along the shelves. Five minutes later she came down another set of stairs and began to make her way back to her table.

As she passed behind him, she glanced down at the book he was reading.

"*Scusi.* Excuse me."

She was standing beside him, speaking in a whisper. He looked up. His heart was beating disagreeably fast and his tongue had turned to lead. *Cloud-pale eyelids, dream-dimmed eyes* . . .

"You are reading Yeats. Yes?"

"I . . . I . . . Yes. Yes, Yeats. W. B. Yeats."

"Oh, I'm sorry. I was looking for a copy. I have one, but not with me. When you are finished, maybe I can borrow this one."

"What? Oh, no, it's okay, you can have it. Really. I was just . . . sort of filling in time. I really should be reading something else."

She hesitated, but he closed the volume and pressed it into her hand. She smiled and thanked him, then returned to her seat. For what seemed an age he did not move. She had spoken to him. She had let him lend her a book. Not his own book, admittedly, but a book of poems he loved.

For the next hour he tried to concentrate on *Deirdre,* as though reading it might make it possible she would go with him tonight. But the mournful stanzas only saddened and distressed him.

> What's the merit in love-play,
> In the tumult of the limbs
> That dies out before 'tis day,
> Heart on heart, or mouth on mouth,
> All that mingling of our breath,
> When love-longing is but drouth
> For the things come after death?

"Thank you."

She was standing beside him again, holding out the book, smiling. He took a deep breath. His mind had filled with palaces and gondolas and sheer, blind terror.

"I . . . I was going to go across to the buttery for a coffee. Would you like to come?"

She put the book down.

"I'm sorry," she said. "But I have an essay to finish. They take me a long time."

He saw her turn to go and thought it was all over. But she hesitated and turned back.

"Maybe tomorrow," she said. "If I finish my essay on time."

She finished it and they went for coffee to Bewley's instead, which was nicer anyway. By that evening he had two fresh tickets for *Deirdre.* She met him outside the College gate and they walked down to Lower Abbey Street together. She was wearing a loose coat over a black cashmere dress, and in her ears were tiny jewels that he thought must be diamonds. He had never seen anything so lovely or so perfect.

He sat through the play like someone in a trance. He remembered only Deirdre's words to Naoise, as they wait for King Conchubar to come for them:

> Bend and kiss me now,
> For it may be the last before our death.
> And when that's over, we'll be different;
> Imperishable things, a cloud or a fire.
> And I know nothing but this body, nothing
> But that old vehement, bewildering kiss.

He walked her home that night through autumn-weary streets, thinking of vehement kisses, of breath on clouded breath, yet afraid even to hold her hand. They talked about the play, which she had found hard to follow, about Yeats, about their studies. She lived in Rathmines with an Italian family who thought she was at a girlfriend's rooms at Trinity Hall.

"Shall I see you again?" he asked when they arrived.

"Of course. You don't think I borrowed that book just to read some old poetry?"

"You mean . . ."

She smiled and reached up to kiss him. Not vehemently, but enough to bewilder him thoroughly.

"I love you," he said.

"I know." She smiled.

"Was I that obvious?"

She shrugged.

"Kiss me again, Patrick. And this time close your eyes."

Autumn turned to winter, the sky over Trinity grew silent and heavy with snow. They were lovers now, both liberated and enslaved by the unexpected emotions that had come to rule their lives. Snow came, and rain, and days of bright, limpid sunshine when they walked for miles along Sandymount Strand or across the frosted solitudes of the Phoenix Park.

She did not live in a golden palace, though she admitted that ancestors of hers had indeed built the famous Ca' d'Oro, the House of Gold, whose exquisitely gilded exterior had once made it the most famous of the many *palazzi* on the Grand Canal. He found a book on Venice in the library and discovered that the Contarinis had been the noblest of the city's noble families. Eight of them had been Doges. They had owned palaces everywhere.

Her family now lived in what was, certainly, a *palazzo*, but not so grand as the Ca' d'Oro. She promised to take him to Venice that summer, to meet her parents and the rest of the Contarinis. He wondered what she would make of Brooklyn or his uncle Seamus.

He wrote poems for her, atrocious things that filled him later with acute embarrassment and aching sadness. One commemorated a walk they had taken early one morning on a bright day in winter, along the beach at Sandymount. That had been the scene of their first quarrel, an event that had left him hurt and puzzled long afterwards.

Light lay on the sea like lozenges of silver. Far in the distance, beyond Dun Laoghaire, the Wicklow Mountains were veiled and elegant in an early morning haze. He held her hand. Above them a seagull stooped through a world of violet and gold.

They sat side by side on the sand, looking out to sea.

"When the summer comes," she said, "we'll spend every day on the Lido, just gazing at the Adriatic. And in the evenings we'll find somewhere to make love."

"It sounds perfect," he replied. "But not every day. I want to see Saint Mark's. And Santa Maria della Salute. And . . ."

She put her finger over his lips, then bent and kissed him gently. He drew her to him, his right hand cupping one breast. As she lay against him, he unbuttoned her shirt, then bent down to kiss her skin. As he did so, he noticed a small pendant on a fine chain round her neck. Taking it between finger and thumb, he lifted it closer.

The pendant was made of gold. It was circular. One side was engraved with her name, "Francesca Contarini," the other with a curious device: a seven-branched candlestick with a cross for the central column.

"I haven't noticed this before," he said. "What is it?"

Without warning, she snatched the pendant away from him and pulled it over her neck. Angrily she took it in her fist, then drew back her hand and flung it hard, into the sea.

"Francesca! What's wrong? What is it?"

She stood, trembling, buttoning her shirt with a shaking hand. He got up and tried to hold her, but she pulled away from him and started walking quickly along the beach. Bewildered, he ran after her, but she pushed him off. He could hear her crying.

He walked behind her until she tired. Her sobbing had grown softer. Behind them, their footsteps were already being eaten by the encroaching waves. Finally she stopped and let him put his arm round her shoulders.

"What is it, darling? I didn't mean to upset you."

She turned a tear-stained face to him.

"Please, Patrick. Never ask me about this again. Promise me. Swear you will never mention it."

"I only . . ."

"Swear!"

He did as she asked and she seemed to grow calmer at once. She put her arms round his neck and kissed him on the forehead.

"I'm sorry," she said. "I didn't mean to be angry with you. Don't ask me to explain. It has nothing to do with us. Nothing."

For a long time afterward, he thought the pendant must have been the gift of another man, a lover left behind in Italy; though she had sworn to him that there had been no one serious before him, and he had believed her. The pendant tormented him from time to time in the years to come. But he never asked her about it again.

THE LIVING

And it came to pass, that at midnight the Lord smote all the firstborn in the land of Egypt, from the firstborn of Pharaoh that sat on his throne unto the firstborn of the captive that was in the dungeon.

—Exodus 12:29

DUBLIN

ONE

Dalkey, Co. Dublin
January 1992

Three in the morning. The darkness inexplicably charged, the silence heavy and drugged. There would be another storm. It lay in his bones, like electricity, moving in a slow current. Outside, the cold chattered briskly, saying things he did not want to hear.

Light fell on light: across his desk, a tiny pool of yellow shining on ancient paper; through the window, a street lamp etching shadows out of the dim room. He could hear the sea in the distance, the tide coming in, small waves taking possession of the land. Or a single wave, repeating and repeating ceaselessly, until there was no more land, only water.

He had chosen the house for its view. It looked straight out onto Dublin Bay, and all last summer he had watched the sea perform its endless, slow ballet, as though it danced for him and him alone. Now, in midwinter, he was no longer sure he had chosen wisely. The sound of waves made him restless, filling him with a terrible loneliness and a sense of foreboding. It was at moments such as this that he wondered if he had done the right thing in coming back to Ireland.

He rubbed his eyes. The crabbed and faded script was a strain to read, even with the help of a magnifying glass. Yellow light and ocher paper blurred. Fragmented letters ran across the page like frightened ants.

"C'mon, Patrick. You hadn't killed him, somebody else would've had to do it."

Voices snagged at him, like branches sharp with thorns. The past was still angry and unforgiving.

"He was coming in. He'd had enough. There was a signal: Damascus station intercepted it. Why wasn't I told?"

"There was a slipup. It happens. You know it happens. What's it matter? Wasn't like he didn't have it coming. Somebody would have done it sooner or later. Not you, then somebody else."

In the distance, waves possessed the shore.

He stood and went to the window. At forty-two, Patrick Canavan possessed very little. He paid rent on a house overlooking the Irish sea: what little there was of his CIA pension took care of that. No wife, no children, no memories he could share with friends, no friends to share them with.

He opened the window all the way, pushing the sash up hard. Out of the night, out of the padded and frozen darkness, the sounds of the world rose up to him in waves: the stark lapping of water on stone, a train in the distance, loud on frosted rails, a ship's horn, the bell on a rocking buoy.

Far out on the abandoned waters of the bay, he saw lights: ships coming in from the dark sea, from France and Spain and Italy, headed for Dun Laoghaire or Dublin Harbor, an armada of tiny lights on a wind-darkened tide. The fog that had kept them out at sea so late had lifted, leaving a vast and empty darkness rich with stars. Out on the final edges of the night, a small boat passed like a firefly and was suddenly lost.

His eyes traveled over the darkness, and he thought how complete it was, how everything was dipped in it. *How could twenty years make such a difference?* he asked himself. Times change, people change, people die; but it was more than that.

He saw Beirut again, as though the darkness had become a screen for memories. On his left, the Syrian guard post plastered with posters of Asad, to his right the abandoned al-Saqi Hotel, now occupied by a Hezbollah group from Bi'r al-ʿ Abd. He saw the Jeep turn the corner, the boy from Amal firing, low from the hip. And, in slow motion, Hasan Abi Shaqra running from the alleyway towards him, his own gun lifting, pointing, firing, Hasan falling at his feet, blood turning to dust on the dry earth. *"He was coming in. He'd had enough."*

"Come back to bed, Patrick."

Ruth stood in the doorway, naked, her eyes dim with sleep. He turned from the window, blinking away the sunshine and the blood, suddenly cold.

"I was working," he said, wondering why he felt a need to explain himself to her.

"It's after three. I woke up and you weren't there. Come back to bed."

He felt irritated by her presence, by the demand she made on him. It was so long since he had shared anything with a woman. He closed the window, shutting the world out.

She took him back to bed, her nakedness futile against his indifference. They lay there for a long time, shivering between cold sheets. Light from the street lamp filtered through the thin bedroom curtains, staining the bed with its unnatural light. Her arm lay beside his, almost translucent, like alabaster.

"Do you love me?" he asked, but she was asleep again, and he had not really wanted an answer. There was a sort of love between them, he supposed; and a physical passion that could still make him cry out, as though in pain. He tried to convince himself that the gulf between them was merely one of age—she was more than ten years his junior—but he knew it was really something he had built inside himself out of all the little emptinesses of his life.

Getting involved with Ruth had been a big mistake. He thought he loved her, but that wasn't the problem. Ruth belonged to the Agency, the way everyone did at first, the way he had at the beginning. That was the problem. Or part of it, at least.

They'd become involved at a party three, maybe four months earlier, not long after his arrival in Dublin. An old friend from Langley, Jim Allegro, was here on special attachment with the Irish Ranger Squad, liaising on antiterrorist tactics. Jim had heard of Patrick's arrival through the grapevine and contacted him. "I'm having a party tonight—come by and meet some people."

The party had been dull: pieces of cheese and tinned pineapple on wooden cocktail sticks, stale French bread, cheap Australian red in boxes, wall-to-wall Dire Straits. The guests were the usual crowd: anemic third secretaries from the embassy, a handful of spooks you could spot in a nudist colony, and awkward locals downing Guinness at a rate of knots. As usual, all the intelligence hounds were sniffing one another's rears in a pack. She was sitting in a corner, going through Allegro's bookcase like a censor looking for smut.

"You won't find anything in there," he said. "Jim's cleaner than an operating table."

"On the contrary," she replied, "that's precisely where all the messy things end up."

How had he guessed she was in the trade? She didn't look the type. Not that there was a type—but if there had been, she wouldn't have been it. She was too well dressed for one thing. The sort of clothes that had their labels on the inside, if they had labels at all. A single piece of discreet jewelry, a mere hint of expensive perfume. But for the accent, he would have taken her to be French. She was petite, with short blond hair, a downturned mouth, and tiny ears like shells.

Her next words had been, "Shall we get out of here?" She had taken the initiative from the beginning, otherwise he would never have got as far as "go." They had driven down the coast in her small blue Mercedes. Everything was autumnal: the air, the sea, their mood. She drove too fast for the narrow Irish roads and too skillfully for it to matter. It was dawn when they arrived back at his house. "You have appalling taste" was the last thing she said before leading him to bed.

After leaving the CIA, he had returned to Ireland to finish the doctorate he had abandoned eighteen years before. Coming back to Dublin had been like a physical blow: the old places, all the memories rushing at him, striking him deep in the pit of his stomach, and him helpless before their onslaught. Rathmines, Ranelagh, Donnybrook, Ballsbridge—the names had leaped out of maps and off the fronts of buses at him, each with its own sweet or bitter flavor, its own particular weight of memories and associations.

He had returned with such hopes, such expectations. Dublin would restore him to youth, or something like that. Dublin would revive in him the ideals of twenty-four years ago. Well, that had all been a fantasy, and he knew it now: even if the city had been preserved in aspic all these years, nothing of the past would have returned to him, or at the most a glimmer, a teasing reflection in a rusted mirror.

His years at Trinity had shaped his life. He had lived and worked in a palace of gray stone, surrounded by dreams and poetry. Not the past only, but a present that seemed not wholly real. It had been less the magic of the place than the enchantment of youth: he had come to understand that in time. But then he was aware only of snow falling on dark, pitted cobblestones, and sunlight on mullioned windows, and the bell in the Campanile ringing out against the shadows at dusk as he walked through soft-lit courtyards to Commons. And Francesca. Always Francesca.

Now he was back, but the magic and the poetry had gone. He had tried to find them again in Ruth, but all that remained was a sense of bewilderment and shame. Pressed for a reason, he could have given a dozen. But at heart he knew there had only ever been one reason for his inability to love or be loved: Francesca's death. But that was the past. He had to come to terms with that. In the dark he lay listening to the sound of his own breathing, unable to surrender himself to sleep.

He slipped out of bed again, knowing sleep would not come. There had been so many nights like this: they just had to be endured. He crossed to the window, as though drawn by the pale lamplight. A man can resign from the Agency, but his mind and body never relax.

He heard the footstep just as his hand reached for the curtain. A single step followed by silence. He stiffened and lowered his hand. Silence. Cautiously he eased back the edge of the curtain and bent his eye to the crack.

His dark-adjusted eyes found the man almost at once. On the opposite side of the street, away from the lamp. He was cold and restless and looked like someone who had been standing there a long time. Waiting for something. Or someone.

TWO

Patrick let the curtain fall. For half a minute he stood by the window, forcing himself to be calm. Ruth was still asleep, her heavy breathing plainly audible to him across the room. Moving quietly in the darkness, he found his trousers and the thick sweater he had been wearing the day before. His shoes were beside the bed.

Downstairs, he paused in the kitchen. A row of gleaming, wooden-handled Sabatier knives hung on a magnetic rack. He selected one with a six-inch blade and slipped it into his belt. It was razor-sharp: he knew, because he had honed the entire set three days earlier.

The back door led into the garden, but he knew better than to go that way. There might be more than one watcher, and the odds were that a second man, if any, would be at the rear of the house.

A side window gave onto the drive. He unlocked the dead bolt and opened it without a sound. A blast of cold air took him unawares. The wind was rising. There was a roll of thunder, very far away, moving behind unseen clouds. The storm was coming.

He dropped to the ground, poised against possible attack. Here, beside the house, the darkness was complete. Clouds came up fast, obscuring the stars. He crouched, listening. Beneath the pounding of his heart, he heard cold waves turning on the shore. Above him, branches shifted. His skin felt taut and nervous. In spite of the cold, he was sweating.

Crossing the gravel of the drive took an eternity. Then grass, then the fence dividing him from the next house. A frosted lawn led down to a low wall on the other side of which lay the road. From here he could still see the street lamp, but there was no sign of the watcher. Automatically, he checked the knife: the other man would carry a gun, he was sure of that.

Though he knew the darkness hid him, he felt utterly exposed as he sprinted across the road, carrying his shoes. On the other side, he vaulted the sea wall onto the path that wound along the beach. The tide was well in now, a heavy swell pushed by rising winds. The thunder sounded again, nearer this time, a low, animal growl threatening violence.

He kept to the sand, crouching low. The waves covered any sound. The man was still standing where Patrick had last seen him, in the shadows just beyond the lamp. His back was to the sea. He moved restlessly, trying to keep warm. About six foot, Patrick reckoned, and well built. There would be a car nearby, perhaps another man waiting in it.

Patrick removed his shoes again. It was bitterly cold, but he had to be sure of silence. He slipped behind the wall, then over, never letting his eyes wander from his target. The frost felt like daggers on his bare skin. With his right hand he slipped the knife from his belt. Thunder like stones in the sky. Darkness closing in. The sea tormented, moving landward from the night.

He was behind the man now. Without a sound, he set his shoes down. Faint as gossamer, his breath hung in front of his face, trembling. He braced himself and reached with both hands at once. His left grabbed a clump of hair, pulling the man's head back fiercely, while the right brought the knife round hard against his throat. He could feel the blade touch flesh, the Adam's apple neat on steel.

"Kneel."

The old voice out of the darkness; his own voice, and yet not his voice.

The man grunted, about to scream, his throat bulging unseen against the blade. Then, slowly, his legs buckled and he lowered himself to his knees. Patrick moved hard behind him, a knee in his back, the knife well poised, the long throat taut. He could feel the stranger's fear, acrid in the sea air, in the electric presence of the storm.

"Take your gun and throw it to the ground. Please don't force me to hurt you."

The man struggled for words.

"No . . . gun . . . I . . . swear."

"Who are you?"

Silence. The wind moving, cold as death.

"Who sent you?"

The knife again, a trickle of blood, frost on the blade. Silence. Death hovering breathless in the thin air. The man's fear was rapidly giving way to something else. Defiance? Indifference? Transcendence?

"Why are you watching me?"

Silence. Then a roll of thunder that echoed across the bay.

He switched to Arabic.

"Min ayna ta' ti? Where are you from?"

No sign of comprehension.

He tried Persian.

"Az koja amadi?"

No answer.

Suddenly lightning flashed, turning the world to light for an instant. An image fixed itself in Patrick's mind: a dark-haired man, his head held back, a knife against his throat, a thin line of blood across bruised flesh.

Patrick blinked, and in that instant the stranger made his move. His right hand came up, grabbing Patrick's wrist, knocking the knife away. He swung in sideways, his hair twisting painfully in his captor's grasp, his left arm pivoting, his fist striking out hard. Patrick rocked, loosening his grip. The man staggered with him, then dropped forward, using his head to butt Patrick, knocking him down. At that very moment the storm broke. Like a river bursting through a dam, rain came flooding out of the sky, thick and cold and heavy.

Patrick heard the man's feet ring out on the hard ground. He rolled onto his knees and started scrabbling for his shoes. The rain smothered and blinded him. His clothes were already soaking. Frantically, he passed his hands over the road. He found one shoe, then the other, and hurried to pull them on, leaving the laces untied.

The stranger had headed off to the right. Patrick followed, hampered by rain and darkness. Thunder again, then seconds afterward another flash of lightning. Stenciled against the night, he saw a car and a man opening the door. He stumbled forward, desperate now.

There was the sound of an engine rasping, unwilling to ignite. He had a chance. Panting, he ran through the darkness. The engine turned again and died. A lace caught beneath his foot and sent him off balance, pitching forward in a heap, skinning his hands badly on the rough ground. He heard the engine cough, then hold. Biting back the pain, he hauled himself to his feet, staggering across the last few yards.

He crashed into the car as it pulled away from the curb, turned, ran, snatched for the handle. The door opened and he threw himself into the seat as the vehicle picked up speed. The driver had not yet switched on his lights. Rain and darkness flooded the windscreen.

Patrick reached for the wheel, pulling it toward him. The driver braked suddenly, sending them into a spin. The car mounted the curb, tilted, and crumpled against the sea wall.

Panicking, the driver opened his door and stumbled into the road. He slipped, then picked himself up and began to run.

Patrick threw his own door open, but it stuck on the wall, leaving a gap too narrow for him to squeeze through. He wriggled across the gear stick, then out through the driver's door. Wind and rain grabbed him, tearing him back into their world. He spluttered, catching his breath, and broke into a run.

Another clap of thunder prepared the way for a stroke of lightning that lasted seconds. Out at sea, raging waves were frozen, as though the light had carved them in an instant out of raw ice. A ship appeared, running for harbor, hopeless and alone on crystal waves. He saw the man jump the wall, heading for the beach.

The sand was already filled with rain. His feet sank in it. It was like treacle, clawing at him, pulling him down. He moved as though in a dream, no longer certain why he was here. The world had vanished and been replaced by nightmare. He could hear waves crashing on rocks and wind tearing the sky to shreds. A crash of thunder rolled across the void. Jagged bands of lightning grew out of nowhere like the sudden branches of giant trees. The man was only yards ahead of him, scrambling among white spray at the edge of the rocks.

Patrick shouted, but the wind snatched the words from his mouth, leaving him breathless. The man was crazy. The rocks he was climbing on would soon be covered as the tide came farther in: he could find no shelter there.

Waves were already dragging at his ankles. He pushed farther out into the freezing water, unable to see a thing, his eyes blinded by the last flash of lightning. The water was already at his knees.

The first rock caught him unawares, striking him in the shin and almost sending him flying into the sea. He scrambled onto it, crouching down, finding his way to the next by touch. He was no longer sure which way the land lay and which way the sea. At any moment he might lose his grip and go spinning into deep water, at the mercy of cold currents, battered on dark rocks, pulled down into darkness.

He slipped on kelp and pitched forward into a freezing pool. A voice came to him out of the maelstrom, thin and anguished. The wind drove away all semblance of meaning. There was no way of knowing whether the words had been a threat or a cry for help. Out here, there was nothing but the wind and the sea.

Another rock, the rough edges of barnacles, rain and spray mingled in a single sheet of water, a wind like barbed wire against the skin. He saw a shadow darker than the rest, something crouching at the edge of the rocks, where they joined the sea. Scarcely balanced himself, he lunged forward and made a grab for the man.

They fell backward onto a broad wrack-covered rock. He heard his opponent gasp as the breath was forced from his lungs.

"Who are you?" he shouted, anger forcing his voice above the storm. The man remained silent, struggling in his grasp.

Overhead, a clap of thunder seemed to burst the sky open. Lightning tore the darkness away like a thin veil. Patrick saw a white face, the eyes opened in terror, and a hand across the face, as though to ward him off.

Suddenly, his opponent pushed him back, slipping out of his grip on the wet rock. He flopped down into a gap, twisted, and tried to stand. As he got to one foot, a huge wave crashed into him, throwing him off balance. He lost his footing completely. There was a loud cry, inhuman, passionate, past articulation. Patrick reached out. But there was nothing. Another bolt of lightning crossed the sky. The rock ahead was empty.

The tide was still rushing in. There was nothing Patrick could do for the stranger, not in a sea like that. He turned and started crawling back along the rocks. There were no lights on the shore to guide him. In the madness, he could have been moving away from the land, out to sea and certain death. He lost count of the number of times he slipped, crashing heavily onto the rocks. It would be so easy to break a leg and be trapped until the sea took possession of everything and dragged him out into its depths.

Lightning again. The world stark, insane. He got his bearings and dropped into the water, desperate for balance. Even here, the undertow was fierce, like ropes that tried to pull his legs from under him. The water rose up to his chest now. He felt tired suddenly, as though the sea had sapped him of all strength.

Aching, he gave himself to it, half swimming, half drowning. Salt water poured into his mouth, filling his stomach, weighing him down. His arms and legs moved sluggishly, as though he was swimming in another substance, in quicksand or mercury, thick and deadly, pulling him down.

Suddenly, he felt land beneath his feet. Coughing and spluttering, he threw himself forward. His head went under, then rose again. He fought to regain his balance. His feet found purchase on the sloping beach. Spewing up water, he staggered through the last few yards of angry waves, coming at last to rain-drenched sand. A few feet more and he threw himself to the ground.

All around him, the world was bedlam. But he scarcely noticed. All he could think of, all he could see polished on the darkness of the night was the white oval of the watcher's face and his hand raised, pushing him away. And on the man's inner wrist a tiny circle tattooed in black, inside the circle a cross flanked by two smaller crosses, all in red.

It was impossible, he thought. A nightmare from the past, a nightmare that could not possibly have followed him here, to this place, to this moment.

Behind him, in the darkness, the sea moved, rank and heavy with drowning men and the bodies of great fish sinking to its rotten bed. They were devouring one another down there, men and fish and all manner of swimming and crawling things.

THREE

He lost track of time, lying wet and out of breath at the foot of the sea wall, as though cast up there by nauseous waves. Slowly the rain subsided and the thunder became a distant rumbling as the storm passed on into the Wicklow hills. Aching to his bones, he picked himself up and clambered back over the wall onto the road.

The car was still where he had left it, against the wall. Its engine had stalled. He had supposed someone would have heard the crash and come out to investigate or phoned for the Gardai, but the road was deserted. If any sleepers had been awakened, they must have imagined the crash a clap of thunder and gone back to sleep. He pulled the door open and slipped into the driver's seat.

He knew he should rush back to the house for a hot shower and a change of clothes, but first he had to search the car. His mind was in turmoil. He had seen the symbol on the watcher's wrist only once before, years ago, during a mission in Egypt. To see it again here in Ireland filled him with the deepest foreboding. He had thought that episode buried forever: he should have known that sands shift and the buried past returns to life.

He switched on the interior lights and looked round. The car was a small Citroën hatchback, tidy and quite new-looking, probably rented. There was nothing on the rear seat or the shelf behind it. Leaning across the passenger seat, he opened the glove compartment.

Inside, he found a map and a small book bound in black leather. The book was a copy of the New Testament in Greek with an interlinear English translation based on the Revised Version. Its pages were well thumbed, and here and there in the margins someone had made textual notes in pencil. He put the volume down and turned to the map. It was a standard Geographia map of Dublin, from Ballymun and Santry in the north to Tallaght and Glenageary in the south.

His own street, situated in the extreme bottom right-hand corner, had been ringed several times in red ink. There were three more rings: one in

Ballsbridge, not far from the American Embassy; one round the west end of Merrion Square, opposite the National Gallery; and one in the Liberties, just off the Coombe.

He felt his heart go cold. The first two rings held no significance for him; but the third, circling St. Malachy's parish church, told him all he needed to know.

Taking the map and book, he got out into the rain. It was only a drizzle now, the storm's rich anger spent or gone elsewhere. He only paused to check the boot, finding it empty as he had expected, then set off home.

Ruth was waiting up for him. She was crouched over the table in the kitchen, cradling a mug of tea, more for the comfort of it than from a need to drink. He sat down facing her, wordless, shivering, soaking, afraid of her gentleness more than anything.

"The storm woke me," she said. "You were gone again. I thought you might be in the study. I looked everywhere for you."

She did not ask where he had been, merely told her story and fell silent. In the half-light her shaded face seemed perhaps lovelier than a woman's face had ever appeared to him. For that moment, in that place. He wanted to sit with her, hold her, talk with her. He thought he loved her after all: it was, at least, what he wanted. To love her, to be here with her. But there was no time tonight. The circles round St. Malachy's, like the circle on the stranger's wrist, could mean only one thing: a man was in terrible danger. Patrick had no choice.

"I have to go out again," he said.

She looked at him intently, understanding beginning to dawn.

"What's going on, Patrick? Whatever it is, it doesn't concern you. You're finished with that stuff."

"Come upstairs," he said, "I have to change. I'll catch cold if I have to stay in these wet clothes."

She followed him, clutching her dressing gown about her as though it could ward off the sudden terrors of the night. The world pressed against her, heavy and cold, its saturated breath dank in her nostrils.

He made straight for the bedroom and picked up the telephone from the table by the bed. Ruth stood in the doorway, watching. It was bitterly cold.

The phone in St. Malachy's presbytery began to ring. De Faoite's hearing was poor, and he would be asleep, unless wakened by the storm. Patrick felt his heart beating, keeping time with the burring of the telephone. He waited two minutes, then hung up.

"Okay, Patrick—so, suppose you cut this out and tell me exactly what's going on here?"

He tried to ignore her, starting to take off his wet clothes, but she grabbed him by the arm and forced him to look directly at her.

"Don't fuck about with me, Patrick! I have a right to know what's happening. For Christ's sake, you're not even in the trade any longer."

"It has nothing to do with that."

"Oh no? Then why all the sudden mystery? Walks in the middle of the night, mysterious phone calls. Come on, Patrick—I've been through all this. If you're in danger, I'm in danger, so don't play games."

He held her clumsily, unable to respond, or perhaps afraid to do so. Outside, the sea still raged against the shore. Water lay against water, wave against wave, an unbroken ocean round the world, closing in on him, connecting him to his past. Beirut, Alexandria, Bandar Abbas—everywhere the sea, everywhere waves beating furiously against the land.

"It has nothing to do with you, Ruth. Honestly. It's something out of my own past. Something I have to handle myself."

"Who were you ringing?"

"Eamonn De Faoite. He's the parish priest at St. Malachy's in town. Sometimes he teaches Semitic studies at University College and Trinity. He was my teacher back in the sixties when I studied here. I think he's in danger. I wanted to warn him."

"Warn him? About what?"

Patrick shook his head.

"I don't know. I . . ." He paused. "Listen," he resumed. "About eight years ago, I was in Egypt. The Agency was looking for support among the Coptic Christian population, as a sort of balance against the Muslim Brothers. There'd been anti-Coptic riots back in the early eighties; Sadat had exiled Pope Shenuda to Wadi Natrun; Islamic fundamentalism was spreading.

"I was in a small village in the Delta. Myself and a local agent. The people we were staying with were Copts. They woke us very early one morning. Something had frightened them. They asked if I would go to the next village, a place called Sidi Ya'qub. They kept saying that something terrible had happened, that they wanted me to go to see if what they had heard was true. When I asked them to tell me what it was, they just threw their hands up and shook their heads. Finally, I agreed. I took the Jeep and drove over to Sidi Ya'qub."

He paused. Outside, the troubled sea gave its voice to the storm.

"It was one of the stupidest things I ever did. I very nearly got myself lynched. What had happened was this: Sidi Ya'qub had a school. The building was situated a short stretch outside the village proper, on a low ridge. Some men had come the previous afternoon and herded the children together, put them in a bus, and driven them off. About thirty children altogether.

"When I arrived, the village was frantic. They had been looking for the children all night. The police had been called in, the Muslim Brothers were there in force, everyone was acting crazy. Anyway, I stayed and gave a hand. I knew why the Copts in the next village were afraid: if anything had happened to the children, they would very likely be blamed. And if what had happened turned out to be unpleasant, they knew things could get very nasty."

He hesitated.

"Yes?" she asked.

"Well, it did turn out to be unpleasant. Very unpleasant indeed. They found the children shortly after noon, in an old temple about a mile from the village. It's not much of a temple, not the sort of place that puts you on the tourist trail. I went out there with everyone else after word came in that the children had been found.

"There was a stone basin in the center of the temple. Basalt, I think. And very large. It had been badly damaged, but it could still hold perhaps a hundred gallons or thereabouts."

He closed his eyes. The memory of the temple and what had been found there was sharp in his mind now.

"The . . . the children were lying in a circle round the basin. Their throats had been cut and the basin filled with the blood. The basin wasn't full, but the blood in it was deep. Their teacher was there as well. He had been drowned in the basin. The children had been stripped and tied with thongs. And someone had marked their foreheads with a circle, a circle containing three small crosses. That was when I had to get out, when they saw the crosses." He paused. "I heard later there was very nearly a massacre at the village where I'd been staying. They left just in time, before their neighbors got there. They've never gone back."

Ruth stopped him.

"I don't understand what this has got to do with you and Eamonn De Faoite."

"I think they're here," he said. "The people who killed those children. They're here in Ireland. And I think they mean trouble. I've got to get to Eamonn. Now, tonight."

"How do you know they're here? What happened?"

"I saw one of them. I chased him."

"An Egyptian?"

Patrick shook his head.

"No. That's the strange thing. I don't think he was an Egyptian. I think . . . I'm sure he was Irish."

"What happened to him?"

He told her.

"And you think they could be watching De Faoite?"

He shrugged. He had dressed now and was eager to be off.

"It's possible. Listen, Ruth, I've got to go."

"I'm coming with you."

"No, I'd rather you stayed here to watch the house. There may be another watcher."

She stepped away from him. Behind her, the bed had grown cold. Its crumpled sheets reminded her of a hotel room.

"That isn't the reason, is it?"

He had already turned toward the door.

"I don't want you involved, Ruth. I'm treating this as personal business: it has nothing to do with the Agency."

"You think so?" She was growing angry again.

"Okay, yes, I think so." But he was lying, desperate to avoid the thought that the past was drawing him in again, that no one ever truly escapes from that delicately fabricated world. "Don't get involved, Ruth. Don't get the Agency involved. I'll be back when I've seen De Faoite."

"Suit yourself. But don't expect me to be here when you return."

It was still raining when he left.

FOUR

He drove distracted through a world of lights and shadows, like a ghost passing through someone else's dream. The final stages of his journey took him through a landscape of broken fanlights, rusted railings, and dark tenement walls on which someone had written FUCK in foot-high letters, time and time again. It was an invocation of sorts. But who was listening?

The Liberties were the oldest part of the city, and not even the dark could cover the squalor and neglect on every side. As Patrick walked down the Coombe toward St. Malachy's, he could smell yeast from the nearby Guinness brewery, mixed with a rotting odor that came up from the quays. A thin, freezing mist had started to move in off the sea and was working its way slowly along the streets.

Above him, in a tenement, a curtain was twitched aside. Unseen eyes watched him pass, then the curtain fell back into place. A dog barked angrily on his left. Open doorways, stained and rotten, graffiti on the walls, a smell of urine from the hallways, broken windows, broken lights, broken lives.

Eamonn De Faoite had been parish priest of St. Malachy's as far back as anyone could remember. Every morning for almost sixty years he had left his scholarship upstairs and come down onto the streets to face his little world. The Liberties were his Calvary, he had told Patrick once: they had broken him and scourged him and nailed him to themselves, year in, year out, an eternal Easter. He had tended generations of the poor and the almost poor: baptized them, married them, said mass for them and their children, received their stammered confessions, administered the last rites, buried them in deal-board coffins. And still no resurrection.

Patrick approached the presbytery carefully, his senses alert for any sign of a watcher: a parked car, a shadow that moved, a sound. There was nothing. Keeping himself close to the house walls, he reached the door. There was nothing for it now: if someone was watching, he would just have to let himself be seen.

He knocked on the presbytery door. His visits to De Faoite had not often brought him here. They normally met at Trinity College or the Chester Beatty Library in Ballsbridge: the old priest kept his worlds quite separate. Perhaps that was what kept him sane.

"I'm not a good man," he had once told Patrick. "I find it hard to be a priest. I hate poverty. I loathe petty crime and the mess people make of their daily lives. If I had it to do over again, I don't think I could face it. Do you know, if I believed in reincarnation like these Indian yogis, I think I'd go crazy. Imagine—having to come back again! Jesus, Patrick, doesn't that give you the creeps now?"

Patrick knocked again. Perhaps hating his vocation was what made a man a saint. He didn't know: he was one of the people who made messes of their lives. He suddenly realized that he had not been to confession in twenty years. There were a lot of messes to get off his chest. Mist swirled round the enamel-painted door. Why didn't De Faoite answer? There was a light on in the upstairs room that served as the old man's study.

There was no answer to his third knock. As he turned to go, he noticed that another light was burning in the church next door. He opened the iron gate and went through. The old church loomed out of the darkness, faintly menacing in a veil of mist. It had been built in 1689, and much of it was now in a state of serious decay. De Faoite had started a restoration fund and issued appeals for money, but who was going to dig into his pocket to gild a church among the tenements?

Above the door, a weather-worn statue of the Virgin gazed down at him. The face was almost featureless, without nose or eyes or expression. On her head she wore a crown, and on her lap a deformed child, its limbs eroded by wind and dirt, stretched a fingerless hand toward a faintly delineated breast.

The door opened to his touch. There was a smell of wax and incense, mixed with an underlying odor of damp. Beneath an icon of the sacred heart, a red lamp flickered in the draft from the door. He slipped inside noiselessly, feeling alien and ill at ease. When had he last set foot inside a church?

Faint shadows moved beneath the ceiling. At the far end of the church, above the altar, a single lamp hung on a copper chain, shedding a dull sepia light to the top of the sanctuary steps. Nearby, half a dozen candles had burned to stubs at the foot of an alabaster statue of the Virgin.

He called De Faoite's name, but there was no answer. Mist followed him into the church, rolling gently across the floor. He closed the door behind him.

"Are you here, Father?"

A faint echo rang from the ceiling, hidden in darkness. Automatically, he dipped his fingers into the holy water stoup and crossed himself. The church was unheated, and tonight it felt like an icebox.

Perhaps the priest had been called out to hear an urgent confession from one of his parishioners. There were three confessionals against the west wall. Patrick made his way to them. They were all empty.

He called again, but his voice was swallowed up in the damp, sacral silence. He was wasting his time here. Best to find a telephone and ring De Faoite again. He turned and started to go.

There was a low sound. It seemed to come from the direction of the transept, possibly the sanctuary. Patrick froze. In the shadows, nothing moved. A candle sputtered and went out. He took a cautious step forward.

"Is there someone there?" he called.

No one answered. He felt the hairs ripple on the backs of his hands and the nape of his neck. Why was he afraid?

The sound came again, a little louder. It was like a moan, scarcely human. An animal, perhaps. A dog or a wounded cat.

He padded through the darkness toward the transept. Above the host, a red flame shuddered. He strained to see in the gloom.

There was something on the altar. Something living. He felt his breath catch in his throat, sour and frightened.

"Eamonn," he whispered, "is that you?"

The thing on the altar moved. Patrick climbed the steps, the scent of incense heavy in his nostrils. The air felt sickly, raddled with holiness. As he drew near, he saw that the white altar cloth was stained. Like juice or wine, a long streak of red had soaked into the cloth. Memories rushed in from his childhood to dismay him, the horror of the chalice of blood, the horror of the flesh offered up as bread, the horror of Christ bleeding from seven wounds across the altar. The thing on the white table was a man.

They must have tied him before dragging him here. They could not have done what they had done while he was loose: he would have struggled, in spite of his age. He seemed unaware of Patrick's presence, unaware of anything but the pain surrounding him. But he was conscious, that was the horror.

Patrick's fingers fumbled with the ropes. He felt bile rise in his throat, burning him. They must have hacked out the eyes: the sockets had filled with blood, like rock pools after high tide. Like a basin of blood in an abandoned Egyptian temple.

"Eamonn," he said, "it's me, Patrick. Can you hear me?"

The old priest moaned again but showed no other sign of recognition. The ropes were tight, lashing the frail body like the threads a spider uses to secure its prey. But they were not needed now. The old man had no strength left in him.

"Who did this, Eamonn? Why? Why?" He was crying. Tears touched the altar cloth. His hands trembled, loosening the knots. He looked up and saw the figure of Christ, suspended in semidarkness, a wooden figure nailed with wooden nails. The old man groaned and tried to move.

"It's all right, Eamonn. Don't try to speak. I'll get an ambulance. We'll get you out of here."

The last knot came undone and he pulled the ropes loose. There was nothing more he could do here. He had to get an ambulance. Taking off his coat, he rolled it up and placed it under the priest's head as a pillow. He knew he should wipe away the blood from De Faoite's face, but he had a horror of the bleeding sockets.

"You'll be all right, Eamonn. We're going to get you to hospital. I've got to go to ring for the ambulance. But I'll be back soon."

As he looked up, he caught sight of something on the back wall. Above the altar pyx, someone had scrawled a message in large black letters. There were three lines. The words meant nothing at first, then, with a shock of recognition, he saw that the letters of the first line were actually Hebrew and that the inscription was in the same language. The second and third lines were in Greek.

עין תאת עיע שן תאת שן יד תאת יד רגל רגל תאת רגל

Και ει 'ο οφθαλμοσ σου σκανδαλιζει σε, εξελε αυτον και βαλε απο σου.

The first line was easy to translate:

Eye for eye, [it read], *tooth for tooth, hand for hand, foot for foot.*

He was less familiar with Greek, but the inscription was not difficult:

And if thine eye offend thee, pluck it out, and cast it from thee.

The third line was less familiar. He guessed it came from the Book of Revelation:

Behold, he cometh with clouds; and every eye shall see him,
and they also which pierced him.

The paint was still wet. It had run in places. The writer had been in a hurry. But not too much of a hurry. Underneath the lines of writing, the same hand had drawn a circle. In the center of the circle were three upright crosses.

"Eamonn, if you can hear me, nod. I'd like to know if you're aware I'm here."

Suddenly De Faoite's hand reached out and grabbed Patrick by the wrist. He pulled him down toward him. His lips were moving, trying to form words. His breath came in jagged lumps. Saliva ran across his lips and chin.

"*Pass . . .*" It was scarcely a whisper. Patrick bent his head closer, his ear against the old man's trembling lips.

"I can hear you, Eamonn. What is it? What are you trying to say?"

Again the lips moved.

"*Pass . . . Pass . . . over . . .*"

"I don't understand."

"*Soo . . . soon . . . Pass . . . over . . . soon.* Find . . . Balzarin . . . Gave   him   papers. . . . Knows . . . something . . . Ask . . . Balzarin . . ."

De Faoite's hand relaxed and let go of Patrick's wrist. His body fell back limp. At the foot of the Virgin, another candle gave itself up to darkness.

FIVE

The footstep was soft, but magnified in the stillness. Patrick whirled round. Shadows. Darkness that was not quite darkness. A sound high up in the ceiling: mice? bats?

"*Al-salām alaykum,* Patrick. You're a long way from home."

The soft voice sounded exaggeratedly loud in the hushed emptiness. It had come from a clump of shadows in the central aisle. Patrick took a step back, almost tripping at the foot of the altar.

"What's wrong? Getting nervous? You were never nervous, old friend."

The voice was so familiar. Familiar yet strange, as though someone had borrowed it. The greeting had been Arabic, but the speaker was not an Arab.

"Alex? Is that you?"

"Who were you expecting? Jesus Christ? That famous Jew who abandoned the working classes for"—a figure stepped out of the shadows into a pool of weak light; he gestured vaguely with a gloved hand— "for this." What did he mean? The wood? The plaster? The cheap candles? The silence?

"What are you doing here, Alex?"

Patrick's voice was stiff and unwelcoming.

"We're on neutral ground now, Patrick. Relax."

The newcomer held out a hand, but Patrick stayed where he was. Aleksander Chekulayev had been KGB station chief in Beirut during Patrick's last spell of duty there. They had met several times before that, twice in Cairo, often in Baghdad, once in Najm al-Sharq, a dirty café in Damascus where Patrick had contracted food poisoning. His stomach remembered the fat little Russian in the same mouthful as it did rancid hummus. According to the political winds, they had been rivals, enemies, friends, partners in crime—sometimes all at once. Alex had tried to have him killed on one occasion. There is no such thing as neutral ground.

"What is it, Alex? What do you want?"

"I was about to ask you just that myself."

Chekulayev took a cautious step forward. Patrick could see him more clearly now. The Russian seemed grayer than he remembered. Beneath its natural pallor, his skin appeared as though covered in a fine gray dust, and his eyes were circled by darker lines, like the hair-thin cracks on a Raku bowl. Patrick wondered if the grayness was the price or the reward for a lifetime of thought and lies and insinuation.

Glasnost had sniffed at Chekulayev's edges and drawn back, perhaps more saddened than frightened. He was too old to change, too young to have learned how. The system might mellow, but he could wait. In the end, it would grow gray like him. In a sense, he was the system.

The Russian nodded in the direction of the altar.

"May I see?"

Patrick shrugged. At least he had no reason to think Chekulayev was responsible for this particular mess.

"Don't worry, Patrick, I'm quite alone." He came forward slowly, like a mourner approaching the bier to view the deceased. Patrick stood aside to let him pass. The Russian stepped up to the altar and stood for about a minute, his head bowed, as though in prayer. When he turned, his face was grim.

"Not a pretty sight. You knew him?"

"Yes. He was the priest here."

"Yes, of course, the priest." Chekulayev looked round, as though aware for the first time he was in a church. "The letters on the wall. Hebrew and Greek. You understand them, of course."

"Word for word, yes. But why they were put there, who wrote them—I've no idea." High above, the mice moved slowly in the darkness. Or were they bats after all?

"*Oko za oko, zub za zub.*"

Patrick looked puzzled.

" '*An eye for an eye, a tooth for a tooth.*' Someone wanted revenge. A spiritual revenge . . . by very earthly means. What commandment had your priest sinned against, Patrick?"

"Most of them, I should think. Or none of them. What difference does it make?"

"To me, none at all. But perhaps it made a difference to someone. What's this all about, Patrick?"

Patrick stared at the Russian, as though challenging him.

"C'mon, Alex—what are you telling me? That you didn't know what you'd find here, didn't know I was here—is that it? I suppose you're just in Dublin on holiday and dropped in here for an early morning tour of one of the city's less visited churches."

Chekulayev said nothing. It needed only a camera to transform him into the archetype of a certain type of tourist. His fawn coat and burgundy scarf were neatly pressed, his shoes reflected the light of the candles. He could have been a businessman on leave, meddling in holiness for his soul's pleasure.

"Let's sit down, Patrick. I feel exposed up here, like an actor on a stage. All those empty pews back there, all those shadows piled up behind the pillars—they make me nervous. Let's sit down."

Patrick shuddered and looked away. He remembered—how many years ago?—a performance of Eliot's *Murder in the Cathedral*. Where had it been? St. Patrick's? Christchurch? He forgot. But he had not forgotten those final images: Becket by the altar, pierced and bleeding, the knights-tempters with their reddened swords, the chorus of the women of Canterbury chanting in the shadows:

"The land is foul, the water is foul, our beasts and ourselves defiled with blood. A rain of blood has blinded my eyes."

A rain of blood. An eye for an eye. And now Alex Chekulayev come like a ghost out of nowhere to haunt his present. Was there no escape?

They walked together to the back of the church and sat in the rear pew, like penitents come to wait their turn for confession, ringed by shadows.

"If I believed in anything," said Chekulayev, "I would become a Muslim. Churches are such gloomy places, don't you think? They give me the creeps. But mosques are all right. No statues, no memorials, no dead men nailed to crosses. It's morbid, don't you think, this religion of yours?"

"You were going to explain how you come to be here."

Chekulayev reached inside his pocket and drew out a pack of cigarettes. He held them out to Patrick.

"No, thank you."

The Russian shrugged and took one before returning the pack to his pocket. He jammed the cigarette into a small ebony holder ringed by a thin line of ivory and lit it. He used a match, cupping the flame in thick hands. For a brief moment, his face was lit up, like an icon in darkness, faded and gray and peeling. The face had matured, thought Patrick. Or perhaps just aged.

"Russian," Chekulayev said, meaning the cigarette. "At my age, you get used to things. And my people get suspicious of agents who acquire a taste for Western comforts. Just as yours are wary of a man with a penchant for leftish ideology. We never ask what a man thinks—that's far too abstract. It's what he wants that makes him dangerous." He breathed out a thin pillar of smoke. Patrick wondered if there was still a Russian word for "sacrilege."

"A few weeks ago," Chekulayev began, "I came to Dublin from Egypt. I was following rumors, a lead I'd picked up in Alexandria. Perhaps you've heard the rumors yourself. Tell me or not, as you like—it's your decision.

"Anyway, tonight I followed a man to the coast. He drove a little Citroën. A very careful driver. A little slow: not easy to follow. He parked his car on a road by the sea. After a while, he got out and walked down the road a little; then he began to wait. I waited too. You understand, Patrick. In this business of ours, waiting is of such importance.

"But our friend was not too clever. He let himself be seen. Someone attacked him." The Russian put the cigarette to his lips and inhaled slowly. He did not look at Patrick.

"I think you know what happened after that," he continued. "When you came out the second time, I followed you. That's the truth, Patrick. You led me here yourself."

Patrick felt the pew beneath his thighs, cold and hard. It reminded him of long masses he had sat through as a child, of the confessional's dank odor, of guilt, remorse, and tears. And of the terrible boredom of life.

"What made you show yourself, Alex? Didn't you want to follow me anymore? Didn't you want to see where I might lead you?"

"I decided it was time we talked. Time we shared our thoughts. We can help one another. Don't you agree?"

Patrick said nothing. Across the vanishing rows of silent pews, he could still make out the unmoving figure of Eamonn De Faoite, inexplicably murdered. In the early morning stillness, the small church filled with ghosts. Men he had killed or allowed to die. Men he had betrayed, men he had bought and sold, all dead or as good as dead, all unshriven, all unforgiving. Hasan Abi Shaqra coming to him for amnesty, his blood shattered across the dust like bright red shards of glass, abandoned eyes opening and closing in unbelief.

"I'm no longer with the Agency, Alex. It's true, whether or not you choose to believe me. I know nothing of your rumors, I never saw the man you followed before tonight. I'm not lying to you."

Up aloft, tiny feet scratched on wood. Years ago, someone had seen a vision here, a statue moving or oozing blood, or perhaps the Virgin herself, pale in a blue veil—Patrick could not remember. What did it matter anyway? Nothing had changed. And a priest lay dead on the altar.

"Please tell me what you know, Patrick. We aren't children. I don't believe in coincidence."

"I've told you. I'm no longer in circulation. If you don't believe me, have it checked out. One phone call, that's all it'll take."

Chekulayev lifted the cigarette from his lips. He did it without affectation or self-consciousness.

"You were always too trusting, Patrick. That's a great fault in an agent.

Perhaps you thought I was your friend. Some of us thrive on that conceit, that we are brothers beneath the skin, allies beneath our ideologies. It was easy to think that in Beirut. They hated us all without discrimination. They took us hostage, killed us. We were all unbelievers, all without salvation. And such a camaraderie that gave us: my enemy's enemy is my friend. Such talk. Such foolishness.

"People like us don't have friends, Patrick. We can't afford to. For me it would be the final luxury, something more insidious than American cigarettes or French perfume. Friendship has a smell of decadence, it lies on the skin longer than attar of roses. They would smell it on my body and whip the skin from my flesh and the flesh from my bones to exorcise it. So please don't ask me to believe you. Tell me the truth instead. Tell me about Passover."

Patrick started. Not "pass over," but "Passover." Was that what De Faoite had said? What did it mean? He said nothing. This was such a game. They were playing such a game. "Tell me what you know. Tell me the truth." Like children at charades, they mimed and signed to one another with grotesque gestures. But, unlike children, they sought to confuse, to mislead, to pervert one another. In this world, truths became falsehoods, falsehoods truths, until all became a single, consuming lie.

Like a worshiper, rapt at the sight of God's blood winelike in a gold chalice, he stared ahead, saying nothing. Chekulayev made a small gesture with his cigarette, a little red gesture that pinpricked the darkness. There was a footstep in the shadows behind them. Something hard and cold pressed against the nape of Patrick's neck. He heard the unmistakable sound of a pistol bolt drawn back.

"I think," Chekulayev whispered, as though in belated recognition of the dim sanctity of the place, "I think you had better come with me."

SIX

The house looked like every safe house he had ever visited or lived in: a little shabby, a little damp, a little sad. They took his blindfold off once the car was safe inside the garage. A dull green door led into the house itself. Chekulayev went ahead, saying nothing. Cheap carpets patterned in lilac, flocked wallpaper, damp-stained cornices: a cut-price haven for the morally dispossessed. Safe houses are like railway platforms: not places but moments in time.

There had not yet been time to feel afraid. That, he knew, would come. Ordinarily, Chekulayev would never have dared pick him up and bring him here. There were unwritten rules, and abducting the opposition's agents on neutral territory was one of the least bendable. The Russian must be worried. Worried about something big.

They followed a dingy wooden staircase to the top of the house, on the third floor. Chekulayev opened a door and preceded Patrick into a small, sparsely furnished room. A couple of armchairs upholstered in drab green Dralon, a coffee table bearing the ring marks left by hours of unrelieved boredom, a landscape print that might have represented anywhere from the Urals to the hills of Wicklow.

On the wall facing the door a little lamp burned on a copper bracket. Chekulayev took hold of it and pulled it toward him. A second door opened in the wall. The Russian stood back and ushered Patrick through the opening.

"Please," he said. "After you."

Patrick stepped inside. This was a smaller room, its walls soundproofed, like a radio studio. It held a metal table, bolted to the floor, and two uncomfortable wooden chairs. A bright bulb was screwed into the dead center of the ceiling, protected from tampering by stout wire mesh. The floor was uncarpeted. In one corner sat a toilet bowl with a plain wooden seat. A large mirror had been built into one wall. There was nowhere to wash or shave. He turned just in time to see the door close heavily behind him.

• • • •

Chekulayev shared the interrogation with a woman. Her full name was
Natalya Pavlovna Nikitina, and Patrick noticed that Chekulayev, when
addressing her, never omitted her patronymic. He guessed her age to be
about forty and her rank in the KGB at least that of major. She and
Chekulayev took turns through the days and nights that followed, leaving
Patrick little time for rest.

Natalya Pavlovna, Patrick assumed, would have cover as a first secretary
or assistant attaché at the embassy on Orwell Road. She was thin, patient,
and given to long silences. Her long black hair was always tied back in a
bun, held in place by pins. She dressed plainly and always in black, as
though in constant mourning. Her long pale neck gleamed like alabaster.

Patrick thought her anorexic at first, but in time revised his estimate:
Natalya Pavlovna was an ascetic. The pale limbs, the vestigial breasts, the
alabaster neck reminded him of a ballerina. But this woman was dedicated
to a different dance and moved to a different music. Where Chekulayev
feared the lash that would open his skin and bring to light his inwardness,
she welcomed its lacerations. Where he was sensual and used deprivation
as a threat, she was abstinent and treated the rigors of interrogation as a
discipline out of which truth, chastened and polished, would finally
emerge.

Patrick had no way of telling how much time passed. No natural light
entered the room. The powerful bulb in the ceiling was never extinguished.
Patrick would waken from a broken, desperate sleep to see Natalya
Pavlovna or Chekulayev standing by his side, ready to begin another session.

The worst were those with the woman. She had served her apprentice-
ship on the women's block in Leningrad's Kresty prison, before the block
was turned into a psychiatric wing. There she had learned the rhythms of
pain and the cadences of despair. She understood the finesse that left the
skin unbroken and the mind in tatters. She spoke the language of betrayal
in all its vernaculars. But the language of her heart was suffering: she knew
it in herself and taught it to others, unself-consciously.

From the Kresty, she had been transferred to Moscow's Lefortovo
prison, where she had worked on dissidents like Solzhenitsyn and Bukov-
sky. She talked at length about her experiences there. Above all, she
remembered the great nets the authorities had stretched across the gaps
between the landings, to prevent inmates from throwing themselves to
their deaths.

"Think of me as a net," she would say to Patrick. "I'm here to help you,
to stop you falling. There's nothing to be afraid of."

The room became a nightmare. Floor and walls and ceiling merged into a landscape without shape or dimension. The light never dimmed or flick-ered. Soon after Patrick's arrival, an orderly had taken away his clothes and given him a long white shift to wear instead. No sounds reached him from outside. He knew he could not be heard, even if he screamed.

It was clear from the outset that the mirror was a one-way glass through which they kept him under constant surveillance. He would sit facing it for hours, like an animal in a zoo, staring at his captors. At other times, he turned his back on them and stared at the other wall.

Food was left for him in bowls while he slept. It came regularly enough to stave off real hunger pangs, but not often enough or in sufficient quanti-ties to satisfy. It never varied: white rice, a few beans, cold black coffee. The empty bowls were removed while he slept again, which was seldom. The coffee kept him high and awake for long periods. When he did sleep, he was restless and easily wakened. He quickly became disoriented. He suffered from constipation, then bouts of severe diarrhea that kept him huddled for hours over the toilet. He would wake from disturbed dreams, shaking and nauseous.

Sometimes they would let him sleep ten or fifteen minutes, then wake him by banging loudly on the door. That would continue for hours: each time he began to nod off, the banging would start, until he grew agitated and angry. By the tenth or eleventh time, he would be so tired and con-fused that he started weeping from sheer frustration. Afterward, he would feel ashamed of his tears: he was determined to show his jailers no signs of weakness. But the tears came, whether he wished them or not.

He dreamed of De Faoite incessantly, of the wounded and bleeding altar on which he lay, inarticulate, like a tortured animal. The priest would rise and open cracked lips and whisper a single word over and over: *"Passover, Passover."* And in the dream flakes of plaster would crumble and fall from the high vaulted ceiling, white and sharp as snow, drifting across the bloody church, blanching its floor and walls, bleaching it of all corruption.

"Talk to me, Patrick," Natalya Pavlovna would say in a hushed voice, like one of the nuns he had known as a child, praying, alone with God. "Tell me about yourself. Tell me about your past. We have plenty of time, all the time in the world."

But he sensed an urgency in her voice, a frisson of alarm that belied the patience with which she approached her task. She never spoke of things directly, never asked leading questions. Her inquisition was roundabout, yet Patrick knew it hungered for a certain and sudden quarry.

At first, Patrick would not respond to these overtures. He kept a deter-mined silence, as though vowed to it. That was his novitiate. But as time passed and he lost track of night and day, present and past, dream and reality, he came to crave Natalya Pavlovna's visits more and more. In the end, he felt only gratitude for her presence and an overwhelming desire to please her.

At times he would wake out of some twisted dream or nightmare to find his mind preternaturally sharp, and in such moments he knew his gratitude to be no more than Natalya Pavlovna had contrived. But he could not wholly throw it aside. Lack of sleep and repeated caffeine buzzes kept him off balance. His resources were diminished, his resistance increasingly difficult to summon. There were moments when he felt he loved her, her soft, reassuring voice, her dark, questioning eyes.

It was not love, of course, but fear mixed with gratitude. And yet at times he could feel a shiver of sexuality pass between them. Even nuns on their hard beds wake with a shudder of desire. Often when she visited, he had the beginnings of an erection. Her subtlety was like a finger drawn along his flesh. They experienced a growing intimacy. Her questions were a lover's hands, stripping him bare. He would wake up sweating, dreaming of betrayal. But who was left for him to betray?

On several occasions, she asked him about his sins, major and minor, old and new. It was a way into his soul, and from his soul to his heart, and thence to his mind, where he kept all his recollections of names and dates and places. Natalya Pavlovna cared nothing for theology. Sins were nothing to her, or at best keys with which to unlock the doors of Patrick's mind.

"Think of me as a priest," she would murmur, "as a father confessor. How long is it since your last confession?"

And Patrick—who had indeed been many years absent from the confessional, and who did indeed suffer from a guilty conscience and the creeping footsteps of unquiet ghosts—unburdened his spirit gladly and without remorse.

Natalya Pavlovna never rushed, never applied overt pressure, though it was becoming increasingly clear that she was working against time. From sins religious they passed to sins secular, from morals they ascended to pragmatism and the absolutism of the state.

The sessions with Chekulayev were more down to earth. Unlike the woman, he was not interested in the state of Patrick's soul. After a session with Natalya, Patrick found it almost a relief to be faced with Chekulayev's directness.

He knew the names of Patrick's principal agents in Egypt and Lebanon, most of his contacts in the PLO and Hezbollah, and several of his agents of influence in Syria. He had details of CIA houses in Cairo and Port Said. He could recite details of several important cases in which Patrick had been involved, including some that had gone wrong, wrong enough to lead to unnecessary loss of life. He knew about Hasan Abi Shaqra.

What he sought, of course, were the gaps. The things he knew were nothing to those of which he was ignorant. But Patrick knew when to talk and when to keep silent.

"Tell me about Shifrin." Chekulayev returned time and time again to Patrick's old mentor, his station chief in Cairo. "When did he tell you about Passover? What does he know about the Brotherhood?" Patrick did not answer, for the simple reason that he had nothing to offer.

Natalya Pavlovna, however, possessed the skill to blur the difference between what she knew and what she did not. Each time they spoke, Patrick sensed his resistance weakening. He had talked and he wanted to talk more. He longed to confide in her. The white walls pressed in on him like the blocks of a hydraulic press. He thought they were growing closer. But he could not bring himself to measure them.

"Tell me about Passover." Natalya Pavlovna returned to the subject with increasing frequency. She seemed almost nervous. Her thin hands lay on her lap like pale, crustless crabs, naked and exposed. "What do you know of Migliau? Is he here? In Ireland? What have you heard? Have they set a date?"

To all of these questions Patrick could only plead complete ignorance. His head ached and he longed for darkness. Even with his eyes closed, the bright light lanced his brain like a thin blade.

"I've told you. All I know of "Passover" is that De Faoite mentioned it before he died."

"You mutter it in your sleep. I've heard you many times." This admission that she eavesdropped on Patrick's moments of slumber did not seem to cause Natalya Pavlovna any awkwardness. She knew Patrick assumed it, expected it. Sleep was not sacrosanct. In the religion they shared, nothing was sacrosanct. They were like husband and wife now. Surely there could be no more secrets between them.

He woke three or four times to find himself alone. By the fifth he was sure something was wrong. He was starving: why did no one come? He shouted and banged the walls, but there was no response. Exhausted, he fell asleep again. When he awoke, nothing had changed.

He called out again. *You can hear me, you bastards, you can hear me!*

"Where are you, Chekulayev? Where are you, Natalya? Why don't you answer?"

But no one responded to his entreaties. A ball of fear settled in his stomach.

He crouched down by the wall, disoriented. So, they had changed tactics. Isolate him, deprive him of all human contact, starve him. He felt helpless and afraid. How long could he go on? His cupboard was bare, at least of those things Natalya Pavlovna really wanted to hear. Would lies suffice?

He thought of ways to pass the time, mind games to blot out his growing distress. First, he taught himself to recite the Lord's Prayer backward, first in English, then in Latin, as he had learned it as a child. After that he composed elaborate, meaningless poems in Arabic, in which each word began with the same letter and each line ended with the same rhyme. And he wrote letters in his head to everyone he had ever known. Still no one came.

For a long time he stood defenseless at the mirror. He watched himself curiously, as he might have watched a monkey in a cage: his unshaven face, his red-rimmed eyes. Perhaps this was all there was left: himself and his reflection. If he vanished, he wondered, would the reflection remain there, like a wound after the knife has gone? He banged hard on the glass, bruising his knuckles.

"Chekulayev, you fucker! Stop playing games! Get your ass in here, I want to speak to you!" His voice sounded cracked and hollow, crashing against the tight walls and falling to the floor. For the first time, he was gripped by a fearful claustrophobia. It took him by the throat, forcing him painfully onto his knees, pressing him in onto himself. He began to sob. Tears coursed down grimy cheeks into his beard.

Time passed. He grew calm and called again. Still no one came. There were no sounds. It was as if he had been buried alive. He pushed the thought out of his head. *You're still in the interrogation room. They're out there, watching you. Hold on.*

He used the toilet and cleaned himself with a strip torn from his thin garment. There was no more paper.

The fear grew more intense. More than ever, he had lost track of time and place. If he did not leave soon, this tiny chamber would become his tomb. He sank back on the floor, shaking. Surely now Chekulayev would decide that he had had enough. There was no need to continue the farce. He was broken. He would confess. Natalya Pavlovna would understand. There would be no gloating, no rebukes. Just relief that their ordeal was over. But no one came.

He was not sure when the thought first came to him that something was wrong. He had conducted interrogations himself, he knew the score. Isolation was a valuable tool: it could break a stubborn spirit. But there were limits to its usefulness. It could drive someone over the edge for days or even weeks. His captors did not have that sort of time: he was certain of it. They wanted answers now. Something was amiss.

He took a chair and stood with it for a long time in front of the mirror.

His intention was clear. Still nobody came. Turning his head away, he lifted the chair by its back and swung it in a long arc. It crashed against the mirror with a roar of fragmenting glass. Something sharp flew against his cheek. He let the chair fall. The room beyond was empty.

SEVEN

Careful as glass, he stepped into the tiny room. There was an audio console on his right, fitted with two rows of tapes: one group to record, the other to play back. The console was illuminated as though someone had been there and gone a moment ago. A pad lay in front of the console, covered in Cyrillic longhand. On top of it someone had left a pen with the top unscrewed. A bank of green and red digital counters glowed like fairy lights against burnished metal. A single tape was spinning like a circus wheel, its free end flapping against the controls. On top of the console someone had left a half-finished cup of coffee. Patrick lifted it up. It was stone cold, days old.

As he set the cup down, his hand brushed the console. He heard the sound of breathing, then a voice, whispering, close by.

"When will you understand? When will you believe me? I don't know anything. I can't help you. I can only tell you what I know."

His own voice. A second tape had started to turn. He shuddered and switched off the toggle he had accidentally touched. Silence regained control.

He waited, tense, behind the door, expecting someone to come, holding the cup in his hand, the nearest thing he could find to a weapon. Cold coffee lay spilled on the floor, a dull, khaki pool soaking into the carpet. There was an electric clock above the console. It said twenty to ten: night or morning, he had no way of knowing. He let five minutes pass. No one came.

The door opened into the little anteroom through which he had passed on his arrival. Like the interrogation room, the monitoring cubicle was disguised behind the brown-papered wall. The door closed behind him, and it was as though neither his cell nor the cubicle beside it had ever existed. He stood in an ordinary room, breathing ordinary air. He had only the white cotton shift to remind him of his ordeal.

He paused on the landing, uncertain what to do. Sense told him to go directly down the stairs: with luck he could make it to the front door and

DUBLIN   57

be on the street before anyone came. But a more deep-seated instinct told him that no one was going to come. To leave without knowing why could only be dangerous. If his instinct was wrong, at least he had the element of surprise.

In a junk room on the third floor he found a long-handled hammer. It felt lethal in his hand and gave him renewed confidence. The other rooms —all bedrooms—were empty. A glance through one curtained window told him it was ten o'clock at night. Outside the streets were endless, mocking, scarred with rain. There was no way down.

He descended the stairs to the second floor, willing himself to move slowly, fighting back an urge to run until he reached the street. He heard a sound like music, a muffled, almost ethereal sound. It was music, and yet not quite music.

On the landing, he hesitated, listening. Now he realized what the sound was: a gramophone needle stuck in a record groove was playing the same snatch of music over and over again.

The sound came from a room on his left. He opened the door. Here, as elsewhere, the light had been left on. A coffee table with English-language magazines, two easy chairs, an empty glass that had been knocked to the floor. In one corner, a cheap gramophone ground out its single phrase. He stepped across and lifted the needle. The sleeve stood on a shelf nearby: the Elmer Bernstein recording of Seán O'Riada's *Mise Éire,* played by the RTE Concert Orchestra. Someone had been getting into the spirit of things.

Next door was a bathroom. Stainless steel and dingy porcelain, a toilet like the one upstairs, a razor on a shelf. He closed the door.

There were six people in the next room, five men and one woman, Natalya Pavlovna. They sat facing him in a row, their eyes fixed on the door. No one spoke. No one asked him to come in. He stood in the doorway for a long time, returning their stare. Such strange postures, such tortured expressions. No one moved a muscle. Patrick closed the door behind him.

Whoever had tied them had done a good job: not too tight, not too loose. Just right. Once they were firmly fastened in their chairs, of course, the rest had been easy. They had probably bought the plastic bags and rubber bands in Quinnsworth's. They could not have cost more than a pound.

Behind the plastic, the faces were chalk white. Natalya Pavlovna's alabaster neck was creased and swollen. A small patch of cerulean blue had appeared on her left cheek. Chekulayev's tongue protruded like a rubber cork, black and ugly.

The heads had been shaven. Hair lay discarded on the floor, an innocent reminder of old barbershops. Patrick stepped up close. On each scalp three figures had been inscribed in ballpoint pen: *666.*

He looked up. On the wall behind, the same pen had been used to write a single line in Greek:

Τισ ομοιοσ τω θηριω; και τισ δυναται πολεμησαι μετ αυτου?

Patrick recognized it. The words came from the Book of Revelation:

Who is like unto the beast? who is able to make war with him?

He glanced at the shaved heads and remembered another verse from the same chapter:

Let him that hath understanding count the number of the beast:
for it is the number of a man;
and his number is Six hundred threescore and six.

666: the number of the Beast.
He prayed nobody he knew was behind all this.

EIGHT

They were walking through St. Stephen's Green, a little like lovers, a little like strangers. Everywhere, sculpted faces watched them pass: Mangan and Markievicz, Emmet and Tone and Kettle—poets and freedom fighters turned to civic amenities. There was a little sunlight: not enough to send the clouds packing, but sufficient to lift people's spirits an inch or two. Buskers had played for them at the top of Grafton Street, *A Raibh Tú ag an gCarraig*, the pipes muted, the tin whistle sweet and swollen with its painful melancholy. They had taken lunch at the Shelbourne, then crossed the road directly into the park.

Everything seemed normal here: children played or fed the ducks on the tiny lake, lovers embraced on benches, old men in shabby coats lingered by the bandstand, as though waiting for it to fill again with music. It was not yet spring, but the air held a promise of change. On Grafton Street, old Lord Mustard danced to jazz tunes in a silly hat.

Sometimes she held his hand, at others she folded her arms and walked ahead of him, as though impatient to be somewhere. She was wearing a long fur coat from Zwirn with Pancaldi shoes, and for the first time he thought she looked out of place. She wore them as a means of distancing herself from the squalor of her occupation, from the everyday demeaning acts she performed in the name of reason. He thought of her clothes more as symbols or guarantees of loyalty: Ruth Ehlers could not be bought. Not, at least, for money.

"I want you to leave, Patrick," she said. Beside them, a fountain of green and bronze bulrushes threw water high into the February sky. "I mean it: don't get involved in this thing any further."

It was the first time she had referred to the subject all day. Oddly enough, it seemed to bring her closer, as though she felt easier dealing with an impersonal matter.

"I am involved. I was involved from the beginning."

"But that's as far as it goes. Let somebody else handle it now. You gave this all up, remember?"

"I've been recommissioned, Ruth. That's what this amounts to. You don't just walk away from a friend's body."

They were standing beside the white marble relief of Roisin Dubh, beneath Mangan's placid bust. Ruth stroked the pale face with a gloved hand.

"Yes, Patrick, you do. If you want to stay alive. Listen, I've been putting the pieces of this thing together."

"And?"

"A few weeks ago, we intercepted a signal from a Soviet AGI ship off Malin Head. When I say 'we,' I mean the radio intercept station at Hacklaw in Scotland, run by the British. They passed it on among a pile of routine stuff to the NSA's liaison office at Benhall Park. Benhall passed it to us."

He had heard about AGIs—Auxiliary General Intelligence vessels, *Okean*-class ships the Soviets kept moored off the coast of Donegal. Their main function was to keep track of U.S. nuclear submarines using Holy Loch as home base.

"Usually," Ruth went on, "these are low-grade signals intended for their agents in Ireland. Routine stuff, usually something to do with the IRA. But this one had taken Benhall three days to crack. I got to see it the day it arrived. If I'd known then . . ." She paused. A gust of wind caught her scarf. It flew across the marble face like a multicolored veil, before she caught it and wound it round her neck again.

"The message came from the very top, Patrick—from Moscow Center, from General Kurakin, chief of the First Directorate. It was addressed to the *rezidentura* in Dublin. It began with apologies for sending the message by such an insecure route, but there had been no time to arrange for anything better. Dublin station was to drop everything it was doing and get ready for the arrival of somebody very important. The code name was unfamiliar to us. He was known as 'Obelisk.' "

Patrick had been watching a bird preening itself on a nearby bush, a robin escaped from a Christmas card. He turned and took Ruth's arm, tightly, drawing her away from the marble figure down the path.

"It's cold," he said, "let's go back."

They headed for the bridge over the little lakes.

"You know who I'm talking about, don't you, Patrick? You know who 'Obelisk' was."

"Of course. Chekulayev. It's his old name, it's always been his name."

"We didn't know that. Not then. No one thought to check on their Middle East agents. It didn't seem obvious, not then."

They came out onto the street, into the midafternoon traffic, and headed up toward Baggot Street.

"There were no more messages from Center after that, not through the AGIs anyway. We notified Irish intelligence, kept a lookout for ourselves, but he slipped through. We think he was dropped off the coast from a sub one dark night. Or maybe he just flew into Dublin airport, God knows. Patrick, we didn't think about the Middle East. Maybe I should have guessed—knowing you were in Dublin."

"You weren't the only one who knew I was here."

"No, but . . . I had more reason to think about you."

They were walking arm in arm now. Away from the open spaces of the park, she seemed smaller. Her breath hung white and momentary on the frozen air. He could feel it burn his cheek when she turned to speak.

"We knew he'd arrived," she continued, "because a few days later we picked up a signal from the *rezidentura* using the same code as the earlier message. That was careless. The signal was signed 'Obelisk' and referred to something called 'Passover.' He'd started work, he said. Two days later, you disappeared."

She held him more tightly, as though frightened he would vanish again, like smoke, like warm breath on cold air, like a thought started but not completed. An elderly nun smiled at them in complicity as she hurried past. Only the celibate truly understand the meaning of passion.

"Even then I failed to make the connection. 'Obelisk,' 'Passover'— Jesus, Patrick, it should have been obvious."

"Nothing's obvious in this business. Look, what's so worrying about all this? Dublin station knew Chekulayev was here, nobody warned me, I found out the hard way. So, why the sudden panic?"

"No panic, Patrick. Just sensible precautions." She paused. "I haven't told you everything. We got the NSA to feed the code name into their computer system at Fort Meade. They carry records of all diplomatic and SIGINT traffic in and out of Ireland. That includes all their own intercepts from Menwith Hill and Morwenstow in England, which covers all Intelsat V communications through Elfordstown, as well as anything GCHQ feeds in. They use a word-recognition program that can handle four million characters a second. We asked them to track the word 'Passover' in about a dozen languages over the past month."

"And?"

"We got nothing. Not a damn thing. We tried 'Obelisk' and 'Chekulayev' —still nothing. Somebody suggested 'Easter,' but all that gave us was a couple of routine messages from the Vatican to their nunciature. Then the penny dropped. I fed your name in."

As though by mutual accord, they stopped. They were just crossing the bridge over the Grand Canal between Lower and Upper Baggot Street. Like half-finished wire casings, frozen trees flanked the water's edge, stretching into the distance in either direction. He let her speak.

"You got three mentions. Number one was from somebody in Tel Aviv to a friend in the Israeli embassy, wanting to know what the hell you were doing in Dublin. The second was peculiar. It was a radio message using a diplomatic wavelength and a standard code, but the transmitter was located somewhere on the west coast, near Galway. It was beamed somewhere toward southern Europe—northern Italy or Yugoslavia, perhaps. You'd been seen visiting Eamonn De Faoite. Someone had run a check on you and discovered you were with the Company. They thought you still were."

She turned and look down the canal, in the direction of Mount Street. Trees like gutted candles, lifeless, without flame. Water like base metal, flowing silently between grass and concrete.

"You said there were three. Three messages."

"Yes." She hesitated. He noticed how she bit her lower lip, small white teeth on the red flesh. "We think it was the reply to the second, a telephone call. All the NSA can tell us is that the call originated in Venice, Italy. The number's untraceable. It went to a number outside Oughterard, a little place not far from Lake Corrib, to a holiday cottage. It was taken by an answering device." She paused.

"Yes?"

"The cottage has been empty all winter, Patrick. Locked up. Or so the owner says. We sent someone to check. There was no answering machine. The telephone was disconnected."

"What was the message?"

"It was in Italian. The speaker left instructions that you were to be eliminated along with Eamonn De Faoite. Your house was to be searched for papers, papers De Faoite might have given you."

"When was it sent?"

"Three weeks ago. About twenty-four hours before you found De Faoite murdered." She turned to him, tense, angry, almost weeping. "For God's sake, Patrick, the cottage wasn't empty when our people got out there. There was a child, a boy of ten. What was left of him. The heart had been cut out: they found some of it later in a garbage can. It had been burned. He . . . The doctor thought he'd been dead about a week. We got an ID on him yesterday."

All about them the world seemed ordinary. Traffic passed in a constant stream. Only yards away, a small queue had formed at the Bank of Ireland cash machine on the corner of Haddington Road. And they stood on the bridge talking of children with their hearts ripped out.

"His name was Alessandro Clemente, the son of Paolo Clemente, the Italian Minister of Foreign Affairs. The boy had been kidnapped from outside his private school off the Via Galvani in Rome. That was about two weeks before the body was found. The Italians were keeping the whole thing quiet. It was hard enough finding out what we did."

"What about this guy Clemente, the father? Is he speaking? Does he know what all this is about?"

"He isn't speaking to anybody, Patrick. He's dead. His wife found him in his study with a shotgun rammed down his throat and most of his head decorating the wall. This was about ten hours after the report of the boy's death reached him. We did discover one thing, though. There was a note on his desk. Not in his own handwriting, so his wife says. It was just one line. I'm told it's from the Book of Leviticus. *'He hath given of his seed unto Molech, to defile my sanctuary, and to profane my holy name.'*

"Just what the hell is going on here, Patrick?" She was crying, hot, stinging tears that lined her cheeks. Not for the boy, not for Patrick, but for herself. She had lifted a stone of marble and seen the horrors that slithered to and fro beneath. "What the fuck is going on?"

NINE

Back in her flat on Pembroke Road, they sat on a long couch in front of the fire, close but not quite touching. Beneath high ceilings, shadows moved on Mondrians and Van Doesburgs and Fontanas, line upon measured line, shadow upon shadow. In one corner, a painted sculpture by Dhruva Mistry, half man, half beast, kept careful watch. On the hi-fi, Klaus Nomi was singing an aria from Saint-Saëns's *Samson and Delilah*.

Only the fire seemed real. A fine odor of warm peat crept through the room. Red and yellow and gold flames cast bright reflections on brass and copper. Ruth had made mulled wine filled with heavy spices: cloves and cinnamon and aniseed, with orange and lemon peel. They sipped the wine and listened to the music, and Patrick thought how unnatural everything had become, how far removed from a world in which the bodies of pale children decayed in summer cottages, and priests, like Oedipus, were blinded on high altars.

"It troubles me that God can allow such things," he said.

"I thought you didn't believe in God."

He watched smoke spiral upward, imagined it gray and nebulous on the darkening air outside.

"I don't," he replied. "But that's just it, don't you see? I can't believe in a God who lets things like this go on. Oh, and things worse than this. Much, much worse. Any other god I could believe in, but not this one. To be omnipotent and hold back, to be capable and do nothing. Just watch. Watch and judge. I remember . . ."

She twisted a little toward him, her eyes fixed on his profile.

"I remember," he continued, "something I once read. It was in a book of Islamic theology: *'These to heaven, and I care not. These to hell, and I care not.'* What sort of God is that? And the Christian God isn't any better. He lets children die on the street in Calcutta just so people can say what a wonderful woman Mother Theresa is. At least Molech kept his depredations to a reasonable level."

"Who was Molech, Patrick? What did it mean, that verse they found on Clemente's desk?"

"Molech? He was a Canaanite god. Phoenician, if you prefer. He had a taste for children. Their parents used to take them up to his altar at a place called Topheth. That was where they did it—the burning, the sacrificial offering. To keep the crops from spoiling. To make their cattle fertile. For whatever reason—for whatever seemed important to them."

She shuddered and looked aside.

"They burned them?"

"Yes. So the Old Testament says. Maybe it's just biased, a load of propaganda about Canaanite atrocities—who knows? But I don't remember anything about cutting hearts out."

The fire in the hearth leaped and twisted, throwing a cloud of sparks high into the chimney. Ruth leaned against him, touching him for the first time since entering the apartment. He responded, putting his arm round her, drawing her to him.

"My parents were enlightened," she said. "Or thought they were. Rich liberals with black friends, Jewish friends, intellectuals. No gay friends, of course: they weren't *that* liberal. They had old money, so they could afford some eccentricities. They voted Democrat, donated to the ACCL, signed petitions to end the war in Vietnam. I was brought up to be nice to the maids and gardeners, and every Christmas I gave some of my toys to the local orphanage. They sent me to a succession of private schools, and Europe twice a year, and Vassar when I was old enough, because it had gone coed. And a year in Switzerland, to be 'finished' as they put it.

"The trouble is, where do you go from there? When I grew up, nobody was dropping out any longer. I was liberal all right, but I had my own trust fund. With a private income, you can afford to be liberal. Even with Ronald Reagan in the White House. Especially with Ronald Reagan in the White House."

She put her head on his shoulder.

"I got married, but that didn't solve anything. I don't suppose it ever does. Mr. Ehlers was a nice guy, as nice guys go. But after you've fucked about seven hundred times in a row, and taken your fifteenth vacation in three years, and put this year's finishing touches on top of last year's finishing touches on the bidets in the guest bathrooms, even nice guys can pall a little.

"So I dropped out. Since I couldn't be a hippy any longer, I joined the Company. My parents were furious. But I wanted to prove something to them." She paused, biting her lip. "Funny, I've forgotten what it was." She pulled him to her, frightened, angry with her fear. "Tell me, Patrick, tell me what the fuck it was! It wasn't this—so what was it?"

She was crying painfully now, her doubts grown inarticulate with rage. He kissed her eyes, tasting the bright, metallic tears. He knew the flavor well, it ran in his own veins, bitter, galling, cold as ice. His lips stumbled drunkenly down her cheeks, his hands fumbled across her breasts, clumsy, like a child's. She pulled away briefly, then returned to him, her lips to his lips, her breath confused and harsh, mingling with his breath, with the heavy odor of wine and spices.

They had not made love since his return from the safe house. He had been distant, colder than usual, without response. Now, with a suddenness that dismayed him, the pent-up fears of his confinement focused on a raging physical need. To enter her would free him from everything. Like a prophet surprised in solitude by a sudden, tumultuous god, he cried out, aghast at the brightness of his vision. He felt her hand descend like a bird's wing, light and trembling, to his thighs, her fingers moving on his growing flesh.

He closed his eyes and saw Natalya Pavlovna, the thin body, the piercing eyes. He thought of her naked beneath him, the small, flat breasts, the bruised nipples, the churning breath. She had come to him like a lover, seeking out his sins, and he had never touched her or been touched by her. He reached out a hand for Ruth, stroking her leg, higher and higher until he heard her gasp.

She twisted, sliding down, pulling him to the floor with her. Her eyes were closed, she could not bear to look at him or have him look at her, her heart was pounding, uncomfortable and fast. His fingers touched her, now light, now pressing urgently. Her breath came quickly, she wanted to cry out, to expel the awful thing that had lodged inside her: a dead child gutted and cast aside like an unwanted fish on a harbor wall.

He undressed her passionately, but as though in a dream: her top, her skirt, her underthings. Her skin felt hot and fevered to his desperate touch, he could not sense her presence in the room with him. Imperceptibly, they had begun to move to different rhythms. She made love to exorcise the ghost of a child she had never met, whose silent, ravaged heart had entered her dreams and wrought havoc there; he to find a dream that might make waking more bearable.

Her nakedness appalled him, her need to be touched, her vehemence in lovemaking. Her exorcism called for rage, his for forgetfulness. As she undressed him, he felt his sense of unreality deepen, as though the shedding of his clothes entailed in some fashion a loss of identity. His head felt light, almost detached from his body. And yet his thoughts were clear, almost unbearably so. He felt her hands, hot and restless, move across his back and chest.

What happened next was unpredicted and unrehearsed. It was rather as if he had been staring at one of those trick pictures, the sort psychologists use to test perception, in which a duck becomes a rabbit or a beautiful woman reveals herself as an old crone.

An almost imperceptible shift occurred between one breath and the next. He looked round to see that the fire had burned low and the room was now bathed in candlelight. He could not even be sure it was the same room. There were heavy hangings on one wall where there had been none before. Outside, the sound of traffic had vanished. It was chillier than it had been a moment earlier.

He was still naked, still tumescent, still crouched above the form of a naked woman on the floor. But the woman was not Ruth. Her hair was jet black, tousled, in heavy braided folds across her face. She was small-breasted, with narrower hips and more abundant pubic hair. Even as he looked, she brushed back the hair from her face.

"In ainm Dé, a Phádraig, lean ort! For God's sake, Patrick, don't stop now," she said.

He did not know how he knew, but the language was Irish, Leinster Irish of the eighteenth century. But that was impossible—she could not be speaking Irish. He knew her, knew her as well as he knew himself: it was Francesca. Only that was impossible too: Francesca was dead, she had been dead twenty years.

He stumbled back, slipping, then raising himself on one hand.

"Cad tá ort, a Phádraig? Cad tá ort, a stór? Patrick, what's wrong? What is it, darling?"

Standing, he felt his head spin. The candles moved and the room lurched. He was falling, he could feel himself spinning through space, then the floor crashing against him and the breath pumped out of his body.

When he came round, Ruth was standing over him, a wet sponge in her hand, a look of deep concern on her face.

"Patrick, what's wrong? What is it, darling? How do you feel?"

He put his hand to his head. Out of nowhere he had a pounding headache. His stomach felt queer. It reminded him of migraines he had experienced in his teens.

"I'm . . . all right," he murmured. "Just . . . blacked out. My head feels terrible: I think it's a migraine."

She raised him to a sitting position against the sofa.

"Shall I get a doctor? Has this happened before?"

"It's all right. I'll be okay. This used to happen when I was younger. I'll be better after a sleep."

But nothing like this had happened before: a hallucination, blacking out. His body was covered with sweat and he had started to shiver. Ruth helped him onto the sofa.

"Stay there," she said. "I'll fetch a blanket."

He shifted himself to a more comfortable position. As he did so, he noticed something on his stomach, a long, fine line. He took it between finger and thumb and lifted it. It was a hair, a black hair about two feet in length.

TEN

Archbishop Pasquale Balzarin stood at the window of his second-floor study, watching the shadows lengthen on the lawn. Sunlight lay plaited through blades of untrampled grass. A bird soared overhead, lost in circles of its own making. On the lawn, a peacock passed, precise and shadowless, its feathers warm against the twilight. It walked through its own world, untouched by the worries of the man who watched it, a thing of beauty merely.

Why now? he thought. *Why now?* Arthritic fingers pressed nervously on the white beads of his rosary, investing the question with an element of prayer. Outside, the peacock screamed, turning its fan against the encroaching darkness.

Balzarin had been papal nuncio to the Republic of Ireland for three years now. During his last visit to Rome, he had heard whispers. Fazzini was certain to step down from his curial office on his seventy-fifth birthday. If Balzarin sat tight a few months more, he would step into Fazzini's shoes and, of course, his cardinal's hat. He wanted that more than he had ever wanted anything.

Correction. What he wanted most of all in the world was to get out of Dublin. Out of its rain and mist and perpetual gloom. He was sixty now and wanted to spend his last days in the sun, preferably in his native Italy, best of all in Rome. After all, he did have fifteen years to go before he was officially expected to retire.

There were moments on the verge of sleep when he cursed St. Patrick for ever having brought the faith to this place at all. The whole thing was a horrible mistake. Christianity was a Mediterranean religion: God's son would never have volunteered to dwell among the cairns and cromlechs of this mist-soaked wasteland.

He returned to his desk. A copy of the most recent edition of the *Annuario Pontificio,* the Vatican Yearbook, lay open at the first of many pages dealing with the Secretariat of State. It did no harm to keep up to date on who did what, who had been moved, who had passed on to a higher service. Casually, he flicked over a few pages, then, consulting the index, turned to the section devoted to the Archives. He studied the entry for a few moments, made an annotation in pencil on a pad, and closed the book.

There was a knock on the door.

"Avanti!"

Father Assefa Makonnen stepped into the room. He was the nuncio's *addetto,* roughly equivalent to a second secretary. An Ethiopian, he had been sent to Dublin a year ago, to encourage links between the Irish Church and the Third World. It had taken him less than six months to learn that some of the church hierarchy in Ireland thought this *was* the Third World.

"I'm sorry to disturb you, Your Excellency, but your visitor has arrived."

Balzarin sighed and pursed his lips. He had forgotten that a visitor was due. He glanced at the clock on the mantel. It was fourteen minutes to five.

"Show him in," he said.

As Makonnen turned to go, Balzarin called him back.

"His name, Father, what is his name?"

"Canavan, Your Excellency. Patrick Canavan. An American of Irish descent."

"Ah, yes," Balzarin whispered. "The American."

The clock whirred guiltily and struck the quarter hour.

It had taken Ruth over two hours this morning to fix up this interview with the nuncio. Strings had been pulled, favors promised. She was still unhappy about Patrick's pressing on with his inquiries but had decided trying to dissuade him was futile.

Makonnen introduced Patrick to the archbishop and saw him into a chair before seating himself nearby, pen and paper on his lap in readiness for note taking.

Patrick hesitated. They no longer made them like Balzarin. The nuncio was a patriarch from his purple skullcap to his highly polished boots. He seemed to have borrowed the parts for his face from a range of Renaissance painters, but the overall effect was uniform: a look of thin, aristocratic disdain that wore the holiness of his office with ill-disguised impatience.

"I'm very grateful, Your Excellency," Patrick began, "that you found time to see me."

Balzarin gestured briefly with his hand. Patrick was not sure whether the movement meant "Don't mention it" or "Get on with what you have to say," but he rather thought the latter.

"I'm not sure . . . Has Father Makonnen explained to you the reason for my visit?"

The nuncio adjusted a photograph on his desk. On one finger, a ruby ring caught light from the fire.

"You are a researcher in Semitic languages at Trinity College. You were a friend of the late Father Eamonn De Faoite, the parish priest of St. Malachy's, here in Dublin. You are"—he glanced at the clock on the mantelpiece—"fifteen minutes late for your appointment. How can I help you?"

Patrick shifted awkwardly. Out of the corner of his eye, he caught a reassuring smile from the secretary.

"I'll come straight to the point, Your Excellency. Before he died, Eamonn De Faoite told me he had given you some papers. I believe those papers relate in some way to his death. With your permission, I would like to examine them."

Balzarin did not move. But Patrick sensed the effort he made to control his features. Shadows licked at his pale skin, cast by the flickering flames in the open hearth. The nuncio fixed his eyes on Patrick, as though he possessed a faculty beyond sight, that enabled him to read his visitor's thoughts. He was nervous, but when he spoke, his voice betrayed nothing of his inner feelings.

"I think you are mistaken, Signor . . . ah, Canavan. I did not know Father De Faoite. He did not give any papers to me. If these were important papers, surely he would have given them to his own bishop. They would not concern me. I am the papal nuncio: parish affairs are no concern of mine."

Patrick coughed. In spite of the blazing fire, he felt cold. It was growing dark outside. He glanced across the room at Makonnen. The Ethiopian's smile had gone and been replaced by a searching look directed at Balzarin. Patrick tried again.

"I have every reason to believe that Eamonn De Faoite's death was no parish affair. To my certain knowledge, it already involves at least one national intelligence bureau. At a very high level." Just how high it went, he had no way of knowing: but Chekulayev was not someone they would waste on parish politics.

"An intelligence bureau?" Balzarin seemed disturbed and more than a little interested, in spite of himself. "Could you be more specific, Signor Canavan? You are referring to the CIA?"

Patrick shook his head.

"At this stage, I think it's better I don't answer that."

"You are being deliberately mysterious, *signore*. Let me repeat, your friend left no papers with me, nor have I any other papers in my possession relating to his death. Father Makonnen tells me he died a little over two weeks ago. According to the bishop's office, there was nothing unusual about his death. He was an old man who has now gone to his heavenly reward. I really cannot see what interest either his life or his death could hold for what you term a 'national intelligence bureau.' I am a busy man, *signore*. You will excuse me if I ask Father Makonnen to help you out. Thank you for coming. I'm sorry I could not be of greater help."

The Italian rose, intending to bring the interview to a close.

"Please sit down, Your Excellency. I haven't finished speaking."

Patrick watched Balzarin's face turn an episcopal purple. The nuncio remained standing, momentarily lost for words.

"Eamonn De Faoite was murdered on the altar of his own church," whispered Patrick. "His eyes were gouged out and he was left to die in severe pain. His killers had daubed verses from the Bible on the walls. And you tell me there was 'nothing unusual about his death.' "

Slowly, as though lowered there by a mechanism from above, Balzarin sank back into his chair.

"*Come* . . . ? How . . . did you obtain this information? All details of De Faoite's death were kept from the public. The circumstances were much too . . . disturbing. This is a Catholic country, *signore*. There are some things that are better left unsaid. Do you understand me? This is not a matter of politics or scandals or reputations; it is a matter of faith. As representative of the Holy See in Ireland, it is my duty to ensure that the Church's image is not harmed unnecessarily. The Church has many enemies in this country, both here and in the north. I have no intention of letting you or anyone else play into their hands."

Balzarin talked himself back into a position of control. He leaned across the desk. The light was fading rapidly now, but nobody moved to turn on a lamp.

"Let me ask you again," he said in a voice from which all signs of perturbation had been rigidly excluded. "How did you come by your information concerning the manner of Father De Faoite's death?"

"I found him. He died trying to tell me about something called 'Passover.' He said you had papers that explained what it is about. I don't care a damn if nobody ever knows a thing about his murder. That isn't important. But those papers are."

"And I repeat, I know nothing of any papers. Frankly, I think you may be making a mystery where there is none. You say Father De Faoite spoke of Passover to you. He was dying. Like yourself, he was an expert in Semitic languages. No doubt he had some papers referring to the Jewish festival of that name. Or to the Book of Exodus perhaps. His death was the work of a madman. If you were there, you will not need me to tell you that. I can understand that you are disturbed. But I cannot let your personal distress do damage to the Church. Do I make myself clear?"

Patrick knew the archbishop was lying. He could see it in his eyes and in his manner. His assurance had turned to bluster. He knew something, something that he and others wanted to remain a secret.

From his pocket Patrick drew out a small slip of paper. He had drawn a circle on it, and in the circle inscribed three small crosses. Gently, he laid it on the nuncio's desk.

"Will you please tell me if this means anything to you?"

Balzarin switched on a green-shaded desk lamp and reached for a pair of wire-framed spectacles on his blotter. Patrick noticed that his hands shook as he put the spectacles on. He watched him narrowly as he bent to look at the paper. In the corner, he could see Makonnen watching as well.

The color drained from the nuncio's face. His lips moved, whispering something inaudible. He looked up. In his eyes Patrick could see a haunted expression.

"Please leave, Signor Canavan. You are meddling in things you have no knowledge of. Please do not come again or try to contact me. Forget about this business. It is essential for you to forget about it. Otherwise . . ."

Balzarin stood abruptly.

"Father Makonnen will see you out. Good-bye, *signore.*"

Pausing only to remove his spectacles, the nuncio turned and left the room through a side door. His footsteps echoed briefly in the room beyond.

On the lawn, a peacock cried out. Suddenly, there was silence. And in the silence darkness ruffled the leafless trees.

ELEVEN

Midnight. The world suspended, lightless, blind. Dawn was hours away, almost unbelievable in its remoteness. Assefa Makonnen woke out of an uneasy sleep. Had there been a sound? Above his bed, a red light flickered beneath a painting of the sacred heart. He lay listening to the wind as it circled the building, creeping in and out among the trees. It was very cold.

The priest switched on his bedside light. Out of the darkness, a stark white room emerged. He rubbed his eyes and sat up. What had woken him? The cold? The mental unease he had felt ever since the American's visit? Or had it been a sound after all? He listened intently, but there was only the wind.

He turned out the light and tried to go back to sleep, but sleep would not come. His mind was troubled. Over his head, the red light flickered incessantly. He would open his eyes and see it, like a red eye glaring at him. As a child in Asmara he had taken comfort from it in the cold hours before dawn. It had watched over him throughout his years at the Ethiopian Seminary in the Vatican, and later at the Accademia Pontificia, where he had trained to be a papal diplomat. But tonight it seemed angry, almost accusing. He switched on the bedside light again.

Something was wrong. Why had Balzarin lied to the American? Makonnen knew he should tackle his superior about the matter. But he also knew that he did not possess the courage to do so. The archbishop was a powerful man. It was only a matter of time before the Holy Father elevated him to the rank of cardinal. Back in Rome, Balzarin would be in a position to make or break lesser men. To make matters worse, the nuncio's father had been murdered in 1940 while serving as a provincial governor in Italian East Africa—in northern Ethiopia, to be precise. From his first day in Dublin, Makonnen had been aware that his presence was barely tolerated.

But a priest had died under dreadful circumstances and someone was trying to cover it up. Makonnen knew that not even the local police had been notified. The bishop had gone directly to Balzarin, and the nuncio had taken the matter entirely into his own hands.

There had been papers. Makonnen had handled them: after De Faoite's death, he had been instructed to take them to Rome in the diplomatic pouch. He had flown straight to Fiumicino airport on the twenty-fifth of January and headed directly to the Holy See. There he had handed them over personally to Cardinal Fazzini in the Secretariat of State. Fazzini had dismissed him with a wave of the hand and told him to take the next flight back to Dublin.

He had come back troubled. But, until today, his training had retained the upper hand over his emotions. They had taught him obedience: at school, at the seminary, at the Pontifical Academy. Obedience had never irked or shamed him before this. But tonight he felt it like a gag across his mouth, choking him.

The American had spoken of interest on the part of a "national intelligence bureau." In all likelihood he meant the CIA. The man at the United States embassy who had arranged Canavan's audience was reputed to be their chief intelligence officer. And the Agency had cooperated with the Holy See often enough in the past. Why, then, had Balzarin reacted as he had? Just what did the archbishop know? Makonnen thought he might find the answer in Balzarin's office.

He took his spectacles from the bedside table and slipped them on. The bed was warm, and he was reluctant to venture out. The climate here was the only thing on which he saw eye to eye with Balzarin. He steeled himself and swung his feet out of the covers onto the cold floor. He slept in socks, a woolen vest, and a thick jumper given him in November by a Sacred Heart of Mary sister from Tallaght. Sometimes he thought the only thing between him and abandoning his vocation was Sister Nuala's jumper. That and the socks.

His soutane hung on the back of the door. Shivering, he pulled it over his head and fastened his belt tight round his waist. This was the stupidest thing he had ever done.

As he opened the door, he glanced round. On the wall facing the bed hung a plain wooden crucifix he had brought from Ethiopia. The black Christ stared at him with burning eyes. Makonnen returned his gaze. "What would you do?" he asked beneath his breath as he closed the door behind him.

The nunciature was plunged in darkness. The building was almost empty. Two of the staff had gone up to Armagh the day before to consult with Cardinal O'Fiaich on the latest Anglo-Irish debacle. The *chargé d'affaires,* Father Kennealy, was attending a conference in Cork. Only the nuncio, Makonnen himself, and a visiting Jesuit from the Holy Office were sleeping on the premises tonight. The visitor was in a guest room on the top floor.

The study was on the floor below him, near the nuncio's private apartment. Makonnen hesitated on the landing, listening carefully. He wondered again if he had been woken by a sound. It was highly unlikely that someone would have broken in: the nunciature, a new building just off the Navan Road in the north of Dublin, was well protected by the Gardai. Perhaps the wind had disturbed something in the grounds.

The carpeted stairs muffled his footsteps. He clung to the banister with his right hand. On the high wall to his left, the portraits of former nuncios hung like a row of judges, their massive gilded frames barely visible in the darkness. Makonnen thought of his tiny home on the outskirts of Asmara, the ancient churches cut in rock, the tattered vestments of the priests, God's poverty, Christ's poverty, the world's poverty. And all around him in the dark endless riches jostling for space. For the first time in years, he felt out of touch with the world and with himself. Did God walk in such silent corridors? He shuddered and continued down the stairs.

There was a light under the door of the nuncio's study. Balzarin must be working late, something he normally never did. Makonnen hesitated. Now he had come so far, he did not like to turn back.

His feelings on the stairs had somehow hardened him. He remembered his arrival in Rome, fresh out of Africa, dark-skinned and alien, trying to find his way in a universal church run by white men. At first, the glamor of the place, its symbols of imperial and ecclesiastical might, its gilded cupolas and icy prelates had disturbed and compromised his faith. With time, he had grown a skin against such things. But underneath, close to his flesh, they were an irritation.

He would confront Balzarin and be damned. What was the worst they could do? Send him to some backwater without hope of promotion? There were worse things in life. He stepped up to the door and knocked hard.

There was no answer. He waited half a minute and knocked again. Still no reply. Hesitantly, he took hold of the handle and pressed it down. The door was unlocked. It swung open without a sound.

The nuncio was seated at his desk, his face partly hidden in shadow, eyes fixed on the door. Makonnen hesitated.

"Your Excellency . . . I . . . ."

Balzarin did not move.

"I thought I . . . heard . . . ."

Makonnen took a couple of steps into the room. Something was wrong. The nuncio's face was twisted in a grimace, whether of pain or terror he could not tell. The eyes were wide open, unblinking, drained of life.

The *addetto* stepped up to the desk. Balzarin was unquestionably dead, a small glass phial clutched in his right hand. The desk lamp lay shattered on the floor. That must have been the noise that had woken Makonnen. He bent forward and felt the nuncio's cheek. The flesh was still warm.

He closed the nuncio's staring eyes and reached for his hand in order to take the phial. The hand was resting on the desk, on top of a pile of papers. Makonnen glanced down. A mauve-colored file lay open, its papers scattered. Without thinking what he was doing, he began to gather them together. Carefully, he inserted them into the file and closed it. On the cover were two words: *La Fratellanza*, The Brotherhood. Beside the word someone had drawn a circle, and in the circle three small crosses.

TWELVE

He used the direct line. It would be almost two o'clock in Rome. The phone rang at the other end, giving no indication of the caller's urgency. It was several minutes before anyone answered.

"*Pronto? Parlo col Vaticano?*"

"*Si. Che cosa desidera?*"

"*Sono Padre Makonnen, l'addetto dalla nunziatura di Dublino. Vorrei parlare con il Cardinale Fazzini, per favore, interno 69.*"

"*Ma guardi che a quest'ora il cardinale dorme.*"

"*E molto urgente. Per favore, provi.*"

"*Mah, se proprio vuole. Attenda un momento.*"

69 was the number for Fazzini's private line, only to be used in extreme emergencies. Just as he thought the operator would cut in to tell him to try again in the morning, there was a click and a terse voice answered.

"*Pronto. Qui parla Fazzini.*"

He hesitated for only a moment. This was important. Important enough to get a cardinal out of bed for.

"Your Eminence, this is Father Makonnen, *addetto* at the Dublin nunciature. I . . . I'm sorry to disturb Your Eminence at this hour, but . . . there has been a terrible tragedy."

In spite of himself, he found his voice fading away. He glanced round at the still figure of Balzarin, stiffening in his chair. For the moment he had left aside his private worries. He was a diplomat again, his only wish to avoid a scandal that might harm the Church. The irony of his situation could wait till later.

"It is two o'clock in the morning, Father." Fazzini's voice was sharp, edged with sleep. "Whatever your tragedy, surely Archbishop Balzarin is capable of dealing with it until a more suitable hour."

Makonnen took a deep breath.

"I regret . . . to tell Your Eminence . . . that Archbishop Balzarin is dead. He . . . I think he took his own life. *Si è suicidato.* I . . ."

"Are you alone, Father?"

"Yes, I . . . The other staff are away. The present housekeeper chooses not to sleep in the nunciature. She is not expected until ten o'clock. The only other person here is Father Diotavelli from the Holy Office. He's still asleep. If . . ."

"Listen to me carefully, Father . . . what did you say your name was?"

"Makonnen."

"Listen carefully, Father Makonnen. If you are correct and the archbishop has indeed taken his own life, I am sure you understand the need for . . . discretion. I take it you have informed no one else of this . . . unfortunate discovery."

"Yes, Eminence."

"*Va bene.* See to it that Father Diotavelli is kept in the dark. The last thing we want is those bastards from the Congregation for Doctrine getting wind of this. They poke their noses into everything and find excuses for endless investigations. Keep Diotavelli out of this at all costs.

"Now, this is important. I do not wish to distress you further, Father, but you must tell me how the archbishop . . . managed things."

"He . . . I think he took poison, Eminence. There was a small container."

"*Veleno? Bene.* There is no blood, the body is not marked in any way? *Nessun segno sul corpo?*"

"No."

"Very good. The archbishop: you found him in bed?"

"No, Eminence. In his study. I'm phoning from there."

There was a pause. Makonnen glanced up. On the wall above the desk a crucifix hung on a single nail. The figure of Christ was small and pale and wounded, his body slumped in the resignation of death. In the chair beneath sat Balzarin, red-faced and irresolute, mocking the pale image.

"Father Makonnen, you must somehow get the body of the archbishop to his bed. It is the best way. Remove all traces of the poison. When everything is straightened, telephone the archbishop's private doctor. I will already have spoken to him: he will understand. There must be no autopsy. The certificate will say Archbishop Balzarin died in his sleep of natural causes. *Morte naturale. Capisce?*"

"I understand." It was standard procedure. Bishops did not commit suicide. Nuncios, like popes, died in their beds.

"One thing more, Father. Did the archbishop leave a note of any kind? A letter, anything?"

Makonnen hesitated.

"No," he said. "Not in his study. Perhaps in his bedroom, I'll take a look. But . . ."

He paused.

"Yes?"

"Eminence, there was a file. It was lying open on his desk when I found him."

"A file, yes. What sort of file?"

"It . . ." He remembered the papers he had couriered to Fazzini the previous month. The cardinal must know. He would explain everything. "It has a symbol on the front, Your Eminence. Three crosses in a circle. Your Eminence—someone visited the archbishop today. An American. He asked about that symbol. About the papers that came from Father De Faoite. At the time I thought Archbishop Balzarin seemed distressed."

There was a long silence at the other end. When Fazzini spoke again, his voice had changed.

"Father Makonnen, I must tell you that this is not a matter to be discussed over the telephone. I am very grateful for this information. Until I see you in person, however, I cannot give you any details. All I will say is that the archbishop had become involved in . . . certain matters not in keeping with his position. You must make sure the file is secure. The Church could be gravely damaged if any of this leaked out.

"Wait where you are and I will send someone to help you. Do not telephone the doctor until they come. There may be other documents, we must be extremely careful. Do not touch anything else until help comes. Do you understand?"

"Yes, Your Eminence."

"I shall wish to see you tomorrow in my office in Rome. Take the first flight. In the morning you will summon the other staff members back to Dublin. Do not contact them yet." There was a brief pause. "This American, Father. Did he give his name?"

"His name? Yes, Eminence. It was Canavan. Patrick Canavan."

"Very good. He may have to be contacted as well. His life may be in danger. Did he leave an address?"

"I'm not sure. Just a moment, Eminence, I'll check." What did the cardinal mean, "His life may be in danger?"

Addresses were kept in a small filing cabinet in one corner. Makonnen opened it and started looking under "C." There it was: "Patrick Canavan, 104 Pembroke Road, Ballsbridge." He returned to the phone and gave the address to the cardinal.

"You have done very well, Father. *Sono molto contento di te.* Please be patient. Try not to worry, everything is being taken care of. Wait for help to arrive. And pray for the soul of Archbishop Balzarin. Try not to judge him. We are all human. We are all tempted. Satan is powerful, Father. The Beast is everywhere."

"I understand, Your Eminence. I'll do my best. Thank you for your help."

"Good-bye, Father Makonnen. Thank you for calling me."

The phone went dead. Makonnen replaced the receiver with a shaking hand. Against his will, he was being drawn into dangerous waters.

Moving the archbishop's body was not easy. With a shock, he realized that this was the first time he had ever handled a corpse. It took all his strength to drag Balzarin across the corridor into his private apartment. They were cheek to cheek, like lovers in a silent dance. The nuncio's flesh lay cold and clammy against his skin, intimate and nauseating.

He lifted the body into bed and arranged the sheets. But try as he might, nothing could dispel the impression of unnatural death. Balzarin's lips were curled back from his teeth in a tortured grimace. And Makonnen could not banish his fear that, at any moment, the dead eyes would open again in horror and outrage.

Makonnen looked in all the obvious places for a note, but there was nothing, not even a sign that the nuncio had started to write one. To avoid thinking of the silent bedroom, he busied himself checking that all was in order in the study. He pocketed the phial that had held the poison. The file he slipped into a large brown envelope, ready to take to Rome. He went carefully over the other papers on the desk, to be sure that there was nothing else that seemed out of place. As far as he could tell, all was in order.

He found himself restlessly pacing the floor of the study. Several times he started to pray, as the cardinal had asked him to, but the words came sterile to his lips, as though Balzarin's death had killed something in him too. On his knees in the stillness of the study, he found himself bereft, without resources, impotent in the face of a darkness greater than any he had known. He felt as though something bestial had ravished his innocence.

Still restless, he decided to fill in the time packing for his journey to Rome. His best flight would be the nine fifty-five Aer Lingus departure, direct to Fiumicino, arriving at one thirty-five that afternoon. He picked up the envelope containing the file and took it upstairs to his room.

There was little to pack. He had done this so often, he had it down to a fine art. He did not know how long he would have to stay at the Vatican, but however long his visit everything would be supplied for his simple needs. He slipped the file into his overnight case and zipped it closed.

Back in Balzarin's study, he checked each of the filing cabinets in turn, just to be sure there was nothing obviously missing. Satisfied that all seemed in order, he sat down to wait for the help Cardinal Fazzini had promised. And then he remembered the nuncio's private safe. Fazzini would want to know the contents. But where was the key?

He looked through the drawers of the nuncio's desk, but none of the keys he found fitted the safe. He found Balzarin's key ring in the pocket of his trousers, but the key he sought was not on it. He tried the housekeeper's keys on a ring in the kitchen, but nothing matched. Just as he was about to give up, he remembered feeling something round Balzarin's neck as he carried him to his room. He returned to the bedroom: the key was on a chain, hanging beside a little gold crucifix.

The safe was packed solid with papers. Some seemed extremely old, others quite new. He carried them across to the desk, feeling a sense of guilt at this intrusion on a dead man's privacy. And yet, not an hour earlier, had he not come down to this room for the express purpose of prying?

His attention was drawn at once by two large folders, their dark blue covers overprinted in gold. Each bore a golden circle and three gold crosses, and above them another symbol, two crossed keys, like those in the papal coat of arms. He took one to the desk. It contained about a dozen pages, on each of which several photographs had been pasted. Those at the front were old, many dating from the last century. As he got nearer the back, he came closer to the present day.

The photographs passed slowly through his hands: black and white butterflies pinned to a moment in time. They looked at him out of their rectangular cells: pale faces, dreaming eyes, opening and opened lips. He could not tear himself away. They willed him to look, to pass judgment, to remember.

The men in the photographs were, for the most part, senior clergy: bishops, archbishops, cardinals, the heads of seminaries, the chiefs of curial congregations. They were all Italian, all middle-aged or elderly, each one facing the camera disdainfully, mocking its trivial vanity with a chilling pride. Transfixed, he leafed through the pages, unable to find any pattern or meaning in them.

There was the sound of a car engine drawing up on the gravel path outside. Thank God, someone had come at last. He stood up, preparing to go to the door. As he did so, he let go of the folder. It shifted, opening at one of the later pages. He glanced down and paused, his attention drawn at once by the photograph at the top left corner. It was Balzarin, portentous, smiling, dressed in purple. Beside him, in red robes and virgin lace, he recognized the thin, unsmiling features of Cardinal Fazzini.

THIRTEEN

Makonnen felt his heart go cold. Though he was still unable to make sense of any of this, instinct told him he was in terrible danger. Outside, the engine was switched off. He heard the car doors open and close.

He ran to the window and looked out. Security lights illuminated the area around the entrance. Two men were walking toward the door. They were not priests, or were not, at least, dressed as such. There was something purposeful about their movements, something that reminded him of . . . what? Undertakers?

Without even pausing to think, he snatched up the bundle of papers from the safe. The doorbell rang.

He looked round desperately for something to carry the papers in. His briefcase! It was in his own office down the corridor. Clutching the papers to his chest, he ran out of the room. The corridor was unlit save for the bar of light coming from the open door behind him. His office was two doors down. He put the papers on the floor and went in. As he opened the door his chest heaved. Panic fluttered in his stomach. Downstairs, the bell rang a second time. What if it woke Diotavelli?

Hurriedly, he emptied his briefcase. There was something else he had to do, but for the life of him he could not remember. Blood pounded in his brain. Suddenly, it came to him. He ran across to his desk and opened the top drawer. Lying on top was his diplomatic passport. He snatched it out and thrust it into his soutane, then turned and dashed out of the room. He bundled the papers inside and snapped the case shut. He heard the sound of a key turning in a lock, then the familiar creak of the front door opening.

The file! It was still in his bedroom. He ran up the stairs two at a time, his heart like lead in his chest, weighing him down. On the stairwell dark portraits glared at him in disapproval. He could hear doors being opened below, footsteps on the stairs.

In his room, he unzipped the case and transferred the file to his briefcase. Hurriedly, he took his overcoat from its hook on the door and slipped it on. His hands were shaking with fear. And yet his mind was preternaturally clear: he had to escape and go with what he knew to someone he could trust, someone who had the authority to ask questions he could not. As he turned to go, his eyes fell on the wooden crucifix on the wall. He hesitated momentarily, snatched it down, and thrust it into his overcoat pocket.

He switched off the light and opened the bedroom door. Outside, the landing was still shrouded in darkness. He turned right, away from the stairs, heading down the corridor in the direction of the fire escape. At that moment the lights flashed on. Like a badger trapped at the entrance to his hole by a man with a torch, Makonnen froze. Gripped by an agonizing fear, he turned to face his hunter.

Diotavelli was standing on the stairs, dressed in a nightshirt.

"*Che succede, padre?*" he asked in a sleepy voice.

"*Niente, niente!* Please, go back to bed."

But Diotavelli was not to be so easily placated. It was three in the morning. He had heard a doorbell ringing. He was sure there were sounds of someone moving about downstairs. And here was a member of the nunciature staff, fully dressed and carrying a briefcase, sneaking about in the dark. The Jesuit came down to the landing.

"*Che cosa sta succedendo? Che cosa state facendo qui?*"

"An emergency, Father. I have to go out. Please be quiet: you'll wake the archbishop."

At that instant a man appeared from below. He was dressed in black tight-fitting clothes, like a mountaineer. A tight hood was pulled over his head. In his right hand he carried a pistol fitted with a silencer.

Whatever Diotavelli may have lacked in physical courage, he made up for in self-confidence. He had served the Holy Office for over twenty years, hunting out heresy in all parts of the globe. He was accustomed to respect and obedience. Men with guns were nothing to a man who had faced down the minions of Satan.

"*Nel nome di Dio! Chi . . .*"

The stranger simply raised his gun and fired. He did not deliberate. He did not take aim. Makonnen watched in horror as Diotavelli bucked as though he had been punched hard in the chest. His feet left the ground, blood spurted from his chest. There was hardly any sound: a whisper from the gun, a broken cry, the smack of the bullet tearing flesh, then silence everywhere even before the body reached the ground.

The Ethiopian saw the killer move as though in slow motion. He watched the gun dip and turn, saw light reflected off the barrel, the man's eyes reaching for him, snatching him, holding him, the gun lifting in an arc toward him. His body twisted heavily as if through treacle, and he threw himself sideways. He heard his voice cry out, saw the muted flash in the barrel of the silencer, felt the floor crash hard against his shoulder.

His hand moved without conscious direction to his pocket. He saw the gunman turn—slow, unhurrying, taking his time. His fingers gripped the crucifix, like a talisman to take with him into death. Hurried lips whispered, *"Jesus"*—there was no time for prayer.

The killer raised his hand, aiming for a head shot. Makonnen jerked away from the bullet, crashing against the wall. He came up gasping, the crucifix in his hand now, as though to ward off evil. As the gun swiveled for his head a second time, he drew his arm back and hurled the cross at his attacker. The sharp edge caught the man on the forehead, suddenly bright with blood, and fell back to the floor. The gunman cried out and dropped his weapon.

By then Makonnen was on his feet. The light switch was a step away. He flicked it up and turned to run, his black skin and black clothes invisible in the sudden darkness. Someone shouted behind him and there was a low hissing sound, repeated and repeated. He kept on running.

The fire door at the end of the corridor gave on to the fire escape. The cold night air tore his breath away. A heavy gust of wind snatched at him, knocking him off balance. He stumbled and fell down the first flight of steps, winding himself further. A light came on in the corridor along which he had escaped. Behind him, he could hear feet pounding and a hoarse voice calling him to stop.

The briefcase had dropped somewhere in the course of his fall. He fumbled for it on the hard steps, in the unremitting darkness. There was a sound of feet on metal stairs. The wind howled round the corner of the building. His fingers found the briefcase. Lifting it, he half ran, half fell down the next flight. A metallic crash marked the path of another bullet.

At the foot of the stairs he paused only momentarily. The garage was to his right, by the side of the house. Kennealy had taken the Volvo, Stephens and Corcoran the Volkswagen. That left the nuncio's Mercedes or his own bicycle. He had a key for the Mercedes on the ring in his pocket but realized it would be foolish to take such an easily traced vehicle. The bicycle would be slower, but silent and almost invisible.

Keeping to the grass by the side of the house, he ran as fast as he could, the heavy briefcase dragging in his hand. Behind him, he heard his pursuer's feet move from metal to gravel. Then the sound of a second pair of feet, moving round from the front of the house. The thin air slashed his lungs. He staggered, fell, picked himself up, and ran again. He had only feet to go. There was a shout to his rear, followed by the hiss of the gun firing. A window in the garage shattered with a brittle sound.

The bicycle was in its usual place by the garage wall. Here in the nunciature he always left it unlocked. He rammed the briefcase into one of the panniers and grabbed the handlebars, pushing the machine across the reluctant gravel, mounting as he ran. A man appeared in front of him, running. He swerved, missing him by inches. The bicycle was picking up speed. Gasping for breath, he pushed the pedals, knowing his life depended on it.

He was round to the front of the house. The running footsteps behind him were fading as he pulled away from them. Now he was on the drive. The ground rushed away beneath him like a dream of freedom. He glanced up and saw stars where the wind had sucked away the clouds.

With a sigh of relief he made out the figures of the two Gardai manning the gate. He braked and stepped off the bicycle. The policemen turned and watched him approach. One of them switched on a powerful flashlight. The beam caught him in the eyes, dazzling him.

"Father Makonnen, is that you?"

He nodded and the guard turned off the light.

"What on earth are you doing out here at this time of night, Father?"

Makonnen recognized the voice as belonging to Sergeant Dunn. He had not remembered that the sergeant was on night duty this week.

"Sergeant Dunn, I . . . have . . . to speak . . . with you."

"Take it easy, Father. You're all out of breath. Whatever is the matter?" Dunn spoke in what Makonnen had been told was a country accent, Mayo or Limerick, he could not remember which.

Taking deep breaths between sentences, he tried to explain as well as he could, without sounding hysterical. The two policemen listened in silence. When he finished his story, he realized he was shaking. All around, the wind blew, shaking the trees on Navan Road.

Suddenly, there was a sound of feet approaching along the drive.

"Sergeant," Makonnen began, "that's them! They're coming this way."

"It's all right, Father, we'll deal with this. You're in safe hands. There's nothing to worry about."

"Wouldn't it be better to call for help? Those men are armed."

"I wouldn't worry about that, Father. Constable O'Driscoll here and myself are both well enough armed ourselves. Aren't we, Seán?"

"Right enough, we are, Pádraig. Don't go worrying; now, Father. We'll talk to these lads."

The first man came into sight. It was the man who had killed Diotavelli. He drew near. Makonnen noticed that he still carried his gun.

Dunn was the first to speak.

"Good morning, sir. It's terribly windy, isn't it? Would this be the man you're after looking for, sir?"

Makonnen looked round. He felt the strength leave him all at once. O'Driscoll was pointing his Uzi straight at him. And Dunn had placed a large hand tightly around his arm.

FOURTEEN

He stubbed out his cigarette on the bark of the tree. Above him, in the darkness, unseen branches shook in the wind. He shivered and pulled his collar up. From his vantage point behind the tree, he could just see the gate of the nunciature. His body tense, he craned forward, trying to get a better view without showing himself.

Since leaving the nuncio that afternoon, Patrick had been working on the assumption—or, rather, the certain knowledge—that the man had something to hide. From long experience, he knew that someone who has been rattled will take some sort of action. Balzarin had been rattled. Badly.

Patrick had taken up his position in the lane opposite the nunciature in order to watch who came and went. By now it was early morning, and he had decided that his stakeout was not going to pay off. He was close to throwing in the towel and going home: he felt cold and tired and hungry, and at the moment a telephone bug sounded like a much more pleasant proposition.

But then he had been stirred out of his lethargy by the arrival of the car, a Ford Sierra with military number plates. The driver had stopped and spoken briefly with the Gardai on duty at the gate, then driven on into the grounds. Patrick had still been trying to decide whether or not he should risk going in himself when Makonnen came out and started what looked like an earnest conversation with the two policemen.

But now things were hotting up considerably. The priest did not appear any too pleased by the arrival of the men in black. They smelled of military, and Patrick was willing to swear that at least one of them was carrying a gun.

He moved out from behind the tree, eager to get a better view. Nobody was looking in his direction anyway. Makonnen was arguing with the Gardai about something: he could hear his voice between gusts of wind. One of the guards had the priest by the arm and seemed to be holding him against his will.

The second soldier—if that was what he was—spoke briefly to the first, then disappeared back up the drive. There was the sound of an engine being started. Moments later, the car reappeared and the first man began to bundle Makonnen into the back. There could be no question now: the priest was struggling desperately. He had a case of some sort, which his assailant dragged from his hand and threw onto the front seat. Makonnen was no match for his opponent: a heavy shove and he tumbled into the rear of the car like a broken doll.

Taking advantage of the confusion, Patrick dashed back down to Navan Road, where he had parked his own car. He had hardly got himself behind the wheel when the Sierra emerged from the lane and turned sharp left onto the road. He threw himself flat a split second before the car's head-lights spilled across his window.

When he came up, the Sierra had already reached Nephin Road. As he watched, it turned left, heading north into Cabra, toward the Tolka Valley. He rammed the key into his own ignition and turned it. By what seemed a miracle, the cold engine started. Keeping his lights off, he followed the other car.

Trailing someone without a backup team is hard. At half past three in the morning, it is virtually impossible. Too close and you may as well walk up to your target and shake hands. Too far back and they get lost in a maze of streets.

As Patrick turned into Nephin Road, the Sierra had just passed the railing of John Paul II Park. He kept his eyes firmly on the rear lights ahead, like a mariner steering by two red stars. Suddenly, he lost them. The car had turned left at a roundabout onto Ratoath Road, cutting back along the rear of the park. Where the hell were they heading? McKee, Clancy, and Collins barracks were all a short drive south of here, the Department of Defence was off to the northeast in Drumcondra.

He turned at the roundabout, wishing he could decide on a probable destination. He would rather take a different route and avoid the risk of being spotted. There was nothing out here but the Royal Canal and the Tolka River.

At that moment the car ahead stopped. Automatically, Patrick stalled his own engine. The empty street filled with the sound of wind, sudden and desolate. Up ahead, the lights went out.

The Sierra had parked in front of a level crossing over the main Cork railway line. The area round the crossing was well lit, and Patrick could see three men get out of the car. Makonnen, the smallest of the group, was in the middle, his arms pinned by the others.

Patrick opened the glove compartment and reached in. The gun felt cold and unfamiliar, an old friend from whom one has grown distant after many years. He took it out, gripping it tightly, like a small animal he had brought to bay and conquered. It was a Heckler & Koch P7M8, his old handgun from Beirut. He preferred it to the Brownings and Berettas he had previously used: he found it light, compact, and extremely accurate. It was permanently fitted with a 310 Target Illuminator.

He stepped out of the car and was almost bowled over by a sudden blast. But the wind was an advantage: it would drown his footsteps, making it easier for him to get close to his quarry without being detected. From their behavior, he was certain they had no idea they were being followed.

He saw them pass the level crossing, then vanish into shadows. Quickly, he made up the distance. For a moment he thought he had lost them. Then he saw the steps leading down from the road to the bank of the canal.

This was Long John Binns's old waterway, a disastrous eighteenth-century rival to the Grand Canal in the south of the city. Its glories were long gone. Weeds and rushes grew tangled in its waters; its banks served for lovers' walks and children's races. Tonight, darkness lay stretched across it like a fine, unpatterned carpet. No lights flickered on its wind-tossed water. No night birds skimmed above the towpath in search of prey.

He caught sight of them as they went through a low gate onto the towpath. He was much closer to them now. Makonnen was arguing with his captors, his voice desperate and afraid. Patrick had no doubt why they had brought him here.

They did not go far. Patrick watched as the man on Makonnen's right forced the priest to his knees, in a posture of prayer. He crept closer, concealed by bushes. Makonnen's voice came to him with sudden clarity, brought to him on a gust of wind that blew across the canal. It was a prayer, though Patrick did not know the language. Yards away, an old lamp cast a soft yellow glow down the path, too little to read by, but enough to show Patrick what was happening. He fumbled beneath the barrel of his H & K and switched on the illuminator.

Makonnen finished his prayer and crossed himself. The man on his right raised the silenced pistol to his temple. Patrick was already targeted, the illuminator's powerful laser beam dropping a sharp red dot on the killer's cheek. He squeezed the cocking mechanism and pulled lightly on the trigger in a smoothly practiced movement. The shot echoed across the open fields and was swallowed up in silence. A second later, there was a sound of splashing as the dead man plunged into the canal.

The second man spun round, one hand reaching inside his jacket for his gun, his eyes scanning the area from which he thought the shot had come.

Patrick did not reveal himself.

"Drop the gun," he shouted.

The man tensed, as though about to run.

"We have you in our sights," Patrick added, shifting the odds. "Throw the gun down and put your hands on top of your head."

Without warning, the man swung himself sideways out of Patrick's line of fire, taking Makonnen with him. When he came up again, he held the trembling priest in front of him, and his pistol was held hard against his head.

"If you so much as fucking look at me," he shouted, "I'll give the Church another martyr!"

Patrick beaded him with the laser, but he did not dare fire: the mere reflex of death would be enough to blow Makonnen's head off.

"I want you out here," shouted the gunman. "Now! All of you! I want to see you!"

Patrick stood, keeping the pistol trained on his target.

"There's just myself," he said. He could sense the gunman's uncertainty.

"Don't fuck with me!" the man screamed. He was frightened and wound up, and Patrick knew the pressure on that trigger was already half a pound too much. He had seen more than one gun fired accidentally under stress.

"I'm not screwing you," Patrick replied, shouting to make himself heard over the wind. "I'm alone. There's no one else with me."

"Get rid of your gun!" The man tightened his grip round the priest's neck, pulling him closer to him. "I said, get rid of your fucking gun!"

"You know I can't do that. If I drop the gun, you still have the priest. You can still shoot him. Now, get this clear: he's all I want. I'm not interested in you. Let him go and you walk out of this. Kill him and you're a dead man. You can walk away from here or you can float, like your friend. It's your choice."

"I'm giving the fucking orders here! I'm saying who walks out of this and who doesn't. Whoever you are, just put your gun in your pocket and get the fuck out of here. Don't get mixed up in this. You're out of your depth. Do you understand? You're in deep waters."

All this time, Makonnen had been mumbling prayers in a frightened voice, Hail Marys in a mixture of Latin, Italian, and Ge'ez, the liturgical language of the Ethiopian Church—a babel of invocations to ward off Fazzini's pestilential Beast. Suddenly, his voice broke off in mid-prayer and he began to turn his head, slowly, against the pressure of his captor's arm, until his face looked directly at the gun, the barrel sleek and cold against his forehead, right between his eyes.

"Now!" he whispered. "Kill me now, quickly, while I'm ready. Hurry, do it for the love of God!"

Patrick saw the man hesitate.

"No!" he shouted.

The man struck Makonnen hard across the face with the end of the silencer, then swung the gun around, aiming at Patrick. He fired twice in quick succession: silent shots, wide of their mark.

Patrick's bullet struck him in the teeth, an imperfect shot, but mortal. His head jerked back, his finger clenched the trigger, firing wild shots into the wind. Makonnen leaped away, leaving him to topple sideways into the canal. The dark waters broke and formed again. A ripple surged outward from the point of impact and was erased by the wind. The silence that fell was absolute.

FIFTEEN

Milk-white light filtered through long curtains, simple, without form or substance. He had once thought the Holy Spirit must be like that: a simple descent of dove-white sperm, light spun from light, the Word made luminosity. Out of habit, his eyes traveled up to the wall above his head. It was bare: no red light, no crucifix.

He could not remember coming here: the bed in which he lay, the room, the plain rust-colored carpet, all were unfamiliar. His head was aching, and it hurt to open his eyes. He turned away from the light and pulled the bedclothes over his head. Sleep returned.

He dreamed he was in a tomb. His body lay cold and anointed on a marble slab. On the wall someone had painted the outline of a fish in red. Around him, hooded figures chanted a litany in a language he had never heard. Candles flickered like gemstones in the dark. Echoes moved across the walls like shoals of fish twisting and turning beneath the tide.

Suddenly the voices fell silent. The candles were extinguished. There was a sound of a rock being rolled into place, a heavy rock. He could hear sounds of hammering, metal upon stone, orchestral almost. Then the hammering fell silent and he was utterly alone. And at that moment, in the darkness, in the silence, he heard someone moving.

His eyes opened and he was in the strange room again. He turned and squinted at the light from the window. In his head, he could still hear the sound of hammering.

Suddenly, memories of the night before flooded back with appalling intensity: Balzarin's dead face, white and uncomprehending; Diotavelli gunned down in his arrogance, his nightgown bright and angry with sudden blood. He relived the chase through the house and grounds, the wind that tore his flesh, the capture, the drive to the canal. But after that all was blank, as though someone had dipped a sponge in water and wiped it across his brain.

He threw the bedclothes aside and stood up. He had been sleeping in his underclothes, something he never did. His outer garments lay draped across a wooden chair.

Crossing to the window, he drew back the curtain. Squinting in the sudden brightness, he looked across green fields to a steel-blue lake. Wooded hills girdled the shore, and above a serried tracery of leafless trees rose a pointed tower of dull gray stone. In the water, the pale images of clouds moved slowly on the breeze like white smoke.

What was this place? Who had brought him here? He dressed quickly and made his way to the door. A small landing led onto a flight of un-carpeted wooden stairs. Through an open door on his right he could see a washbasin and part of a bath. The next door was closed. He opened it and found another bedroom, much like the one in which he had woken.

Coming out onto the landing again, he heard the sound of voices talking quietly below. Cautiously, he started down the stairs. A flagged passage led to an open door and a smell of fresh coffee.

He paused in the doorway. A man and a woman sat facing each other across a scrubbed pine table on which lay a heap of papers. He recognized the American, Canavan, but the woman was a stranger. Canavan looked up and caught sight of him. He smiled and pushed back his chair, standing.

"Father Makonnen. I hope you've slept well. How are you feeling?"

"I . . . I'm feeling a little confused. Last night . . . I can't remember very well. Where am I? What are you doing here?"

"It's all right, there's nothing to worry about. I guess you could do with a coffee and maybe something to eat. Oh, I'm sorry, you haven't been introduced. This is . . . my friend Ruth Ehlers, from the American em-bassy. She knows who you are already. This is Ruth's house, or her week-end cottage, I should say."

The priest remained standing. Yesterday's events were crumpled and blurred in his head.

"I don't remember coming here," he said. "I was . . . I remember going to the canal. Two men . . . drove me there. Then . . ."

"Come and sit down. You'll feel better when you've had some coffee. How would you like it?"

Canavan took his arm and guided him to a chair.

"I . . . Black, please. With a little sugar."

He sat down. Deprived of the conventions of the seminary or the nuncia-ture, his world was coming apart. He still had not said his morning prayers.

"Coming up. What about some breakfast? We've got mushrooms—Ruth picked them this morning. There's wholemeal bread from Bewley's, plenty of real Irish butter, black cherry jam."

"Just the coffee, please. You said 'breakfast'—what time is it?"

"Well, perhaps 'breakfast' isn't really the right word. 'Lunch' would be more appropriate. It's just after twelve o'clock."

"How long have I been asleep?"

"We got here just after five. You were still pretty agitated. Ruth gave you a couple of sleeping tablets."

"I see." Makonnen paused and looked round the room. It was clean and bright, with tall windows that looked out on the lake. "Tell me," he asked, "where is 'here'?"

Patrick glanced out of the window.

"Don't you recognize it?"

"No. I don't think I've ever been here before."

The woman spoke for the first time. She was beautiful, he thought, but troubled by something. He had been trained to resist beauty, but not distress, and he found himself unwillingly drawn to her by it. She wore a soft dress of European manufacture, without the gilding he had come to expect in American women. Even his African eye, calibrated more to the nuances of poverty than style, could sense how finely her limbs were habituated to well-cut garments.

"This is Glendalough," she said. As she spoke, she raised one hand nervously to her cheek, and he noticed how her fingernails had been chewed. What was making her so ill at ease? "The valley houses an old monastic city founded by St. Kevin in the sixth century. That's the round tower you can see just above the trees. It used to be the belfry. And a place to hide when the Vikings came burning down everything in sight. There are ruins all round it. You'll see it all later."

The priest nodded. He had heard of the place and often planned to visit it. There were close links between the early monks of Ireland and those of his own church.

He turned to Patrick, who had just finished pouring coffee into his cup.

"What is going on, Mr. Canavan? Why have I been brought here?"

He was not angry, just frightened, torn from everything familiar.

"We were hoping you would provide some answers to your first question yourself, Father. As for why we brought you here, surely you know your life is in danger?"

"Danger. Yes, I understand." Again he could hear footsteps pounding after him in the dark. He had to force himself not to look round. "I remember . . . what happened in the nunciature, then being taken to the canal. But everything after that is a blank. You must know what happened."

"Yes."

"I'd like to know."

Patrick paused. "Very well," he said at last.

While he ate, Patrick told him all he knew, and in turn prompted him to explain the events that had led up to his capture at the gate of the nunciature—Balzarin's death, the phone call to Fazzini, the arrival of the gunmen.

When the priest finished, Ruth poured more coffee for everyone. Back in his chair, Patrick indicated the papers strewn across the table.

"So these don't include the papers De Faoite sent to Balzarin?"

"No. I took those to Fazzini in person. These are all from the nuncio's safe, except for that mauve file, which I found on his desk."

"The one he was reading when he killed himself?"

"Yes, that's right."

There was a pause.

"Have you looked at these papers, Father?" The question was put by the woman.

"Only at one of the folders of photographs."

"I see. We haven't gone through those yet. We thought you might help us identify some of the people in them."

Makonnen sighed. As the coffee cleared his head, he began to understand just how deep had grown the waters in which he was swimming.

"Please, can you tell me what this is all about? I want to know. I am willing to help you, but I must know what is happening."

Ruth looked at Patrick, then back at Makonnen.

"Father," she started, "I have to insist. Whatever Mr. Canavan or I tell you must remain absolutely confidential. You must swear not to reveal it to anyone else without our permission. Do you understand?"

The priest shook his head.

"I'm sorry," he said, "but you must know that is impossible. I am a priest. I have taken sacred vows. Under my vow of obedience, I would be obliged to reveal any information I possessed to those set in authority over me."

Patrick leaned over the table. Something in his manner told Makonnen that he and the woman were lovers. But he sensed an awkwardness between them, like an electric charge that was constantly ready to flare up.

"Forget it, Ruth," said Patrick. "We can trust him." He turned to the priest. "All we're asking, Father, is that you be discreet. Your vows do not require you to volunteer information, do they?"

For the first time, Makonnen smiled.

"No," he replied, "they do not."

Patrick leaned back.

"Then I think we can begin."

SIXTEEN

Patrick went first. He spoke carefully, as though conscious that he had to forge a bond, a sense of trust between himself and the priest. The fact that he had saved Makonnen's life and gunned down the two men who had threatened it was meaningless. For all Makonnen knew, he had fallen among fresh thieves, subtler and more well-meaning than the first, but thieves and killers for all that. Good Samaritans are not supposed to carry guns.

"Father Makonnen," he began, "I think we may assume that, by now, Cardinal Fazzini has been alerted to the fact of your disappearance. He will not know how you came to make your getaway, and I imagine it will be some time before he learns what happened to the men he sent to kill you. In the meantime, he has to deal with some awkward details, the most embarrassing of which is likely to be Diotavelli's body. Ruth will find out what she can through the American embassy, but it's unlikely to be very much.

"One thing is certain. If you return to the nunciature or the Vatican, you're as good as dead. That you are in essence ignorant of Fazzini's machinations is of no concern to him. You know too much, and you must be silenced. If it is any consolation, that applies to me as much as it does to you."

Makonnen remembered Fazzini's request for Canavan's address.

"Did anyone . . . ?"

"Why do you think we're here?"

The priest leaned forward.

"What if I go to someone else in the Vatican, someone I can trust?"

Patrick shook his head.

"Not until we know more about what's going on and who is involved. You're a marked man in every way. But in principle, yes: we shall need access to the Vatican, and for that we shall need your help."

"Please," Makonnen pleaded, "what is this all about?"

Patrick betrayed hesitation for the first time.

"The simple answer to that question is that we don't know."

"When you visited the nuncio yesterday, you said that a national intelligence bureau was involved in this. I assume you meant yourselves, the CIA."

Patrick smiled.

"At that point, no. I was referring to our distant cousins, the KGB." He spoke of them as a priest might, after Vatican II, have spoken of "our separated brethren" in the Protestant churches. That was the first intimation Patrick had of how close they stood to one another, the spy and the priest—hand in hand almost, fingertip to fingertip, bullet to book, initiates into the most ancient of mysteries.

"But I now think the CIA is involved in some way." He exchanged glances with Ruth. "To make things entirely clear, my own role in all this is, as far as I know, entirely personal. But I did at one time serve as an agent with the CIA, and the possibility of that connection cannot entirely be disregarded."

He paused. Makonnen looked at him curiously, as though hearing his confession. Patrick felt uneasy, thinking back to the grille in his church at home, the priest's voice prompting, seeking out sin like a scalpel probing for tumors.

"Miss Ehlers is a sort of monitor," he went on. "She serves directly under the CIA chief of station at the embassy here. Her job is to monitor intelligence traffic into and out of the various embassies in Dublin. Most of that traffic is intercepted by the National Security Agency listening station at Menwith Hill in Yorkshire. They pass it on to the British through their liaison office at Benhall Park in Cheltenham."

Ruth broke in.

"Patrick, I don't think Father Makonnen needs . . ."

"Please, Ruth, I know what I'm doing." Patrick spread his hands in a placating gesture. "The father is a diplomat. If you imagine that anything I'm telling him is not already intimately known to his superiors in the Vatican, you're being very naive about the Catholic Church." He turned back to Makonnen.

"Benhall Park puts this material together with what GCHQ gives them from their own monitoring stations at Hacklaw and Cheadle, as well as their telecommunications intercepts from Caroone House in London. It's actually more complex than that, but the point I'm trying to make is that Ruth's material is extremely comprehensive and extremely reliable.

"Mostly she's involved in assessing data for its relevance to the Irish situation. She checks through translated Arab material, for example, to see if it refers to possible links between, say, the Libyans or the PLO and the

IRA. And you're probably aware that your own transmissions are checked for much the same reason."

Patrick did not have to spell out his meaning. In the late seventies, the Vatican nuncio in Dublin, Archbishop Gaetane Alibrandi, had attracted notoriety for his repeated contacts with IRA members. Alibrandi's motives had been noble enough—to understand and, perhaps, to intercede with men of violence. But the unfavorable attention the nunciature had then drawn had not diminished under his successors.

"Then you knew Balzarin was up to something. You were trying to draw him out."

Patrick shook his head.

"No. Until yesterday afternoon, I had no reason to suspect Balzarin of anything. He had some papers I wanted to see, that was all I knew. But when I spoke with him, he behaved like a man with something to hide. After I left the nunciature, I phoned Ruth and asked her to run a check on it. Phone calls, diplomatic telegrams, radio messages—everything. I think she'd better tell you what she found herself."

Ruth hesitated. For some reason the priest made her anxious. For all the range of her parents' friends, she had had little contact with Catholics and almost none at all with priests. Like many women, she found their conscious option for celibacy a rejection of something essential to herself. She supposed men felt the same about nuns. For the first time in years, her social skills betrayed her. She was ill at ease and aware that she showed it.

"Father Makonnen," she began, "you probably know that your people —I mean the Vatican State—and the CIA regularly exchange intelligence information. As Patrick . . . Mr. Canavan so kindly pointed out, you naturally understand that we also like to keep ourselves independently informed of any items of interest that may for any reason have been omitted from our regular briefings. And I'm sure your own intelligence people have their ways of informing themselves of some of our less well kept secrets."

She hesitated. There was no telling how Makonnen might react to what she had to tell him. She took a deep breath and plunged on.

"Yesterday," she said, "after Patrick phoned, I went across to the embassy and looked up some old computer files. Patrick has explained to you that we were looking for something with the word 'Passover.' He didn't mention that, on one occasion, we ran the word 'Easter' through as well. 'Pasqua' in Italian. Well, all we came up with were a few messages to and from the nunciature. Nobody even bothered to read them. After all, what could be more normal than the Vatican talking about a major Christian festival?"

She paused and glanced out the window. A large bird circled the tower, its wings catching fire momentarily in the early afternoon light.

"But someone had been careless. Maybe 'Passover' isn't the sort of word our translators usually have to handle. Anyway, it turns out that *Pasqua* isn't just Italian for 'Easter.' It's also the word Italian Jews use to refer to 'Passover' if they happen to be talking to Christians: *Pasqua Ebraica*—the Jewish Easter.

"So I went back through the messages involving the nunciature. The first two could have referred to either Passover or Easter, it wasn't clear. But the third was more puzzling. It was dated February 3, it was in code, and it was signed, not with a proper name, but with a sort of pseudonym—*Il Pescatore*, the Fisherman." She paused. "Does that mean anything to you?"

The priest thought for a moment. She saw the faint shadow that crossed his eyes, sensed his hesitation.

"No," he said. "No, it means nothing to me."

But she knew what he was thinking, that Peter had been the first Fisherman of the Church. And the first Pope.

"The message was addressed to Balzarin in person. It instructed him to have courage. All was going well. Plans had been completed. *Pasqua* would take place in exactly one month, on March 3." She paused. "Someone should have noticed that Easter this year isn't until April 17."

Makonnen listened with growing bewilderment. Where was this leading? He fumbled with the beads of his rosary, moving them nervously in a form of silent prayer. He felt compromised and abandoned, like a child on the verge of adulthood.

"And the Jewish Passover starts on March 3?" he asked.

She shook her head.

"No. That's what's puzzling. Passover begins a few days before Easter. But in the message *Pasqua* definitely means 'Passover,' not 'Easter.' The writer speaks about 'the day the children of Israel fled from captivity in Egypt.' And both De Faoite and Chekulayev spoke quite clearly of 'Passover.' "

Makonnen got out of his seat. He felt trapped, as though this Fisherman in the Vatican had him fast by a long line and a hook. He went across to the window and looked out, at the gray tower and the winter trees, at the dark water, the gathering clouds. Even in winter it was green here, green and wet beyond all his childhood imaginings. *Why is the world so desolate,* he thought, *so empty even when it is full?*

"Why are we talking about this here?" he asked. "Why are you telling me? You have a huge organization: men, computers, files. I'm just a priest, I can't help you."

Ruth glanced at Patrick. Her expression was one of exhaustion, of despair almost.

"We can't do that, Father," Patrick said quietly.

Makonnen turned and looked at him.

"Why not?"

In answer, Patrick picked up the file Makonnen had found on Balzarin's desk. He opened it and took out a sheet of paper. Gently, he laid it on the table for the priest to read. It was a small sheet of headed notepaper. At the top was a small round shield, underneath which was inscribed a biblical quotation: *And ye shall know the truth and the truth shall set you free.*

Makonnen came to the table and picked up the sheet.

My brother [the letter read], *I have received your letter and that of the Pillars. May God bless you and all you seek to accomplish in His path. The hour of Passover will soon be upon us. Rest assured of my prayers and my assistance. If there is anything you or the brothers need that I can supply, do not hesitate to ask. All that is mine is yours: you know that. I have given the instructions you requested. You will not be interfered with. Give my greetings to Cardinal Fazzini. In His name,*

Miles Van Doren

"I don't understand," said Makonnen, handing the letter back to Patrick. "What does this mean? What's this shield at the top?"

"The shield," Patrick said slowly, "is the official seal of the Central Intelligence Agency." Ruth was looking away, her eyes fixed on the distance. "The words are from the Bible: you can see them any day of the week if you walk into the entrance lobby of the Agency out at Langley."

"And this man, Miles Van Doren—who is he?"

Ruth watched a cloud pass like a veil behind the tower. She had chosen this place for its silences. But the world had followed her and was filling her gray spaces with its own sounds.

"Miles Van Doren," she said in a voice so quiet Makonnen had to strain to hear it, "Miles Van Doren is my father. He is the presidential adviser on foreign intelligence and a deputy director of the CIA."

SEVENTEEN

In spite of the fire it was growing chilly in the room. Ruth threw on another block of peat and poked the ashes, sending bright sparks up the chimney.

"I'm going out," she said. "I'd like to take a walk about, see that everything's all right out there. I might go on down to the lake."

She took a green Barbour jacket from a hook near the door and slipped it on.

"Take care. Don't walk too far. We'll look after things in here." Patrick knew what Ruth meant when she said she would see that everything was all right. In this business, constant vigilance was the price, not so much of freedom as of life itself.

The door closed gently behind her. Patrick indicated the easy chairs by the fireplace.

"Let's sit down over here."

For a while they sat, drinking coffee, watching the flames rise through the soft peat. The priest needed time to digest what he had just been told, to understand that his ordeal was not over, that it had only begun. When the coffee was finished, Patrick found some sherry in a cupboard, an old Manzanilla, very dry and very pale. It would have been better chilled, but he poured it anyway. They began to talk, returning before very long to the mystery that had brought them there.

"Chekulayev was killed," Patrick explained, "by the same people who killed Eamonn De Faoite. Eamonn knew about Passover. The papers he sent to Balzarin must have contained details: names, places, dates—whatever he'd been able to dig up."

"Why would he send them to Balzarin?"

Patrick shrugged.

"My guess is that he knew something about Fazzini, maybe the Vatican connection in general. He must have thought he could trust Balzarin. Eamonn was a clever man, but in some ways very simple. He would have regarded the nuncio as the proper person to approach on a matter that concerned the Vatican."

"It wasn't the correct procedure. His own bishop . . ."

"Perhaps so. But Eamonn was never one for correct procedures. And if he thought there was no time to lose . . . Anyway, we'll never know now."

"What about these papers?" Makonnen gestured toward the pile on the table. "The ones I found in the nunciature. What have you found in them? Apart from . . ."

Patrick sipped his sherry and put the glass down on the floor. He went to the table and brought some of the papers back to the chair.

"Several letters," he said. "Some of them date back years and relate to different stages in Balzarin's career. There are letters from various cardinals and bishops, by no means restricted to the Vatican or Italy; a number from Italian government officials or influential people in countries to which Balzarin had been posted; a few from bankers, industrialists, the heads of finance houses; two from military officers. The most recent ones are Irish: a senator, a judge, and a member of the board of the Bank of Ireland."

As he took the file of letters from Patrick, Makonnen commented in Italian.

"*Era piduista.* He belonged to P2."

Patrick shook his head.

"No, I don't think so. There may be a connection, but I can't see any evidence of that as yet."

Makonnen had been referring to P2 *(pi-due),* a secret and powerful Italian Masonic lodge whose public exposure in 1981 had led to the collapse of Aldo Forlani's coalition government. P2's influence had reached as far as the Chigi Palace. Many feared that its power had not been wholly broken.

As the priest looked through the letters, Patrick continued.

"All of these letters refer in one way or another to an organization known as the Brotherhood or, more simply, the Brothers. There are several references to a tomb, which members seem to venerate. More than one correspondent mentions the Pillars.

"We also found a diary in Italian, written in what we think is Balzarin's own handwriting. That will have to be translated in full, but even at a glance we can see there are going to be problems: people are referred to by initials or titles, places by abbreviations. Some of the entries have been heavily crossed out, as though the keeper of the diary had second thoughts about them. Which makes us think, of course, that what is left may not be as revealing as we would like."

He handed Makonnen a medium-sized volume bound in soft burgundy leather. A small label inside the front cover declared that it had been manufactured by Olbi's in Venice, but it bore no other distinguishing feature.

"Father," Patrick went on, "I'm going to be frank with you. We are all in terrible danger. Two days ago, Ruth and the team working with her at the embassy received strict instructions to drop the case. They were told it was being handled at a higher level. We no longer believe that to be true. With any luck we may be safe here for a day or so, but that's the most we can hope for.

"As I told you, we think you are personally at considerable risk. I don't want to sound offensive, but you have to understand that here in Ireland you are conspicuous, even if dressed in a layman's clothes. There are almost no black people in this country. For that reason, you can't afford to move around freely.

"Fortunately, Ruth has money and contacts. We intend to take you out of here tonight and find somewhere safe for you to stay until this is all over."

"And how long will that be, Mr. Canavan? A week? A month? A year? You say 'until this is all over.' But how long has it been going on? Some of the engravings in that folder date back to the eighteenth century."

Patrick paused before answering. Even in the warm room, before the fire, he felt cold. The hallucination—if that was what it had been—of two days ago still troubled him. He wondered if he should see a doctor. Or a priest.

"Father, I didn't want to say this, but perhaps it's better if I do. There's every possibility that none of us may ever be safe again. I can give you protection for a while, but I can't guarantee it forever. Perhaps not even for a week. Our only hope is to find people we can trust, people powerful enough to take action against this group. I don't have to spell out for you just how difficult that may prove to be.

"But at least we can make a start. We can eliminate those whose names we know from letters, and anyone you think you can recognize from their photographs."

He passed the first folder to Makonnen, the one containing engravings and photographs of clerics.

Makonnen did his best. The better-known figures, even those from the past, were easy enough. Some he had seen in newspapers, others in textbooks on church history. One in particular he singled out.

"This man," he said, pointing at the close-up of a severe face that bore the unmistakable stamp of a lifetime spent in positions of authority, of whole generations accustomed to obedience.

"His name is Cardinal Migliau. His family came from Spain after Ferdinand and Isabella expelled the Jews. That would have been at the end of the fifteenth century. They came through Provence to Piedmont, where they settled in and around Turin. But one of his ancestors went on alone to Venice, where he converted to Christianity and made a fortune trading with Egypt and the Levant. He married a girl from a poor branch of the Grimani family, but for all that remained an outsider.

"His sons and grandsons continued to trade with the Sultan, mainly in pepper. They bought land at Montebelluno and a villa by Palladio near Maser. By 1645, when the Great Council put noble status up for sale, they had enough money and enough influence to get their name entered in the Golden Book. They are one of the last noble families surviving in Venice."

Makonnen paused, his eyes fixed on the photograph.

"Migliau was made Patriarch of Venice three years ago," he said. "It wasn't a popular appointment, but the Pope insisted. He may not be liked around St. Mark's, but he has considerable influence in the rest of Italy. In many quarters people are already speaking of him as *papabile.*"

"I'm sorry?"

"*Papabile.* A suitable candidate for the papacy. If the present Pope were to die soon—which God forbid—there is no doubt that Migliau would be the favorite of the conservatives."

"I see." Patrick paused. "What about the men on this page, do you know any of them?"

Makonnen looked carefully, but there was no one he recognized. By the time they reached the end, Patrick knew they would need the services of a good photo library.

The second folder contained prints and photographs of nuns, their costumes indicating a variety of religious orders. Makonnen gave up quickly on these.

The last item was an album rather than a folder. Patrick had left it on the table, where it could be viewed more easily. He got up and arranged two dining chairs side by side.

It was an old volume, elaborately bound in a fashion popular in France in the seventeenth century. The binding had been carefully removed from its original contents and resewn onto pages more suitable for holding engravings and photographs. On the first leaf, someone had inscribed in copperplate the words *I Morti.* The Dead.

Underneath was a Latin inscription in the same hand: "*An ignoratis quia quicumque baptizati sumus in Christo Jesu, in morte ipsius baptizati sumus? Consepulti enim sumus cum illo per baptismum in mortem . . .*" Patrick recognized it as a passage from Romans: "*Know ye not, that so many of us as were baptized into Jesus Christ were baptized into his death? Therefore we are buried with him by baptism into death.*"

He turned the page. A row of faces stared at him, the dead staring at the living, across more than centuries. The paper felt old and slightly mildewed, as though it had been buried for years in a tomb. He felt it beneath his fingers, fusty and slightly rotten.

The arrangement of the pages that followed differed from that in the folders. At the top of the first page was a name: Benedetta di Rovereto. Patrick recognized the name as Venetian, an old family, nobles from the thirteenth or fourteenth century. Underneath and on the next page were arranged engravings and then photographs of young women, the earliest from perhaps the second half of the seventeenth century. There were seven in all.

As he looked at each face in turn, he became aware of a family resemblance between them. The clothes changed, the hairstyles altered, but the eyes, the noses, the chins all spoke of a common ancestry. They might have been sisters or cousins, except that decades and centuries separated them. Did they all carry the same name? Was that it? A single name carried through several generations in the same family?

The next set of portraits were of men. The name at their head was Giovanni Carmagnola. Again Patrick saw the resemblance running through their faces like a single thread drawn through a many-patterned fabric: a feature disappearing here, only to return later, less pronounced but unmistakable; a second dying away to be replaced by another; a third persisting in each generation, like insect fossils creeping unchanged through strata of ancient rock.

Page by page, the dead were ranged in front of them, living only in a single moment. Who they were, what they represented, what their deaths signified remained a riddle. Had they all died young, soon after these portraits were drawn or these photographs taken?

Patrick turned the pages as though hypnotized, drawn from picture to picture, as though a child, having taken him by the hand, was leading him through vast chambers hung with the portraits of his ancestors. On average, there were about seven or eight pictures to each name. But some names had fewer, beginning at a later date, while one or two had more and went back much further, to the sixteenth and even fifteenth centuries.

The etchings showed their subjects in formal poses, usually seated, often beside a statue of the Virgin or a crucifix. Even across a range of generations, there was little variation. The photographs largely followed the formalities of the earlier drawings, but here and there a note of innovation had been introduced. Some stood in front of the portrait of a predecessor, others before a family tombstone.

He had just passed the halfway point when he felt his mouth go dry with fear. For a moment he did not even know what it was that had frightened him. His hand froze on the page as though turned to stone.

"Mr. Canavan, what's wrong? What is it, Mr. Canavan?"

He heard Makonnen's voice, but it sounded dull and remote, as though it reached him from behind high walls. He did not reply. He felt as if he had been struck dumb.

There was no need to look at the name at the top of the page. The faces coalesced into a single face, the eyes became a single pair of eyes, the mouth a single mouth. At first he thought another hallucination had begun, but as the moments passed he realized that what he was seeing was wholly real.

Her photograph was at the bottom of the right-hand page, the very last in the series, the most recent. It was both fresh and painfully familiar. In a box at home, buried beneath dust and trivia, he had an album of his own, filled with photographs like it. Francesca alone, Francesca with a group of friends, Francesca and himself together, on the banks of the canal, taken by Paolo on an autumn evening twenty-two years ago. They had been in Venice together on holiday, staying with her family. A year later, he had returned to bury her among mist and cypresses, in a vault of crumbling stone on the cemetery island of San Michele.

EIGHTEEN

A crack runs through the center of the universe. Images of Francesca fly through his brain like moths—moths with jagged tearing wings, hungry for light. He fears the onset of further hallucinations, of madness, of desperation. Another reality, a phantom world, takes on form and substance all about him. It threatens to suck him into itself, to drag him down like a crippled ship, into eternal cold and darkness. He fears ghosts, sees mottled faces touch the edges of his vision and shy away again.

But there is nothing ethereal about the picture: it is physical, tangible, as solid in its materiality as himself. His fingers can touch it, just as they can touch the table or his own face. He clings to it like a drowning man to wreckage. It is not a ghost. It will not shimmer in the darkness. It will not go away.

Slowly, a piece at a time, the world fits itself together again.

Breathing hard, Patrick slipped the photograph out of the old-fashioned corners that held it and closed the album. Makonnen watched him, perplexed and a little frightened. What could be in the photographs that disturbed the American so much? Patrick glanced at the photograph again, then put it into his jacket pocket.

"Father," he said, turning abruptly, "will you please stay here in the cottage? I want to go out to look for Ruth. She's been gone a long time."

Beyond the window, the first signs of approaching evening had appeared. Patrick took his Burberry down from the wall and pulled it on. It was a city coat, out of place here in the country. He lacked Ruth's ability to blend into her surroundings.

At the door, he paused.

"Father, please lock the door when I've gone. Only open it to Ruth or myself. You'll find a shotgun in the cupboard behind you."

"I can't . . ."

"I don't expect you to fire on anyone, but I would suggest you hang on to it. If anybody looks like making trouble, try waving it at them. Look as though you mean business. I won't be long."

He tied the belt of his coat tightly and pulled the collar up against the cold. As he stepped through the door, he shivered. Behind him, he heard Makonnen turn the key in the lock.

She was nowhere in the garden. He called her name gently at first, then loudly, but there was no reply. At the end of the garden, a low gate led onto the road. He looked up and down it: a tractor trundled slowly in the direction of Laragh, towing a cart stacked with bales of hay. The light was fading from the air. In three quarters of an hour it would be dark.

He crossed the road and walked down to the path behind the hotel. An atmosphere of melancholy had settled over everything. It suited his mood perfectly. The lake was to his right, out of sight from the path. Closer at hand, the round tower and the cluster of slate-gray ruins that circled it were visible through the trees.

Out of season, the ruins were deserted. He saw a bent figure among the gravestones and called Ruth's name; but it was an old woman in a head-scarf arranging winter flowers on a recent grave. He nodded and went on. New graves gave way to old, domes containing plastic flowers to moss and lichen. In place of sharp inscriptions in English, the slabs bore faded lettering in Latin or Irish. *Or do Diarmait*, A prayer for Dermot. *Or do Pádraig*, A prayer for Patrick. He turned his head, but the old woman had vanished.

He had come here once with Francesca. It had been spring: the end of March or early April. He remembered pink blossoms on the trees and sunlight on gray stone. The following day, he had written a poem for her. He could still remember its opening lines:

> By a sharp stone in Glendalough
> I saw a raven stand and shiver in the wind;
> and I saw Kevin walk
> over dark waves
> from shore to sorrowing shore.

Even now, in that dank, unlovely graveyard, his fingers stained with innocent blood, and the years lying like a great wilderness between, the words of the poem came back to him out of the past. The words came, and with them images they conjured into life in the thin air of the present: long hair falling against a dimly-lit shoulder, gray eyes in the half-light of a book-lined room, white teeth against soft lips, the slope of rounded breasts against thin fabric. And a gold pendant engraved with the sign of a seven-branched menorah, topped by a cross.

As he walked down to the lake, his thoughts turned restlessly to the photograph in Balzarin's album. That it was Francesca he was absolutely sure. An entire section of his memory was devoted to her face. Already the photograph from the album had lodged there, among a thousand other images. Calmer now, he considered it again, trying to understand what it could be doing pasted among the rest. More than that, he struggled to see how, if at all, this changed things. Was this the real connection, the knot that tied him to De Faoite, Chekulayev, and their killers?

Turning a corner, he slipped on damp grass and fell awkwardly against a gravestone, winding himself. As he started to pick himself up, he noticed that the lettering on the stone was worn and illegible. Nothing remained to identify the white bones underneath: no name, no age, no date of birth or death.

And in the next moment, as he straightened up, leaning his weight against the weathered stone, a thought of the purest horror came to him. He staggered, dizzy, almost retching. For the second time in less than an hour, he felt his world lurch and crack from side to side.

It can't be true! he thought. But in his heart he knew it was. He reached inside his jacket and took out Francesca's photograph.

It had not been obvious at first. There had been tombs in so many of the photographs. And his thoughts had been fixed on Francesca herself. But now, as though emerging from the winter mists that had once shrouded it, he saw quite clearly the tombstone in the background.

Francesca had been photographed standing in front of her own grave, alive, half smiling, a ghost trapped in a trick of sunlight.

NINETEEN

In the west, the sun had started its long journey toward the Atlantic. There was a sound of birds preparing for night. The wind was rising again, bending the naked tops of the trees. There was still just enough light to see by.

He continued on down toward the lake. His first priority now was to find Ruth. She had not responded to any of his calls, and he was growing anxious.

The lake came into view directly ahead of him. This was the smaller of the two lakes at Glendalough. Dark hills ringed it about, and along its fringes tall, slender reeds waved like ripples of woven silk. Across its surface, a solitary white bird glided, its feathers touched red by the setting sun. Light and water fused in its wake. In the shadows along the shore, a bittern boomed, welcoming the darkness.

He looked up and down the vast expanse of reddening water. The light made searching difficult, and he knew her green jacket would camouflage her at any distance. Cupping his hands together, he hollered loudly. But only a faint echo came back, as though mocking his concern. Perhaps she had already started back toward the cottage, taking a different path than usual.

Taking the left-hand path, he walked quickly along the lakeshore. As he turned a bend, he saw her several yards away. She was sitting among the pebbles near the water's edge, her back against a large rock. A few minutes more and she would have been invisible, merely a dark green shadow fading to gray. He called her name and hurried in her direction.

He noticed the blood before anything else. A small pool of it lay at the base of the rock. Then he saw the angle at which her head was bent.

Her hands had been trussed firmly behind her back and a gag thrust hard into her mouth so she could not cry out. The gun had probably been silenced. The blood had dried around the tiny bullet hole in her forehead. Most of the bleeding had been through the larger exit hole at the rear. Her eyes were still open, staring across the lake, as though watching the gliding bird. He closed them and then stood looking at her, wondering what to say. He felt awkward and embarrassed. She would have known, he thought. She would have known exactly what words were appropriate. But the only sound was the lake stirring beneath a cold north wind.

He stood up and looked across the gray water. It shivered furtively but told him nothing. He clenched his hands, the nails cutting into his palms, drawing tiny flecks of blood.

A sudden sound brought him back to himself: a helicopter passed by overhead, swooping low, as though looking for a place to land.

Jesus! he thought. Makonnen was still in the cottage, alone.

Tearing himself away from the lake, he turned and ran to his right. A shortcut went over the fields, across low stone walls and down to the road. He ran jerkily, avoiding rocks and tussocks scarcely visible in the rapidly thickening darkness. The thin air scoured his lungs. Underfoot, the ground was damp and yielding, dragging at his feet. He scrambled through bracken, up a steep slope. The helicopter passed again, taillights winking, one red, one white.

At the top, he climbed the last wall and dropped down to the road. The cottage lay to his right, with three bends of the road between. He headed toward it, at walking pace, his heart pounding, forcing himself to remain calm.

As he drew near the gate, he made out the silhouette of a man standing outside, just on the grass verge.

"Is that you, Michael?" he said as he approached within speaking distance. The man did not reply.

"Sure, and I thought you was me friend Michael," he said, drawing closer. If the man was looking for an American, he hoped the phony accent and the darkness would deceive him.

He reached one hand into his pocket and saw the telltale stiffening as the stranger reached inside his coat. He drew out a pack of cigarettes and the man relaxed.

"Have you got a light, sir?" he asked, taking a cigarette from the pack. "Jeez, and I could do with a smoke!"

The man fumbled inside a pocket briefly and took out a box of matches. Patrick stepped up to him, the cigarette in his mouth. The stranger struck the match. As it flared up, he saw Patrick's face and realized too late his mistake. Patrick punched him with all his strength, full in the guts. As the man jackknifed, breathless, Patrick brought his knee up hard, connecting with his chin. There was a crisp snapping sound and the man toppled backward onto the road, striking his head hard against the tarmac.

Patrick found the gun and slipped it into the waistband of his trousers.

He straightened and looked up and down the road. No sign of anyone. But the helicopter might have landed nearby and dropped more men. He had to act quickly. Quickly and silently.

Between the gate and the cottage lay about two hundred yards of garden, mostly overgrown. There were lights in the kitchen, which lay to the right of the front door, to Patrick's left. He could also make out a light in one of the upstairs bedrooms.

He removed his Burberry: it would only serve to give him away in the darkness. Beneath it he wore a dark jersey and slacks. Bending, he rubbed his hands in clay and smeared his face with it.

Keeping away from the path, he moved toward the cottage, a shadow gliding through the darkness. His eyes were accustomed to the dark, and he was familiar with the terrain. So far, things were going in his favor.

There was a clump of rhododendrons near the front of the cottage. Crouching low, he moved up behind them. He could just make out the shape of a single man keeping watch by the door. A strange car had been parked next to Ruth's Volvo.

Turning to the left, he skirted the house. All was quiet at the back. There was no rear entrance, just a pair of low windows. He could go in through them—but that would leave the guard at the front and anyone in the vicinity he was able to call for help. He decided to deal with the guard first.

A month ago, he and Ruth had set rabbit snares among the trees at the rear of the cottage. It would be difficult locating any of them in the dark, but he thought he knew his way well enough to try. He found the large ash tree that had been partly burned by tinkers the year before. There should be a snare a few paces to the left.

It was still there. He fumbled in the grass, untying it from the stake that held it in place. Moments later he had a length of heavy wire. It was far from ideal, but it would do. He found a handkerchief in the pocket of his trousers and ripped it in two. Wrapped round the ends of the wire, the strips made reasonable handles.

On tiptoe, he crept to the corner of the cottage on the far side from the kitchen and glanced round. The man was still by the door. He carried an automatic rifle in one hand. Patrick's problem was to get behind him without being seen.

There was a sound of muffled voices. A man's voice was raised in anger, rough and menacing. He could just make out Makonnen's reply. The priest was still alive. But for how much longer?

The guard was making an elementary mistake. His attention was fixed more on the area to his right, where he had illumination from the kitchen window. Patrick lowered himself to the ground and began to crawl toward the man, keeping himself close in to the wall.

Suddenly, the man turned his head and looked off to the left. Patrick halted and held his breath. Things were still in his favor: turning from the lighted area to the pitch-dark on his left, the guard's eyes had not adjusted. Patrick waited until he looked away again, then started crawling once more.

This was the worst moment, the moment he had to make his mind up to kill. Any hesitation could prove fatal. He thought of Ruth, of her blood freezing on gray stones by a dark lake. His hands gripped the wire and he started to rise.

The man turned, his eyes opening wide in horror. Before he had time to recover or call out, Patrick was on him, slipping the wire over his head and jerking it tight against his throat. The wire cut into his hands, softened only by the thin cloth of the handkerchief.

There was a clattering sound as the rifle dropped to the ground. The man reared up and backward, hands thrust to his throat, fumbling help-lessly. Patrick felt the wire dig into the flesh and pulled harder, ignoring the pain in his hands, the pity he felt for his victim. There was a low gagging sound, the guard grew frantic, twisting, throwing what was left of his strength into a final effort. But Patrick held firm, sliding the wire back and forward, slicing it deeper into the soft throat, as though slicing cheese.

He felt the man go limp and caught him as he fell, lowering the body to the ground. His hands stung, but that was all he felt. No remorse, no anger, no disgust. Those would all come later, if at all.

For over a minute he crouched in the shadow of the wall, gun at the ready, watching the door. No one came. He heard voices again: the rough voice, then Makonnen's, pleading, and finally a third, precise and cold and measured. He wanted to take at least one of them alive.

He opened the door slowly, desperately trying to remember whether or not it creaked. It did not. A moment later, he was in the passage. The kitchen door was on his left. He took a deep breath and reached for the handle, praying his luck would hold.

TWENTY

Surprise was on his side. The door opened to his right, giving him a clear line of fire along the main kitchen area. There were two men with Makonnen, dressed alike in dark green anoraks. One was standing, the other seated at the table, facing the priest. Patrick swung round the door, moving directly into a firing posture, legs apart, arms at head height.

"Freeze!"

Everything shifted into slow motion. The standing man threw himself sideways, pulling Makonnen with him to the ground. As the chair went from under him, the priest slipped, toppling away from his assailant. There was a shot. It went wild, missing Patrick by several feet. He fired back through the table, two shots in quick succession. The man on the floor grunted and fell silent.

At the table, the second man remained unmoving. Patrick trained the gun on him.

"Put your hands flat on top of the table! Don't move a muscle!"

He took a step into the room.

"Father Makonnen," he called out, "are you all right?"

There was a brief silence, then the priest replied.

"Yes. Yes, I am."

"What about him?" He meant the man on the floor.

Another silence. When he finally spoke, Makonnen's voice was accusing.

"I think he's dead."

"In that case, help me tie up his friend. I want to take him with us. He has some talking to do."

For the first time, the man at the table spoke. His was the cold voice Patrick had heard through the window. Even now, he was emotionless, bleak. He was tall and gaunt, aged about sixty, with pearl-white hair worn a little long. It had been a long time since he and Patrick had last met.

"You're wasting your time, Patrick. There's nowhere to run to. Not now. Why not give up? While you're still alive. We don't want to hurt you,

Patrick. We just want you to keep some things to yourself for a little while. It's not your fault, you weren't to know."

Patrick did not reply. Keeping the gun trained on the man, he helped Makonnen to his feet. The priest was bleeding from one temple but seemed otherwise unharmed. Patrick was nervous. Had there been only four men, or were there others, already alerted by the shooting?

"Are you alone?" he asked the white-haired man.

The stranger smiled but said nothing. In the grate, the fire had burned low. A faint smell of cordite hung on the air. Darkness crowded thickly against the windowpane.

Patrick stepped up to the man and leveled the pistol at his temple.

"I asked if you were alone. Believe me, I will shoot you if I have to."

He cocked the pistol. The man smiled at him: cool, deliberate, unconcerned.

Makonnen stepped forward.

"Mr. Canavan, you . . ."

"Please, Father, let me handle this."

The priest held back, uncertain how best to act. Canavan had seemed a moral man, or, if not that exactly, one determined to prevent unnecessary killing. And yet he had to his knowledge killed three men already and was threatening to shoot a fourth.

The man in the chair held Patrick's gaze unwaveringly. It was not a simple lack of concern that showed in his eyes, but something more: certainty, conviction, acquiescence? Yes, thought Patrick, perhaps that was it: a willing acceptance rooted in an absolute certainty of his own rightness. But what did Miles Van Doren have to feel righteous about?

"Why did you have her killed?" Patrick demanded. He had to struggle to keep his voice steady. "She was your daughter. Your own daughter."

Van Doren looked at him caustically, much as a cat looks at a noisy child, with studied disinterest. His eyebrows were thicker and darker than his hair, and they canopied his eyes, darkening and enriching them. His skin was meager, stretched over the bones of his face like waxed paper. Tiny veins ran threadlike in a clumsy mesh beneath the surface of the skin, purple against its gray terrain, like rivers clustered incongruously on a map of a pale and lifeless desert.

"Don't get excited, Patrick. You're mixed up in something you don't understand. This isn't Agency business. Shall we say that Ruth was . . . a sort of payment? A debt, a sacrifice. I had no choice. She knew things she had no right to know. She'd got in too deep. Just like you, Patrick. You should have dropped it after the business with Chekulayev. There's too much at stake for us to play games."

Patrick was growing nervous. He sensed that Van Doren was playing for time.

"On your feet," he snapped. "We can talk about this later, once I've got you out of here."

"I've told you already, Patrick, you're wasting your time. Put the gun away. You've nothing to worry about if you act sensibly. I have influence, I can see to it that you come out of this unharmed. Otherwise . . ." Van Doren shrugged his shoulders.

Patrick started to reply, but his voice was drowned by a sudden roaring. The air filled with it, and a second later an eruption of light tore the darkness apart, as though a giant hand had ripped a thick, black curtain from top to bottom.

Patrick recoiled from the window, half blinded by the blaze of light. Van Doren took his chance. He pushed back his chair, grabbing for Patrick's arm. The gun went off, missing Van Doren's head by inches. The shot was blotted out by the roaring from outside as the helicopter steadied itself for a landing on the lawn.

Patrick was pulled off balance, toward his assailant. Van Doren spun him round, yanking his right arm painfully behind his back, forcing the gun to drop from numbed fingers. Outside, darkness rushed back as the helicopter set down, throwing dead leaves and twigs high into the shuddering air.

Holding Patrick's arm high against his back, the shoulder close to breaking point, Van Doren used his free hand to draw a gun. He rammed it against the nape of Patrick's neck, without words, not quite gentle, not quite hard. As he did so, he bent forward and kissed the top of Patrick's head: a soft kiss, such as a lover might lay on his sleeping partner.

Outside, the pilot switched off the engine. A profound silence washed through the night. Patrick could hear his heart beating, strokes away from sudden death. He could sense Van Doren's tension, knew that his finger was tightening on the trigger, that it was over, that the kiss had been an act of betrayal, or perhaps contrition.

"Please drop the gun." It was Makonnen who spoke, nervous, yet firm. "Don't make me shoot you. I don't want to, but I will if I have to. Believe me."

Van Doren did not relax his grip, either on Patrick's arm or the pistol. He glanced round almost casually.

Makonnen had taken the gun from the man Patrick had shot. His hand was not entirely steady, but he was too close to his target to miss.

"What happened, Father?" Van Doren asked. "Have your scruples suddenly deserted you?"

The priest shook his head. He was not a man given to sudden revelations or moral shifts.

"You misunderstand," he said. "I would not have had Mr. Canavan shoot you in cold blood. But this is not cold blood. To save his life, I am willing to take yours. Do you understand now?"

Patrick sensed Van Doren's hesitation. Makonnen took another step forward. Feet ran across the gravel outside. Someone shouted.

Van Doren half turned, shouting in reply.

"I'm in here! I've got Canavan, but the priest is armed. Be careful."

There was a crash as someone kicked the door open. Two men in green anoraks burst into the room carrying automatic rifles. Makonnen did not flinch or even turn his head. He held the gun in both hands now: his grip was growing steadier by the second.

The newcomers hesitated. They leveled their rifles at the priest, but knew the risk of opening fire.

"Put the gun down, Father," said Van Doren. He continued to hold Patrick in a painful armlock.

"I will fire," said Makonnen. "Tell your friends to lower their rifles."

"Be reasonable, Father. If you kill me, my men here will gun down both of you half a second later. What will that accomplish? You will simply die with my blood on your hands."

Makonnen wavered. Van Doren gazed straight at him, as though daring him to shoot. He dropped the pistol to the floor.

One of the newcomers stepped up to Makonnen and grabbed him roughly by the arm.

"Take him out to the helicopter," ordered Van Doren. "I'll take Canavan. We'll take them both to Migliau. He has some questions he wants answered." He turned to the second of the gunmen. "You'll have to stay here with Mark until I can send someone back for you: there won't be enough room in the copter for six. Go and tell John to start the engine. We'll be straight out."

The man turned and went outside. A moment later, they heard the whine of the helicopter engine being restarted. Patrick was jerked round and pushed toward the door. Makonnen followed with the other gunman.

As they walked toward the helicopter, Van Doren slipped the gun back into his pocket. Patrick stumbled on the gravel, but the older man kept his grip. They bent down, ducking under the rotors. At the door, Van Doren let go of Patrick's arm to enable him to climb into the machine.

Patrick had been waiting. The instant his arm was free, he spun, grabbing Van Doren around the waist. Before the other could do a thing, Patrick lifted with all his strength. There was a sickening crunch as the rotor blades whisked Van Doren's head to cream, followed the next second by a high-pitched whine as the rotor mechanism became unbalanced. Blood sprayed everywhere. Van Doren's body jerked twice and went limp. Patrick dropped it and ran out from beneath the crippled rotors, straight for Makonnen and the man holding him.

The gunman had frozen in horror. Before he could recover, Patrick had knocked both him and the priest to the ground. There was a shot as the other rifleman opened fire over their heads. Patrick whirled, snatching the automatic from the ground, and raised it, pulling on the trigger. The gunman staggered and fell back.

"Come on, let's get out of here!" He bent down and pulled Makonnen to his feet. The man he had knocked down made a grab for his leg, but Patrick sidestepped and kicked him hard in the teeth.

Ruth's Mercedes was standing where she had parked it, just in front of the cottage. The key would be in the ignition, where she always left it. Patrick ran toward it, half pulling, half pushing Makonnen with him. He bundled the priest into the passenger seat. There was a burst of automatic fire from behind them. Patrick turned and fired back wildly, then ran on round the car, into the driver's seat.

"Take this!" he yelled, thrusting the rifle into Makonnen's hands. "Use it if you have to, to keep them back."

The priest sat trembling, his lips moving in repeated prayer. He was sick and numb. Patrick tossed the rifle into his lap and turned the key. The engine started first time. Another burst of fire just missed them as Patrick let in the clutch and roared off in first. He only remembered to put the lights on after they had turned onto the road and driven halfway to Laragh.

THE DEAD

"Jesus Christ, who is the faithful witness, and the first begotten of the dead."
—Revelation 1:5

VENICE

TWENTY-ONE

No sound. A great and bitter silence over everything. Blackness punctuated by small yellow lights like corpse-candles on a stretch of lonely marsh. He was in the darkness moving, and the silence all about him, insistent and faintly menacing. As he moved, his eyes began to clear, and he was able to make out something of his surroundings.

He was being rowed in a small boat of some sort. It lay low in the water, gliding soundlessly across a patterned solitude of light and dark. He felt it rock softly from side to side as it moved through the water in a straight line, creasing the surface gently with its prow. With a start he recognized the prow's distinctive shape: the bladed *ferro* of a Venetian gondola.

He cast a quick glance backward. At the stern, a tall gondolier, dressed all in black, angled himself across his long oar, twisting it in that curious Venetian fashion through its wooden rowlock. Somehow he knew the rowlock was called a *forcola*, but he could not remember having learned the word. A light hung from the pointed stern, leaving a trail of broken gold on the water behind. But the gondolier's face remained hidden in shadow, beneath a soft, wide-brimmed hat. He turned his head, facing in the direction of travel once more.

His seat was a high-backed chair, delicately molded and decorated with gilded dolphins and brass sea horses. His hand brushed against the cushion on which he sat: it was thick velvet, soft to the touch. He leaned back, expecting to hear the plash of water or the turning of the oar against the *forcola*, but there was nothing. He must be in Venice, but where exactly? And who was rowing him? And why? He tried to form the questions, but his mouth would not open.

At that moment, the moon slipped out accommodatingly from behind heavy clouds, throwing a bland, whitish light across the trembling water. He was on the Grand Canal, gliding down the very center of the great channel, flanked by tall houses and gilded *palazzi*. Everywhere he saw pointed windows, many of them covered with awnings and aglow with candlelight. There were torches on poles where the *fondamente* and *rive* straggled down to the edge of the canal. Outside the palaces, massive lamps hung at the landing stages, casting strange flickering light on the mooring poles and the little craft tied up at them.

There was something terribly wrong. He could not at first tell what it was, only that something was false, that there had been a change of sorts. But whether the physical world had undergone a transformation, or there had merely been a shift in his own consciousness, he could not say.

Other craft bobbed or darted past them—slim *sandoli* rowed with cross oars, and long, black-painted gondolas, many complete with *felze*, the curved black cabins that kept the passengers' identity secure from prying eyes. Light *traghetti* ferried people from bank to bank, weaving their way skillfully through the other traffic.

He recognized the facades of *palazzi* on either side. Francesca had taught him well, pointing them out to him on their many trips up and down the canal. In art and architecture, as in love, she had been his guide. He noticed that they were traveling from north to south, away from the *terraferma* toward San Marco and the lagoon. On his right, he could make out the Fondaco dei Turchi, a crumbling ruin that had once housed the headquarters of Venice's Turkish merchants. Almost facing it, on his left, stood the Palazzo Vendramin-Calergi, where Wagner had died, mad and alone.

The names of the palaces and the families who had inhabited them passed through his head like gray ghosts: Bastaggià, Errizo, Priuli, Barbarigo, Pesaro, Fontana, Morisini—a litany of the dead, their great houses rising like tombstones out of the moon-touched water. He knew something was amiss. But what?

They reached the Ca' d'Oro, with its gilded reliefs and bright capitals twinkling in the light of a hundred torches, each of its tall windows bright with a thousand candles. Between the gold, panels of red and blue, cinnabar and aquamarine, shimmered in the moonlight.

The boat passed on, down to the Ca' da Mosto, marking the beginning of the bend where the canal turns down to the Ponte di Rialto. Slowly, they rounded the broad corner. The bridge came into sight like a great ship, lights burning in the windows of the shops that formed its central section. Suddenly, in the distance, west of the bridge, the sky was filled with flashing lights. Fireworks exploded soundlessly above the Campo San Polo. Rockets turned the night red and gold. Fireballs burst, scattering showers of rainbow-colored sparks across the sky. Fire cascaded like rain, illuminating rooftops and pinnacles and the tops of high towers.

In the light of the fireworks, he caught clear sight of the facade approaching on his left. He recognized the building as the Fondaco dei Tedeschi, a sixteenth-century complex that had contained the lodgings, offices, and warehouses of the old German merchant colony. The side and front of the building glistened with color. Two great frescoes covered them, the work of master artists. He remembered their names: Giorgione and Titian, both commissioned after fire destroyed the original edifice in 1505.

And there, he knew, quite as though a part of his brain that had been sleeping until then had come fully awake and whispered the awful truth into his ears, there lay the real horror, the true madness. There should not have been frescoes. Giorgione's was long fallen into ruin, a mere fragment left in the Accademia gallery, his only documented work. Titian's was no more than a haze of faded colors on the Fondaco wall, a reminder of past glories, nothing more. The Fondaco itself was a post office now, drab, artless, without vibration.

He thought back to each of the places they had passed. The Fondaco dei Turchi should not have been in such a state of disrepair: it had been rebuilt in the last century and later turned into a museum. There should have been a forest of television aerials on the roof of the Palazzo Vendramin. The gilding and the colored paints had long ago flaked away from the golden palace of the Contarinis.

And now the madness settled in him like a snake, coiling and uncoiling through his body. He had seen no *mostoscafi*, no *vaporetti*, not a single motorized craft anywhere on the canal. Gondolas had not carried *felze* since the last century. There had been no *imbarcaderi* crowded with passengers waiting to board the water buses. No police boats, no *vigili urbani*, no ambulances, no electric lights.

He looked up. They were about to go under the bridge. High above, looking down at him from the bridge, dark figures huddled against the parapet. They wore black capes and tricorne hats, and on their faces low white masks, beaked, like birds of prey: the *bauta*, the carnival costume of the eighteenth century.

The gondola slid without a sound beneath the low arch. The lights were blotted out. All became darkness.

TWENTY-TWO

"Are you all right?"

Patrick sat up in bed, shaking. Someone had turned on a light. Makonnen. He heard his voice again.

"Are you all right, Mr. Canavan?"

He was sweating. When he closed his eyes, he could still see the canal in darkness, the white masked faces peering over the bridge.

"Yes," he whispered. "I'm okay. Don't worry. Everything's all right."

They were sharing a room in a small *pensione* on the Rio della Verona. On the day before, they had flown to Rome from Glasgow and taken the first train to Venice.

"What time is it?" Patrick asked.

"It's after four o'clock. You were shouting in your sleep. In Italian. You were shouting in Italian."

"What was I saying?"

Makonnen hesitated.

"I . . . don't know exactly. I couldn't make out all the words. Once you cried out, *'Chi è lei? Dove mi sta portando?* Who are you? Where are you taking me?' "

Those were the words he had tried to shout to the gondolier. He had not forgotten. He had forgotten nothing. The gondola, the dark facades, the bridge lit up by fireworks: his memory of them was real, and as clear as that of the hallucination he had experienced in Dublin. But this had been a dream, surely nothing more.

"What are you frightened of, Mr. Canavan? What is it?"

Patrick felt the sweat growing cold on his skin. The night was chilly. He could feel the all-pervading damp of Venice rising from the small canal outside.

"You know what frightens me," he said.

"No," replied the priest. "I do not mean that. That frightens me too. That is natural. You are right to be frightened. But there is something else. Something else is frightening you."

Patrick did not reply at once. He had not told Makonnen about Francesca's photograph or his discovery that the object in front of which she was standing had been her own tomb. There had been no time to think properly about it. Nor had he spoken of the hallucination he had had in Dublin.

"Tell me, Father," he began, "do you believe in ghosts?"

Makonnen looked at him uneasily.

"Ghosts? I've never really thought . . . You must know that the Church does not encourage tampering with the supernatural." He paused. "Do you think you have seen a ghost? Is that what you are frightened of? A ghost?" There was no mockery in the priest's voice, no hint of a rebuke. Men could be frightened of the dead, that was natural. In Ethiopia, in many parts of Africa, the dead were not so separate from the living.

Patrick shivered.

"Listen, Father. I'm not sure I believe in a God, much less in spirits. But . . ."

Carefully, he explained to Makonnen what he had found. He took Francesca's photograph from his pocket and showed it. The inscription on the stone was clear, there was no mistaking it. Only Francesca's identity remained in doubt. For Makonnen, but not for Patrick. When he finished, the priest did not speak at first. They lay silently in their cold beds, listening to the water lapping the edges of the canal.

"Is that why we have come to Venice?" Makonnen asked finally. "To find this woman? You think she is still alive, that something very cruel has happened to you. Is that it?"

"I came here to find Migliau. To discover what he knows about Passover."

"But you want to find the truth. You want to find this woman, if she is still alive. If she is not, after all, a ghost. That is so, isn't it?"

Patrick nodded. It was true. Until this moment, he had not admitted it to himself. That was why he had chosen Venice over Rome as a place in which to start their investigation. But he did not speak of the hallucination or the clarity of his dream. Were they connected in some way? He might have to see a doctor. Perhaps the stress of the past few weeks, combined with the pressures that had led him to leave the Company . . .

"Turn out the light, Father. Let's get some sleep. We have to start early in the morning."

He woke at seven, unrefreshed. Makonnen was already up, whispering prayers in a corner, underneath a small bronze crucifix. He was dressed in clothes Patrick had bought for him in Belfast, on the day after their escape from Glendalough. A heavy, rust-colored sweater, brown tweed trousers, and dark tan brogues. He still seemed uneasy in his new clothes, as though he wore his priesthood like a carapace between his flesh and the alien, layman's garb he was forced to wear. At first, indeed, he had been reluctant to exchange his clerical dress for new garments, but Patrick had persuaded him that it was essential for his safety. Somewhere, hidden eyes would be watching for a black priest. Makonnen could not change his blackness, but he could at least avoid drawing attention to his vocation.

From Glendalough they had headed straight for Dublin. There had been no immediate pursuit: clearly, Van Doren's messy end had disabled the helicopter and thrown his surviving agents into confusion. Patrick had driven like a madman down twisting roads, with Makonnen beside him, very still, very subdued, staring into the cone of light ahead as though transfixed by something ungodly torn out of the surrounding blackness.

In Dublin, they stopped long enough to draw money from a cash machine and to hire a fresh car from Boland's on Pearse Street. They left the Volvo near Trinity College: with any luck, it would be days before anyone realized it had been abandoned. By seven o'clock they were heading north on the Swords road. An hour later they were nearing the border.

Instinct made Patrick cautious. The Irish border is simplicity to cross— and simplicity to watch. He knew an unapproved road that turned east after Dundalk. It ran high along the cliffs overlooking Dundalk Bay, then down toward Newry, skirting Carlingford Lough. He knew it would be impossible to travel that way at night. The road turned and twisted, and in parts only feet separated it from the cliff's edge: without lights it would have been suicide. But lights would have drawn the attention of British border patrols watching for illegal traffic.

They spent the night in a guesthouse in Dundalk and left early the following morning. Patrick waited until the main road was clear of traffic before turning right. The road was little more than a country lane with a tarred surface. It rose through a series of bends before opening out over the sea. There were mountains beyond it. And the river coming down to meet it, dressed in silk. A red sea, and a green sea, and a blue sea, catching fire, and the mountains heavy and full of mist.

Soon after that they crossed the border, though there was no marker to say that they had done so. No one challenged them. And before long they were back on the main road, heading into Newry.

They passed in silence through a changed world. Makonnen was in a black mood, a mood that matched the landscape. There seemed to be a church on every corner: a blind and obsessive religious force lay like a dull cancer at the heart of the country's darkness. By the roadside, as regular as traffic signs, tin plates had been nailed to the trees. They bore painted admonitions for the ungodly: "Prepare to meet thy God!" "Christ Jesus died for your sins." "Ye must be born again."

After a short stay in Belfast to cash money and change cars, they headed for Larne. They reached the harbor in the middle of the afternoon and crossed on the ferry to Scotland. No one stopped them. There were no security checks to pass through at either Larne or Stranraer. For the first time since leaving Glendalough, Patrick had started to breathe a little more easily.

There were regular flights to Rome from Glasgow. They stayed overnight in order to take the seven-forty British Caledonian/Alitalia flight via Amsterdam, rather than pass through Heathrow. Makonnen still had his passport. His arrival at Fiumicino airport would be recorded, but that could not be avoided. At Rome, they took the first *rapido* to Venice, arriving after the fall of darkness. Only forty-eight hours had passed since their escape from Glendalough. It seemed much longer.

"Did you sleep in the end?" Makonnen had finished his prayers and was standing now, slightly defensive, as though some trick of light had revealed Patrick to him with another face.

"Yes. Very well, thank you."

"You did not dream again?"

Patrick shook his head. Curiously, he still remembered his dream. This had never happened to him before, such clarity, such breadth of detail.

"I think we should have breakfast," he said. "I want to discuss our plans."

This was the first time either man had mentioned the making of plans. Each stage of their flight had run into the next, each destination the one before, as if some force of nature were driving them. There had been no planning, no intent.

They breakfasted in a small downstairs room facing the canal. Patrick gazed through the window, watching the dull winter light fall heavy and unannounced on the high water. There was nothing special about the view: just the weathered facade of a small *palazzo*, grained and marbled with age and damp. But it told him all he needed to know: that he was in Venice once more, that he could be nowhere else. It was as if he had never been away.

Yellow plaster fell away from bare brick, like skin exposing bone. In places, heavy iron staples pinned the bricks together. Grilles covered half the windows, giving the whole the semblance of a prison or an asylum. High up, a single window lay open where someone had hung a carpet out to air. A large white cat sat on a low windowsill, eyeing the dirty water malevolently with one blue and one yellow eye; God alone knew how it had contrived to get there or how it would get away again.

Patrick felt tired. The weight of the past was so heavy here, it lay on everything and everyone. Even in the center of Cairo or the *suq* in Damascus, he had not felt so strongly the presence of the past. Here, he could believe that a crack might open up between it and the present, a fissure between the thick walls separating the years from one another. He looked away from the scene outside and poured strong black coffee into Makonnen's cup.

"Father, there may be risks in what I am about to ask you to do. If you don't feel able to take them, you just have to say. I don't want to force you to do anything."

The priest looked up from his coffee and gave a rather glum smile.

"I'm afraid I have already been forced by circumstance. I did not choose to come here. I did not choose to be involved in any of this. But I am here. I am involved."

He sipped from the cup and spread a little butter on a brioche.

"Incidentally," he said, "I don't think you should let anyone hear you referring to me as 'Father,' do you? My Christian name is Assefa. And perhaps I can call you Patrick."

Patrick nodded. They were the only guests in the small dining room, but even Venetian walls—especially Venetian walls, he thought—have ears.

"Very well. Listen. It will have to be your job to investigate Migliau. Find out what you can: his daily routine, his movements over the next few days, anything unusual that people may have noticed."

"But I can't just turn up at the basilica and start asking questions. Maybe you could do that. You could pose as an American journalist or a writer. American journalists are a sort of infestation—nobody thinks twice if he sees one crawling in his direction, unless it's to get out of the way. But who ever heard of the Ethiopian press?"

Patrick slipped a piece of *focaccia* into his mouth and washed it down with a sip of coffee.

"Is there anyone you know in Venice? A personal friend, someone from the seminary or the Accademia?"

Assefa pondered. His friends from the Accademia Pontificia had all entered diplomatic service, mainly abroad. He had lost track of most of his friends from the seminary. And then he remembered Claudio. Claudio Surian. He had been in his fourth year of training for the priesthood when, quite abruptly, he had abandoned his vocation. He and Assefa had been close friends, but not even Assefa had known how serious Claudio's problems had become. Claudio had refused to answer his letters and made it clear that a visit would be out of the question.

"Yes," he said, "I have an old friend here. He is not a priest. But he may know the answers to some of your questions. And I am sure he will know how to find the answers to the rest."

"Excellent. But you must be sure to swear him to secrecy. He must understand that your life is in danger. Tell him enough to make him appreciate that fact, but no more."

"I understand. Don't worry—he will be very discreet." Assefa drained his cup and reached for the pot. "What about you?" he asked. "What do you intend to do?"

Patrick glanced at the wall on the opposite bank. It was so close, he felt he could reach out and touch it. The past was like that, close enough to hold. Yet a man could drown in the waters that separated him from it.

"I also have some old friends to see," he said. "If they are still alive. And if they will see me."

Assefa reached out his hand and laid it on top of Patrick's.

"Be careful, Patrick," he whispered. Someone had come into the room and was sitting down several tables away. "You have said several times that my life is in danger. You have saved it twice already, and I am very grateful. But I am more afraid for you than I am for myself. Only my life is in danger. But you, Patrick, I fear that your soul is in peril."

TWENTY-THREE

The water taxi dipped and bobbed through heavy waves, throwing up a light spray in its wake. Out in the open, it was growing choppy. A fine drizzle fell, reducing visibility and covering the windows of the small cabin with a veillike condensation. The *motoscafo* had taken the most direct route for San Michele, down through Cannaregio, along the Canale della Misericordia, and out into the lagoon.

Wherever the truth might lie, Patrick's search began here at Venice's cemetery island. He had to start where he had left off twenty years earlier. When news of Francesca's death reached him, he had been in Dublin. She had gone to Venice to visit an aged aunt, while he stayed behind to catch up on work after the Christmas vacation. The telegram had reached him a week later: TERRIBLE INCIDENTE. FRANCESCA MORTA. FUNERALE DOMATTINA. ALESSANDRO CONTARINI.

He had already arrived in Venice before the reality of her death hit him. It had been like a punch, heavy and hard, leaving him breathless and filled with a dull, incomprehensible pain. They said she had drowned while rowing alone in the lagoon, that her body had been recovered by fishermen who had witnessed the accident. The next day, tired and numb, he had followed the funeral barge in a gondola draped in mourning. There had been mist all along the Grand Canal, and a deep chill over the lagoon.

Her father, mother, and brothers had been polite but distant. They had never approved of the relationship and saw no reason to grant him further access to their tight family circle. They were Contarinis, descendants of doges, rich, vain, and powerful. They had made it clear that he would not be welcome to stay on once the formalities of mourning were over, and the day after the funeral he had returned to Dublin with his grief still intact: unshared and ultimately unacknowledged, it had festered in him for years and left wounds that would never heal.

As the little *motoscafo* approached the landing stage on the northwest corner of the island, Patrick caught sight of a mournful procession directly ahead of them. A cortege of gondolas festooned in black struggled to keep pace with the motorized hearse that led them. In front, the chief mourners stood rigidly in the thickening rain, all dressed in heavy black coats. Among rows of black umbrellas, one stood out, bright red, like an obscene gesture. Dark plumes hung bedraggled above the hearse, drenched in sea spray and drizzle.

They hung back until the mourners had landed. Patrick had come full circle. It would not have surprised him to have recognized the faces in the procession, or to have seen one of them beckon to him, summoning him to the graveside.

The mourners wound their lugubrious way past tall, dark cypresses and frowning monuments of granite and marble. The bier was draped in black and gold and topped with winter flowers. At the front of the procession, a tall priest walked with his head bent, reading prayers from a rain-drenched book.

Patrick told the driver to wait and stepped off onto the landing stage. He passed directly through the cloister bordering the church that stands guard over the entrance. Death began here, in the form of huge stone plaques, lovingly inscribed and less lovingly covered in graffiti.

The cemetery itself was carefully laid out. It dated from the end of the eighteenth century, when Napoleon had decreed that the dead of Venice be brought here for burial. It was a small city, an intricate maze of streets and lanes and passageways. Rain-sleek domes and gabled roofs and the pinnacles of dark mausoleums formed a jagged line against a slate-gray sky. Tall tombs of white Carrara marble towered over the modest resting places of the middle classes and the pitiful headstones of the poor. Gates of wrought iron led up to heavy, studded doors. But no one passed in or out, and there were no windows anywhere.

In the streets, no one played or laughed or sang. Here and there, visitors paused to read the inscription on a monument or bent to lay flowers against a gravestone. Patrick could not remember exactly where the Contarinis had built their family vault. He walked up and down the rain-soaked paths, growing more confused with every turn he took. The rain fell in a steady stream. Everywhere he turned, another vista of silent tombs opened before him. The blank faces of angels met his gaze, and Virgins of white marble, and Christ crucified in stone. He felt cold. Bitterly cold.

It took him a miserable hour, trudging from mausoleum to mausoleum, before he found the tomb. He turned a bend and saw it looming out of the rain at the end of a long pathway: a gray stone monument in the Roman style, flanked by obelisks and guarded by gaunt sphinxes with the faces of women.

As he approached more closely, he noticed that it had grown shabby from neglect. The fence surrounding it had rusted and fallen in places.

Weeds grew where there had been grass. The steps leading to the door were cracked and overgrown. Perhaps he had made a mistake after all. But the family name was still there, carved in tall letters above the lintel: CONTARINI.

He felt alone and terribly afraid. Involuntarily, he looked over his shoulder, back along the cypress-bordered path that led to the tomb. No one was there. A shiver ran through him. A regiment of ghosts had gathered round and were pressing against him, inhaling his breath, kissing his lips, licking his flesh for warmth. And on the dank, decaying steps Francesca's ghost stood waiting with pale eyes.

He shook his head and was alone again. Nervously, he stepped up to the gate. It would not yield to his efforts: a heavy, rusted padlock held it solidly shut. He gave up and walked along the fence to a spot where several bars had broken away. Squeezing through, he found himself on spongy ground, among grasses that rose to his knees. As he approached the steps, his chest felt tight and his breathing grew thick and hampered.

"Dio ha chiamato a se la nostra sorella Francesca . . ."

He remembered the priest at Francesca's funeral, assuring the mourners of everlasting life. They had gathered round the tomb, in no particular order, while the priest stood on the steps, facing her coffin, proclaiming the resurrection of the flesh in a house of bones.

"Ma Cristo, primogenito di coloro che risorgono, trasformerà . . ."

Standing alone and unconsoled, waiting for her brothers to carry her into the tomb, Patrick had felt his faith melt away like mist fading across the lagoon. Afterward, he had entered the mausoleum to join the line of friends and relatives filing slowly past the niche in which she had been placed. He had wanted to see her again, but the coffin had been firmly closed. The slab bearing her name and the dates of her birth and death was already in position. He had touched it and bent to kiss it when someone jostled him from behind and he stumbled forward, leaving her forever.

That night, her father had summoned him to his study and offered him money. At the time he had thought it simply a payoff, a *douceur* like that paid to an awkward and undesirable suitor to see him out of a favorite daughter's life. But Alessandro Contarini's daughter was dead. There had been nothing crass or indelicate about the offer or the manner in which it was made: only *arrivistes* are clumsy in such matters. The wealth of the Contarinis went back centuries and their nobility even further.

"Patrick, per favore, non fare l'orgoglioso. Please, Patrick, try not to be so proud. Accept my offer. You need a vacation, time to be by yourself, time to recover from your loss."

The count's words had been thoughtful, almost kind, but Patrick had sensed behind them the steeliness of an ultimatum. He refused the money

but left the next day. It was only after his return to Ireland that he realized
for the first time that he had seen none of Francesca's family shed a tear
during the whole of his short visit. He had never contacted them again, nor
they him.

He thought the heavy door might be locked like the gate, but with a
little effort it swung partly open. The door was made of cypress wood and
set with panels of heavy bronze portraying scenes of classical and Christian
life. Grave figures processed with palm branches or sacrificed at flower-
decked altars. Both men and women were dressed in flowing Roman garments, pulled over their heads and reaching to their feet. High up, Adam
and Eve crouched naked and guilty beneath the Tree of Life. Moses led the
Children of Israel out of Egypt. Abraham laid his only son on a high altar,
bound as a sacrifice.

In another panel, Jesus raised Lazarus from the dead. And in the center
a group of weeping disciples laid the body of their crucified Lord in the
tomb. It did not immediately strike Patrick that there was something very
strange about that scene.

He had bought a small flashlight in a shop on the Merceria before
looking for the water taxi. Switching it on, he squeezed through the half-
open doorway.

He found himself in a vast, unlit chamber hung with cobwebs. The beam
of the flashlight swept steadily over the walls. Behind marble slabs, generations of Contarinis slept. In one corner, empty niches waited for their
inhabitants.

Slowly, he made his way from slab to slab, reading the inscriptions. He
found the resting place of Lucrezia Contarini, the aunt Francesca had been
visiting when she died. Next to it Francesca's mother Caterina had been
interred: *La Contessa Caterina Contarini. 25 febbraio 1920–18 marzo 1977.
Hic jacet pulvis cinis et nihil: Here lie dust, ashes, and nothing.* She had died
six years after Francesca. Withered flowers stood in a dry vase beneath her
faded photograph.

But however hard he looked, he could not find Francesca's tomb anywhere. He started again at the beginning, systematically following the
slabs, going from one to the next with the care of an archaeologist. Nothing. He felt his flesh go cold. It could not be possible. He had been here,
his fingers had touched her name. With a trembling hand, he removed her
photograph from his pocket. The slab was just as he remembered it. And
there, just beside it, was the edge of another slab. Only a few letters were
visible, but they were enough to tell him that the second tomb was that of
Francesca's grandmother. And that Francesca's mother now lay buried in
the niche where her own coffin had been interred. *Hic jacet pulvis cinis et
nihil.*

TWENTY-FOUR

Outside, the rain still fell in a steady stream. The cemetery seemed to have emptied of people, and as he traced his way back past weeping angels and the idealized busts and photographs of the dead, he noticed that the funeral cortege had already embarked on its journey back to the city. Venice lay hidden behind a gray curtain, separated from its dead by a wintry channel of rain-lashed water.

In the cloisters he found a young Franciscan monk who offered to take him to the sacristan. The original monastery of San Cristofero was long closed. Now a small contingent of working monks was attached to the island's church, a building of severely classical appearance, designed by Coducci in the fifteenth century. The monks' chief function was to smooth the path from Venice to the grave. They tended the cemetery and supervised the burials, greeting each funeral party as it arrived, stoical or weeping, at the landing stage.

The *sagrestano* had a small office off the main cloister. The room was virtually bare, devoid of either luxury or grace, a sort of antechamber to the tomb. Grimy windows looked out directly onto the necropolis. The young monk asked Patrick to be seated, then turned and disappeared on sandaled feet. Ten minutes later, the *sagrestano* appeared in the doorway and introduced himself as Brother Antonio.

Pulling back his rain-soaked cowl, he drew a chair up to the green-painted metal desk that provided the room's only working surface. He was well advanced in years, with a few pathetic wisps of gray hair adhering to a wrinkled bald head in nervous imitation of a tonsure. There was an almost shocking gravity about him that tended almost to severity. Perhaps a long life among the dead had impressed on him too deeply the blatant horrors of earthly existence. Or perhaps he had simply grown old and crabby by degrees, like anyone else. Small, deep-set eyes scrutinized Patrick a full half minute before he spoke.

"Buon giorno. Posso parlare Italiano?" he asked. His voice was scratchy and asthmatic.

"Ma certo."

"This is unusual," he said. "We receive few foreign visitors here on San Michele, especially at this season. The island is not on the tourist itinerary. Each year a few lovers of the Russian ballet come to pay their respects to a man called Diaghilev, who is buried in the Orthodox plot. And even fewer bring flowers to the tomb of an Englishman called Baron Corvo. I suppose they have read his books. I could not tell you. I have not read any of them myself. I am told they are mischievous books. And that he was a man of great depravity. And not even a baron."

He paused, sensing Patrick's impatience.

"I'm sorry, *signore,* but you must understand that this is San Michele, not Père Lachaise or Montmartre. We have no Chopins here, no Prousts, no Delacroixs, no Oscar Wildes. You must go to Paris for that. But our church is very fine. It is the earliest example of Venetian Renaissance architecture. There are three altarpieces by Carona and a bust of Bernini's. The son, I mean, not the father. One of the younger monks would be happy to show you round."

Patrick shook his head.

"I haven't come here to look for celebrities," he said. "I came to find the tomb of . . . an old friend. But I need your help."

The old man relaxed a little. Looking for tombs was something he understood. His breathing grew a little easier.

"I see," he said. "My apologies, Signor . . ."

"Canavan."

"Signor Canavan. From time to time, tourists call at the island. They expect to be entertained, to be shown the sights. They weary me a little. But an old friend—that is different. That is very different. I shall be pleased to help you." He folded his wrinkled hands in front of him. "Now, your friend—what was his name?"

"Her name. She was buried here twenty-one years ago. I've gone to the family tomb, but there's no sign of her ever having been there."

Brother Antonio nodded.

"And the family—what is their name?"

"Contarini. Her father was Count Alessandro Contarini."

A momentary shadow seemed to pass over the monk's face, then it was gone. He nodded gravely. *"Contarini, si. La grande tomba romanica.* In the southwest sector. You say you have been there."

"Yes."

"And you found no trace of this friend."

"That's correct."

"Perhaps you are mistaken. Perhaps she was never buried in the family vault. That sometimes happens."

Patrick shook his head.

"She was buried there. I know—I was at the funeral."

Brother Antonio shifted uncomfortably in his chair. He looked shrunken inside his ample habit, rather like an apple that long exposure to the air has dried and wrinkled.

"I take it, Signor Canavan, that you understand something of how this cemetery . . . works. It is not like most habitations for the dead. We have very little space. Of course, we try to do our best to create new land on the east of the island. But space is limited, and in the meantime people most inconveniently insist on dying and being born. We bury them every day, the old and the young, the rich and the poor, and still they keep coming. Praise God, *signore,* we are not pagans here. We do not burn our dead or leave them out to rot. And we shudder to think of the crabs and lobsters at the bottom of the lagoon.

"Normally, unless their families are prepared to pay a good deal, the common dead are disinterred at the end of twelve years. We throw away their little headstones and dispose of their bones. In the old days, a barge called here every month to transport them to a little island farther out in the lagoon, Sant' Ariano, near Torcello. Sant' Ariano was the city's ossuary until several years ago. Now we have enough room to bury everyone in a common grave to the east of the main cemetery."

The monk fixed his eyes on Patrick.

"Does that seem bizarre to you, Signor Canavan? Primitive, perhaps? I know it is not what you Americans would do. You try to keep your dead forever, in lead coffins. But our custom is different. The bones are nothing to us. Not many years ago, we used them to refine our sugar. We Venetians have a sweet tooth, you understand. And we are a little in love with death."

Patrick broke in.

"Surely what you have just told me applies only to what you just called the 'common dead.' The Contarinis are wealthy, their tomb is one of the biggest on the island. If anyone rests in peace here, surely the Contarinis do."

Brother Antonio looked uneasily away. Patrick followed his gaze. Through a window of cheap glass, a confusion of tombs barricaded the sea. Above the window, an unpainted crucifix hung on cracked plaster.

"No one rests in peace on San Michele, Signor Canavan. Least of all the Contarinis. There is sea all around us. There is damnation. There is a resurrection to come."

The old man's vehemence surprised and wounded Patrick. More than anything, he was looking for a sign that Francesca was at peace.

"I'm not speaking of their souls, Father. Just their bones. Surely once they have been interred, no one will remove the bones of a Contarini." He did not refer to the possibility that one of them, once buried, might walk again.

The monk paused and returned his gaze to Patrick.

"No," he said. "You are quite right. The Contarinis rot in undisturbed splendor." There was a note of mockery in his voice. He sighed. "What was your friend's full name?"

"Francesca. Francesca Contarini. She died in 1971. On January 5. She was brought here for burial on the sixth."

"Have you evidence of that?"

"No, of course not. But I thought that you, perhaps, might have a record."

For just a fraction of a second, Patrick saw the monk hesitate.

"These are family records, *signore*. Requests to examine them are normally made through the families concerned. If the Contarinis . . ."

"Please, Father, I don't have time. Francesca was . . . a very dear friend. It's over twenty years since I visited her grave. I'm only in Venice for a few days."

The *sagrestano* seemed about to refuse. Instead he sighed and eased himself slowly to his feet.

"Very well," he said. "But perhaps we will find nothing. Or learn that her bones have joined a million others in the heap out there. God knows, there will be a terrible muddle when the resurrection comes. No doubt I shall be in there with the rest of them, trying to sort myself out. I pray God my bones are not mixed with those of an amputee. I might lose an arm or a leg in the confusion."

As he spoke, going over/what was no doubt an old and favorite joke, he creaked across to a row of shelves running the length of one wall. They bore over one hundred leather-bound volumes, arranged in groups of years.

"What year did you say?"

"Nineteen seventy-one. The sixth of January."

The monk took down one of the more recent volumes and carried it back to the desk. He started to open it, then paused.

"This friend of yours," he said, "she was not—forgive me—she was not a suicide?"

Patrick shook his head firmly.

"It was an accident. She drowned. I saw her buried here, I followed her coffin." He struggled to keep control.

Father Antonio opened the ledger and began to leaf through the pages, muttering under his breath all the while.

"*Maggio . . . aprile . . . marzo . . . febbraio . . . ah,   gennaio! Bene. L'undici . . . l'otto . . . il sette . . . ah, ecco! Il sei gennaio!*"

His finger crept slowly down the page. Patrick noticed that the nail was black, in places turning yellow.

"Taglioni . . . Trissino . . . Rusconi . . . Lazzarini . . ." The old man intoned the names as though reading a roll call. "Bastiani . . . Giambono . . . Ah, so sad, a baby, that one. I remember them, they were very unhappy. . . . Malifiero . . ."

Patrick held his breath. The old man's finger reached the bottom of the page and rested there, trembling fractionally, like a leaf that senses a storm building in the distance.

"There is nothing," he said. "No entry of that name."

"There must be some mistake."

"No mistake. Unless you have given me the wrong date."

"Look again. Try the fifth, or the seventh."

Brother Antonio shrugged his thin shoulders and resumed his search. Again his gnarled finger traveled down the names of the dead and the details of their interment. And again it came to rest. He shook his head limply.

"Surely," Patrick urged, "you must remember. It was a big funeral, an important family, their only daughter. There were reports in the newspapers, I remember."

"I'm sorry," said Brother Antonio, closing the ledger. He seemed ill at ease. "I have no recollection of such a funeral. But there are so many every day, the details slip my memory."

"You remembered the baby, the one you said was so sad."

"For its sadness, yes. But a Contarini—that would not be so great a tragedy."

Patrick changed direction.

"What about her mother? Do you remember her funeral?"

"Perhaps. What was her first name?"

"Caterina. Her maiden name was Querini. She died on the eighteenth of March 1977. I think she was buried in her daughter's place."

The monk replaced the first ledger and took down a second.

"That would be unusual," he said, "but not unheard of."

He consulted the ledger.

"Contarini . . . Contarini . . . *Ecco, ci siamo!* 'Contessa Caterina Contarini, of the Palazzo Contarini, Campo San Polo 2583. Born 25 February 1920, died 18 March 1977. Buried in the Tomba dei Contarini, plot no. 7465, 21 March 1977.' "

He looked up.

"That is all, Signor Canavan. There is no mention of a daughter. All is in order, as you see."

He walked back to the shelf and replaced the volume. For a few moments, he stood facing the rows of ledgers, as though hesitating before taking yet another from the shelf. Then, abruptly, he turned to face Patrick. His face was hard and set, betraying a determined effort at self-control.

"Signor Canavan, please forgive me. I am an old man. My sight is feeble, my hearing is growing dim. Soon, very soon, my name will join all the others in these ledgers. The ink will dry and before long another ledger will be added to the rest. Every day, several times, my successor will take the new ledger from its place and add more names. Sometimes the sun will shine. Sometimes, like today, there will be rain, or a heavy mist among the cypresses. The gondolas will come and go as they have done all these years. Nothing will change. San Michele will grow a little fatter with its dead, the bones will lie more heavily in the earth. Perhaps, in time, Venice will sink beneath the sea and no one will come here anymore. But at heart things will be as they have always been."

The old man paused. He took a couple of steps toward Patrick, his back bent, his thin hands clasped painfully in front of him.

"Let the dead rest in peace, Signor Canavan. Where they come from and where they go are no concern of yours. The mausoleum of the Contarinis is already falling to dust. There is grass on its stone, and moss. It does not matter who sleeps there and who does not. They are beyond your reach, all of them. Go home, *signore.* Pray for us. And we shall pray for you."

He paused a brief moment longer, then pulled his cowl about his wizened head and walked stiffly to the door.

"Do not return, *signore.* There is nothing here. Nothing but grief."

Patrick watched as the old man opened the door and walked out into the glistening rain.

TWENTY-FIVE

Makonnen was waiting for him at Florian's as arranged. The priest seemed ill at ease among the gilded mirrors and red velvet banquettes of the cafe's luxurious interior. He was in a corner, drinking an *espresso ristretto* from a tiny white cup. Between sips, he stared haplessly through a window painted with mermaids at the people passing down the long arcade beside the Piazza San Marco.

Patrick sat down beside him and asked for a Fernet-Branca.

"Have you had lunch?" he asked Makonnen. The priest shook his head.

"Would you like some?"

"Not really. I'm not very hungry."

"Nor am I. But I suppose we'd better have something."

When the waiter arrived with Patrick's drink, he ordered one plate each of *prosciutto crudo* and *bresaola,* with a bottle of Recoaro. The waiter took the order with a flourish, gave an almost imperceptible glance of disapproval at Makonnen, and left. Opposite, in a corner, an elderly grande dame sat at a table alone, watching her rouged and prunelike features ripple in a rococo mirror as she lifted a cup of hot chocolate to pursed lips.

Apart from them and the old lady, the cafe was almost empty. In Venice, no one much minds the *acqua alta* when a spring tide brings the sea sweeping into the city and floods the piazza. But on a cold day toward the end of winter, when rain rushes in from the Adriatic and there is no shelter to be found anywhere in the streets, those who can do so stay at home and warm themselves at their stoves.

"Did you find your friend?" asked Patrick.

Makonnen nodded. He seemed a little distrait.

"Yes," he said. "He still lives in his old house. His mother died last year, and he stays on there with his father. The old man's eighty-five now, and Claudio has his hands full looking after him. He can't afford a housekeeper or a nurse, so he has to do everything himself. He washes and dresses him, helps him to the toilet, feeds him." Assefa paused, staring at his empty cup.

"It's strange," he continued. "But it's like a vocation for him. He seems to lead a celibate life. Never thinks of himself. Every moment, he's there to help the old fellow. Like a saint. We were so ashamed for him when he left the seminary, as though the priesthood was the only thing that mattered in life. Some of us thought he was damned, that he had damned himself by turning his back on the Church. And now he wipes an old man's backside and thinks nothing of it. Not as a penance or anything like that, but as a sort of love."

"He sounds like a good man, your friend."

"No, that's just the point. He's not a good man. He'd hate to hear you say that. Truly he would. He drinks a lot and swears, and I think he has terrible tempers. And he hates the Church. But you'll see for yourself. He wants to meet you. This afternoon."

Patrick sipped his Fernet-Branca, grimacing as its bitterness reached his palate. The grande dame lifted a jeweled hand to her scrawny chin and glanced at them coldly. Pale steam rose in lazy spirals from her chocolate.

"What did you tell him?"

"Only what you told me to, that my life is in danger, that we need help."

"Is he able to help us? Did you tell him what we need to know?"

Makonnen nodded.

"Yes. He has contacts. Old friends from the days when he was an altar boy. And more recent friends. He's a Communist now, or says he is. Before his mother died and he had to look after his father more, he belonged to some left-wing clubs in Cannaregio."

An English family came in, shivering, handing their Burberries and streaming umbrellas to a patient waiter. There were four of them, a husband, wife, and two blond-haired children aged about seven, one boy and one girl. They seemed self-conscious, almost timid, as the English always do in foreign parts. The dowager eyed them through gold pince-nez, as though irritated to be thus disturbed by tourists out of season.

"What about you?" Makonnen asked. "What did you find?"

Patrick decided it was time to explain about the photograph of Francesca he had found in the album. He made his story as down-to-earth as possible, offering no theories, inventing no hypotheses to account for what he believed the photograph showed. He brought it out and passed it to Makonnen.

"Is this the ghost you asked me about last night?"

Patrick nodded.

"What do you believe? That she is dead? That the figure in this photograph is indeed a ghost?"

"I don't know what to believe," Patrick replied hollowly. "Not even you know that."

Makonnen nodded, agreeing.

"What did you find at the cemetery this morning?" he asked.

Patrick described his fruitless visit to the island, his conversation with Brother Antonio. He heard himself speak, yet it seemed as though he stood somewhere apart, watching, listening. Detached from his surroundings, he watched the English family seat themselves, the contessa sip her chocolate, the waiters come and go like acolytes in a glazed and gilded temple.

He had come here many times in the past with Francesca, to escape the crowds in the summer, to listen to the orchestra play old dance tunes, to watch the world reflected in the mirrors, everything back to front and yet somehow more real than life, more intense.

He wondered if Ruth had ever come here. She would have fitted in, he thought, a figure out of Henry James or Fitzgerald. Americans like that were almost an extinct species now. Hollywood and Disneyland and Burger King had all but wiped them from the face of the earth. And now Ruth had joined them, a victim of a different kind of greed. It seemed crass, but he thought he loved her more now that she was dead. It had been that way with Francesca too. Would Assefa regard that as a sin? he wondered.

"Are you all right, Patrick?" The priest leaned over the table, a look of concern on his face. Patrick came out of his reverie.

"I'm sorry. I must have drifted away. I was thinking about Ruth."

"That's all right. You don't have to explain."

The waiter brought their food. They ate in silence, washing the meat down with glasses of mineral water. They were almost finished when Patrick noticed the grande dame pay her bill and take her coat and umbrella from the waiter. Instead of going straight out, she came across to their table.

"You an American?" she asked Patrick. With a shock, he recognized the accent—Boston or maybe Cambridge. His *contessa* was a character out of James after all.

He nodded.

"Take my advice," she hissed, bending over him and clutching his shoulder with a clawlike hand. Close up, her skin was taut and mottled with age. Her breath smelled of chocolate. "Next time you come here, leave the nigger outside. He doesn't belong."

Before Patrick could respond, she had turned and was stalking toward the door. At their table, the English family sat and talked about a thatched cottage they had just purchased somewhere in Surrey. The door closed and their tinny voices filled the little room.

They took a water bus as far as Santa Marcuola and walked the rest of the way into Cannaregio. The rain had eased back to a drizzle. Here and there a handful of cats had ventured out to look for scraps. As they headed down toward the Ghetto, the streets became tighter and the houses taller, hemming them in. An old woman in a tattered overcoat passed, carrying shopping in a plastic bag. In a doorway, a blind man sat scraping lines in the ground with a white stick. They passed over narrow bridges, across side canals in which rotting vegetables and dog turds floated. Everywhere there a smell of poverty and neglect hovered in the air. And a deeper, more insidious smell, age mingled with despair.

Claudio Surian and his father lived on the top floor of a six-story tenement. On the street outside, scruffy children played with a battered football. From a broken gutter water trickled down the front wall, leaving a dark, rusted stain on the ancient brickwork. The house had never been very beautiful, but once it had possessed a certain dignity that was now almost wholly eroded. Assefa pushed open the huge wooden door that led into the courtyard.

A stone staircase led up to the apartments. Assefa and Patrick climbed slowly, their feet slipping on worn steps made slick by the rain. A faint smell of urine greeted them on each of the little landings. On the wall opposite, a shutter was pulled back and a woman's head looked out. She watched them climb, her eyes suspicious, her expression hostile.

Someone had sprinkled disinfectant on the top landing. Assefa knocked on a heavy door from which all but a few scraps of red paint had worn away. After about a minute, there was the sound of a key turning in the lock. The door opened several inches onto a chain before being pulled back more widely to admit them.

Patrick's first impression of Claudio Surian was that he had tried to commit suicide and failed. There was a look of resignation in his face, especially marked around the eyes. It was the face of a man who knows that his despair is rational and therefore unavoidable, who has considered hope among other crutches and rejected it as useless. He seemed ill. His thin cheeks exaggerated what his eyes betrayed. But his clothes were neat and tidy, and he was clean-shaven.

"*Entrate, vi prego,*" he said.

To Patrick's surprise, the voice was pleasant, almost kindly, with not a trace of the sourness or bad temper he had expected. He shook hands with Surian and followed Assefa through the door.

The room was dimly lit, except for one area over what appeared to be a workbench. The walls were covered in masks—some white, some painted, others half and half. There were masks in the shape of suns and moons, masks with tall hats, checkered masks with stars for eyes. There were several examples of the plain white *bauta*, some complete with tricorne and long black veil. The best examples were masks of the Commedia dell'Arte

—the black half mask of Arlecchino, Pulcinella's long nose and pointed hat. In the center of the floor stood a steaming caldron filled with papier maché. Small tins of paint, bottles of thinner, and brushes covered the workbench.

"I'm sorry," Surian said, finding chairs for his visitors. "I have very little space. This room has to serve as my workshop. My father is resting in his bedroom. If you don't mind, we'll talk in here."

The only source of heat was a small kerosene heater in one corner, but the room was warm, even stuffy. A haze of cigarette smoke hung over everything like a bluish mist on the lagoon.

"So many masks!" exclaimed Patrick.

Surian snorted.

"It's our boom industry, didn't you know? No tourist leaves Venice without at least one mask. About fifteen years ago, there were only a dozen or so mask shops in the whole of Venice. Now there are nearly three hundred." He sat down on a rough wooden stool. "I'm building up stock now for the summer season. I sell my masks to shops on the Strada Nuova mostly, and a few places near the Rialto."

"But these are much better than the average tourist masks."

"Thank you." He smiled wistfully. "It isn't what I wanted to do with my life—but I'm sure Assefa has told you that." He paused and drew his stool closer to his visitors. "I understand you want information about our good Cardinal Migliau."

Patrick nodded. "I'm willing to pay you for your time."

Surian laughed.

"What makes you think you could afford me? I won't be patronized, *signore.* If I help you, it's on Assefa's account. He says he's in danger. Is that true?"

"Yes!"

"For something he did?"

"For something he knows. Something we both know."

"But you won't tell me what it is?"

Patrick shook his head.

"It's very complicated. There's no need for you to know, and I think you could be in danger if you did. Please trust us."

Surian looked at Patrick keenly.

"Vaffanculo!" he swore, his manner changing abruptly. "I don't trust anyone, least of all an American. You fuckers have airbases all over this country, all over Europe. You pull the strings and we dance. And if there's a war, we'll do the dying while you watch. So please don't ask me to trust you."

"Claudio, please . . . he's trying to help me," Makonnen pleaded, in an effort to pacify his friend.

"Sure he is. And from what you told me, he needs a little help himself. But before I start helping strangers—and I include you in that, Assefa—I want to know what's going on." Pausing, he reached into his shirt pocket to draw out a tin of tobacco and some Rizla papers. He began to roll a cigarette, carefully teasing the strands of tobacco onto the thin sheet.

"What are you?" he asked. "CIA?"

"This is private," Patrick argued.

"Nothing's private to the CIA. Go and ask for my file, if you haven't done so already. See how private life is here."

"This isn't a CIA matter," Patrick insisted. "Except . . ."

There was a querulous shout from an adjoining room.

"Claudio! Claudio! Corri qui, sbrigati!"

Surian excused himself and went through a door on his left. Patrick heard the sound of a raised voice behind the thin partition.

"Con chi stai parlando, Claudio? Che è questa gente? Ti ho detto che non voglio amici tuoi a casa mia!"

Then Surian's voice, abruptly gentle again, patience in every syllable, placating, pacifying.

"Nessuno, papà. Solo vecchi amici—se ne vanno subito. It's no one, Father. Just some old friends. They'll be gone soon."

A minute later, the door opened and Surian returned. He took his seat once more without a word and finished rolling his cigarette. He replaced the tin in his pocket and took out a box of matches.

"Do you mean to harm Migliau?" Surian asked. He lit the thin cigarette and raised it to his lips.

Patrick hesitated.

"It's nothing to me if you do," Surian said, blowing a ribbon of acrid smoke into the air. "Perhaps you would be doing some people a favor if you . . . put him out of the way."

"I don't want to kill him. I just want him to answer some questions, that's all."

"And you think he will answer you?"

Patrick shrugged.

"Perhaps. I might have to be a little rough with him."

Surian smiled sardonically.

"I'm sure. Well . . ." He pulled on his cigarette. "I wish you luck."

"You aren't going to help?"

"I didn't say that. Yes, I'll help if I can. Migliau's bad news. A lot of people would like to see him out of action. There's just one problem."

"What's that?"

Surian stubbed the last of his cigarette out on the edge of his stool.

"I made some inquiries after Assefa left this morning. A friend of mine works in the local office of the party newspaper, *L'Unità*. He was a little surprised when I told him I wanted information on Cardinal Migliau. What do you think he told me?"

Patrick said nothing.

"Early this morning, his best contact in the Carabinieri was in touch. Nobody is supposed to know, but it seems that Cardinal Migliau has been missing for three days. He was last seen going to his bedroom in the Palazzo Patriarcale on Monday. On Tuesday morning, his servant found the room empty. The church authorities waited twenty-four hours for a ransom note, then contacted the Carabinieri yesterday. A GIS squad arrived in Venice yesterday evening from Lavarno. Now, *signore*, suppose you tell me just what's going on?"

TWENTY-SIX

It was dark by the time they left. The rain had stopped, but the atmosphere still held a muggy dampness, through which a nagging chill crept like neuralgia through bone. Patrick walked with Makonnen and Surian as far as the Rio Terrà San Leonardo, where they parted company. The priest and his friend continued along the main street to the Lista di Spagna, where Surian had arranged to meet the reporter from *L'Unità* in a cafe.

Patrick headed down to Santa Marcuola, where he took the water bus across to the opposite bank, disembarking at San Stae. From there he plunged into a maze of narrowing lanes and alleyways, losing himself in their bewildering complexity. Yet he was never really lost. Each time he took a wrong turning, it came right in the end. He was guided by a directional instinct he had picked up during the two summers and single winter he had spent in Venice with Francesca.

Little had altered since then. Shops had changed hands, street lights stood where none had been before, a few buildings had received fresh coats of paint. But the configuration of passages and bridges was just as he remembered it.

Deeper and deeper he sank into the skein of alleys and canals, twisting and turning, yet always heading in the general direction of the Frari. It was not late, but the streets were nearly deserted. He passed a small *pasticceria*, where a group of men stood drinking coffee and talking in low voices at the counter. A scrawny cat ran across his path, darting from one doorway to the next. He paused on the next bridge, to take his bearings.

Surian's news had rattled him. He had managed to convince the mask maker that he knew nothing about Migliau's disappearance. But he could not rid himself of the nagging thought that there was a connection between it and the recent events in which he himself had been involved. Had Migliau been kidnapped? Certainly, that seemed more probable than that the cardinal should have taken flight simply because Patrick had uncovered some photographs in Dublin.

There was, however, a third possibility: that Migliau's disappearance was in some way connected with Passover. If that was true, it could mean that fear of exposure had panicked the Brotherhood into bringing the date forward. For all Patrick knew, Passover could be starting at this very moment.

He walked on, wetting his feet from time to time in unseen puddles. People were at home, watching television, eating. He felt hungry, but he wanted to get this over before it grew much later. The *calle* through which he was walking seemed familiar. The house was not far now. But the closer he got, the slower his steps became. He looked round nervously, as though expecting to see Francesca tailing him. These were her streets. If her ghost walked anywhere, it walked here.

The house faced onto the Rio delle Meneghette, but the land entrance was at the end of the Calle Molin. The Contarinis had bought the *palazzo* in 1740, when the last of the Grimani-Calergis died without issue. It was by no means the largest or the finest of the many *palazzi* in which different branches of the Contarinis had lived over the centuries. But it was the last of them and, in some ways, the closest to the family's heart—the closest, even, to the secret they had kept alive for generation after generation.

Seen from the back or the side, like all Venetian mansions, it was unprepossessing. An old street lamp cast a baleful glow over a low wall from which the plaster had fallen away. Behind the wall, Patrick knew, there lay a courtyard, and beyond that the rear of the *palazzo* itself lay draped in a cloak of shadows. Here, leading onto the street, was a rickety door from which the paint had peeled, exposing the wood beneath. A corroded knocker shaped like a Moor's head hung crookedly in its center.

Patrick grasped the knocker tightly and banged several times. Hollow echoes rang along the *calle*. Footsteps sounded farther back, then a door closed with a loud crash. But in the Palazzo Contarini, all was silent and dark. He raised the knocker and banged again, three times. A church bell rang in the distance, as though in mockery.

All at once he heard the sound of bolts being drawn deep within, and a door opening, and slow feet limping across the flagged courtyard. He pictured it, its blue and black and yellow tiles worn down with age, the ancient well-head carved with lions and a leaping unicorn. The footsteps reached the outer door and stopped.

"Chi è? Che diavolo volete a quest' ora?" The voice was that of an old woman, thin and petulant, speaking in the lugubrious accent of the Veneto.

"My name is Canavan. I want to see Alessandro Contarini. I want to speak with him."

"Alessandro Contarini è morto. Dead! Please go away!"

"Tell him I have to speak with him. He will remember my name.

Canavan. Tell him my name is Patrick Canavan. He knows who I am. He will know what I have come to speak about."

"I tell you the count is dead! There's no one here. No one at all. Go away."

Suddenly, a light went on in an upper window. He saw a shadowed face against the glass, then a hand throwing the window open.

"*Chi è, Maria? Che cosa vogliono?* What do they want?" A man's voice this time, old and tired, but aristocratic.

"He says his name is Canavan. He is asking for the count."

There was a long pause. Then the man at the window called again.

"Tell him the count is dead. There is nothing for him here."

Patrick cupped his hands round his mouth. "I've come to talk about Francesca! You owe me this. Your family owe me an answer!"

There was a longer pause. In the alleyway, a crippled dog went past, dragging its hind legs. Patrick felt the rotting and the paralysis all about him, pervading the city. Death and decay, and a terrible stillness of the will that had lapsed into inertia.

"Let him come up," the man replied at last. "I'll speak with him."

The window closed heavily. Patrick waited by the door. The dog had dragged itself into a space between two houses and lay down whimpering. Was it in pain? Patrick had no strength for compassion; there were no empty spaces left inside him. He heard a key turning in a heavy lock.

The old woman swung the door open, stepping aside to let Patrick through. She carried a hurricane lamp in one hand, but her face was turned away, shrouded in a raddled weave of shadows. She held back until he had passed, then closed and locked the door.

A shaft of yellow light fell across the courtyard from the window on the second floor. Patrick's eye followed it up to the window itself. He could just make out the indistinct shape of someone standing near the glass, peering down into the courtyard.

The old woman slipped the key into her pocket and stepped in front of Patrick. As she did so, light from the lamp slanted across her face, revealing a little of her features to him. A sliver of memory scraped his flesh.

"Maria? Is that you, Maria? It's me, Patrick Canavan. Didn't you know my name? I used to come here with Francesca. All those years ago—do you remember?"

"*Non mi ricordo di lei.* I don't remember you. No one came here with the Lady Francesca. The Lady Francesca is dead."

But she did remember: he could hear it in her voice, sense it in the way she held back from him, as though afraid. What was she frightened of? The past?

They entered the *palazzo* through a low doorway on the ground floor.

Generations ago, this had been where the family stored merchandise and laid their gondolas to rest through the long winter months. Not many years ago, when Patrick had last been here, there had still been boats and oars and curiosities from the Contarini past: the marble heads of doges, three plaster angels, cracked and wound with string, great seals of state bearing the motto *Pax Tibi Marce*, several candelabra, each filled with a thousand candles of yellow wax, the remains of a fifteenth-century altarpiece, glittering with gold and lapis lazuli, a gaming table from the Ridotto casino, puppets dressed in faded Commedia dell'Arte costumes, and a miniature theater in which they could perform. He had gone there several times with Francesca, to make the puppets dance and sing, to sit in a chair in which the last Doge of Venice had sat, and to make love silently, away from the sharp eyes of her ever watchful family.

Now the long rooms stood cold and empty. As Patrick followed Maria to the staircase, something small and gray scurried past, fleeing the light. There was a noise of scampering, then silence again.

The stairs led to the *mezzanino*, once the floor on which the Contarinis, like all rich merchants of the Serenissima, had conducted their business. Even in Francesca's day, there had been busy offices here. But now, like the floor beneath, it was hollow and echoing, and smelled terribly of neglect. Patrick thought of the weed-choked mausoleum on San Michele. He could not understand what was going on. What had happened to the Contarinis in such a short space of time? Had they suddenly lost their wealth? Or had some other, less material calamity overtaken them?

Finally, they arrived at the *piano nobile*, formerly the heart of the house, where the family had slept and eaten and entertained their many guests. Maria opened wide the curiously carved door that led into the great central room, stretching the length of the floor and fronting the canal outside.

The room was lit by three weak electric bulbs suspended from a cobwebbed ceiling. In the center, the old electric chandelier hung dull and unlit, festooned with long strands of web and choked with dust. On every side, the ravages of long neglect were apparent: chairs and sofas, ottomans and taborets, their fabric damp and rotting; unpolished tables and sideboards on which the bodies of dead cockroaches lay in shiny carapaces; broken ornaments heaped together on an uncarpeted floor.

But something else caught Patrick's eye. When he had last been here, the rear wall had been hung with a great Gobelins tapestry sequence, almost as long as the room itself. The tapestry was no longer there, but in its place a mural had been revealed. Patrick could make out few details, but the general theme was clear. The mural was divided into panels, each depicting a scene from the life and ministry of Jesus. Something in the style reminded him of the work of Tiepolo; certainly, the fresco dated from the eighteenth century, no earlier. The figures were lightly drawn, turning pigment to light and story to form with great skill.

Clad in the damask robes and jeweled turbans of Ottoman Turks, the Wise Men laid tribute at the feet of the Infant Jesus. In the next panel, Mary and Joseph fled to Egypt while, in the background, Herod's soldiers smashed the skulls of the newly born against marble pavements and pillars of brass.

Toward the center of the mural, the artist had woven the Stations of the Cross into a continuous narrative sequence: the flagellation, the first, faltering steps on the Via Dolorosa, the first fall, the nailing to the cross, the deposition. And finally, the scene at the tomb, as the disciples bring his mutilated body to be buried.

Patrick faltered, recognizing in this last scene the original for the representation on the door of the Contarini mausoleum. And at last he saw what he had missed on San Michele. It was obvious and simple, and it took his breath away. In most versions of the entombment, there are four besides the crucified Christ: Joseph of Arimathea, Nicodemus, and the two Marys. Here, there were twelve disciples and no women. But it was the figure of Christ that filled Patrick with horror. For, in this painting, Jesus was alive and bound and struggling as they carried him to his grave.

TWENTY-SEVEN

"The artist was Tiepolo. Not Giambattista, but his older son Domenico. The style's a little lighter, less allegorical. He painted it in 1758, just after he finished work on the Villa Valmarana. That was a few years after his father came back from Germany, of course: my grandfather used to say Giambattista helped him with some of the larger figures."

The voice was that of the man who had called to Patrick from the window. He was seated at the far end of the room on a high-backed chair. The electric light made him look drained. He seemed smaller than Patrick remembered. His hands were white against the arms of the chair.

"What happened to the tapestries?" Patrick asked.

Alessandro Contarini smiled.

"They were sold. I believe they fetched a lot of money. More than you can imagine. Much more than even I could afford. I think you will find them gracing the walls of a bank somewhere in Texas. Or is it California?" He smiled again and looked directly at Patrick, as though the location of the tapestries were a confidence between friends.

"Tell me," he went on, "do you think that is possible? Will the walls of a bank in Texas become more graceful simply because they have been covered by antique tapestries?" He paused, folding his hands sweetly on his lap, like a well-behaved child. "Perhaps not. Perhaps not."

He lifted one hand as though to admonish the thought of grace in such an alien and uncultured place, then beckoned, a nervous gesture, more Asiatic than Italian. So soft and so deliberate.

"Please, Signor Canavan, come closer, let me see you better." He made a faint, dismissive gesture with his hand. "Leave us, Maria. We wish to be alone."

Patrick heard the door close behind him with a muted click. He took several steps toward the count, approaching within a few feet of him.

"*Basta!* That's far enough, Signor Canavan. I can see you well from there. You'll find a chair near you—please sit down."

The chair was grimy but fairly dry. Patrick brushed it gingerly before seating himself on the edge.

Alessandro Contarini had aged dramatically in the past twenty-one years. Patrick remembered him as a handsome man in his late fifties, with smooth gray hair brushed back from his forehead, exquisite clothes, and skin that was still almost without wrinkles. Now he looked like a desiccated replica of his old self: his skin was gray and mottled, his cheeks hollow, his eyes sunken and haunted. Thin white hair straggled untidily down to his neck. The exquisite clothes were stained and torn, the polished white teeth that had once smiled so patronizingly had turned yellow or disintegrated to blackened stumps.

"I'm sorry you do not find the *palazzo* as you last saw it," he said. His voice was strained and hesitant, with a tight, wheezing note; yet, beneath the surface, Patrick could detect something of the old hauteur.

Patrick said nothing. The image from the fresco had embedded itself in his mind: a group of hooded figures circling about their helpless victim, dragging him toward a stone sarcophagus in a dark tomb set about with vines.

"It was something of a shock to see you standing there tonight," the old man went on. "Did you know that someone was here this morning asking about you? No, I can see from your face that you know nothing about it. That is very curious, is it not? How long is it now? Twenty years?"

"Who came here?" Patrick asked. "What did they want to know?" He was frightened. Who the hell could have known so quickly that he was in Venice?

The count ignored his questions. "It must be more than twenty," he said. "And now you come to my attention twice in one day. You aren't famous, are you, Signor Canavan? You haven't won a lottery or killed a president? No? And yet important people come here asking questions. They wanted to know about the past, about your friendship with my daughter. And now the past turns up on my doorstep howling demands into the night, 'You owe me an answer!' "

The old man paused.

"Is that all you think I owe you? I seem to remember that, when we last met, I offered you money. That was immodest of me—I apologize. Perhaps we understand one another better now. You were a child then, little older than my son Guido. And yet your grief was real, not a child's grief at all. I am sorry you were hurt, sorry you were made to suffer. Please forgive me." He sighed, passing a long white hand over his cheeks.

"At my age, nothing is left but forgiveness. So many things left unsaid, undone. And so much said and done that I regret. It will come to you in time, Patrick Canavan."

"Where is Francesca?" Patrick asked softly.

"Francesca is sleeping. Francesca is dead."

Patrick shook his head.

"Don't lie to me," he said. He wondered why he was so calm, why his voice had fallen to little more than a whisper. "There's no need to lie any longer. Just tell me where she is, that's all I want to know."

"You speak as though she were alive."

"I've been to the tomb on San Michele. There's nothing there. And I have a photograph."

He took the crumpled picture from his pocket and passed it to the count. Contarini looked at it for a long time.

"Where did you find this?" he asked finally.

"Does it matter?"

The old man shrugged.

"Perhaps not. Well—what is it you want?"

"An explanation."

"There are no explanations that would make sense to you."

"Suppose you let me be the judge of that." Patrick hesitated. He leaned forward, softening his voice. "Signor Contarini, I don't think you understand. I loved your daughter once. I believe she loved me. Twenty-one years ago, she was taken from me. Someone, for reasons I cannot even guess at, pretended she was dead. I was summoned here by you and made to go through a mock funeral. I saw no reason to ask questions then. I left when you asked me to leave. But I will not leave tonight without answers."

Contarini handed the photograph back to Patrick. His hand was shaking, and Patrick noticed tears at the corners of his eyes.

"Signor Canavan, please believe me: Francesca loved you as much as you thought, and maybe more." He looked up. His face bore a look of infinite, irredeemable sadness. "I think"—he faltered—"I think she still loves you. Or at least your memory."

The count straightened and looked directly at Patrick.

"Do not try to find her, Signor Canavan. She can never come back to you, never return to the world you inhabit. For you and your world, it is as though she had died. Don't try to change it. Leave things as they are."

Patrick took a deep breath. Contarini's words were like a finger tearing back a scab, exposing an ancient wound. He had thought the pain of Francesca's loss something wasted and bereft of strength, but in a moment it had returned with renewed vigor, like a blunt knife suddenly sharpened, cutting his flesh.

"Why?" he whispered. "Why?"

The count did not reply at once. He sat in his high-backed chair like a faded Renaissance prince whose court has deserted him.

"Signor Canavan," he began, "there have been Contarinis almost as long as there has been a city called Venice. Eight doges of the Republic bore our name. We owned palaces and ships, warehouses and trading houses here and throughout the Mediterranean. From the beginning we sat on the Great Council and the Senate and the Council of Ten. Now there is only myself, an old man waiting to die in a house that is already a ruin. Nothing you can do or say now can hurt me or help me.

"But you want the truth, and the truth is precisely what I cannot give you. It is, I suppose, too shocking. Not for me, perhaps; but others would find it so. And in their rage, they would do what the many-headed crowd has always done: destroy what they do not understand."

The old man paused again. His pale eyes scanned the dimly lit room as though seeing it for the first time.

"There are ghosts here," he said. "This room is full of them. Some of them I can see, others only hear. Perhaps they are not literal ghosts: I do not think they could harm us, at least not in any physical sense. But they are real all the same. Listen, Signor Canavan, let me tell you about them.

"Centuries ago, when Venice was still a vassal of Byzantium, a group of merchants defied the Emperor's ban on trade with Egypt and sailed to Alexandria. They filled ten ships with spices, silks, and carpets and came home rich men. One of them was my ancestor, Pietro Contarini. Two years later, he and another man returned to Alexandria; but this time they had not come for spices or cloth. They stole the mummified remains of St. Mark and smuggled them back to Venice. The mummy was laid to rest beneath the high altar in the Basilica—and Venice became a great pilgrimage center."

The count fell silent. On the canal outside, a motor-powered boat chugged slowly through the night. The sound of the engine filtered past heavy shutters into the room, rising briefly, then dying away as the boat turned a corner and vanished.

"Pietro Contarini," he continued, his voice reduced almost to a whisper, "brought something else back to Venice along with the body of the saint. He had discovered something which, to him, was infinitely more valuable than the bones of a holy man. Pietro's discovery was not a relic or a piece of merchandise or a box of treasure—it was the truth. A truth so devastating that he kept it to himself for the next forty years."

Patrick fixed his eyes on the count's pale lips as he related his tale. In the shadows of the room, he imagined others crouched and listening.

"On his deathbed, however, Pietro told one of his sons, a man of over forty himself by then, Andrea. In those days, merchants were still trading regularly with North Africa, in spite of the objections of the Pope and the

Byzantines. Andrea took a ship to Alexandria, then made his way overland to Palestine. To Jerusalem and the Holy Sepulcher."

In the room, nothing moved. Even the shadows held still. Outside, all was silent. Patrick could hear his breath coming and going in the stillness.

"Over five years passed before Andrea returned. He had seen with his own eyes what Pietro had only heard about. And he had met the keepers of his father's secret. In the few years that remained to him—for he died six years later of the plague—he confided in members of his family and a few carefully chosen friends.

"That, Signor Canavan, was the beginning of our rise to power. Pietro's secret was, indeed, more precious than silks or spices."

Contarini paused.

"But power has a price," he resumed. "A man cannot have power and riches, yet possess his own soul. No more a family. The Contarinis, the Barbaros, the Grimanis, the Sagredos . . . all the noble houses who came to share our secret—all paid their price. Our families, our private affections, our faith, even our souls . . . all for the sake of a truth the multitude could neither understand nor tolerate."

He fell silent, folding his sallow hands together like the wings of a giant broken butterfly. A tremor passed through them and grew still. Outside, the lapping of water against stone was the only sound.

"How," Patrick asked, "does this explain Francesca? Her death, her being alive?"

Contarini sighed. It was a deep sigh, almost a moan.

"Don't you see? Francesca was my price. Her happiness was the sacrifice I had to make. And you were her sacrifice—all she had, all she wanted."

"For this?" Patrick rose angrily, gesturing violently at the crumbling, damp-stained walls, the broken and rotting furniture.

The count shook his head. The long white hair had fallen across his face like a veil.

"No," he said. His voice had changed in timbre, acquiring vigor from some hidden reserve. He raised a hand and pointed, jabbing again and again at the great fresco.

"For that, you fool! For that!"

TWENTY-EIGHT

Patrick left the *palazzo* in a daze. Contarini's anger had subsided into a fit of coughing, and Maria had hurried in to tend him and chase his visitor away. He had left quickly, chased by shadows, harried by ghosts, out into the awful night.

The crippled dog still lay crouched in its corner, shivering with cold. Patrick felt torn between disgust and pity. He wanted to throw stones at it or break its neck. Its misery appalled and frustrated him: to drive it away or put it to sleep were the only options he could stomach. But he did neither. He lacked both courage and conviction.

Instead, he turned his back on the dog and the palace of the Contarinis and walked quickly out of the *calle*.

What blasphemy had Pietro Contarini brought back from Egypt? Witchcraft? Black magic? An early version of the Cathar heresy? Was that all it had been—a juvenile perversion of the Church's rites, a Faustian dialogue with imaginary forces of evil? Or something more banal, perhaps: some tired excuse for illicit sex, Pietro's wet dreams made all too abundant flesh in an orgiastic cult.

But Patrick was sure it was not that simple or that banal. The KGB are not renowned for their interest in the supernatural, and Contarini's story would have provoked little more than amused smiles in the air-conditioned corridors at Langley. And yet both agencies were in this up to their necks. A lot of people had died—and as far as Patrick could see, none of them had been the victims of an occult attack.

A freezing mist had moved in off the Adriatic and crept across the city while Patrick talked with Contarini. It had worked its way slowly along the streets, and now lay flat on the surface of the canals, obscuring the rounded backs of bridges and drifting into every *calle, fondamenta,* and *rugetta.* Like wisps of white smoke, its tendrils wandered through the sleeping streets, curling about the infrequent street lamps, blurring and softening what little light there was. In archways and *sottoportici,* thick masses of it lay like predators, waiting for the unwary.

Patrick turned his collar up against the chill air. In his agitation, he had taken a wrong turning shortly after leaving the *palazzo*. Now the mist was playing with him, teasing him, leading him farther and farther astray. His footsteps echoed between the close-packed buildings on either side—a desolate sound that only emphasized how alone he was in this half-deserted city.

He picked up speed, but the farther he walked the less familiar his surroundings seemed. Reason told him to knock on the first door he came to and ask the way. But it was after midnight, and the bolted doors and shuttered windows he passed held out no prospect of a warm welcome.

After a while, he came to a deserted square. He found the name on a blue and white plate high up on one corner: Campo dei Carmini. But it meant nothing to him. Along one side of the little square, the dark facade of a baroque church loomed menacingly out of the mist. Its troubled pillars and sinister windows reminded him of the tombs on San Michele, as though the church had been constructed for the dead and not the living.

Leaving the square, he paused to read the name of the street he had just entered. As he did so, he heard a sound behind him. It had resembled a foot scraping against stone. And it had not been an echo.

Pressing himself against the side wall of the church, he listened carefully for the sound to be repeated. He could not be certain, but he thought it had come from the square. Contarini had said that someone had been asking questions about him. Was there someone out there now, following him?

He moved on, walking more slowly now, straining to distinguish between his own footsteps and the echoes they raised, listening for the telltale sound of someone tailing him. If he could lead his shadow on, then double back and move in from behind, he might be able to collar him. But the mist and his own disorientation limited his freedom to act.

A narrow alleyway opened out onto a bridge. In a window opposite, a light was burning. He crossed the bridge, then halted, waiting. The silence was thick and oppressive: he wanted to call out, to tear it to pieces without remorse. It came again: a single scrape in the alleyway. Through an arch, he caught sight of another canal: the passage ran down to the water and, as far as Patrick could see, ended there. If he could trick his pursuer into heading that way, he might be able to trap him.

He headed slowly down the passage. "Don't lose me now, for God's sake," he whispered. The mist thinned out a little here, but he had to step carefully lest he mistake the edge of the bank and plunge into the water. His guess turned out to be correct: the passage ended at the water, and there was no path either to right or left.

Intuition had suggested that someone would have left a boat tied up here, otherwise there would have been little point to the small landing area at the end of the passage. Through the mist, he could make out the shape of a small *sandolo* covered in a heavy tarpaulin. He pulled the boat nearer with the painter and slipped over the side, almost losing his footing on the slippery cloth.

He crouched down in the shallow vessel, thankful for the mist, just able to see the end of the passageway over the edge of the bank. And there, at last, an unmistakable footstep! He felt tension build in his stomach and all through his muscles.

A shadow moved. Patrick held himself ready to spring. Everything depended on how close his pursuer came to the edge: far enough, and he might be able to grab him and pull him over. At least he had the element of surprise. The mist parted and the shadow became a dark figure. Patrick held his breath. *Come closer, damn you! To the edge. Come on!* The figure hesitated, frightened perhaps that he might lose his footing in the mist and fall. Patrick felt the *sandolo* rock uneasily beneath him: it made a poor platform from which to launch himself at his pursuer.

The figure paused, then turned abruptly and began to walk back along the *sottoportico*. Patrick flexed his legs and jumped onto the bank, falling on his knees. As he landed, he saw the figure look round and catch sight of him. He scrambled to his feet in time to see his pursuer stumble into the mist.

"Stop!" he cried. "I want to speak to you!"

There was a sound of running footsteps. Patrick broke into a trot. He reached the street again just in time to see the mist fold round a moving shadow. Footsteps rang out like bullets in the darkness. Patrick set off in pursuit, following the sound.

He ran breathless through a maze of alleyways, across bridges, along narrow embankments, the sound of footsteps luring him on, deeper and deeper into the swirling mist. Sometimes he thought he had lost his quarry: he would take a false turn and all but lose the scampering footsteps, then suddenly he would come out along a different passage and hear them ahead of him once more. Twice he caught sight of the running figure ahead of him, a dark blur in the mist.

Out of breath, he stopped on a little bridge to catch his wind. Leaning against the metal balustrade, he looked up and caught sight of someone on a second bridge, just yards away. The mist parted momentarily, giving him a clearer look. His head felt light. He could feel the blood pounding in his temples, his heart pumping wildly in his chest, making him giddy. Had he been mistaken? He looked again, but the mist had swept back. There was no one on the other bridge.

"Francesca!" he called. "Francesca, *fermati!*"

Running footsteps sounded on the *riva* just beyond the bridge where the figure had been standing. Patrick felt a new energy sweep through him. He dashed off the bridge, almost falling down a short flight of steps in his haste.

The footsteps were on his right now. Spinning, he hurried down a mist-choked alleyway, coming out onto a wider street just in time to see the figure vanish again. Gasping for breath, he set off in pursuit. A sharp, stitching pain flared up in his side, making him bend almost double. Gritting his teeth, he pressed on. His legs were like lead, and his head was swimming.

"Fran . . . cesca . . . *Per grazia di Dio . . . fermati!*"

His breath was coming now in harsh, labored gasps as his lungs struggled in the damp air. A broken paving stone caught his foot, sending him sprawling on his face. Winded, he lay for half a minute, his head spinning, fighting for each breath.

Closing his eyes against the pain, he pushed himself up and took a step forward. A pang of pure agony stabbed through his gut. Lights exploded in his head. His legs buckled and gave way. He felt himself falling, his body out of control, then all feeling left him and he was plunging, disembodied, through the deepest blackness he had ever known.

He opened his eyes. It was still dark, but the mist had cleared. His head ached intolerably, and his eyes were painful. Blinking, he thought he could make out stars in a black sky. He was lying on his back against something hard. With an effort, he pulled himself to a sitting position.

On either side, dark buildings slipped by as though in a dream. There were no lights anywhere, but as his eyes accustomed themselves to the dark, he could make out the pattern of the Grand Canal. He was in the mysterious gondola again, being rowed alone by a nameless and faceless gondolier. They were farther down the canal this time, heading for St. Mark's. The torches and candles of his previous dream had been extinguished, and the water was empty of other craft. All was silent as before.

It disturbed him that he could remember everything of his earlier dream, that he knew it had been a dream, and that he was certain, as he had been before, that he was not at this moment dreaming. And yet he could neither hear nor speak.

The gondola began to veer toward the left bank. As they drew close, he thought he recognized the twin-arched windows and ornamented upper storey of the Palazzo Corner-Spinelli. The boat slipped into a narrow side canal and made its way slowly through a labyrinth of channels, some only wide enough to permit the passage of a single craft. Unseen, they passed the backs and facades of tall houses. Here and there, Patrick could see a taper in a high window. Once, he caught sight of a woman watching them from a low balcony, her blond hair combed loose in long, weeping tresses, and pale breasts cupped in tired hands, like offerings.

They slid beneath low bridges, the gondolier stooping down to get through. Once, in the distance, he could see through a gap between tall houses part of a wide *campo*. A bonfire had been lit, and in the center of the square, a group of blind men wielding long knives chased a frightened pig in ever decreasing circles. Then the scene was blotted out by a high wall covered in ivy. The gondola slipped deeper into the maze.

They passed near an embankment on which a crippled dog dragged itself painfully along. Patrick was sure the dog reminded him of something, but he had forgotten what it was. He realized that, although he could neither hear nor speak, he was not wholly cocooned from his surroundings. He could feel the chilly air against his skin, and, if he dipped a hand into the water, it would come out wet and cold. And yet he sensed some sort of barrier between himself and this world. He had been brought here as a spectator, not a participant. But what was it he had been brought to see?

The boat slowed suddenly, and Patrick noticed that they were turning in toward the bank. Out of the darkness loomed the canal gate of a large *palazzo*. Two torches flared on either side, held fast by iron brackets, and a third was held by a servant dressed in a *bauta*, waiting just inside the open gate. Above the gate, a large molding represented a lamb carrying a cross.

They swung in to a low flight of stone steps, and the gondolier tied up skillfully at the nearest mooring post. The gondola twisted round and scraped against the steps. The servant stepped forward, holding his torch high.

At that moment, something happened to Patrick's ears, as though an invisible blockage had been removed. He could hear the sound of water lapping around him, and the wooden hull of the gondola scraping the steps. Like the dog he had seen earlier, the scraping sound reminded him of something. He stepped out of the gondola onto the first step. The servant bowed from the waist, then straightened. Patrick noticed his eyes, gazing at him from behind the mask: the lids were heavy, the pupils glazed and flecked with tiny specks of gold.

"*Abbiate la grazia di seguirmi. I signori vi attendono.* Please accompany me, sir. Their lordships are awaiting you."

TWENTY-NINE

"Can you hear me, Signor Canavan? Please nod if you can hear me."

The voice sounded muffled and remote, but the words were English. Why were they speaking English?

"Please try to answer, Signor Canavan."

He tried to open his eyes, but they felt as though someone had stuck them together with glue. His lips would not move.

"Is all right, Signor Canavan. Just let me know if you can hear me."

He nodded, and, as he did so, experienced a wave of intense nausea. The nausea gave way to blackness. Then out of the blackness the face of the servant in the *bauta* came toward him. The mouth opened as though in speech, but Patrick could hear nothing. The face was swallowed up by blackness.

"Can you hear me now, Signor Canavan?"

This time his eyes opened. He saw a blurred face staring down at him, a man's face, wearing a look of concern. The words were English, but the accent was Italian.

"Yes. Who . . . ?"

"My name is Dr. Luciani. You are in the Ospedale Civile. *Capisce?* Do you understand?"

Patrick nodded feebly.

"You were brought here last night. *Una signora* . . . a lady brought you here after she find you in the street. You were unconscious. Can you remember anything? Did you have accident?"

Patrick shook his head. He felt as though last night's fog had been concentrated and decanted into his skull. His stomach was nauseous. It was like a migraine, only worse.

"You mean—not have accident . . . or not remember?"

"Mi ricordo . . . la nebbia. . . . I remember . . . mist . . . running . . . a gondola."

Patrick had replied in Italian; strangely, he found it easier, as though English had become foreign to him.

"Ah, parla Italiano. Benissimo." The doctor paused. "Signor Canavan, I want to carry out some tests. They are merely to establish whether or not you have suffered some injury to your brain. You may have fallen or been struck. Do you understand?"

"Yes."

"Later, I would like you to have an X ray. And possibly an EEG. Just to be sure. But at this stage, I only wish to test your reactions to stimuli. There's nothing to be worried about."

Patrick's sight was clearing. His head still throbbed, but his thoughts were less confused. Memories of the night before were beginning to flood back: Contarini in his kingdom of rats and ghosts, a lame dog whining among shadows, the fresco on the wall of the *palazzo.*

A nurse came forward to assist the doctor. Patrick was in no condition to argue as she and Luciani began to prick and prod various parts of his anatomy. They flashed lights in his eyes, took his temperature and blood pressure, examined his ears for signs of blood, and tested his reflexes.

He remembered getting lost in the mist, then chasing someone who had been tailing him. What then? Had someone attacked him? Without warning, the image of a bridge formed in his mind, and on it a shadowy figure, half hidden in mist.

"Doctor! . . ."

"Please, Signor Canavan, relax. We'll soon be finished."

"No, please. . . . You said . . . a woman brought me here. *Una signora.* . . . What was she like? What did she look like? *Per piacere . . . è importante . . . molto importante."*

The doctor shrugged.

"I'm sorry, I didn't get a very good look at her. You were my first concern. When I went back to reception, she had gone."

"What age was she? Young, old?"

"Did you know her? Is that it? She said you were a stranger, that she had been out late and found you in a state of collapse."

"What age?"

"About forty, I think. Quite thin, she was quite thin. And smallish, not a tall woman. I'm sorry, I can't remember. Perhaps one of the nurses . . ."

Patrick lay back, helpless. Images of the dream that had followed his collapse were forming in his brain: dark water peeling back beneath the sharp prow of the gondola, stone steps thick with moss, a huge pig, bleeding, running in tightening circles, eyes flecked with gold behind a carnival mask. . . . He was frightened that the dream would pull him back into unconsciousness again. Desperately, he forced his eyes to stay open.

"I miei vestiti . . . Where have you put my clothes?"

"It's all right, don't worry," the nurse reassured him. "They're in this locker by your bed. Everything's safe, don't fret."

"La mia giacca . . . my jacket, please look in the pocket. A photograph . . . there's a photograph."

The doctor looked up impatiently from his examination and motioned to the nurse.

"Take a look while I finish this. It may help jog his memory."

The nurse found Patrick's jacket and went through the pockets carefully. Everything was there—wallet, passport, keys, money—everything except the photograph.

By midafternoon, Patrick's head had cleared completely. Dr. Luciani allowed him a little light food, and the nurse propped him up in a half-sitting position. They left him in a side ward, with nothing for company but a battered television permanently tuned to a children's channel. He asked them to contact Makonnen at the hotel, and an hour later he arrived, anxiety written all over his face.

Patrick smiled and reached out a hand.

"If I didn't know better," he laughed, "I'd say you were looking pale."

"I am pale," Makonnen answered, sitting down. "I didn't know what to do last night, when you didn't come back to the hotel. You said you'd be back before midnight. I thought of contacting the police—but what could I tell them?"

"I'm sorry. Things got a little . . . difficult. I found . . . Francesca's father." He paused. "Assefa, I think they may be on to us. Someone was asking about me at the Contarinis'."

"How could they have found us so quickly?"

"I don't know. Anyway, we'd best move to another hotel. Or better still, find lodgings through your friend Claudio. By the way, what did his reporter friend have to say last night?"

Assefa shrugged.

"Migliau is still missing. There has still been no demand for a ransom. It's as though he'd vanished into thin air. The Carabinieri are growing frantic. The official view seems to be that he was kidnapped, but that something went badly wrong. They expect his body to turn up in a canal any time now. However . . ."

"Yes?"

"That's the official view. Claudio's friend has other ideas. His name is Aldo Siniscalchi. I've arranged for you to meet him. You'll like him: he thinks, asks questions, gets impatient. For several years now, he's been keeping a file on Migliau. Well, not just Migliau, but the Church in Venice generally." He paused. A nurse looked in, glanced curiously at the American and his visitor, and left again.

"Patrick, did you know that three of the eight popes elected in this century have been patriarchs of Venice? As I told you before, some people think Migliau may be number four. He got to be what he is now chiefly through family connections, but Siniscalchi thinks there's a lot more to him than a coat of arms.

"He got interested in Migliau originally because of the cardinal's extreme right-wing stance. Migliau has never hidden his opinions: he has been consistently outspoken in his opposition to reform in the Church or, for that matter, in society at large. No birth control, no abortion, no divorce, no married priests, no women priests—the usual stock in trade of an ecclesiastical reactionary."

Patrick smiled.

"I take it you don't see eye to eye."

Makonnen shook his head.

"No. But I have no choice. God did not do me the favor of ensuring that I was born in Europe or America. From the Third World, things look very different. Don't get me wrong—I'm actually quite conservative in many matters. I don't approve of Claudio or the Communism he has espoused. That's not the answer. But the Communists are right about some things. You can't preach the gospel to a man with an empty belly. You can't enthuse about the kingdom of God to someone living in daily fear of arrest by a right-wing death squad. And for the record, I don't think you can promote the growth of democracy by bolstering up dictatorships."

"And Migliau thinks you can?"

"He doesn't see the relevance. For him, the Church's mission is to save souls, not lives. To rebel against the state, even if that state is steeped in injustice and bloody to its elbows, is a cardinal sin. To practice birth control, even when you and your family are starving, is to contravene God's eternal law."

"But that's little more than the Pope himself has been saying for years anyway."

Makonnen sighed.

"You don't have to remind me. How do you think Migliau got to be Patriarch of Venice? But he wants to go further. If he had his way, he'd turn the clock back in ways you can't imagine. Even I had no conception until last night.

"He'd declare Vatican II invalid, abandon the principle of collegiality, reintroduce the Tridentine mass. He'd ban all dialogue with other churches, prohibit relations with non-Christian religions, restate the dogma of Jewish culpability for the death of our Lord. With Migliau as Pope, the

Church would take a major step backward. There'd be an Index of Prohibited Books again, heresy trials, widespread excommunication."

Patrick shook his head in disbelief.

"You can't be serious."

Makonnen raised his eyebrows.

"No? What makes you think I can't? Compared with thirty or forty years ago, the Catholic Church is positively giddy with modern thinking. And yet people like you—even people like myself—think it's all but standing still. Men like Migliau are scared stiff. They see what the reforms have done, what they are still doing; they think forward another thirty or forty years, and in their imaginations they see the end of the Church as they know it: no mass, no priesthood, no hierarchy, no papacy—perhaps not even a God. I think that's an exaggeration, in fact I know it is—but try telling that to a hard-liner like Migliau."

Patrick shrugged.

"So Migliau's a Catholic fundamentalist afraid of change. What's new? Conservatism and the Catholic hierarchy are scarcely strangers."

"Perhaps. But Migliau goes yet further. One of the cardinal's greatest fears is that fundamentalist Protestants will start to negotiate for political influence in Europe just as they have been doing in the States. If that happens, they will draw away a lot of the God-fearing right whose support would be essential for a moral and religious revolution. Migliau knows he has to get in first.

"Siniscalchi has evidence that the cardinal has had meetings with politicians from the extreme right, not just here in Italy, but in France, Spain, Germany, Austria, and possibly elsewhere. There are no documents, of course, nothing that L'Unità or any other paper can publish. But one report suggests that Migliau has offered to do a deal. If he becomes pope, he will instruct his bishops in each of those countries to see to it that their flocks vote for his candidates. Once in power, they will pledge political and legislative support for his campaign against modernism in all its forms. Migliau will be the first pope in centuries with more than encyclicals as his weapons. He'll have a police state at his disposal."

THIRTY

Patrick felt the breath thicken in his chest. It sounded plausible, too plausible.

"You say Siniscalchi has evidence of this?"

"Of a sort, yes. But hard proof, no."

"Can he get hard proof?"

"Yes. He knows someone who has access to Migliau's office. He wants to see you tonight—he may have something for you then."

"You said he disagreed with the police theory about a kidnapping. What's his explanation for the disappearance?"

"Just that the kidnapping theory doesn't hold water. No one on the right would dare lay a finger on Migliau. Nor, to be honest, would they want to. The same goes for the Mafia. That leaves the left. Siniscalchi has more contacts than the police with left-wing factions and terrorist groups—or so he told me—and he swears that Migliau's disappearance is as much a mystery to them as to anybody else."

"What does that leave?"

"It leaves the possibility that Migliau has dropped out of circulation from choice. For reasons known only to Migliau and whomever Migliau confides in. He thinks it could tie in with our problem, though he doesn't know how."

Patrick paused.

"How much have you told him?"

"I . . ."

At that moment, the door opened and Dr. Luciani came into the room. He smiled and introduced himself to Makonnen.

"I wonder if you would mind waiting outside, Mr. Makonnen. I'd like to have a word with your friend."

When Assefa had gone, the doctor sat down on the edge of the bed and looked at Patrick.

"Well, Signor Canavan, how do you feel?"

"Much better, thank you. Completely well, in fact. If you don't mind, I'd like to leave as soon as possible."

A frown creased Luciani's high forehead.

"Actually, Signor Canavan, I do mind. You may feel well, but I would like you to stay here for at least another twenty-four hours."

"What for?"

"Just observation. There are a few more tests I would like to run. In a few days' time, I would like you to have a CT scan. We don't have the equipment here, but the hospital in Mestre has had a scanner installed recently, and I think I can have you booked in there for an appointment later this week."

Patrick felt a stab of alarm.

"Is that necessary? Is something wrong?"

The doctor shook his head vigorously.

"No, no. I have no reason to think so."

"Then . . ."

Luciani interrupted.

"Signor Canavan, have you been experiencing . . . any auditory or visual disturbances recently?"

"I don't understand. Disturbances?"

"Perhaps hallucinations would be a better word. *Allucinazioni.* Any of the senses could be affected. You might taste or smell something that was not there. A food or a perfume, flowers perhaps. Or it might be a sound— music, a voice . . ."

Patrick looked away. He heard water lapping, smelled a woman's body, warm and close.

"No," he lied. "Nothing like that."

"You are sure? Think very hard."

"Yes, I'm sure. Why do you ask?"

The doctor hesitated.

"On the basis of what happened to you and the test results I have had back, I think you may be suffering from a form of focal epilepsy. Please, don't be alarmed. It need not be serious. And there are other possible diagnoses. I only want you to help me."

"But it may be serious. That's what you're trying to say, isn't it?"

Luciani did not reply at once.

"Signor Canavan, I have no wish to alarm you. Diagnosis in such matters can be extremely difficult: that is why I would like you to undergo further tests. And even if a firm diagnosis is made, establishing the etiology—the cause—will be far from simple.

"The most common cause of focal epilepsy is a lesion of the temporal lobe of the brain. That is why I want you to have the EEG and, if possible, the CT scan. If there is a lesion, it will normally give rise to hallucinations of some kind. The lesion may be minor or, at your age, it may be a tumor. I say that, not to frighten you, but to convey some notion of the potential seriousness of your condition, and, therefore, of the need for your cooperation. Tell me, have you had episodes like this before?"

Patrick hesitated.

"No. Not exactly. . . . There have been dreams. *Dei sogni.*"

"What sort of dreams?"

Patrick attempted to explain. When he finished, Luciani nodded.

"Very well. I would like to speak about your case with one of my colleagues here. He is a specialist in neurological disorders. I think he may be able to see you sometime this evening. In the meantime, there will be a nurse on hand at all times: let her know if you need anything, or if you experience any fresh symptoms."

At the door, he paused.

"Signor Canavan, I think I should tell you that there is a Carabinieri inspector downstairs. His name is Maglione, from the station at San Zaccaria. He has been waiting for permission to interview you." He glanced at the floor. "Do you have any idea why he wants to see you?"

"No, I . . . There must be some mistake. I've done nothing."

"Please don't play games with me, *signore.* We found a gun in the pocket of your jacket. It has been placed in the hospital safe until we decide what to do with it. Now, I can ask this gentleman from the Carabinieri to leave; but if he insists on seeing you, I may not be able to stop him. As your doctor, I would prefer you not to be placed under any unnecessary stress at the moment. Frankly, I'm worried in case it triggers another attack. But I cannot refuse a reasonable request from the police. So, you tell me: what shall I do?"

Patrick thought quickly.

"Let him come up," he said. "I've got nothing to hide. But I'd like a little longer to speak with my friend, Mr. Makonnen. It's a private matter, and it is important to me. I promise you it has nothing to do with a criminal offense of any nature."

Luciani took awhile to make up his mind.

"Very well," he said at last. "I'll tell Maglione he can see you in ten minutes. Will that be enough?"

"Yes, I think so. Thank you."

As he left, Luciani spoke briefly to Makonnen, who was still waiting outside.

"Assefa, please close the door," said Patrick as he entered.

"What is it, Patrick? Are you all right?"

"Yes, of course. I'm fine. Listen, Assefa—we don't have much time.

There's a policeman waiting for me downstairs. God knows what's going on, but I don't intend to hang around here to find out. You've got to help me find a back way out of this place."

"But the doctor said . . ."

"I don't give a damn what he said. I can't stay here. Nor can you. Passover starts in a couple of days. We don't have any time to lose."

THIRTY-ONE

They walked to Cannaregio through the clamorous dim light of midafternoon. Like refugees nearing an ill-marked border, they looked about them constantly, at every moment fearful of arrest. Every face, every gesture seemed to threaten betrayal or discovery.

Gradually, they left the more populated streets behind and began to relax. Patrick told Assefa what had happened after leaving him the night before. He described the chase after someone he had thought was Francesca, his collapse from exhaustion, and his dream. When he finished, Assefa walked beside him for a while in silence. They crossed the Rio di Noale onto the long stretch of the Fondamenta della Misericordia. A boat carrying refuse passed, headed for the Canale della Sacche. The driver waved at them and smiled. A faint smell of rotting garbage hung in the air for a moment.

"You say you passed a square in which men were chasing a pig," said Assefa at last.

"Yes. Blind men. With knives."

"With knives, yes. And this scene—did it mean anything to you?"

"Mean anything?" Patrick could sense his friend's unease. He watched the heavy boat piled high with rubbish chug out of sight. "Why should it mean something? It was the sort of thing you see in dreams. Nonsense, really." But he knew that could not be true. Nothing else in his dreams had been nonsense, they had all made perfect sense: and he could remember the details with all the exactness with which an invalid remembers pain.

Assefa shook his head.

"No, Patrick. Not nonsense. In the eighteenth century—are you listening, Patrick? This is important—in the eighteenth century, on each of the two Sundays of the carnival every year, the city would arrange for blind men to gather in a square in order to slaughter a pig. It was a sort of spectacle, something for the *nobili* to laugh at, to feel superior about. Are you telling me you've never heard of it?"

Patrick shook his head.

"And yet you dreamed of it. You knew nothing about it, yet you dreamed it was happening."

By the time they reached the Ghetto area, it was almost dark. Centuries ago, the Jews of Venice had been confined to this section of the city, the first of a multitude of ghettos throughout the world. Now, only a couple of synagogues survived on the edge of squalor. As they passed the Scuola Canton, Patrick wondered what Migliau would do with the Jews if he came to power. Would he return them to their ghettos, force them to wear the letter O on their chests or yellow hats once more, make them pay over and over for the supposed crime of killing his God? For a moment, he dismissed such thoughts as ridiculous: not even a pope could bring the Middle Ages back again. And at once he remembered the small plaque that faces the main synagogue in the Calle del Ghetto Vecchio, commemorating the deaths of two hundred Venetian Jews at the hands of the Nazis.

There, just ahead of them, was the tenement in which Surian and his father lived. In a city where a new building is almost a contradiction in terms, the block seemed not merely old but ailing, as though infected by some insidious and wasting disease.

Drawing closer, they noticed a small knot of people milling about around the front entrance. At first he took them for a group of casual loiterers, but it was soon apparent that they had a purpose in gathering there. A handful of schoolchildren, satchels still in their hands, skittered about, excited yet curiously silent. The rest of the crowd was made up mainly of women and old men. Patrick and Assefa were about to push through the crowd when they noticed a policeman at the center. He was trying to take a statement from one old woman, but everyone else insisted on talking as well.

"*Che cosa è successo? È morto qualcuno?*"

"*Poveretto, si è ammazzato.*"

"*Chi era? Tu lo conoscevi?*"

Patrick's first thought was that someone had taken note of their visit here yesterday. But that would scarcely explain the crowd or the excited jabbering. At that moment, a small boy tried to squeeze between Patrick's legs, in order to get to the front. Patrick reached down and grabbed him by the neck. The child squealed and tried to wriggle free. A woman looked round at them and laughed. Patrick smiled at her reassuringly.

"Hang on," Patrick said to the boy. He could not have been more than five or six. "Where do you think you're going?"

"*Stronzo, lasciami andare!* Lemme go! Get yer friggin' hands off of me!" shouted the little brute.

"Not until you tell me where you're going."

"Inna house, where d'you think?"

"What for?"

"See the man."

"The man? What man?"

"The dead man, stupid. Jumped out the winder inter the courtyard. Lemme in."

A chill passed through Patrick. Without another word, he let the boy go. His hand was numb and useless.

"It may not be him, Patrick." Assefa had moved to Patrick's side. But his voice carried no conviction.

They squeezed their way through the crowd. No one challenged their right to pass. The main door stood open, leading into the courtyard.

Only a weak light managed to struggle past the high walls. The windows round the courtyard were lit up, as though in celebration of some festival. Indistinct faces stared out into the gathering dark, some curious, indifferent, but each drawn by the same fascination with violent and unexpected death.

The child's courage had failed him a couple of yards inside the entrance. He was standing nervously, unable to take another step, yet rooted hard to the spot by morbid curiosity and a last pale ghost of bravado. On the other side of the courtyard, a huddled form lay unmoving on the ground. Patrick and Assefa went across. Someone had covered the body with an old bed-spread. Blood had spilled out from underneath, forming a dark, sludgy pool on the concrete. Patrick bent down and raised the edge of the coarse fabric.

An imperfect, wounded light sloped across the lifeless face beneath the cloth. Patrick's first thought was that someone had played a joke on them. The face staring up at him was not human at all, but a dummy's face, white and hard, with painted eyes and varnished cheeks. It was the face of Arlecchino, cracked down the center and smeared at the base with common blood. Patrick's fingers fumbled at the mask, pulling it back to reveal Claudio Surian's face. The back of the skull had caved in: fragments of white bone jutted out awkwardly, as though desperately trying to break free of their harness of blood and flesh.

It was dark by the time they got to the Lista di Spagna. Assefa still felt numb. Neither he nor Patrick thought for a moment that Claudio had jumped to his death. They were pilgrims come to a dark temple: godless, blind, sick at heart. All about them, veils were being torn and lamps extinguished. The city had become an altar for mad gods, a slab for the perfection of sacrifice. They could sense the blood in the air, smell it in their breath, like rotting garbage, feel it warm and intimate against their flesh.

The shops on the Lista were brightly lit, though less busy at this time of year than at the height of the tourist season, when they took the brunt of the daily excursions arriving at the railway station nearby. *L'Unità*'s offices were in a *calle* near the station. They turned out to be little more than a cluster of rooms above a travel agency, cramped, stuffy, and crammed full of files, typewriters, telephones, and telex and fax machines. There seemed to be no room for human beings, yet half a dozen reporters had managed to squeeze themselves miraculously behind an array of barricades: desks, filing cabinets—anything that might serve to keep colleagues and the world at large at bay for half a minute.

Assefa forced his way past a large, bearded man who was trying to strangle the handset of a telephone while shouting obscenities at it at the top of his voice:

"Porca puttana, andate tutti a cagare, mi avete rotto i coglioni!"

Behind the bearded man, seated at a desk piled high with reference books and about forty discarded plastic cups, a young woman was furiously mangling the ends of her fingers against the unresponsive keys of an antediluvian typewriter.

"Permesso?" Assefa said, but his voice was drowned by the booming of the man at the telephone. He called again, more loudly this time, but there was still no response. The woman remained impregnable behind her desk. Exasperated, Assefa found a copy of Devoto's dictionary, opened it at the middle, and slammed it shut with a bang like a gunshot.

Heads everywhere looked up from work, startled. Only the bearded man seemed oblivious of the report.

"That wasn't very amusing," said the woman at the desk. "What the hell do you want?"

"I'm looking for Siniscalchi, Aldo Siniscalchi. Do you know where I can find him?"

Her mouth opened and closed. She was not a pretty woman, and the action lent her something of the appearance of a fish. She glanced at Patrick, who was standing a few paces behind the priest, then back at Assefa.

"Who are you?" she asked. Abruptly, she had passed from simply brusque to defensive.

"I'm a friend of his. An acquaintance, anyway. Claudio Surian introduced us—we met last night at Bartolini's. Aldo had arranged to see me again tonight, but . . . ."

"I'm sorry," she said. Her voice sounded stiff and unnatural. "I can't help you. Ald . . . Signor Siniscalchi was shot two hours ago outside the *trattoria* where he'd just eaten lunch. He . . ." For a second, she seemed on the verge of tears, then she took control of her emotions again. This was a newspaper office, Siniscalchi's murder was tomorrow's front-page lead.

"Some fucking fascist from Ordine Nuovo gunned him down," she exclaimed. "They've been threatening him for months. He's been doing a series on them. Fascist bastards."

"You're sure?" asked Patrick. His heart was beating in long, uneasy strokes. He felt sick and tired.

"Sure?"

"That it was Ordine Nuovo. You're sure they were responsible?"

"No, of course I'm not sure! They didn't sign their names. But who the fuck else would do it?" Then his accent seemed to register with her. "Hey, who are you anyway? American? CIA?"

"He was following up this Migliau business. Isn't that right?"

She raised her eyebrows, little pale eyebrows that scarcely gave definition to her eyes.

"What has that to do with it?"

"Everything. Forget Ordine Nuovo. Dig up anything you can on Migliau. Find him and you'll find your friend's killers." He hesitated. "And Claudio Surian's as well."

He turned with Assefa and made for the door. Just as he reached for the handle, the woman shouted after him.

"Hey! American! What's your name anyway?"

Patrick turned.

"Canavan. Patrick Canavan. If you find Migliau, tell him I was here. Tell him I haven't finished yet. Tell him I've just started." It was like the child in the tenement, a soft, faint hint of bravado, a muted whistle in the dark.

The woman looked hard at him, puzzled, a little disturbed.

"What's your friend's name?"

Assefa turned and answered her.

"Just a moment," she said. Getting to her feet, she picked her way with practiced ease across a series of obstacles to another desk. After rummaging for half a minute, she surfaced triumphantly, brandishing a fat padded bag.

"He left this for you," she shouted above a din of clattering typewriters and ringing telephones. "Said he wouldn't be here tonight when you called, that he had some big lead to follow up." Her face fell. Again tears threatened to displace her false toughness. "You don't think . . . ? *Cristo!* Anyway, he said I was to give this to you. I think it's a book."

THIRTY-TWO

The book had turned out to be a rare copy of Corradini's *Famiglie Antiche e Nobili di Venezia* or *Ancient and Noble Families of Venice*. It was a respectable, heavy volume bound in dull burgundy leather and edged with gilt—the variorum edition printed in 1873 by Olbi, the Venetian printers. First published in 1791, the *Famiglie Antiche*'s author was Marco Corradini, a man of aristocratic birth and political aspiration who, like so many Venetian noblemen of his day, found himself in penurious circumstances. Unlike most of his fellows, however, Corradini was possessed of brains, a personable manner, and a classical education.

He had compiled his history of Venetian families while serving as personal tutor to the house of Foscari. Through his patrons, he had gained access to a wide range of state and private archives, enlivening his sources with a racy, fluent style. His manner was anecdotal, descending on occasion to the downright chatty, yet he showed a respect for the facts and an eye for the superfluous that rendered his work invaluable.

Patrick and Assefa knew little of all this, save what they had been able to glean from a florid preface by a certain Professor Enrico Battistella of the Accademia Nazionale dei Lincei. They had taken a taxi at the Piazzale Roma and crossed the causeway to the mainland, where their driver had deposited them at a shabby *pensione* near the docks in Porto Marghera.

Coming here, it was as though the magic of Venice had been abolished by a single stroke of a rival magician's wand. The dark industrial streets of Mestre and the gaunt, high-stepping cranes of its port were the apparatus of a different sorcery, and their weary inhabitants the succubi of another, flatter dream. A smell of refined oil wafted through blind and congested streets: there were no spices here, or precious oils, or unguents. Necessity, not vice or luxury, paved the streets of Mestre.

The *pensione* had not asked for proof of identity, nor had it required them to sign its register, if it had one: a small extra payment had taken care of that. Surian had mentioned the place the evening before, when Assefa told him the whereabouts of their first hotel. He had said the *pensione* was sometimes used by members of Prima Linea and other underground groups of the far left. But as far as Patrick and Assefa could see, the clientele was made up chiefly of prostitutes serving the port, their clients—mainly merchant sailors—and a handful of migrant workers from Sicily.

Siniscalchi had placed two slips of paper in the book, the first in the chapter devoted to the several branches of the Contarini family, the second in the much shorter section that dealt with the house of Migliau. In the margin, he had marked in pencil several passages that must have seemed to him worthy of note.

The first of these was a quotation from a document found by Corradini in the Benedictine monastery of San Giorgio Maggiore. The text described it as a chronicle that had been kept on the blank pages of a vellum manuscript of Macrobius's commentary on the "Somnium Scipionis." The chronicle had been kept by a certain Brother Ubertino of Florence between 1223, when an earthquake had destroyed part of the monastery, and 1268, when he recorded that year's disastrous harvest and the famine that succeeded it. Corradini assumed that Brother Ubertino had, like so many others, met his death in the course of the famine. The passage marked by Siniscalchi was dated 1264, on the newly instituted Feast of Corpus Christi.

Assefa read the passage slowly for Patrick's benefit, explaining to him any particularly difficult words or phrases. The chronicle had been written in the Florentine dialect of the period, that was later to dominate Italian as a whole, and Brother Ubertino's language had been tidied up and somewhat modernized by both Corradini and Battistella.

"This last week the flagellanti *have been seen in our streets once more. And this despite the decree issued last month by the Doge and the Consiglio, that none in holy orders, whether lay or religious, should in any wise consort with such as term themselves 'fraternities of discipline,' nor yet sit upon the councils that govern them. There are among them Fraticelli and other Spirituals, followers of the heretic abbot Joachim. And, by our Lady, I think that few of them reck aught of holy discipline or the authority of God vested in our Mother Church. They were first seen here in the year of the plague, a five years past now, having come in a body from Perugia, and it is said they number many thousands and are afraid of no one.*

"You may behold them now on feast days and high holidays, parading in the streets or the piazza before the basilica, and ofttimes before other of the city churches, wearing, as is their custom, black veils of wondrous length, even to the ground, and beating their backs with leathern whips, all the time accompa-

nying their efforts by howling and crying after the manner of wild beasts, or demons come up out of hell."

Assefa paused and asked Patrick if he was following the text.

"I think I get the general drift. Do you know exactly who these *flagellanti* were?"

Assefa nodded.

"Flagellants. The movement started in northern Italy about 1259—that would be the 'year of the plague' the writer refers to. It wasn't long before it spread across the Alps into Germany and elsewhere. Thousands of people joined in religious processions, beating themselves with whips, weeping, seeking salvation. It happened again in the following century on an even larger scale, mainly in Germany.

"The flagellants were influenced by a Cistercian abbot called Joachim of Fiore. Joachim taught that a new age of the Holy Spirit was coming in 1260. A lot of spiritual Franciscans joined them—the Fraticelli mentioned here."

"These people were heretics?"

Assefa shrugged.

"Not necessarily, whatever Brother Ubertino may have thought. Of course, they weren't popular. A lot of people in the Church and in high places generally got a bit nervous about all this talk of the Spirit. It threatened to set up an authority independent of the hierarchy. A bit like liberation theology today, I suppose. Anyway, steps were taken. The movement died out fairly quickly. The Church clamped down a lot harder when it broke out again in the next century."

"So, what has this to do with anything?"

Assefa shrugged.

"Nothing that I can see. Let's go a bit further."

He started reading again.

"Yesterday, I was visited shortly after Lauds by Umberto Trevisan, the young scholar who often comes here to use our great library. He told me that there are already many factions among the flagellanti *and that, for the most part, they are but poor men, cripples, beggars, the feeble-minded, and women, as is indeed common in these manifestations of heresy. But there are among them also certain gentlemen of good family and rich merchants besides that have bad consciences or little sense, and that fear the Devil more than they love God.*

"And he told me privily that he had heard that certain among the Contarinis, the Participazios, the Dandolos, and the Zianis have in secret pledged allegiance to a grim fraternity, wherein are none of the poor or ignoble to be found. This is a most private matter for them, and has nothing in it of public

flagellation or display, such as marks the Spirituals and their imitators, and I think not that they be Spirituals at all. That they meet in private and hold secret cabals is the sum of Master Trevisan's knowledge, for of their rites and heretical dispositions he knows, or pretends to know, nothing. It is my private conviction that they be tainted with the Cathar heresy or are in league with the Knights Templar."

Assefa looked up.

"The next few lines are mainly padding by Corradini about how interesting all this is. But Siniscalchi has put a mark a couple of lines after that, where the author quotes Brother Ubertino again. It's an extract from his entry for the Wednesday following Corpus Christi, about a week after the bit we've just read.

"I received tidings yesterday through Father Domenico, who came to hear my confession, that my friend Umberto Trevisan was yesterday in secret condemned by the three Avvogadori, whereupon he was rowed out to the Canale Orfano, and there his hands were tied behind his back and weights of lead attached to each of his several limbs, to make the faster work of his drowning, as was then carried out. May our Lord have mercy on his soul and give him peace. I thought it prudent not to confess to Father Domenico the matters lately divulged me by my friend, though this lie heavy on my soul. This last night I have spent in prayer for his deliverance out of purgatory, yet I do not rest easy, and shall not again, I think.

THIRTY-THREE

Neither Patrick nor Assefa said a word, yet their thoughts were as transparent to one another as though they had been spoken.

The second passage was an account in Corradini's own words.

"I reckon it neither nice nor proper, howsoever my lord Pisani deem it, to speak in these pages of the peccadilloes of the Nobility or the dissolution of the Rich, lest the common rabble, emboldened by talk of lasciviousness in their Betters, and encouraged falsely by the wanton behavior of some of them that rule them, foment discord in this most serene of Republics. And yet, such is the manner of this Age, wherein Nobility is become Baseness and Baseness Nobility, that of certain families I know not what else I may in truth relate.

"Witness the numbers resorting to Spaderra's and Ancilloto's, the less to drink Coffee, I think, than to murmur against the State; or the rakes that gather nightly in the Casino degli Spiriti and old Cornaro's place, to play at Bassetto *or at* Spigolo *for a heap of gold sequins or a lady's favors; or the Ladies with their* Cicisbei, *betaking themselves in masks and pomaded wigs to see the latest plays at the Fenice or the Malibran."*

"Can't you skip a bit, get to the bit that interests us?"

"I suppose so. Let's see. . . ." His finger ran lightly down the page, he frowned, bit his lip, and at last found something.

"Your Honours, if any among you care to listen, let me unfold to you Secrets that will make your Blood run cold, for herein lies the heart of this matter, that a Family of Jewes are become Lords in Venice, and some of our most ancient Lines fast arrived at the deepest of deep depravities.

"You know well that there are Masons in this City, devoted to secret Worships and abominable Doctrines. And many, I know, deem the Contarinis and Migliaus, the Rezzonicos and Dandolos of that Fraternity. There may be some, I have no doubt, that so incline. But most, I think, hold to a different Allegiance."

Assefa paused.

"This begins to sound familiar," he said.

"Yes," Patrick whispered. "Don't stop."

"I have heard tell—I will not say from whence—that certain of them assemble in one another's Houses, late at night, when the eyes of Men are fast asleep or fixed on Cards in the Ridotto. They travel in hooded Gondolas with muted oars, and are seen by no one, not even their own Servantes, for it is said they row alone to their destinations. What Infamies they practice or what corrupted rites they perform, neither reason may know nor piety guess at.

"But I venture they fancy themselves Hermeticists, or Adepts of the Cabala, followers of Paracelsus, or Illuminati of the Rosy Cross; or, indeed, that they be Deists all, and have imported their foul Mysteries from France, where all such Abominations have their Source. I have heard it asserted that there are among them hieratick ranks, such as Priests, Deacons, and Bishops, and that certain among them dedicate themselves as Monks or Nuns in perpetuity. And these, I understand, their Fellowes call The Dead, inasmuch as they are departed this World before ever their bodies are bereft of Life. I am told they take such as are dedicated to this existence to their Graves, albeit in a representation, and that there are living among us even now persons whose Tombs we pass by daily in our common Churches."

Patrick turned pale. He glanced at Assefa in horror. It was as though a fist of ice had taken his stomach and was tightening its inexorable grip.

"I have even heard it whispered—I will not say by whom—that they emulate the Jewes in this that, on occasion, they will steal a Christian Childe or purchase a Babe from Romanies, to take from it the Heart, that they may make of it a sacrifice. Though I pray this latter report be but idle gossip."

Assefa paused. He noticed how pale Patrick had become.

"Are you all right Patrick?"

Patrick closed his eyes, trying to blot out the image that had formed in his mind, of a naked child, his heart ripped out, lying on a table in an Irish holiday cottage, while black crows hopped sightlessly through the sullen room. When he opened his eyes again, he saw Assefa watching him, concerned.

"It's all right," he said. "There's something I haven't mentioned. I'll tell you later. Please, go on."

Assefa began to read again.

"It is said—though I cannot vouch for it—that on occasion the Illuminati among them repair to an Island in the Lagoon, where a ruined Church is made a sort of Oratory for their Mass. But where this Island lies, or which among so

many Churches now abandoned may be their Temple, I am unable to relate, having but heard this by prima facie *report. Yet one that claimed to have certain knowledge of these matters, albeit he would divulge little enough of them, admonished me to look at the Word of God for sure counsel, and furnished me with Verses that he said would reveal all to the discerning eye. Yet these seven years have I made nothing of them, though I own that the first of them is taken from the prophet Ezekiel:* 'Qui oculos habent ad videndum et non vident: which have eyes to see, and see not.' *Yet, for the delectation of your Lordships and maybe the Profit of any that have sharper eyes than mine, I set them down here as a Curiosity:*

"Abscondita est ab oculis omnium viventium (Job 28:21); 'Ad inferna descendunt (Job 21:13); 'atque abysso subjacente (Deut. 33:13); sumentes igitur lapidem, posuerunt subter eum (Ex. 17:12); En lapis iste erit vobis in testimonium (Josh. 24:27); Quis revolvet nobis lapidem ab ostio monumenti? (Marc. 16:3); super lapidem unum septem oculi sunt (Zech. 3:9)."

Assefa sighed and looked up.

"That's it," he said.

"Are you sure? There's nothing more?" Patrick felt as though all his strength had drained away.

The priest shook his head.

"Nothing," he answered. "It's the end of the section. There's just a footnote that says the last page or two were omitted from the first edition and reinstated by Battistella from Corradini's original manuscript. That's all."

He closed the book and set it to one side. Outside, a factory hooter tore rasplike through the oily slumber of early evening. Assefa and Patrick were sleepers, awakened suddenly to the harshness of day, yet not quite able to dispel the morbid fancies they had just been witnesses to in sleep.

THIRTY-FOUR

They went out that night to find somewhere to eat other than the *pensione.*
A cab took them into the center of Mestre, and they spent the best part of
an hour wandering the rain-dulled streets in search of somewhere that did
not sell hamburgers or french fries. All around them, gray apartment
blocks glowered behind a constant, niggling drizzle. Patrick had never felt
more miserable in his life.

They settled on a place at last, a cramped *trattoria* caught helplessly
between a budget furniture store and a video games arcade. As they ate,
the constant sound of bleeps and roars and staccato firing rushed through
the thin partition wall. The cheese on Patrick's pizza was rubbery. Most of
Assefa's *antipasti* came out of a tin.

Near the end of the twentieth century, assaulted on every side by its
sights and sounds and rancid smells, they huddled over a check tablecloth
trying to solve a mystery at least seven centuries old. Patrick was certain
now that Francesca was alive, that he had seen her the night before, and
that she was out there even now, watching from the shadows. He had
thought once that the shadow in which she dwelled was death, but now he
knew that to have been a lie. The dead do not return. Whatever came back
from those other, crueler shadows, it would not be Francesca.

They ate slowly and talked of this and that, like lovers who have grown
intimate yet jaded. Tragedy had brought them close, and a sense of mutual
danger made elaborate what might have been a simple friendship. And yet,
in reality, neither man understood much of the other or the world to which
he belonged. Patrick's scholarship was, in small measure, a link; but his
Catholicism, with its frequent lapses and furious rejections, was less a bond
than a barrier set between them.

"Those Latin verses," Patrick asked. "Did they make any sense to
you?"

Assefa shook his head wearily.

"Not really," he said. He did not want to talk about them, not even think of them. "I suppose," he went on, "they contain some sort of eighteenth-century play on words."

Patrick nodded. He thought the same.

"Can you translate them?"

"Yes, of course. The first two are from the Book of Job: *'It is hid from the eyes of all living'* and *'they shall go down to the grave.'* The next is Deuteronomy: *'and the deep that crouches beneath.'* Then there was one from Exodus: *'and they took a stone and put it under him.'* Then Joshua: *'Behold, this stone shall be a witness unto you.'* The next from Mark is the only one from the New Testament: *'Who shall roll us away the stone from the door of the sepulchre?'* And the last is from Zechariah: *'Upon one stone are set seven eyes.'*

Patrick slipped a wrinkled olive into his mouth and chewed on it morosely.

"You're right. None of it makes any sense."

Assefa took a sip of wine.

"I thought this sort of thing would have been just up your street."

Patrick shook his head.

"I worked in the field. I gathered intelligence, others made sense of it. I know almost nothing about cryptanalysis."

"Maybe it's some sort of acrostic, using the first letters of the verses. Let's see, that would give us AAASEQS. I don't think that's much use."

"What about the first letters of the words in a single verse?"

"Well, the first one from Job would read AEAOOV. That's no help. The second reads AID. At least it means something in English. Then we've got AAS—that corresponds to three of the letters in the first group we came up with. The one from Exodus gives us SILPSE, which means nothing. Then ELIEVIT, which looks like Latin but isn't. Maybe the first part refers to the prophet Elias. The one from Mark reads QRNLAOM, and Zechariah gives SLUSOS. Frankly, it's all gibberish."

From next door came a round of frantic bleeping that sounded as if someone's spaceship had gone out of control.

Patrick sighed.

"I think you're right. But we'll give it a more careful look when we get back to the *pensione*. At least we know it wasn't done with the help of a computer, so in theory we don't need one to help us unravel it."

"There is one thing, Patrick."

"Yes?"

"Have you noticed that, if we take the first letters of the verses, we come up with seven. And the last verse refers to 'seven eyes.' "

Patrick shook his head.

"Not if you include the very first one from Ezekiel." He put down his fork and took a sip of Pinot Nero. "You're just starting to clutch at straws."

"If you say so. But with Claudio and Siniscalchi dead, where do we go from here, Patrick? You say the police are looking for us. What about giving ourselves up? Maybe someone will listen to our story, start an investigation. This sort of thing would have sounded outrageous not all that many years ago; but since the P2 scandal, people in Italy are ready to believe almost anything."

"Almost anything, Assefa—but not this. Not on our say-so, not without hard evidence. And the fact that the police are interested in us shows that someone in the force is already working for these people."

"So, what do you suggest?"

What was there to suggest? Why even bother to suggest anything? Events would take their course, whether they did anything or not. The result would be the same—death: for them, for anyone who got too close to this thing.

"I don't know," he murmured. "I don't know."

He ordered another bottle of wine. Tonight he wanted to drink as much as possible, to wipe out the bleak images that tormented him. The wine was cheap and acidic, but potent. Assefa watched detachedly as he got drunk. He himself wanted to remain sober. He feared the loss of self, however temporary, the vertigo of spirit that drunkenness entailed. Abandoning his priestly identity had not come easily to him, and in everything that happened now he found a further disjunction between reality and a growing sense of madness. He drank bottled water and listened to the machines next door acting out their own, computerized fantasies.

Afterward, they could not find a taxi anywhere. The drizzle continued, soft and chilling, pale against the street lamps. Patrick walked unsteadily, helped along by Assefa. They followed signs to Porto Marghera, but in reality were lost. This was the real Venice now, the future stamped in glass and reinforced concrete, blunt, sterile, unlovely, devoid of either spiritual or earthly grace. Beyond the streetlights, the drab waters of the Adriatic stood waiting for their final incursion.

"Assefa," mumbled Patrick as they turned into yet another stretch of featureless apartment buildings, "what was the common element in those verses?"

"Forget the verses, Patrick. They don't mean anything."

Patrick staggered and caught Assefa's arm.

"You're wrong. They must mean something. What's the common element in most of them?"

"I don't know, Patrick. You tell me."

"The stone, for God's sake. '. . . they took a stone and put it under him'; 'this stone shall be a witness unto you'; 'Who shall roll us away the stone from the door of the sepulchre?'; 'Upon one stone are set seven eyes.' Don't you see, there must be some connection."

"You're drunk, Patrick. It doesn't mean a thing. Or if it does, it's too late to find out now. Corradini had the verses for seven years and made nothing of them. Let's try to get back to the main road. It's not too late to get a taxi."

"What's the Italian for stone?"

"Pietra."

"And what else?"

Assefa shrugged.

"Roccia?"

"No, not *roccia*. The name 'Pietro.' Peter. And Peter in the Bible is the 'rock' or the 'stone.' "

"I don't see how that helps us, Patrick."

Patrick stopped and took Assefa hard by the shoulder.

"It does. Don't you see, it helps us all the way."

He said nothing more. They found a main road and waited in silence for a taxi to appear. One came past fifteen minutes later and took them back to the *pensione*. The fare was at least double the going rate.

Upstairs, Patrick headed straight for the copy of Corradini, which Assefa had left on the room's rickety table. He handed it to Assefa.

"Here," he said, "look up the chapter on the Contarinis. See if there's anything there about Pietro Contarini. He died somewhere around 870."

"Patrick, I . . ."

"Just look it up, for God's sake!"

Five minutes later, Assefa had found the reference.

" 'Pietro Contarini. This noble-spirited Man was the true Founder of his family's fortune, and the Fountainhead of their prosperity. Born of noble Parents, he was trained up from youth to take his rightful place among the nobili of his Generation. It is related that, at the age of fourteen, he . . ."

"Get to where he dies," Patrick interrupted impatiently.

Assefa read on silently, scanning the lines.

"Here," he said. "It says a bit about his final illness. Shall I read that?"

"No, it's his funeral I want."

"All right, I think that's here.

'He died at last on the thirteenth day of September in the year 869, and was accepted to the bosom of a bountiful and loving Savior, requiescat in pace. And on the day following, his mortal Shell was taken by boat, with hundreds

accompanying, to the monastery Church of San Giacomo, that in those days
flourished on the island of San Vitale in Palude, which lies in the Palude
Maggiore, and is today in ruins. When, in the twelfth Century, the Church
was rebuilt, Pietro's Tomb was much enlarged by his descendants, at the same
time being gilded and faced with marble. I have seen it myself, and deem it a
thing of much beauty, though marvelous decayed.' "

That night, Patrick dreamed the last of his dreams, a long and harrowing
vision that seemed to have neither beginning nor end. He was alone again,
in a square-shaped room draped from end to end in heavy black curtains.
All round the room tall candles burned on silver sticks held on heavy
tripods. That he was in the house to which the gondola had brought him he
was certain. There was a smell of damp in the air, as though the room was
low down, near the level of the canal. And another smell, subtler, uniden-
tifiable, yet somehow disturbing.

He closed his eyes tightly, blotting out the room, telling himself it was
all a hallucination brought on by something called focal epilepsy. He only
had to ignore it and it would go away. He would wake up and it would have
left him. And if it returned, he would have a CT scan and they would give
him drugs to make it go for good. But though he sat and thought of other
things and told himself he was asleep in a flea-bitten *pensione* in Mestre,
the smell of the canal and the thinner odor it concealed persisted in his
nostrils. He opened his eyes at last to see black curtains and candles that
had scarcely burned down.

Suddenly, he heard footsteps approaching. A door opened, a section of
curtain was pulled aside, and a man in eighteenth-century dress entered
the room. He was followed by a second and a third, then others, until the
room was full. Each one, as he entered, bowed slightly toward Patrick,
then moved to stand along the wall. At the end, four women, all veiled in
black lace, came into the room, and joined the men.

Someone began to speak in a low voice, then others joined in, until the
entire assembly spoke in unison. With mounting horror, Patrick realized
that he too was speaking, his voice mingling with the others', rising and
falling in a gentle chant. At first he did not recognize the language, then,
without surprise, realized it was Aramaic.

" 'l tsbqnn' 'lh' bhswk'
'l tlsbqnn' bhswk' bry' wbsryqwth
'l t'lnn' mr'n' b'tr' dy l' bh nwhr'
'l thsyk ynyn'. "

"Do not leave us, O God, in darkness. Do not abandon us to the outer
darkness and its emptiness. Do not bring us, O Lord, to the place without
light, do not close our eyes with its blackness."

The chanting continued for about five minutes in similar vein, a long address to the Deity beseeching salvation from the terrors of the grave. And then the mood began to change. Patrick realized with dismay that he had begun to lead the incantation, speaking short verses to which the others responded. He was fully aware of what was happening, yet powerless to stop himself, as though someone else were speaking in his voice.

Suddenly, the door opened and a man entered, leading a boy of ten or eleven by the hand. The boy was dressed in a red shift. His hair was long and tied back with a red ribbon, and he seemed bewildered. A second man stepped forward from the congregation and took the boy's other hand. Together, they turned him to face Patrick. The boy was trembling. Patrick stared into his eyes. He looked as though he had been drugged or hypnotized.

The men removed the boy's robe and set it to one side, leaving him naked and shivering. Patrick tried to protest, but all power of movement or speech had been taken from him. It was as though he was present, but in another's body, without power over it.

One of the men produced a rope, pulled the boy's arms roughly behind his back, and tied him firmly by the wrists. The second man took a long silver knife from a leather satchel and handed it to Patrick. Patrick watched as his hands received the knife. For the first time he looked down. In front of him was a high marble slab, a sort of altar.

The men raised the boy to the altar. In the room, the chanting started again. The men stepped back into the congregation, leaving Patrick at the altar with the boy.

"We offer you this sacrifice," he intoned.

"Accept what we offer in Christ's name," the congregation responded.

"Take the life that you have given this life, and give us life eternal in return."

"Grant us eternal life with Jesus, the Everlasting Sacrifice."

He watched in horror as his hands raised the knife. Beneath him, the terrified child struggled against his bonds. Why did the boy not cry out? Why did the knife feel so light, so insubstantial in his hands?

Something happened to the boy. He began to scream, loudly, in the tones of an animal at the slaughterhouse that has seen its companions dragged to the knife's edge. Patrick tried to close his eyes, but they would not shut. He tried to drop the knife, but it was as though it had been glued to his hand. He felt his hand move, felt the knife touch the boy's naked flesh, felt a shiver of erotic pleasure pass through his loins, felt the appalling silence crush him as the screams cut short and blood flooded across his fingers.

. . . .

He woke out of blackness into light and looked round for Assefa. But it was still the same room, hung with black curtains, lit with candles that had almost guttered to nothing. He felt sick and dizzy. His hands were sticky. Standing, he caught sight of the altar in front of him, empty now and clean of blood. He could close and open his eyes again, control his every movement as though once more in possession of his own body.

Swaying slightly, as though still drunk, he took several steps toward the door. Was this hallucination never going to end? He pulled back the curtain, revealing the low wooden door through which the others had come. The handle was iron, cold to his touch. He turned it, sweating.

A narrow hallway led to another door. He walked down it softly, as though frightened that he might waken someone. The floor was a mosaic, with spirals of golden angels. On the face of one angel, he saw a drop of glistening blood, still wet.

He opened the door and stepped inside. It was brightly lit by electric bulbs. On the wall facing him, a spotlight gave brilliance to a painting by Moreau. A television set in one corner was tuned to a game show. The volume had been turned off, but from somewhere there came the sound of low music. He recognized it at once as Albinoni's oboe concerto number 2 in D minor, a favorite from his years in Dublin, when Francesca had introduced him to the splendors of Venetian baroque: Vivaldi, Tartini, Marcello, and Galuppi. This had been one of their best-loved pieces, played over and over in a recording by I Solisti Veneti. He looked round, as though expecting to see her come through the door.

Turning back, he caught sight of the television again. The game show had been replaced or interrupted by what looked like a news bulletin of some sort. People milled about in confusion. A SWAT team was tidying up in the background, while police tried to hold back a large and angry crowd. Red and blue lights flashed. Without sound, accompanied only by the ethereal tones of the music, the scene had the appearance of a nightmare snatched out of the unconscious and projected on the tiny screen.

Suddenly, the camera shifted. On the ground, rows of bodies were being lined up by rescue workers. The camera moved in, greedy for spectacle. Patrick saw bloodstained faces, children's faces, shattered bodies, severed limbs. The camera moved along the rows, its hunger growing. The music swelled. He saw small teeth pressed against bloodless lips, eyes fixed in death, hair matted with blood and plaster. He closed his eyes, and still bloody images marched across his vision, the screaming child, the knife, the flesh tearing, his hands plunging into the severed chest, the steaming heart. He opened his eyes and saw the television faces again, saw the room rock, heard the music grow and fade, grow and fade, the walls bulge and close in. As he fell, he heard the voice of the oboe change to a last, despairing scream against the darkness.

THIRTY-FIVE

Between Burano and the mainland lie the mud flats and shattered islets of the northern lagoon. It is a region of the desolate heart, wreathed for much of the year in mists and shadows, dull, remote, full of reeds and marine sadnesses. Its narrow channels are marked by tall *bricole*, long wooden stakes that pattern out the shallows from the navigable deeps. They stand high in the tired sunlight like stumps of an ancient forest from whose branches the birds have long since fled.

They had taken the water bus from the Fondamenta Nuove to Burano. The boat had traveled slowly, as though bereft of purpose, cold and unsteady and almost empty. Four other passengers kept them company: two as far as Murano, the remainder to Mazzorbo. They had gone the rest of the way alone, save for the pilot and his assistant, reaching Burano by midmorning.

Once there, it had proved surprisingly difficult to find a boatman who would either admit to knowing the whereabouts of San Vitale in Palude or show himself willing to take them to its shores. It was as though a curse had fallen on the place. Patrick detected a mute uneasiness in all with whom he spoke. Once, bending to tie a shoelace, he had noticed an old fisherman to whom they had previously spoken watching with an intent and troubled expression. After a little while, the shaking of heads and the sullen silences combined to produce in them a state of despair akin to hopelessness.

They found their man just after lunch in a small bar not far from the little harbor.

"They tell me you're looking for someone to take you to San Vitale."

He was old and rather down-at-heel, with a hard leather face that might have been stretched and molded over a frame in Claudio Surian's workshop. White bristles peppered a weak chin that had once been badly injured and reassembled by a clumsy surgeon. Unfocused eyes suggested longer hours at the bar than at the rudder. He smiled toothlessly and without the least trace of warmth.

Patrick nodded.

"How much?" the old boatman asked.

"I'll give you one hundred thousand. There and back."

"*Vaffanculo!* What you think I am, mister? A fucking gondolier? Listen
—you want a nice little trip up some nice little canals, you want some cunt
to sing some pansy arias, get the fuck back to Venice. Two hundred."

Patrick shrugged. He was in no mood to argue. They had lost enough
time already.

They left Burano in silence, creeping away like thieves whose movements are being watched. Having negotiated his price, the old man had
clammed up. He evinced no curiosity about his passengers or their journey,
expressed neither surprise nor disapproval. The last thing Patrick saw as
their *sandolo* moved away from the harbor was a little knot of fishermen on
the quayside, watching them turn into the channel that led to Torcello.

The only sound was the creaking of the oar turning in the rowlock.
Patrick was reminded of his dreams. This, he thought with a stab of fear,
was the dream's continuation, its working out in the waking world. But
now that he felt himself so close, he feared a denouement, dreaded whatever revelation the next hours would bring. In the swirling water, he fancied he saw figures move across a television screen.

He had said nothing to Assefa about his dream of the night before.
Waking at dawn, he had been covered in sweat and shivering, but he had
not cried out. Images from the dream clung to his mind like flies to an old
web; he could feel the feet of spiders moving close, but however hard he
tried, he could not shake the images free. Above all, the sound of the
child's screams echoed across the empty landscape through which they
passed. He dipped his hand into the water, as if to wash it clean of blood.

A low mist lay on the water like a mask. They were a small black
shadow, a beetle or crab, crawling slowly across the flat white surface,
pushing the mist aside only to see it form again behind their stern. It was
cold out on the lagoon. Patrick and Assefa shivered, regretting they had
not come better dressed. The old boatman seemed impervious to the damp
chill of the place, as though his leathery carapace had been genetically
created for the rigors of life on such desolate waters.

Once, Patrick thought he saw another boat move out from the shelter of
an islet to their west, but when he drew it to Assefa's attention, it had
already gone. Here, beyond Torcello, the channels grew more treacherous
and the *bricole* fewer and less certain. In places, fishermen had set thin
willow wands and rods of bramble to mark off their fish traps.

They ran aground twice on hidden mud flats, and all three men were
forced out, knee-deep in mud, to push the sturdy little craft back into

deeper waters. Here and there, a dismal islet showed the remains of an abandoned wall or gateway, tokens of vanished glories: old monasteries long ago dissolved, forts useless now against a tide of tourists and international business executives, the wattle huts of fishermen, empty for the winter. Once, they passed a tall wooden tripod on whose top a shrine to the Madonna stood custodian over a particularly fretful channel. Faded flowers clung to her feet, and by her hand an extinguished candle marked the devotion of some passing boatman.

The old man raised one hand and nodded past the shrine.

"La palude maggiore. The great marsh. Not far now. Half an hour." They were the first words he had spoken since their departure.

Patrick felt uneasy to be so much at the old man's mercy. Out here, in the lost reaches of the lagoon, where no sound carried and not even a seabird's wing broke the expanse of mud and water, they could be left stranded without difficulty.

They drifted to a halt. The boatman shipped his oar and turned to face the side.

"Why are we stopping?" Patrick asked. Was the old man going to demand more money, now he had them in the middle of nowhere?

But he merely unbuttoned his trousers and proceeded to urinate over the side of the boat. Finished, he rowed on, but his brief action had further impressed on Patrick the man's intimacy with this place: This is my lagoon, these are my waters, I piss in them as I would at home, they don't mind.

Just over half an hour later, the hazy outlines of a low island appeared above the mist. As they drew nearer, it acquired shape and texture. Dark cypresses ringed the fractured lineaments of a squat, twelfth-century church. Closer still, the building developed depth and detail: the style was Ravenna Byzantine, the materials chiefly brick and marble, both much distressed by inclement weather and long neglect. Beside the church, a free-standing campanile had lost its upper story; it jutted up from the cypresses like an admonitory finger placed there to warn the curious away from the island's deserted shores.

The old man beached the *sandolo* in a small cove just west of the church. Whatever landing stage had once served the island had long ago collapsed or been covered by the tangled bushes that in most places crept unhampered to the water's edge. They disembarked in two feet of water and helped the boatman pull the *sandolo* higher up, above the tidemark. The beach was stony and green with water weeds.

"How long you going to be?" The old man spat and took a moldy pipe from his inside pocket.

"Not long," Patrick replied. "We just want to look at the church. Let's say a couple of hours at the most."

The boatman shrugged and started filling his pipe with foul-smelling tobacco.

"Suit yourselves. But I can't stay here all day. I want to get back to Burano well before dark. A man can get lost in these waters. There aren't no lights out this far." He found a small knoll farther inland and sat on it, lighting his pipe and puffing out smoke like a chimney with indigestion.

"If you aren't back in two hours, I'm leaving. And if I leave, you're stranded. Nobody comes here, understand? Nobody. If I've got to come back for you tomorrow, it'll cost you double. No skin off my nose." He spat a gob of brown saliva on the ground and stuck his pipe back in his mouth.

There was no direct route to the church, but after a bit they came across what might once have been a path.

"Why should anyone build a church on its own out here?" asked Assefa. "It seems sort of pointless."

Patrick nodded. "It does now, yes. But the lagoon has a long history. There used to be some important settlements in these parts, before Venice became the centerpiece of the region. Places like Torcello or Mazzorbo, where we called this morning. They were great places once, with cathedrals and monasteries and palaces of their own. I think this church must have served as a monastery church at first, then as a basilica for the surrounding islanders. Then, as Venice took over, people would have migrated there. No other explanation makes much sense."

Assefa looked round at the rough, windswept landscape, the broken campanile whose bell had once tolled daily across bleak and treacherous waters.

"Unless someone wanted a church where no one else would want to come."

Patrick did not answer him. He was thinking of the screams of the boy in his dream. How loud they had sounded, how easily they could be lost in all this wilderness. They carried on in silence.

THIRTY-SIX

Close up, the church was more dilapidated than it had appeared from the sea. Parts of the roof had collapsed, many of the windows were broken, the main doors were unhinged and gaping. Pieces of masonry had fallen from the walls and lay scattered among long grass and reeds. Occasional flooding had left its mark on the lower courses of stone, and in the damp cracks between the brickwork, thick green moss had taken hold. And yet, in view of its age and the length of time it had been abandoned, the building was in remarkably good shape. It was as though, from time to time, someone had come to tidy it up a bit and hold back the elements a little longer.

The main door led directly into a dark, malodorous narthex, a hovel of crumbling plaster and spiders' webs. An archway opened straight out of it into the main body of the church. Beyond the arch, wintry sunlight filtered through a thousand holes, creating a secret paradise in stone, as though another substance had come in place of it. Each brick, each marble fragment, each chipped and fractured piece of limestone shook with its own hue, its own antiphon of light. The ceiling, broken and torn, hung like a canopy of alchemical glass above the empty nave.

Like children coming at last upon a place that adults have long reserved to their own uses, Patrick and Assefa stepped over the dim threshold. The silence unfolded about them like a mass, plain chant rising among rose marble pillars, a solemn litany, stone and light made song. To their right, a great window of perforated alabaster sent shaft upon shaft of nacreous light into the hushed and hollow spaces below. Bushes grew among fallen ornaments, grass wreathed the heads of saints, a heron had made its nest in a baptismal font.

But their eyes were riveted in front. The walls and roof of the apse had suffered least of all, and though the altar had been uprooted and the host removed and the light extinguished forever, it was as if some miracle were still being worked there. Above the stone benches of the priests, above the single window of smoked glass, above the marble cladding, a figure of the Virgin holding her child rose triumphant to the domed ceiling. Fragments of the mosaic had fallen away, yet nothing had marred her beauty. She seemed to float against a sky of gold. She was slender and sad and full of light, and on the blue field of her robe, tiny red flowers lay like drops of a child's blood.

From his jacket, Assefa took a thin white candle. He lit it with a match and set it on a stone in front of the apse. For a time he stood gazing at the Madonna, then he genuflected and recited a quiet prayer. When he had finished, he turned and spoke to Patrick.

"Whatever we have to do, Patrick, let's do it now."

There were several tombs, all in a state of disrepair, around the sides of the church. It did not take long to find Pietro Contarini's: it lay to the left of the spot where the main altar had once stood, an elaborate Gothic sepulcher built in marble and terra-cotta. The paint and gilding had long vanished, limbs had been broken from the figures of saints that stood in its niches, and the casing had cracked in places; but the tomb had remained intact. At the top, beneath a canopy held erect by angels, an effigy of Pietro Contarini lay in slumber. By his head, a marble jar held the stems of withered flowers. They could not have been there more than a year at the outside.

Patrick had no very definite idea of what he was looking for. But he was certain that the tomb held the answers to his questions. He began to go carefully over the reliefs carved in the facade of the monument, and soon a pattern began to emerge. With a shudder, he recognized the first of a series of panels as a representation of Abraham preparing to sacrifice his son Isaac. The boy was strapped and gagged and lay on his back across a large rock, while his father stood over him, knife in hand.

The next panel was more obscure, and Patrick was not at first sure what it represented. A man was sacrificing a goat beside a tall stone pillar, watched by silent onlookers. And then he remembered the story of Jacob, and how he slaughtered a beast at Jegar-sahadutha, where he had set up a pillar of stone and built a cairn of rocks. Someone was making the most of the play on words.

A third panel showed the children of Israel slaughtering lambs and smearing their blood on the stone lintels of their houses: the institution of the feast of Passover. Patrick felt his heart beat rapidly. Things were beginning to fit into place.

Other reliefs followed, most of them portraying scenes of sacrifice from the Old Testament. Above the first row stood a separate register of panels depicting incidents from the life of Christ, culminating in a relief of the Resurrection. Christ the supreme sacrifice, Christ the symbol of eternal life. For some reason, the thought made Patrick uneasy.

But clear as the iconography was, it seemed to offer no further help.

Patrick had hoped for more than a lesson in how the Old Testament prefigured the New. He felt suddenly downcast, as though someone had broken a solemn promise to him.

"Damn it!" he exclaimed. "It makes no sense. Why all the mystery? Why the cryptic verses? Half of them don't even fit these scenes, and the ones that do are scarcely earth-shaking. There has to be something more."

"Not necessarily, Patrick. The religious mind sees significance even in the mundane. Perhaps the man who gave the verses to Corradini just wanted him to understand some esoteric interpretation of our Lord's sacrifice. After all, that seems to be the message of the tomb. It's nothing very new or exciting, but it has its own profundity."

Patrick shook his head.

"No, it isn't that. Not just that. The sacrifice motif refers to something else. I know."

They started to go over the carvings again, as though they concealed a message that they might read if only they had the eyes to see it. Panel by panel, figure by figure, they examined the scenes, trying to relate them somehow to the verses in Corradini's book. Half an hour later, they gave up.

They had brought a little lunch in a box. Assefa opened it and spread the food out on a flat stone. They ate in silence, dejected, beaten, shivering in the damp air. Each man knew that, when they had finished their meal of salami and cheese, they would return to the boat and ask the old man to row them home. They drank by turns from a large bottle of Recoaro water. The food was tasteless to Patrick; he ate slowly, without appetite. When he had taken his last mouthful, he raised the bottle to his lips. As he did so, he noticed the words on the label: *Sorgente Recoaro*—Recoaro Spring. And in that moment he knew.

It had been staring at him all along, like a clue in a cryptic crossword that eludes the conscious mind and caves in all at once to the unconscious. He got to his feet and walked back to the tomb. Assefa watched him, puzzled.

He had not been mistaken. Following the scene of the Passover, there had been one of Moses striking the rock in the desert, causing springs to gush out for the children of Israel. Except that, where there should have been twelve springs—one for each of the twelve tribes, each tribe in turn a prefiguration of one of the twelve apostles—there were only seven. Perhaps the artist had been careless, perhaps he had preferred the number symbolism of the lower figure. But Patrick knew it was not that.

Pietro Contarini had brought something back from Egypt. He had returned there in later years, as had his son Andrea. The scene in the panel showed Moses in the desert, after the Exodus from Egypt. When Pietro

Contarini had been in Alexandria, no one there spoke Egyptian any longer, they all spoke Arabic. And the play on words, Patrick now knew, had not been in Italian or Latin or Greek: it had been in Arabic.

The Arabic word 'ayn has two chief meanings: "eye" and "spring." It means other things besides, of course, but those are its basic meanings. Upon a single rock were set, not seven eyes, but seven springs.

Patrick put his hand on the rock, near the figure of Moses. He felt it give slightly and pushed harder. The panel slid aside. Inside, there was a handle, a great iron ring set in the stone. Inside the ring, carved into the stone, was a circle. And inside the circle were three crosses.

He pulled the ring toward him. As he did so, the facade of the tomb shifted half an inch. He pulled again, harder this time. The stone moved, as though swinging on a pivot. Bracing himself, he pulled for a third time. The side of Pietro Contarini's tomb swung away from the wall, exposing a dark, gaping aperture.

THIRTY-SEVEN

" 'Who shall roll us away the stone from the door of the sepulchre?' " whispered Assefa. He stood beside Patrick, gazing into the hole that had opened in the wall. They could just make out the dim shape of a staircase leading down.

" 'They shall go down to the grave . . . and the deep that crouches beneath,' " said Patrick. The meaning of the verses quoted by Corradini had suddenly become crystal clear.

They had brought flashlights, not knowing how much light there might be in the church to work by or how long they would need to stay. Patrick found his and switched it on.

The walls of the staircase were cased in plaster and covered in an elaborate fresco. A row of figures in antique Roman dress walked in a solemn procession bearing small crosses over their shoulders. Some led small children by the hand, others followed with musical instruments: citharas, tabrets, timbrels, harps, dulcimers, and cymbals. Yet no one danced. Whatever music they were playing was sad and slow.

Patrick set foot on the first step. He had expected the staircase to be mildewed and thick with cobwebs, but to his surprise it was clean and dry, as though swept only yesterday. Though they showed signs of age, the frescoes on the walls beside him were in an excellent state of preservation.

The steps were of marble and little worn. Patrick counted twenty in all. They ended at a rounded archway, much in the Byzantine style of those in the church above, leading into a vast underground chamber with a low, slightly domed ceiling. The beam from Patrick's flashlight swept over a painted universe, confined, huddled deep beneath the earth, independent of the world above.

Assefa joined him, and together they let the light from their torches trace the lineaments of the secret world to which they had descended. Above them, dark constellations turned to fire, and burning stars fell endlessly through a golden sky. Among them, angels in purple robes, their wings ablaze, tumbled in confusion. But at the center, Christ sat in majesty upon a throne of glass. Around him, death and confusion ceased, and a great stillness crept out into the vortex.

Upon the walls, the chaste procession wove its way across the world: past tall towers, across the tops of hills, through forests, over rivers, along the shores of silent, waveless seas. They came from everywhere to join it— men and women in antique robes, kings, journeymen, musicians, priests, nuns, lepers . . . and children everywhere, alone or led by the hand. In the air, birds with strange feathers flew above their heads; on the earth, curious animals watched them pass; and in the oceans, fish with monstrous eyes turned their heads and stared at them.

Whether intended or not, the artist had created a world of deep unease, in which the only comfort lay in the procession and the bearded face of Christ made God, serene in his contemplation of madness.

They followed the procession on each side, up and down the wall, now this way, now that, until they came together to the far end of the chamber, which had been in darkness until now. A great city stood domed and golden on a hill of grass. Above it, the sun shone out of a blue sky. Birds with beaks of jasper sang on tall, columned trees, and angels flew upward, echoing their song. Patrick did not have to ask what city it was the pilgrims had come to. He had seen numerous Byzantine representations of Jerusalem.

But none quite like this. In a complex series of paintings along the front wall of the city, the fresco he had seen in the Palazzo Contarini was repeated and expanded. In the center, three crosses stood, black and naked, on a deserted hill. On either side, the artist had depicted scenes from the life of Christ: the raising of Lazarus, the expulsion of the demons known as Legion, the cleansing of the Temple. But below the crosses, as before, was a painting of an open tomb. Seven men carried Christ, bound and screaming, into the sepulcher.

Below that, the tomb appeared shut, a great stone rolled against its mouth. And near the entrance to the tomb, another stone had been set up, a sacrificial altar. This was the end of the long pilgrimage through an insane world: one by one, the pilgrims were bringing their children to be sacrificed on the stone; one by one, the children were being tied and laid on the stone. And on their left, a figure in a mask was turning a grinding wheel, sharpening long, thin knives.

In the exact center of the room, beneath the face of the risen Christ, stood a stone altar exactly like the one in the painting, draped with a white cloth stained with blood.

It took a long time for Patrick to explain about the murdered child discovered in Ireland, the fresco in the Palazzo Contarini, and the dream he had

had the night before. Assefa listened in silence, with mounting horror. Corradini's hints did, in the end, have substance behind them. At some point in the past, the Contarinis and certain other families had practiced child sacrifice in Venice. Today, they or their successors still kept the cult alive. The question was why. And what was Passover?

It was beginning to grow dark when they left the church. They found the faint path that led back to their landing place and hurried to get there before the boatman decided he had had enough. Behind them, the church huddled in the twilight, protecting its secrets.

The old man was nowhere to be seen. Patrick called, but his voice was swallowed up in the silence. No one answered. He looked at his watch: their two hours were not quite up.

"The bastard's gone!"

Assefa nodded.

"So I see. What do we do now?"

"Wait until he comes back, I suppose. He'll be here in the morning, looking for his double payment."

Assefa wandered down to the water's edge and looked out at the lagoon, at the dim light fading across miles of empty water. He turned to come back, then stopped and looked at something to his right.

"Patrick, come here!"

Patrick heard the urgency in Assefa's voice and hurried to the little beach.

"Look."

The old man's *sandolo* was there, still beached at the spot to which they had dragged it. They went closer.

Someone had taken a heavy stone and smashed the boat's light hull in several places.

THIRTY-EIGHT

There was no earth, no sky; no heaven, no hell. Only darkness, only the sound of waves, and once, far in the distance, the horn of a great ship passing in the night.

It was curious, thought Patrick, how easy it had been to beat them in the end. There had been no need for guns. Without a boat or the means to repair the one in the cove, they were trapped. Trapped and certain of a slow death. They might find water here, but it was highly unlikely that the island would furnish them with the sort of food needed for survival.

The Italian mainland was only a few miles away, but it might as well have been fifty. Boats sailed through the deep channels farther out, and once or twice a day an airplane would pass by overhead; but no one could hear them or see them. Swimming was out of the question: the waters of the lagoon were treacherous to a high degree, the safe channels of this sector known only to a handful of fishermen. An inexperienced swimmer would find himself quickly lost and dragged down by mud and weeds.

The fire burned down slowly into the loose fabric of the night, but neither man had the energy or the will to get up and find more wood. They were physically and emotionally drained, yet sleep refused to come. Patrick feared the onset of further dreams, here above all, in a ruin that was not a ruin, at the heart of his nightmare. He closed his eyes and saw dark shapes creep across the corners of his vision. Another bout of epilepsy? Or phantoms singular to this island, the bloodless ghosts of children without hearts?

Assefa crouched beside him shivering, watching the last flames flicker against the night, wrestling with his own private ghosts. Every priest is haunted by them at some time: thoughts of what might have been, certainties that have crumbled and become doubts, prayers left unanswered, the faces of starving children dying without God. Tonight, they crowded around him like pimps, eager to show him what lay for sale, not in the church or its painted crypt, but deeper still, in his own heart, bloodier and more desolate than any act of martyrdom or sacrifice.

The fire crumbled to ashes, the darkness deepened around them, and still they sat, each wrapped in his own thoughts, waiting for the slow night to pass. Around midnight, Assefa struggled to his feet. His limbs were numb with cold.

"Patrick," he whispered. "Are you awake?"

"Yes. What's wrong?"

"I think we'll die if we stay out here. If not tonight, tomorrow. We should take shelter in the crypt: light a fire, try to get a little warmth. Perhaps someone will come." For some reason, Assefa was impelled to go down to the crypt. He felt the urge like a bodily temptation, but less tangible, less easy to resist. It was common sense, after all. Their survival might depend on it. There is no temptation so undeniable as common sense.

"No," answered Patrick. "I'd prefer to stay up here. You go, if you like."

Assefa hesitated.

"I'll get some wood, at least. There must be brushwood outside the church."

He took one of the flashlights and set off into the darkness. Patrick remained, fighting an almost irresistible drowsiness that could, he knew, prove fatal. Perhaps, as Assefa suggested, morning would bring some sort of hope. There would be light, they could explore the island. And perhaps, after all, someone would come. Plenty of people on Burano knew where they had gone. If their boatman did not return, surely someone would come looking for him. Patrick was sure the old man had been disposed of by whoever had staved in the *sandolo*. He remembered the boat he had seen momentarily the day before. Had they been followed all the way? Or was this simply standard practice when anyone inquired about San Vitale?

The whole thing was beginning to make a sort of crazy sense to him, though he still could not tie together its disparate strands. First and foremost was the notion of sacrifice. That was not too unusual: for many Christians, Christ's death on the cross represented a sublimated, improved form of the Temple sacrifice of Judaism. He was the supreme offering, whose death made redundant all sacrifices of the past: "Neither by the blood of goats and calves, but by His own blood."

Moloch was nothing. How many innocents had died at the hands of Herod in order to save the infant Jesus? How many, like Abraham, had offered up their firstborn to a jealous God? How many had died in Egypt during the first Passover in order that Yahweh's chosen people could leave for a land of milk and honey? And how often had God commanded Joshua, when taking possession of that land, to leave none alive, whether man, woman, or child?

Was that the meaning of "Passover"? A re-enactment of Egypt's sacrifice so that another chosen race could have their freedom? Patrick shivered
at the thought. It was a matter of days now.

He saw a light approaching from the far end of the nave. His first
thought was that Assefa was returning, then he noticed that the light was
different from that of the flashlight his friend had been carrying: it was
larger and rather brighter. He picked up his own flashlight and switched it
on, but its battery had been much depleted. It gave out only a dim, yellow
light that made no impact on the darkness. The approaching light wavered,
then changed direction slightly and headed straight for him.

He switched off the flashlight and got to his feet.

"Who's there?" he called. There was no answer. He took several steps
back to the wall of the apse, and began to circle along it, trying to return to
the main body of the church. The light moved nearer. He could just make
out the indistinct shape of a figure holding it. The figure stumbled and the
light swung wildly for several seconds, before righting itself.

"Who are you? What do you want?" Could it already be someone from
Burano, risking the supposed horrors of San Vitale for the sake of a
drunken friend and two foolhardy strangers?

"Patrick? *Sei tu, Patrick?*"

The voice was soft, familiar yet unfamiliar, little more than a whisper,
yet louder than a cry of pain. His heart seemed to stop, he felt himself
grow dizzy. Stretching out his hand, he steadied himself against the wall. It
felt rough and damp beneath his fingers.

"Where are you, Patrick? I can't see you."

It was a dream, a nightmare rather, the last step down into madness. All
his senses were intact, there was nothing to cocoon him from his surroundings, but he knew he was dreaming. What else could it be?

She raised the lamp higher and he saw her face at last, the ghost's face
he had expected, dark eyes in a pale mask. He remembered a game he had
played with others as a child, a flashlight propped beneath his chin, turning him into a thing of intense shadows and deathlike pallor. But this was
no game, this was truly someone who had been in the grave and returned.

"I'm not a ghost, Patrick. You know that by now. You've been expecting
me. Two nights ago, when you followed me, you knew then. Don't be afraid
—I haven't come to harm you."

He hesitated only another moment, then stepped into the light.

"What have you done with Assefa?" he asked.

"He's all right, I left him down at the cove." She paused, her eyes fixed
on his face. "You've changed, Patrick," she said at last. "More than I
imagined."

"What do you want me to say, Francesca? Fancy meeting you here, hasn't it been a long time, my, my—you haven't changed? I must have been mistaken, I thought you were dead, what a silly mistake? I suppose you meant to keep in touch, but just didn't get round to it. What the fuck, this is just another dream anyway, isn't it? Another hallucination." He was shouting now, near to tears, frightened.

"No, Patrick, I'm not a dream. You know that. Don't ask me to explain, not yet. Perhaps not at all. I'm not here to talk about myself. I've come to take you off San Vitale."

He saw her face more clearly now. What he had said was not true: she had changed. Not aged so much as altered, subtly, less superficially than someone who has merely grown to middle age. Her eyes were not the eyes he had last looked into over twenty years ago.

"Where are you taking me?" He took it for granted that she was in charge. Death confers privileges.

"To the mainland. We've got to get there tonight. Migliau's people will have someone watching. Please, Patrick—I know this is hard for you. It's hard for me too. But you've got to come with me. If you stay here you will die."

Numb, he followed her out of the church, walking several paces behind, her light always ahead of him, bobbing through the darkness. She seemed to know the way. In five minutes, they were back at the cove. Just before they reached the shore, Francesca switched off her lamp.

"The path goes straight down to the beach here," she whispered. "Take my hand, I'll help you down."

Reluctantly, he reached out for her. With a shudder, he took her hand in his. It felt like ice, and for a horrid moment he thought the nightmare was real, that she was indeed dead. But it was only the night air, the cold night air that had frozen his hand as well. She led him down to the beach, just as she had taken him, many years before, to another beach, naked and shivering as the tide turned.

Assefa was waiting for them in the darkness. And beside him a third man stood leaning against a small boat.

ROME

THIRTY-NINE

Rome, March 2

The Madonna was very old and very worn. Her face was a filigree of cracks, the blue paint of her robe was flaking in places, and the gold leaf of her halo had all but disappeared. Whether it was age that had most taken its toll, or adoration, it was impossible to say. But her eyes seemed tired and unfocused, as though the prayers and laments of numberless generations had at last proved too much for her. The spirit, like the flesh, has its limits, and compassion, whatever the theologians say, is not inexhaustible.

Assefa stepped forward and added his candle to those already burning in front of the icon. He stood for almost a minute gazing at her ravished face. She was black like him, and tired like him, and in her crumbling features he found more comfort than in all the city's statues and paintings put together. He sighed and dropped to his knees, turning a plastic rosary between exhausted fingers.

In a shadow close behind him, Patrick stood in silence, his hands clasped before him, keeping careful watch. Santa Maria delle Grazie was a little-frequented church off the beaten track in the Vicolo de' Renzi, just south of the river in Trastevere. No tourists came here, not even the clever sort who toss aside their Baedekers and lose themselves deliberately among alleyways smelling of cats and rotting citrus peel. Even pilgrims were few and far between, a mere handful of cognoscenti drawn by the Black Virgin.

According to legend, the icon had originally been brought to southern France from the Holy Land during the time of the Crusades, by a Templar knight, Guillaume de Pereille. Some said that it was, like so many other Black Virgins, the work of St. Luke. After the Albigensian Crusade of the thirteenth century, it had been carried from Languedoc to Turin, and from Turin to Rome, where it had been housed in its own chapel in Santa Maria delle Grazie and named La Madonna Mora. The more prosaic said it was probably the work of the Roman artist Pietro Cavallini, who was known to have painted a very similar Madonna di Constantinopoli for the Benedictine Abbey in Montevergine around 1290.

Assefa had found the little church early in his seminary days. It had, in a sense, become his private chapel, his place of retreat. At first the Virgin herself had been the attraction: he had sought in her blackness a sort of mirror for himself, a spiritual location for all that was African in him and in danger of being engulfed by the legacy of Greece and Rome. He had prayed to her, and she had answered him in her tired and wounded fashion. But with time the church itself had won his heart: the small side chapels, in which a single light burned before the altar; the shadowed recesses, with their tiny figures of saints on marble pedestals; the odors of beeswax and frankincense, of polish and dry rot, of musty linen and crumbling stone.

In the past, he had directed his feet to this asylum at least once a week. To flee the uninterrupted roar of traffic, the blaring of radios, the incessant chatter of the streets. To escape the cramped and closeted worlds of the seminary and the Accademia Pontificia. And more recently, to still the frenzied babble of his own thoughts.

Now he had been driven here by fear. By fear and loathing and a world of doubts. He felt frozen by doubt, unable to think or act, yet aware that, if he did not act soon, he would fail to avert a terrible tragedy.

Patrick waited patiently in the shadows. He himself felt no need for prayer. It was not a question of belief or disbelief; he had a simple horror of the numinous dark, of the loss of self that all these pleasant odors and muted colors signified. To Patrick, God would reveal Himself in daylight or not at all.

Assefa rose at last. His face was marked with tears, but he seemed less ill at ease.

"I'm sorry," he said. "I've already taken more time than I should."

"That's all right."

"What about you, Patrick? Don't you want to offer a single prayer?"

Patrick shook his head.

"I think it would only confuse me," he said.

"What about your friend?" He meant Francesca. She was waiting outside, keeping watch on the street.

"You know what she thinks, Assefa. That all this is just a travesty, that the truth lies somewhere else."

Assefa sighed.

"Won't you at least light a candle for her? The Madonna may be old, but she isn't deaf or blind."

Patrick drew out a five-thousand-lire note from his pocket and dropped it in the slot at the candle stall. He took a long candle and lit it from Assefa's. As he placed it in the holder, he glanced up at the icon. The fluttering light stroked the ancient gold like a moth's wing brushing flame. The Virgin gazed at him. Had she really been in Languedoc? he wondered.

Had she witnessed the first fires of the Inquisition, the blood of innocent children spilled at Béziers and Perpignan? For the expiation of sins, for the glory of the true Church.

He turned his back on her. Not deaf? he thought. Not blind? Just callous, then.

The photograph Assefa had found in Dublin had in small measure prepared Patrick for seeing Francesca again, but not for touching her or talking with her. More than anything, he found it difficult to accept the changes in her. He now realized that, from that moment in San Michele when he had first taken seriously the possibility of her still being alive, he had thought of her as frozen—a girl of twenty preserved in a magic, timeless realm out of which she would re-emerge to him exactly as he remembered her, young, energetic, and in love.

For him, of course, she had indeed been in limbo: a silent, frosted figure, wrapped away in his memory. The Francesca who had returned to him out of the darkness of San Vitale, however, was anything but a fragment of someone else's past. There were streaks of gray in her hair, and her face was thin and pale and tired. In her eyes he could detect a faraway sadness, as though something deep within her had indeed died all those years ago.

Since her appearance on San Vitale, they had hardly spoken. She had taken them to the mainland in absolute silence, steering by means of small, bobbing lights she had placed along the channels. The man with her had been introduced to them as Roberto Quadri, a lawyer. After beaching the boat, they walked to Caposile, where Francesca and Quadri had left a vehicle, a windowless transit van with bedding on the floor. While Patrick and Assefa tried to rest in the back, she and the lawyer drove through the night to Rome, traveling on the *autostrada* via Bologna and Florence.

Quadri had accompanied them as far as an apartment on the Via Grotta Pinta, a narrow, curving street in the old city, not far from the Campo de' Fiori. The apartment was situated on the top floor of a tall, ocher-colored building in a row of small shops and *trattorie*. It was large, sparsely furnished, and drafty, and it was clearly not anyone's permanent residence. More like a safe house, Patrick thought.

"Who does this place belong to?" he had asked.

"Later," she had replied. "I'll tell you all about it later. But now I want to sleep."

Quadri kissed her lightly on the cheek and shook hands with Patrick and Assefa.

"I will see you all later," he said. "I have to sleep as well. But before that, I have other work to do. *Ciao*, Francesca. I'll call on Dermot, tell him all went well."

Francesca slept until after ten; and in the end both Patrick and Assefa had relaxed sufficiently to give in to sleep as well. Over a breakfast of rolls and coffee, Assefa had asked if he could visit Santa Maria delle Grazie, which he knew was just a short distance away, on the other bank of the Tiber.

Now, they walked back slowly over the Ponte Sisto. The river flowed sluggishly beneath their feet, yellow and muddy, almost out of strength. Assefa walked several paces ahead, preoccupied. Now that he was alone with Francesca, Patrick felt awkward and tongue-tied.

"I feel this is still all a dream," he said. "This doesn't make sense. You were dead: I saw them bury you."

Francesca shook her head. Her hair was tied back in a pony tail, just as he remembered it.

"I was never dead, Patrick. Not . . . in the sense that you mean. In other ways, perhaps. In all the ways that matter." She paused. For a moment, just as they stepped down from the bridge, he caught sight of her profile. At that moment, he knew for the first time that she was truly alive. Other things might alter, but her profile was exactly the same.

"I lost over twenty years, Patrick. I'm sorry, for you more than anything or anyone. Nothing I can do can ever make that up to you. But I had no choice; or I thought I had none. Believe me, I really thought that then."

"And now . . . ?"

"If I thought I could undo a single moment . . . But I can't, so I don't even try. I just try to make amends, that's all."

"I don't understand any of this."

"No," she said. "I know that. But in a few minutes we can get down to explanations. I've asked Roberto and another friend to meet us at the apartment. They'll help me make things clear."

They walked through to the Campo de' Fiori, where several market stalls were still open for business. Francesca seemed to know the stallkeepers well, and bought a quantity of vegetables, cheese, and fish. Next to the fish stall stood an arch leading into a narrow alleyway.

Francesca led them along it, explaining that it was a shortcut through to the Via Grotta Pinta. Halfway along, the alley became a covered passageway, dark and smelling of urine. They passed heavy iron gates on either side, and Patrick noticed that, behind them, the ground was littered with used hypodermics. Francesca glanced behind her.

"You have to take care round here," she said. "Never come this way alone at night. There are muggings, sometimes worse." She walked on, her feet echoing between the passage's narrow walls. "The old *campo*," she went on, "used to be the place where executions were carried out. They burned Giordano Bruno there in 1600. Because he said the earth wasn't the center of the universe, that nothing was finite." She paused and looked back again at Patrick, at the rusting hypodermics. "Do you think it hurts," she asked, "to be burned alive? Slowly, without strangulation? Would ideas help? Like a drug?"

"Ideas?"

"Beliefs, convictions, some sort of certainty." She looked into his face. He thought he saw traces of tears at the corners of her eyes. "Do you think it would ease the pain, believing the universe to be infinite? Do saints or scientists feel less than criminals when it comes to the stake?"

"I can't answer that," he said. "No one can." Assefa stood near them silently.

Francesca said nothing. She looked along the dark passage to a patch of sunlight that indicated the position of the square.

"No," she said at last. "No one has ever been able to give me an answer."

She turned and walked quickly away down the passage.

FORTY

When they got back to the apartment building, two men were waiting for them at the street door. Francesca smiled and greeted them warmly, kissing each briefly on the cheek. The taller of the two was a heavy man of about fifty, dressed in a short leather jacket and lightly checked trousers. His companion was Quadri, whom they now saw clearly for the first time. He was elegantly dressed, in his early thirties, and very thin.

"Patrick, Assefa," said Francesca, calling them closer, "let me introduce Father Dermot O'Malley. Father O'Malley is an Irishman by training but an Italian by profession. He's lived here almost as long as I have. And he speaks better Italian."

The older man stepped forward and shook hands. He was robust, built more like a soldier than a priest. At one time, he had sported red hair, but the life had gone out of it years ago, leaving a thick gray mop that had broad streaks the color of an old russet apple. Patrick fancied his sermons would lean toward the declamatory. He noticed that he did not wear a dog collar.

"You've already met Roberto," Francesca continued, turning to the younger man. "When he isn't rescuing strangers from mysterious islands, Roberto works with Father O'Malley. That's why he looks so tired, isn't it, Roberto?"

Patrick detected the concern underlying the mockery in her voice, and for a crazy instant felt something like a pang of jealousy. But he felt only grief for Francesca now, not love; what right had grief to jealousy?

Quadri shook hands a little formally and stepped back. Patrick thought he looked ill. The handshake had been that of a sick man.

"Patrick," said Francesca, "I hope you don't mind, but Father O'Malley wants you to go with him while I take Assefa and Roberto up to the apartment. We'll all meet here for lunch in about two hours."

Patrick felt a prick of disappointment. He was gradually growing accustomed to the thought that Francesca was not dead after all, and he had been anticipating an opportunity to ask some direct questions about what had happened to her. The questions, he supposed, would have to wait.

"Yes, that's fine," he lied. He wished someone would explain just who these people were and what their connection was with Francesca.

O'Malley had parked his car, a Fiat, farther down the street. As the priest lurched off into a maelstrom of honking traffic, Patrick braced himself for a rough ride and asked where they were going.

"A mystery tour, Mr. Canavan, a mystery tour. Not very magical, perhaps, but I think you'll find it interesting." He spoke in what Patrick recognized as a broad Cork accent, an accent that thirty-odd years in Rome had done nothing to diminish.

"Why just me? What about Assefa?"

"Now, Mr. Canavan, you must have noticed that your friend is not inconspicuous. There are people everywhere looking for the both of you. I don't think they know yet that you're in Rome, and I'd as soon keep it that way. I'm sure you would too. To be honest, I'm taking risks enough with yourself, but Father Makonnen is another matter entirely. He has far too many friends in this city for him to be wandering the streets. As it is, he should never have been out this morning."

The car swung across the Corso Vittorio Emanuele, joining the traffic on the other side like a bee taking its place in a fast-moving swarm. As they headed up toward the Tiber, Patrick took a deep breath. He had guessed where they were headed.

O'Malley glanced sideways at him.

"Relax, Mr. Canavan. Or may I call you Patrick? You'll be perfectly all right with me. We won't stray within a million miles of Cardinal Fazzini's office. Or a number of other offices I could mention but won't."

As they drew closer to the Piazza Paoli, the traffic began to thicken and snarl up. Finally they came to a complete standstill among a pack of honking cars and motorcycles, yards from the bridge. O'Malley slipped into neutral and pulled on his handbrake.

"We'll be here for a little while," he said. "It's a bad time of day. But then, in Rome it's always a bad time of day. Suppose we fill in the time by your telling me how you came to be mixed up in all of this."

Bit by bit, Patrick went through the events that had brought him here, while all around him the traffic roared and drivers took out a lifetime's frustrations on everybody in sight. The priest listened to him in silence, his manner growing increasingly serious as Patrick's story unfolded. He asked no questions, showed no surprise, expressed no sentiments of either outrage or sympathy. By the time Patrick had finished, the brawling, angry world around them seemed to have been switched off, leaving them quiet in the sunshine, ringed by darker shadows and menaced by a different anger.

"How well did you know Eamonn De Faoite?" the priest asked finally.

"Very well. I met him first when I was a student, in my freshman year. He helped me a lot. You speak as if you knew him yourself."

O'Malley nodded.

"Oh yes," he said, gazing out through the small windscreen at rays of sunlight falling on metal and glass, "Eamonn and I were old friends, very old friends. We met when I was a seminarian at Maynooth. He used to hear my confessions." He gave a short laugh. "Jesus, I was never done confessing my sins in those days. I think I had the idea that, since I was going to be a priest, I had to be better than everybody else, get absolution for the most trivial act. Well, Eamonn got me out of that habit soon enough. Mind you, if I thought I had things to confess then . . ."

There was a roar outside as the traffic began to loosen up. O'Malley let in the clutch and moved off, honking loudly.

"We kept in touch after that, a bit like yourself and him. In fact, I think he mentioned your name to me once or twice. From time to time he'd come to Rome for a visit, and we'd have a week or two together then. He never could stand to stay at the Irish College. And I didn't blame him: they think the only food in the world is champ and carrots."

Patrick could tell that O'Malley was struggling to smother powerful emotions, that Eamonn De Faoite's death had brought him intense and permanent personal pain.

They turned into the Via dei Corridori, heading down toward the Vatican. On their left, the massive dome of St. Peter's struggled above the rooftops as though aching to be free of the nervous, jostling streets that hemmed it about like relatives about the bedside of a dying man.

On the Via di Porta Angelica, they turned left through St. Anne's Gate, the Vatican's service entrance. As always, it was almost clogged with cars, vans, and motorcycles. The Swiss Guard on duty waved them through. A second guard on the inner gate took greater care. O'Malley wound down his window and held out a small pass. The guard nodded, saluted, and let them through.

They headed straight along the Via del Belvedere and through a short tunnel into a courtyard where dozens of cars were parked, most of them bearing plates with the letters SCV, standing for Sacra Città del Vaticano. O'Malley drove into a space on the left.

"Have you ever been in the Vatican before, Patrick?"

Patrick shook his head.

"Oh, that's a pity. It's a great place. Maybe we'll have time for a proper tour another time. For your present information, you're in the Cortile del Belvedere, the Belvedere Court. That door on your right takes you into the

Vatican Library. But the door on the left is the one for us. It leads to the Secret Archives."

Patrick raised his eyebrows.

"Ah, you needn't look so surprised," said the priest. "There's precious little secret in there these days. Indeed, I don't think there ever was. If they don't want you to see something in this place, you can be sure they don't leave it lying around somewhere you might stumble across it. But that doesn't mean there aren't nice little discoveries to be made from time to time by them as knows where to look." He glanced at Patrick. "Your friend Eamonn De Faoite knew where to look. More's the pity for the man."

They got out of the car, leaving it unlocked. Theft was almost unknown here, and the Vatican jail enjoyed the reputation of being the least used in the world.

Inside the main door, a stern-faced custodian sat behind a large mahogany table. He looked as though he was aged somewhere between fifty and one hundred and ninety. With a look of irritation, he glanced up from the improving book he was reading and adjusted a pair of bifocals heavily clouded with specks of dandruff. Looking first at Patrick, then at O'Malley, he drew himself up straight in his high-backed chair.

"Yes? May I help you?"

"My name is Father O'Malley. I've come to look at some manuscripts. I take it you still keep some manuscripts here." His Italian was strangely perfect, not tainted in the least by the heavy brogue that colored his English.

The custodian stared at him as though he had just claimed to be the Pope.

"I see. You have a *tessera* of course."

"Sure, what would I need one of them things for? I've better things to do than spend half my life among dirty old books. God knows what I might catch."

The custodian's face, already the color and texture of faded parchment, turned several shades paler.

"I regret that . . ."

"But I've got something better than a *tessera*, if it's a permit you're after. Here, take a sniff at this."

O'Malley took a heavy envelope from the inside pocket of his jacket and passed it to the man behind the table. The custodian picked it up and glanced at it as though it had rabies.

"What's this?"

"Open it and see."

The custodian hesitated, guessing he had been outmaneuvered, then opened the envelope and took out a sheet of thick, letterheaded paper. Less than a minute later, he was bowing and scraping as he escorted Patrick and Father O'Malley to seats at one of the huge black desks in the main reading room. Once they were seated, he approached the prefect, a sort of gargoyle with jaundice who sat upright on a tall, thronelike chair surveying his little, ageless realm, and spoke with him briefly.

The room was empty save for the prefect, his assistants, and a handful of privileged scholars hunched over heavy black volumes as desiccated as themselves. On one wall, a huge clock ticked loudly, a reminder to everyone that, in the end, the calendar takes care of everything.

While an assistant scurried off to fetch the file O'Malley had requested, the priest bent close to Patrick and whispered quietly in his ear.

"The Church has had some sort of archive in Rome since the sixth century. Most of what was in its keeping then was held in the Lateran, but it's said it was all destroyed in fighting at the beginning of the thirteenth century. However, it's my opinion that what I'm about to show you came from there.

"In any case, the archives were kept, after that, either in the Vatican or with the Pope himself whenever he traveled about the country. Later on, the whole lot was moved to the Castel Sant' Angelo for safekeeping. The really important stuff—things like privileges and papal charters—were kept in what was known as the Archivium Arcis.

"Then, in 1611, Paul V founded the Secret Archive, the Archivium Secretum Vaticanum. He had eighty *armaria*, great wooden chests, filled with material from different sources—the Biblioteca Segreta, the Camera, the Archivium Arcis. Until 1879, the archive really was secret, but it was then that Leo XIII decided to let reputable scholars in to study the documents. Some of them look as though they've been here ever since. As you can see, I'm not all that reputable; but I'm not without a little influence either. In my experience, there's nothing in the Vatican that a little bottle of Black Bush in the right hands won't arrange."

He paused as the assistant returned, carrying a small book in his hands. Without a word, he set it down on the desk in front of them and left.

"Now, Patrick, listen carefully. You'll see that the call number on the back of this file reads AA Arm. I–XVIII 6723. All that means is that it comes from the Archivium Arcis, that it's stored in the lower set of *armaria*, series one to eighteen, and that it's item number 6723."

"What is it?"

"Now, don't go getting impatient. If you'll just open it . . ."

There was a hissing sound from the direction of the prefect's chair. They looked up to see the old buzzard holding a bent finger to his lips. O'Malley lowered his voice even further.

"If you look inside, you'll see that it's a copy of a Gnostic gospel written in Coptic. According to a little note in Latin pasted in at the front, it was found among the contents of the Archivium Arcis when everything was transferred to the Secret Archive. Of course, Gnostic gospels weren't exactly popular in those days, so the book sort of rotted away here in its wee box without anyone ever taking a proper look at it."

He looked down at the worn leather cover, the curious Coptic binding tied with thongs.

"Eamonn De Faoite was the first person in centuries to do more than glance at it. And what do you think he found?"

"Suppose you show me."

"Be my guest."

Patrick untied the thongs and opened the little volume. Page after page of crabbed Coptic script in black ink with the capitals in red. It looked dreary and quite unreadable.

"I can't read Coptic."

"Can't you? That's a terrible pity. Neither can I. But look here."

The priest opened the book again, leafing through it until he came to two leaves near the middle. Carefully, he peeled one away from the other. Inside lay a third sheet, unbound. O'Malley lifted it out and spread it on the table in front of Patrick.

"You can read Aramaic, though, can't you?"

Patrick looked down. Unfolded, the sheet was a large piece of papyrus, covered in fine Aramaic writing. Aramaic: the language of much of the Old Testament, the language of Palestine at the time of Jesus.

FORTY-ONE

At times trumpets blow on the high towers. Now on the Tower of Psephinus, now on the tall pinnacles of Hippicus and Phasael and Mariamme. They chase the birds from the sky, and we think the end is come. Simon bar Goria and his men hold the Upper City and much of the Lower also. The Temple and Ophel are in the hands of John of Gischala and his followers. All that lies between has been burned to the ground. There is smoke everywhere. Smoke and the sound of wailing. Some say the Temple has begun to burn.

Patrick looked up. He could hear the sound of the clock ticking and the scratch of a pencil as someone took notes at another table. O'Malley watched him, impassive, like a teacher waiting for his star pupil to show what he is made of.

"Am I to take it that this is genuine?" whispered Patrick.

"I don't know. What do you think? You're the one who reads Aramaic, not me."

Patrick pondered. It was years since he had read Josephus, but there could be no mistake.

"I think it's a description of the siege of Jerusalem in 70 A.D., during the Jewish war with the Romans. But that's impossible. Nothing in writing survived the siege."

"You mean nothing anyone knew of before this."

Patrick nodded. There was nothing inherently implausible in such a document having been rescued.

"Do you think they could fetch me a magnifying glass? This script is very fine."

"Good idea. Make them do a bit of work."

O'Malley summoned an assistant, and minutes later an enormous magnifying glass made its appearance on the table in front of Patrick. He lifted it and continued reading.

Passover has come and gone, but there has been no deliverance. Three weeks ago, the Continual Sacrifice ceased and the altar was deserted. Outside the city walls, the armies of Pharaoh's son are massed. Four legions, and with them Arab and Syrian auxiliaries.

For a moment Patrick was puzzled. Then he understood. The Roman general in charge of the campaign was Titus. His father, Vespasian, had just been made Emperor. So Vespasian was "Pharaoh" and Titus was "Pharaoh's son."

He has moved his own camp to a spot opposite the Tower of Psephinus. The Tenth Legion remains on the Mount of Olives. Their engines of war are the largest and the most terrible: quick-loaders, stone-throwers, catapults. They hurl great stones of white marble into the city. The watchers on the walls cry out when they see them coming, and we flee in terror. On every side, the sound of battering rams rises to the heavens. But our prayers stay here below. They have brought rams to the western arcade of the Temple. The end cannot be long now. Lord, why have you forsaken your people?

Those of the brethren that remain in the city meet daily in the house of John the Zealot, who was blessed by James in the days before his death. We pray no longer for forgiveness, but for understanding. There is one still among us who remembers the words of our Lord, when he came out of the Temple with his disciples. He said to them: "See you all these? I tell you solemnly, not one stone here shall remain on another: all will be destroyed." Even so, it is coming to pass. Then, we pray, all things will be fulfilled, and his promise unto us, that he will return.

Patrick looked up, rubbing his eyes.

"Whoever wrote this was a Christian. Did you know that?"

"Oh, yes, certainly. What you are holding in your hands is without question the earliest surviving document of the Christian Church. I think you'll find your man was a Jewish Christian, not one of Paul's upstart Gentiles."

Patrick nodded. James, the brother of Jesus, had been head of the Church in Jerusalem. He and his followers, unlike Paul and those he converted, had observed the Jewish law and attended the Temple regularly, while teaching that Jesus was the Messiah. Up to the destruction of the city in the year 70, they had been the most important group in the early Church. Then Jerusalem was destroyed and they were either killed or scattered, leaving Paul and his followers free to run the new faith as they wished.

Patrick continued reading.

Of the brotherhood of Jesus that were in the city before the days of Passover, breaking bread together and praying according to the teaching of the apostles, but a few are now left. We pray daily that our brothers who have gone have reached Egypt in safety, and that they will be spared the wrath of these last days.

A party among us, numbering seven, according to the number of deacons presented to the Twelve, have met on this, the eighth day of Loös, to take counsel together in secret. Chief among us is John the Zealot, a holy man fired by the love of God, and a prophet sent to guide the brethren in these days of darkness. He was appointed head of the Twelve by James, the brother of the Lord, in the days before they stoned him to death. Beneath him are seated Eleazar bar Simon, Judas of Gamala, Barnabas the son of Jeshua the Elder, Jonathon, a deacon of Emmaus, Paul of Acrabetta, and myself, Simon bar Matthias, the Levite.

We have named ourselves the Seven of the Tomb, swearing to defend the sepulcher of our Lord, in which are also buried his brother James and his mother. The sepulcher lies hidden among the tombs that lie beyond the walls, to the north of the tomb of Simon the Just. John knows a secret way that passes through the Valley of Hinnom in the south. From there, we shall go by night westward, skirting the camps of the invader, until we come again to the north.

And when there comes to pass that which has been decreed for the city, that it may fall stone from stone, if any still be alive, by God's grace, he shall go unto Egypt, which is Babylon, that he may strike down Pharaoh, even as he sits on his throne, in vengeance for God's Temple, both the earthly Temple and the Temple that was crucified.

And that shall be the true Passover, that God's chosen people shall pass out of the land of Egypt and come into the Land of the Promise. And our Lord shall return. There shall be a new Jerusalem, and God and the Lamb shall be its Temple. Egypt shall fall then, and Babylon, all them that have scattered the children of God among the nations. For Jesus said: "Do not think I have come to send peace on earth: I came not to send peace, but a sword." And so it shall be.

And if all die, let him that comes after take up the sword in our place, that the days may be numbered and the wicked brought to a reckoning. For the Tomb is a sacred trust, and the sword also, that goodness endure and all manner of wickedness perish from the earth.

Patrick looked up.

"That's the main text. There are just a few more lines in a different hand, in Hebrew. They're a bit more difficult to read."

"I'm sure you can manage. Have a go."

Slowly, Patrick deciphered the broken script in front of him.

I, John of Amathus, known as the Zealot, though long baptized, leave here what Simon the Levite has written concerning the last days of Jerusalem, that it may serve as a testimony to others. Of the Brotherhood of the Tomb, I alone remain alive. I shall seal the sepulcher and seek refuge in Egypt, where others have gone before me. I shall carry with me the secret of the tomb, and the secret of him that entered it, and of the manner in which he came to enter it, lest those things be forgotten. There are among the believers who have preceded me still a number that know a little of those matters. If God wills it, I shall choose among them six Elders to lead the Brotherhood. These words I leave for him whom God shall send in the latter days, that he may take up this sword and deliver God's people out of bondage. May he finish what I have begun and determine all things with justice.

Patrick looked up. O'Malley was looking at him intently.

"So now you know," he said.

FORTY-TWO

When they returned to the apartment, the others had already eaten lunch. Francesca prepared fresh pasta and fish and left them in the kitchen to eat it in peace.

When they finally joined the others in the living room, coffee had been prepared. Francesca poured out cups of espresso and passed round a plate of *amaretti*. Father O'Malley was the first to speak.

"You must be wondering by now what this is all about. I didn't like to say too much until I'd had a chance to show something to Patrick." He paused and glanced at Assefa. "Roberto will have explained to you, Father Makonnen, why I thought it best not to have you with us. We paid a little visit to the Vatican Archives, Patrick and I, and there was a fair to even chance that someone there or in the vicinity would have recognized you. At the moment, even an old friend could be unwittingly dangerous to you. I'm sure you understand the reasons for my caution."

Assefa nodded. A sense of personal danger had become second nature to him by now. He wondered how he had got by without it before.

O'Malley sat forward on the edge of his chair. For all his size, he seemed to Patrick a remarkably gentle man. Gentle, but not soft. Patrick sensed something in him, a kind of righteous anger that would tear his gentleness to shreds and burn it if it seemed necessary.

"You'll have to forgive my theatricality in taking you off so mysteriously, Patrick. But I did have a serious purpose in showing you that document. Had you not seen it—the original, mind, not a copy—you might think some of the things I am about to tell you a little . . . farfetched. Unfortunately, they are not. I would give anything to have them so, but they will not be other than what they are."

He paused and folded his hands in front of him as though in prayer.

"Roberto Quadri and I," he began, speaking slowly, "are directors of an organization called FRATERNITÀ. The name is really an acronym: Fondazione per Riabilitazione degli Aderenti e Transfughi delle Religioni Nuove in Italia—the Foundation for the Rehabilitation of Adherents and Fugitives from New Religions in Italy. Actually, the Foundation is just the Italian branch of a much larger network set up by the Church a few years ago to help people who have been harmed in some way by their involvement in new religious movements—what the newspapers sometimes call cults. Moonies, Scientologists, followers of Bhagwan Shree Rajneesh, Children of God, Krishna devotees, Baha'is, Divine Light Missionaries—the list is endless.

"We're only interested in people who think they have suffered through their involvement: disciples who are in and want help getting out, former members who have problems adjusting to the ordinary world again. We find them jobs, give them temporary accommodation, help reconcile them with their families. And sometimes protect them from other cult members who want to get them back or teach them a lesson for leaving in the first place. If someone's in a group and is happy that way, we're just as happy to leave him there. Unlike some organizations I could mention, we don't go in for kidnapping sect members and deprogramming them. That only amounts to brainwashing them to accept what society thinks is normal."

He glanced round the room.

"But since modern society is itself even more abnormal than many of the sects, I see no particular benefits in forcing someone who has found some sort of meaning for himself to return to the lunatic asylum out in the streets."

He paused.

"Sorry, I didn't mean to preach. To continue. Our little group has been in existence about ten years now, but during the last five of those Roberto and I have spent an increasingly large amount of our time with one particular cult. Roberto, by the way, used to be a member of ISKCON, the Hare Krishna movement. He stopped traveling to other planets twelve years ago, studied law, and started helping FRATERNITÀ full time six years back. I think I'd better let him take over at this point."

Quadri put his cup on the floor. Again, Patrick noticed the tiredness, the slow movements of someone critically ill. When the lawyer spoke, however, his voice had none of the languor Patrick expected. He was incisive, clear, and wholly in command of his subject.

"Okay, where do I start? At the beginning, I suppose. So, how did all this start? Not FRATERNITÀ, but this thing we're all involved in." He paused.

"Not long after I started working for Dermot, a woman arrived at our office in Rome. I was on duty. I answered the door and brought her in. She looked to me as though she was in her mid-forties, but something made me think she might be much younger than that. At first, she was in a state of extreme distress—very frightened, very jumpy. She kept looking round, as though expecting someone she didn't want to see. It took a long time before she could summon up enough courage to talk. It took days. Weeks for all the details to emerge.

"We'd just bought this apartment as a refuge for people on the run from the more violent sects, and I brought her here the same evening. After Dermot and I heard her story, we gave her exclusive use. Since the deeds had not yet been transferred to FRATERNITÀ, I was able to make the entire transaction disappear. Not even the other directors knew of its existence. They still don't."

He paused to pour more coffee into his cup.

"For weeks I stayed here in the apartment with her. She was so frightened, she could not be left alone, not for a moment. Dermot came on the second day and every day after that. Sometimes we talked into the early morning, sometimes we just sat with her in silence, reading, waiting for her to talk again. She was on edge, you see, so much on edge. But the more she talked the calmer she became. It was a sort of therapy, you understand, just to tell us what she knew.

"At first we thought, *She's making this up; she's telling lies or she has a vivid imagination.* No doubt we thought other things too—that she was mad at heart, frantic with some grief, perhaps, a lonely woman looking for fears to comfort her, to give her existence meaning and purpose. Well, we were used then to milder sorts of madness, the trivial obsessions of spiritual misfits. Sex is the chief obsession: if they dream, they dream of sex. Some have too little, some too much, others none at all; it makes no difference. But not for her. If she was mad, she was mad with violence. If she dreamed, she had dreams of slaughter."

He paused, as though entranced by the mere possibility of such dreams. "But the more we talked with her, the more we came to know she was not mad. She was sane, you see. Very sane indeed.

"She gave us a list of things we could investigate without drawing attention to ourselves. And everywhere we looked, we found confirmation of what she had told us. Her story held water. I wish . . ." He hesitated, glancing at Patrick, then at Assefa. "I wish now it had been a lie, or she had been mad."

Then his eye caught Francesca's and he smiled, a little wan smile, lonely, private. "Well, perhaps not that. How could we have wished that? Mistaken, let us say."

He paused briefly, fixing his eye on Patrick before continuing.

"Signor Canavan, the document you were shown this morning at the Vatican—you are satisfied as to its authenticity?"

Patrick hesitated.

"I'm not an expert," he said. "But superficially, yes—it seemed genu-

ine. It had the feel of the thing, it felt like . . . what I imagine a document from that period would be like." He paused. "I'm sorry, that isn't
very specific. Well, the Aramaic was convincing, the details of the siege
were historical, as far as I remember them from Josephus. But for any sort
of certainty, you'd have to bring in a paleographer, someone with the right
equipment, with the expertise to do a proper job, to examine the material,
the ink, the script, the language. Ideally, a team of experts."

"Yes," said Roberto. "I know. But that has already been done to our
satisfaction. Eamonn De Faoite examined the letter in the Archives under
the pretense of working on the other documents in that volume. There are
facilities there, excellent facilities. They are not so medieval as they would
like to seem. I have a copy of his report here, if you would like to examine
it."

Patrick shook his head.

"Very well. Perhaps you will give us a description of the contents of the
letter, for the benefit of Father Makonnen, who has not seen it."

Hesitantly, Patrick did as requested. Assefa listened carefully, motion-
less, like a condemned man hearing his sentence read out in court, slowly,
with deliberation, line by damning line. When Patrick finished, he said
nothing. He had come to a redundancy of words.

Quadri spoke again in his quiet lawyer's voice. "As you will have
guessed by now, the Brotherhood to which that letter refers did not vanish
into the mists of time. They are still very much with us. Over the centuries,
they have grown subtle and rich and powerful, and now they are poised to
make a bid for a power and influence even they have never previously
dreamed of." He paused and took a mouthful of hot coffee.

"I think Francesca should explain the rest in her own words," he said.

Patrick turned his eyes to Francesca, only to find her gaze fixed on the
floor, avoiding all contact with the others. He watched her collect herself,
and with a pang recognized the way she drew her brows together, frowning
briefly as she gathered her thoughts.

"There has always been a Brotherhood," she began. "Since the days of
John the Zealot, there has been in existence somewhere a body of men and
women dedicated to the preservation of mankind's greatest secret, the
whereabouts of Christ's tomb. They have had many names, gone under
many disguises, but the Brotherhood itself has always been one and indi-
visible. In almost two thousand years, until I came back from the dead and
poured my heart out in this room to Dermot and Roberto, no one has ever
betrayed them." She hesitated. "No, that's not quite true. They have been
betrayed many times. But no one before this has ever betrayed them and
lived this long."

She looked up and caught Patrick's eye.

"Yes, Patrick, I know," she said. "Long before I betrayed them, I betrayed you. You want me to explain it all, and I don't know how to. Not without telling you more than it may be fair for you to know."

"Let me be the judge of what's fair, Francesca. What happened to you happened to me as well. I have a right."

She did not reply at once. Her hair fell across her eyes, as it had fallen years ago; but now it was streaked with gray, and the eyes beneath it harbored memories unthought of then.

"Very well," she said. "I shall try to explain. But first . . . Dermot— please help me. Father Makonnen . . ."

O'Malley nodded.

"Yes," he said. "I understand." He turned to Assefa. "Father Makonnen," he said, "I know you have been sorely tested in the past few days. I feel I should warn you that, if you stay, you may hear things you might prefer not to have heard. Things that will test, not only your vocation, but your faith. I do not say this lightly. Whatever else, I am a priest like yourself. I know that, if you hear what Francesca is about to tell us, you will not know a full night's sleep for a very long time to come. Perhaps never again. If you prefer to leave, none of us will think the less of you, least of all myself. But it must be your decision."

Assefa got up and went to the window. He looked down into the street, at the coming and going of people and cars, at the world of his vocation. He was thinking of the Virgin he had prayed to that morning, of her blackness and her virginity, like two sides of a coin, knowledge and ignorance, wisdom and unwisdom. To be black was to know things other men could never know. To have suffered always, to have been poor always, to have known no hope of change in your own lifetime. Suffering was a kind of knowledge, pain was a kind of wisdom. Ignorance, like virginity, gave no trouble to the heart. But his own virginity, the denial he had chosen for himself, was a virginity of suffering. He could not turn his back on it as Patrick had turned his back on the Virgin that morning.

"I would prefer to stay," he said.

FORTY-THREE

"They called us the Dead."

Francesca held herself tensely in the chair, as though braced against a storm at sea.

"We were chosen. Chosen out of all the world, they said. A new nobility, a priesthood consecrated by God. So they told us. Our families chose us and the Seven approved their choice. Or disapproved it if they had doubts. Once chosen, there was no going back. It was as if someone had taken a sponge and wiped our names from a slate. From that moment, we were treated as though we were truly dead."

She glanced at Patrick.

"You know that: you rode to my funeral, you watched them bury me, heard them pray for my soul's rest. You think now it was a mere pretense, an elaborate game they played. Perhaps. But their grief was no more simulated than yours. For them, it was as though I had really died. My parents knew they would never set eyes on me again. My brothers, Giulietta my sister, they all knew. So you see, they suffered almost as much as you, dear Patrick. Almost as much as you."

She halted, her eyes nervously seeking his, as though to reassure him, to tell him his grief had not been wasted. But her own eyes held a sadness that frightened him more than simple grief.

"The Dead are a brotherhood within a brotherhood," she continued. "Strictly speaking, they are divided into a brotherhood for men and a sisterhood for women. Like the first Christian monks, like the first Brothers of the Tomb themselves, they live in Egypt, in two order houses close together in the Western Desert beyond the Dakhla oasis. Whenever their services are needed in Europe or America, they are sent for. For centuries, they have been the heart of the Brotherhood. Its eyes, its ears . . . its hands."

She shivered slightly, as though a thin draft had passed unseen through the room. They were close, she thought, closer than they had ever been. Events during the past few months had forced her to show her hand more than had, perhaps, been wise. They were still hunting, still waiting for her to make the one mistake that would put her in their hands. And when they found her, they would have no mercy. None at all.

"Having died once," she said, "they are willing to die again. Or to kill. They are, in a sense, beyond morality. Of course, they have a morality of their own; but they bend it to their own ends, like fashioners of glass who pull and twist and draw it so fine that, in the end, it has no other purpose than to break."

Patrick watched her thin fingers move as though spinning glass filaments. He remembered going with her once to see a craftsman on Murano work with the thinnest of glass, fashioning the legs of tiny insects. He had bought her a glass spider, but by the time she brought it home, two of its eight legs had broken.

"The Dead," she was saying, "are substitutes. By accepting death while still alive, they renew Christ's sacrifice." She hesitated. "How can I explain this? Patrick, when you were in the *palazzo* with my father, did you see a painting on the wall, a fresco?"

"Yes, it showed . . ."

"The figure of Christ bound hand and foot, dragged to the tomb." She paused. "That isn't how the Bible tells us he died, is it? But it's not a painter's fantasy either, nor some ghastly attempt at blasphemy. For the Brotherhood, it is the literal truth. It is the center of their faith."

Patrick remembered Alessandro Contarini as he had last seen him, angry, his long white hair falling loose across his face, his finger raised, pointing again and again at the fresco on the wall and crying: "For that, you fool! For that!"

Francesca hesitated and turned to O'Malley.

"Dermot, I . . ."

"It's all right, my dear. You're doing well. Keep going."

She closed her eyes briefly, then opened them again, as though, in a moment's darkness, she had found strength.

"The Old Testament," she said, "is built around the notion of sacrifice. Bullocks, rams and sheep, goats, turtledoves, pigeons: an endless flow of sacrificial blood.

"But there is human blood as well. Abraham goes to a mountain with his son and prepares to slit his throat as an offering to his God. Moses is sent by the same God to redeem His people from Pharaoh: the price is the blood of Egypt's firstborn. God gives them their Promised Land, and the price is yet more blood—whole cities put to the sword, men, women, and children without distinction. Jephtha returns from his victory over the children of Ammon and the price is his only daughter, to fulfill a vow to God. Hiel the Bethelite rebuilds Jericho and pays with the blood of his sons, Abiram and Segub, cast beneath the foundations and the gate. In time, the Temple reeks of blood."

The unseen storm that raged round her was reaching its height. She fought against it, denying its force in her.

"Christ was born into a world obsessed with sacrifice. The daily burnt offering, the weekly sacrifice on the Sabbath, the monthly offering, Passover; burnt offerings, drink offerings, sin offerings. Within days of his birth the streets were awash with the blood of little children. That was God's price, the ransom that allowed him safe passage to Egypt. In Jerusalem, in the Temple, the altar was red.

"He wanted to change that world, to invest the throats of doves and the necks of rams with a different sanctity. His own life for the world, his own body as a final sacrifice, his own blood as the price of everything, the coin that would buy God's pardon. That is what the Church teaches, what the Church believes. The mass repeats his sacrifice endlessly, flesh and blood on God's new altar."

She looked at Patrick, then at Assefa. Her eyes had a faraway look now.

"That is what you believe, isn't it? That in one man the Temple sacrifice became universal. But the Brotherhood thinks otherwise. The Brotherhood knows the truth."

From the table next to her, she lifted a small book bound in black.

"This is a copy of the Aramaic gospel of James," she said. "It has been in the possession of the Brotherhood since its inception. Any other copies that may have existed have long ago been lost or destroyed. The Brotherhood itself has only ever printed a few hundred copies. I stole this one from my father's library just before I came to Rome. It's an Italian translation. Let me read James's account of the death of Jesus.

" 'He went up to the cross, and they nailed him and hung him on it, as the prophet had foretold. And he suffered greatly from the sixth hour until the ninth, whereupon he cried out with a loud voice and hung upon the cross as one dead. And yet he had not died, but still lived. For when they came to take him down that they might carry him to the tomb, they rejoiced that they found him still alive.

" 'His mother and Mary Magdalene tended his wounds and nursed him by day and night for three months, until he recovered. And in those days but a tiny number of his followers knew what had passed, that he had not died as predicted, but was still alive. For most of the disciples thought he had been buried and had risen from the dead.

" 'For three months, his mother and the Magdalene tended him in secret. They let the Sanhedrin and the Romans think him dead, for in that thought lay his only hope of safety. It was their plan, once he was fully come once *more to his strength and could walk again, that they might find a way for him to take himself out of Judaea, into another country. And he himself desired it greatly, for the cross had broken him, and he could not face the nails again.*

" 'But I, James his brother, together with Simon the Canaanite, Andrew the brother of Peter, and seven others from among the disciples other than the twelve, all of us who knew the truth, thought otherwise. For God's will had been thwarted, and His Sacrifice remained unfinished. Wherefore, we met together in Simon's house that is in the Street of the Water Gate and swore a solemn oath binding us to finish what had been left undone. That night, we came to a place outside the city, where Jesus had been hidden, and took him from there over the cries of the women that watched over him, and carried him to the place outside the city, where Joseph of Arimathea had given a tomb for his burial. And he was bound with cords and his mouth tied with cloth, lest he break free or the Romans hear his cries and send men to investigate.

" 'And we laid him in the sarcophagus that Joseph had inscribed with his name and the circumstances of his crucifixion under Pilate. It was a great anguish to us to treat him thus, but we remembered God's promise to us that He would forgive us all sins through the blood of His son, and the sins of all men. And so we laid him in his place and covered him with the stone and sealed the tomb.' "

She stopped reading and the room filled with a terrible silence. Minutes passed and still no one spoke. At last Assefa turned to Father O'Malley.

"Do you believe this?" he asked.

The priest laughed loudly, breaking the spell of gloom that had settled round them all. "Good God, no," he said. "I can't say it isn't all true, of course. How would I know? How would anyone know? But the world is full of apocryphal Gospels, isn't it? Sure, the Gnostics had Gospels and Epistles and Apocalypses and God knows what coming out of them like eggs out of a chicken. I choose not to believe in the Gospel of Thomas or the Gospel of Peter or the Gospel of the Ebionites, or, for that matter, the Acts of Paul or Peter or Thomas, and the Lord alone knows what besides. So why on earth should I believe this Gospel of James? And if it is true, what difference would it make to anything? If the saints are in hell, I'd far rather be there with them than in heaven with James and his gang."

He paused and looked sadly at Assefa.

"I don't doubt that the Brotherhood exists; I know too much about them and their doings for that. And the papyrus I showed Patrick is proof enough that they go back a long way. But it doesn't mean they know all there is to know."

He smiled.

"Listen, we'll talk about this later. In the meantime, I'll let Francesca get to the end of her yarn."

Francesca laid the book back on the table.

"There's not much more to say," she continued. "The Brotherhood grew, at first in Egypt, later in Italy. My ancestor Pietro Contarini met some Brothers there and was initiated into their secret. By that time, Egypt was under Muslim rule, and the Brotherhood wanted to find a way into Christian territories. From Venice, they spread to Rome, and in Rome they became bishops and cardinals. About the same time Pietro brought the faith to Italy, an Irish pilgrim on his way back from Jerusalem had taken it to Ireland. During the Crusades, French and English knights were welcomed into the Brotherhood by a branch living in Jerusalem, the Guardians of the Tomb itself.

"As the years went by, the Brotherhood grew powerful. My family and others like it in Venice made it the center of their existence. It was a tie that bound them more tightly than any bonds of kinship. Well, in one sense the bond was one of blood. It was not just the secret they shared that held them to one another: it was something darker and more primitive than that.

"When the Brotherhood first reached Egypt, their faith had been tested to breaking point. Jerusalem had been destroyed, the Temple razed to the ground, the Holy of Holies put to the torch. They had no way of knowing how long the tomb of Jesus would remain inviolate, or whether it had already been found and desecrated.

"The Jews of Alexandria were of no help to them. They prayed and wrung their hands, but they were powerless. So the Brothers vowed that one day they would avenge the destruction of their Holy City. And in confirmation of that vow, they put to death their own children, their firstborn sons and daughters, regardless of age. Jesus had not been enough, otherwise the Temple would never have been burned. God was angry, He required more blood. If they were to come out of Egypt once more, like the children of Israel following Moses, Passover had to be repeated. Not the blood of Egyptians this time, but their own blood freely given, a sin offering, reparation for the sins of an entire people.

"So it went on. Of course, they could not put all their firstborn to death in every generation. So the institution of the Dead was introduced. I explained earlier that they were substitutes: instead of physical death, they embraced the grave while still living. From time to time, a child would actually be sacrificed. By then, child sacrifice had become more than a ritual of atonement. The leaders of the Brotherhood, the Seven, knew that involvement in murder would hold their followers together more firmly than any vows. Who would betray such a secret, to bring himself and his whole family into disgrace and worse?"

She stopped speaking. Patrick could see that she was growing agitated again.

"I found out all of this by accident," she said, her voice almost inaudible. "Most of us had no idea, you see. Only the Seven, the apostles immediately below them, the abbots of the Order of the Dead, and the heads of the families ever knew the full truth. But . . . I learned of it and . . . witnessed it. I saw my own father . . . I'm sorry, I can't . . ."

Francesca was shaking now, haunted by a memory she could not exorcise. She had no need for words, the horror was in the room with them, raw and bloody and full of strength. Patrick went across to her, oblivious of the others. He took her hand and lifted her from the chair, taking her gently into his arms, not as a lover, but as someone bound to her by grief.

"What has happened to you has happened to me," he repeated.

But she shook her head and pulled away from him.

"No," she said. "Love doesn't enter into this. Whatever you felt for me, whatever I felt for you, it's all irrelevant. They don't care a thing for love. Not even the love of God. They don't want God to love them, they want Him to reward them in return for what they offer Him. Not love, but power, Patrick. Power and the forgiveness of sins. Power in this world and glory in the next. They will sacrifice anything for that: their feelings, their loves, their children . . . their souls."

He stood watching her, perplexed, frightened, understanding nothing.

"Mr. Canavan." It was Quadri's voice. "Please sit down. We have not finished yet." He turned to Francesca. "Please, Francesca, sit down too. You did well. I'm grateful to you."

He paused and looked round the room slowly. His thin face showed signs of pain. His eyes were full and hard.

"Mr. Canavan, Father Makonnen," he continued. "For several years now, with Francesca's help, a small group of people chosen by Father O'Malley and myself has been investigating the Brotherhood. We have identified several of its leading members, gathered evidence of their activities, compiled a dossier for presentation to the Public Prosecutor when the time is ripe. Because of the size and secrecy of their organization, we have had to proceed with the utmost circumspection. Every step we have taken has been planned and debated most carefully. At every moment we have been aware that a single slip might place our entire mission in jeopardy. An indiscretion, a premature revelation, a careless question—anything might serve to make them aware of our existence. So far, we believe we have succeeded in eluding suspicion.

"We have run a terrible risk in bringing you here today. The Brotherhood knows of you, it has members hunting you everywhere. Francesca is already marked for death. Ordinarily, I would have recommended leaving you to your fate. Our task is too important to be endangered for the sake of one or two lives. That is how we have to be to survive. But we had a reason for seeking you out.

"We want to know everything you may have heard about Passover. One of our people heard of it first over a year ago. Since then, we have done everything in our power to find out more, with almost no success. All we know is that what they are planning is going to be the greatest triumph in the two thousand years they have been in existence; that it is going to take place very soon; and that over one hundred of the Dead have been brought to Italy from Egypt to carry it out. We need your help. Please think hard. If you know anything that may give us a clue, anything that . . ."

He looked round. Assefa had risen half out of his chair. On his face was a look of sheer horror. Slowly, he raised one hand and placed it over his mouth as though he was about to be sick. O'Malley got up and went over to him, taking his arm and holding him steady.

"Father Makonnen, are you all right?"

The Ethiopian took O'Malley's arm, squeezing it tightly, then looked into his face, his eyes wide open, an expression of fear and grief stamped on his features.

"My God," he whispered. "O Jesus Christ, sweet Mary, I know. I know."

"What is it, Father? What do you know?" O'Malley could feel ice in his veins.

"I know what they are planning. God forgive me, I should have thought before this. I know what it is. And I know it will happen tomorrow."

FORTY-FOUR

O'Malley found a bottle of *grappa* in the kitchen. Assefa sipped it in small, nervous gulps, gasping each time the fiery liquid caught his breath. Roberto showed him how to calm himself with slow, rhythmical breaths from the diaphragm. For a while, he sat with eyes closed, breathing gently, letting the tension dissolve. When he opened his eyes again, it was only to stare at the floor; excitement had given way to languor and impassivity.

"Father Makonnen." Roberto spoke gently, yet firmly, as though pressing a reluctant witness to admit what he had seen. "You must tell us what you know. It's very important. Lives may depend on it. Innocent lives."

Assefa shook his head.

"It's too late," he whispered. "What can we do? There's no time."

"Please let me be the judge of that. Tell me what you can."

Assefa looked up. His eyes were full of tears, and in them Roberto sensed a mute appeal, an unspoken plea for reassurance. He had seen it many times in other eyes, under very different circumstances. But the appeal was always the same: "Tell me this is just a dream, that in a moment I'll wake up and find none of this has happened." It was the look of a man who has just been told he is dying of a fatal disease. It was a look Roberto knew very well indeed.

"Very well," said Assefa. "I'll tell you what I can." He paused, then began to speak, choosing his words with care. "For the last few months, the nunciature in Dublin has been involved with a series of highly delicate discussions. I was present at a number of meetings, some at the nunciature itself, others at Leinster House, and some at the Egyptian and Iraqi embassies. You understand that I am only an *addetto*, that I was never privy to any but the lowest-level talks. But Archbishop Balzarin confided in me. I was expected to handle certain items of correspondence."

He paused and raised the glass of *grappa*, then thought twice about it and put it down again.

"About a year ago, the Holy Father decided to begin a series of negotiations aimed at achieving peace in the Middle East. His plan is to start with

Lebanon, since he has direct influence there through the Maronite Christians. If the settlement there proves successful, he intends to attempt a démarche on the Palestinian question or possibly the Gulf.

"His great ally is the new President of Ireland, Mr. MacMaoláin. You may know that, before he became President two years ago, MacMaoláin was a lieutenant general in the Irish defense forces. For several years he was force commander with UNIFIL, the UN Irish Force in Lebanon. He learned a lot then about the politics of the region.

"It seems that he wants the Nobel Peace Prize like his old friend Seán McBride. It happens that he and the Holy Father got to know one another well after the war, when the Pope was studying at the Angelicum, the Dominican university here in Rome. MacMaoláin had an older brother in holy orders who was also writing a thesis at the Angelicum, so he was sent to Rome himself for a year. His parents wanted him to be a diplomat like his father, and they thought a knowledge of Italian would help him get a posting to the embassy in Rome. Of course, he entered the army when he got back to Dublin; but it looks as though he wants to make up for that early change of direction."

Patrick listened intently. Two of the hardest puzzles in this affair seemed to have cleared up simultaneously: why Ireland should have been involved at all, and why Alex Chekulayev had been in Dublin.

"What sort of scheme are they cooking up for Lebanon?" he asked.

Assefa bit his lip.

"I don't have the details, I'm sorry. But Balzarin gave me a broad idea. The Holy Father is of the opinion that people are sick to death of civil war now and will do anything for peace. If we forget about all the different factions, the basic division in the country is between Christians and Muslims. Roughly speaking, the Christians make up about forty-three percent of the population.

"The Holy Father intends to meet with the heads of the different churches, and then with the Muslim leaders. In return for a promise to use his influence in the United States to get the Israelis to agree to concessions on the Palestinians, he will propose a coalition government. Technically, Lebanon will become a Muslim state. But the Christian minority will be guaranteed full representation at all levels of government. It's not that much different from the system established in 1926, except that the Shi'ites will be properly recognized as the majority within the Muslim population.

"God knows if the plan has any chance of working. The Holy Father intends to establish a special Vatican secretariat in Beirut, responsible for supervision of the new constitution in conjunction with a council of Shi'ite, Sunni, and Druse clergy. The Irish have promised to install observers under the auspices of the UN. The hope is that they'll be particularly acceptable to the Shi'ites because Ireland is a nonimperial power supposed to be engaged in a struggle for independence from Britain."

He paused and drained the glass of *grappa*.

"I don't understand," said Patrick. "I can't see how this relates to what we've been talking about."

Francesca interrupted.

"It could, Patrick. The Brotherhood has very strong feelings about Islam. When Muslim armies conquered Palestine and Egypt in the seventh century, the Brothers thought they were a scourge sent by God to teach the churches a lesson, perhaps to prepare the way for their own rise to power. But the Arabs stayed and took possession of the towns and cities in which the holy places of the Brotherhood were situated: the tomb of Christ in Jerusalem and that of John of Amathus in Alexandria, the Church of the Seven at Babylon near modern Cairo, their private catacombs at Qum al-Shuqaffa. The Brothers swore a sort of holy war against the invaders, and through the centuries they did what they could to make life uncomfortable for them."

Patrick thought of what he had seen that time in Egypt, his first brush with the Brotherhood of the Tomb: the blood of Muslim children filling a basalt bowl, a village torn with grief.

"About twenty years ago, leadership of the Brotherhood passed to a bishop named Migliau. He is now a cardinal and the Patriarch of Venice."

Patrick and Assefa exchanged glances. Another piece of the puzzle had fallen into place.

"Migliau," continued Francesca, "has a deep animosity toward Islam. It isn't a rational thing with him, merely part of his general baggage of fears and prejudices. He was furious when the Vatican Council issued a document called *Nostra Aetate*, calling for mutual understanding between Muslims and Christians. And when the present Pope visited Muslim countries like Turkey or Morocco and talked about bonds of spiritual unity between the two faiths, he went crazy. He sent an encyclical letter to all branches of the Brotherhood declaring the Pope an apostate who had betrayed the faith of Christ."

"I don't understand," Assefa broke in. "Surely this Brotherhood has never recognized the authority of the Pope. What difference would it make, whatever the Holy Father said?"

Francesca frowned.

"It's not that simple, Father. At the very beginning, the Brotherhood was entirely at odds with the Church. But in time, as the Church grew more powerful, they came to see it as the public expression of Christianity, designed for the world at large, while the Brotherhood held the truth. The

Church was the shell, while the Brotherhood was the kernel. But now Migliau wants to change all that. He says the Pope has become Antichrist and that he, Migliau, is the true Pope, sent by God to unite the inward and the outward realms of faith. He is quite mad, you see. I think he would consider the Pope's solution for Lebanon a final betrayal. He might try to upset the plan in some way."

"I think he has started." Assefa explained what he and Patrick knew of Migliau's disappearance. The others listened in silence. Even if they could not understand why the cardinal had chosen to vanish, it was clear that his absence was not a coincidence, but a prelude to something more dramatic.

"You said you knew what Passover was," prompted Roberto. Assefa nodded.

"Yes," he said. "I think so. I can't tell you what they intend to do. But I think I can tell you when and where.

"Tomorrow the Pope will act as host to a public conference designed to pave the way for his mission in the Middle East. That's not how it will be presented, of course. Nothing will be said about Lebanon or any of the other projects, not even his hopes or fears or dreams. This will simply be a summit of Christian and Muslim leaders organized by the Secretariat for Non-Christian Religions.

"There will be the Pope himself, the cardinals representing the Secretariats for Non-Christian Religions and the Promotion of Christian Unity, bishops from Catholic dioceses throughout the Middle East, patriarchs of the Greek Catholic churches, representatives of the Maronite, Coptic, Armenian, and Assyrian Christian communities, Muslim shzikhs from the Azhar University in Cairo, Saudi ulema from Mecca and Medina, Ismaili leaders from Bombay and East Africa, and a Shi'ite mujtahid from Lebanon.

"At the opening ceremony, Mr. MacMaoláin will be present, along with the President of Egypt and ambassadors from several Muslim states."

"Did you say the President of Egypt?" O'Malley's face bore a look of deep concern. Assefa nodded.

"Do you remember the papyrus I showed you this morning?" asked the Irishman, turning to Patrick, who was seated on his left. "Do you recall what Simon the Levite said about Egypt?"

Patrick nodded numbly.

"Well, man, come on, what did he say?"

" '. . . if any still be alive . . . he shall go unto Egypt, which is Babylon, that he may strike down Pharaoh. . . .' I . . . I can't remember the rest."

" 'And that shall be the true Passover, that God's chosen people shall pass out of the land of Egypt and come into the Land of the Promise. . . . Egypt *shall fall then, and Babylon, all them that have scattered the children of God among the nations.'* I know the text well, Patrick. It's a good many times I've read it now. But, by God, it never made as much sense to me before as it does this instant."

There was a shocked silence as the meaning of the ancient words became clear. Simon and John and all the dispossessed of Jerusalem would have their revenge. A different pharaoh in a different age, yet perfect somehow for such a vengeance: the ruler of Egypt struck down side by side with the man who had inherited the mantle of the old Roman emperors. And struck down, for that matter, in Rome itself, the Babylon of so many apocalypses.

"Is there anything more we should know?" O'Malley asked at last, his tone subdued and hesitant for the first time since Patrick and Assefa had met him.

Assefa nodded.

"Yes. Two things. First, the conference is only going to last two days. All advance news of it has been kept a careful secret. The press will only be informed at the last possible moment. Just a few of the more important agencies and correspondents have been put on standby, without any details of what will take place. By the time hostile elements in Iran or Libya or Egypt can so much as react, the last session will have finished and the delegates will be on their way home. And the Holy Father will have won a major public relations success. He will be able to say that he has sown the seeds of Muslim-Christian unity, wiping out centuries of mutual distrust and bigotry in forty-eight hours. Whatever the fundamentalists on either side will say, he will have made a gesture for peace. Since Gorbachev came to power, the value of such gestures in international affairs has become very great."

He fell silent.

"You said there were two things."

Assefa hesitated.

"Yes," he said. "Two things. The second is this. At ten o'clock tomorrow morning, a special papal audience will be held in the Apostolic Palace, in the Sala Clementina. All the high-ranking delegates will be there, along with the Irish and Egyptian presidents and members of the Curia who will not be present at the actual conference. But the highlight of the audience will be an event which His Holiness hopes will win the hearts of men and women throughout the world."

He paused and closed his eyes for a moment.

"After he has greeted the dignitaries and seated them round the chamber, the Pope will welcome a party of orphans selected from every country of Europe and the Middle East, but chiefly from Italy and Egypt. Christian children and Muslim children, the hope of a new generation."

Assefa looked at the others one by one.

"Do you understand what I am saying?" he whispered. "Tomorrow morning, the Pope will give his blessing to over one hundred children."

No one said a word. From the street below, a faint sound of feet and voices and engines rose up to them, a thousand miles away, empty, without meaning. Assefa's final words seemed to echo and re-echo around the little room, filling it until there was space for nothing else.

Dermot O'Malley broke the silence. He sat in his chair without moving, listening to the echo wipe away the world outside.

" 'And it came to pass,' " he said in a flat voice from which all emotion had gone, " 'that at midnight the Lord smote all the firstborn in the land of Egypt, from the firstborn of Pharaoh that sat on his throne unto the firstborn of the captive that was in the dungeon.' "

But Patrick did not hear him. He sat rigid in his chair, staring ahead as though he saw something there in the dying afternoon light, a television screen, red and blue lights flashing, a child's face stained with blood, small teeth on bloodless lips, dead eyes, bodies like dolls, scattered across a patterned marble floor.

FORTY-FIVE

They were on the terrace at the rear of the apartment. O'Malley had gone with Assefa to the Vatican. Roberto was on his way to deliver sealed letters to several members of the government and the judiciary. There seemed to be nothing for either Patrick or Francesca to do but wait.

The last light had almost faded from the sky. A pair of kestrels were nesting in the gray dome of Sant' Andrea della Valle directly opposite. As they flew back and forth, their wings caught fire in a strip of sunlight that lay slantwise across the back of the dome.

"That's the male," said Patrick, pointing as one of the birds hovered briefly before darting away in search of fresh building material. "The one with blue wings."

"Yes," said Francesca. The birds set her on edge. She had never been that free, to wing effortlessly in unencumbered air, to turn feathers into light, to be the hunter, not the hunted. "They come here every year," she said. "They build a nest and hatch their chicks and fly away again."

She wished she could just flap a pair of wings and fly away with a kestrel's ease, away from Rome, from Italy, from the past.

"How did you find me?" he asked. "How did you come to follow me in Venice, the night I visited your father?"

She smiled. Not her old smile, he thought. That had gone forever. But another very much like it, wry, enigmatic—not in the manner of the Gioconda, but darker, as though it were not a smile at all but a mask embellishing fear. Fear and great sadness and longings that had grown stale and useless—motifs for an entire life. He thought of the alabaster white masks in Claudio Surian's workshop, the colored mask on his dead face, the *bautas* worn by the figures in his dreams, the elaborate costumes he and Francesca had worn at carnival the year before she died—an entire city cloaked and veiled and sworn to silence.

"Your arrival in Italy did not go unnoticed by the Brotherhood," she said. "They lost you in Rome and put out an alert to all their members. That was how we came to hear that you were here. At first I thought it was some sort of trap for me, but I couldn't understand how you could have become involved. And then we found out who Father Makonnen was and realized it made some sense after all.

"Anyway, I guessed you would go to Venice. The rest was easy. There were two places you could not avoid—my tomb on San Michele and the Palazzo Contarini. Brother Antonio told Dermot you had been on San Michele, and . . ."

"He knows?"

She nodded.

"Only a little. He's an old friend of Dermot's, they used to be in Rome together. Dermot once told him a little, asked for help. Since all burials in Venice take place on San Michele, he's been able to trace back many of the Dead for us, and through them their families. We've uncovered some very useful information that way."

She looked out toward the dome again. The light had gone completely now, leaving the sky a dark shade of purple, heavily bruised. The kestrels were gone. A sound of moving traffic rose up from the city below, like a beast at a zoo, circling its cage.

"So you were there that night, waiting for me?" he said.

"Yes. I was in the *calle* outside. I didn't expect you to catch sight of me in the mist, much less know who I was. I'd no idea then that you had found a photograph, that you guessed I might still be alive."

"You wouldn't have tried to speak to me?"

Her eyes widened.

"No, of course not. For all I knew, you thought I was dead. I still had no idea of the nature of your involvement. From your point of view, my sudden appearance might have been a terrible shock. From mine, there was a very real danger that you could lead them to me."

"But you took me to the hospital."

"Of course. When you called my name, I realized you must know or guess that I was alive. Then you collapsed. I couldn't just leave you there."

Her hand lay unmoving on the terrace railing. His rested beside it, close, yet not touching. Once, holding hands had been the simplest of gestures. But here, tonight, with a grave and a score of years between them, it would have seemed almost a sacrilege.

"I had someone else follow you when you left the hospital," she continued. "Did you know there was a policeman waiting for you?"

"Yes. Was he . . . ?"

She nodded.

"Matteo Maglione. He's their chief man in the Venice Carabinieri. He made a mistake going to the hospital himself. Our man recognized him and realized that you might try getting out the back way. He followed you to Porto Marghera.

"You made your own mistake, of course, when you started asking questions on Burano, trying to find someone to take you to San Vitale. They were on to you straight away. Fortunately, we were just behind them. Too late to save the old fisherman; but at least we got you both off. You took a great risk going there."

"You did as much," he said.

She shrugged.

"I've grown used to it. I don't expect to live forever." She shivered. "Let's go in," she said. "It's getting cold."

They went to the kitchen and made coffee. They needed something to do, something to distract them from the tension of waiting. Above all, there was an unspoken agreement between them not to enter into a discussion of what had happened twenty years ago. For Patrick, grief was beginning to slide into outrage at what had, in the final analysis, been nothing more nor less than a betrayal. If Francesca had left him for another man, his life might never have been as damaged as it had been by her supposed death.

She may have been resurrected, but nothing that happened now could give life back to the years he had wasted grieving for her. Nor, he thought, could anything give new life to the love she had destroyed. Perhaps she had been blameless, the victim of pressures she was powerless to resist. But he was in no position to judge. With a shock, he realized that he had already started to resent the fact that she was still alive. So much of his life had been built around her death, so much of him had been buried with her empty coffin, that he wondered if he could find the energy to make sense of what had after all turned out to be a fraud.

He told her what he could of his life after leaving university, omitting all references to his state of mind. In consequence, all he said was curiously gray and barren, a numb recitation of facts, as though compiled by an agency about someone else. He passed over his wife and children in a few short sentences, said little of his work with the CIA, and simply concentrated on places he had been and people he had known. So much was left unmentioned: his feelings after Francesca's death, the women he had pursued in a desperate attempt to mitigate his grief, the destruction he had inflicted on his marriage day after day until it had grown pale and sick beyond help, the final, protracted struggle with his conscience that had led him to part company with the Agency.

She gave little in return. Mostly, she talked about FRATERNITÀ—how she had come to hear about it, the help they had given her, the work she had done for them in return. Even if Passover had not happened, she told him, they would eventually have taken their expanding file on the Brotherhood to the Public Prosecutor.

"Do you remember P2?" she asked.

He shook his head.

"Only the most basic facts. And I've forgotten most of those."

"The scandal broke in 1981, while I was still in the Brotherhood. In 1966, a man called Licio Gelli organized a Masonic lodge called Raggruppamento Gelli Propaganda Due, P2 for short. By various means, he succeeded in getting some of the most powerful men in the country to join. Members of the Cabinet, several former prime ministers, top civil servants, almost two hundred senior military men, bankers, magistrates, university professors. In their way, they were almost as powerful as the Brotherhood, except that not even Gelli knew that we existed or that his entire organization had already been infiltrated by us.

"Anyway, in 1980 one of Gelli's close friends, a banker named Michele Sindona, was under investigation for fraud. Gelli got mixed up in the case, his villa was raided, and papers were found, including the P2 membership files. It turned into the biggest political crisis in Italy since the war. The Prime Minister resigned and the government collapsed."

She paused and rubbed her forehead as though the tension was giving her a headache.

"Roberto used to talk a lot about the P2 affair. He'd studied it in detail and thought our best plan would be to expose the Brotherhood in the same way. But we had to be in an unassailable position first. We couldn't afford to go public while there were still powerful Brotherhood members unknown to us. The authorities had been lucky with P2: the lists they found at Gelli's villa contained almost one thousand names, the entire membership of the lodge. Short of a miracle, we have no way of obtaining a list like that for the Brotherhood. As far as I know, none exists.

"We have our own files, of course. They're stored in duplicate copies in three separate bank vaults, and Roberto has a master set on computer discs that are kept in a secure location. We're guessing a little, but we think our list is nearly complete. What we have been looking for over the past two years is hard evidence of the Brotherhood's activities. All we need is enough to convince one or two people in the right positions that a series of synchronized raids would be justified: the rest of our evidence would turn up then.

"Your friend Eamonn De Faoite worked for us. He started out translating some things from Aramaic, then he branched out for himself, tracking down the Brotherhood in Ireland. There have always been links. That's why I was sent to Trinity to study."

She hesitated. This was coming close to an awkward subject.

"It wasn't intended originally that I should be one of the Dead. That privilege had been reserved for my older brother, Umberto. But . . . Umberto really was killed in an accident, and I had to take his place. They didn't tell me until I got to Venice. I tried to . . . contact you, I . . ." She closed her eyes, the pain of the memory returning. "They stopped me. I had to leave at once, I had to go to Egypt."

She paused.

"I'm sorry. I didn't mean to talk about this. Not yet."

"It's all right."

She took several deep breaths.

"Eamonn . . . I was talking about Eamonn. He was the first to stumble across references to Passover." She paused. "You say he sent papers to Balzarin?"

"Yes."

"I see. Yes, that makes sense. He told us he had information, but that it was incomplete. I think he mentioned that he had a possible source for more. I remember now that he said Balzarin had approached him, hinting that he knew something about the Brotherhood. We had nothing on Balzarin here. I think maybe Eamonn gave his file on the Brotherhood to him in an attempt to find out more about Passover."

"What about this man Father O'Malley has taken Assefa to see? This cardinal. Can he be relied on?"

"Dermot says he can. Good God, Patrick, we never meant it to be rushed like this. Roberto wanted us to take our time, to muster our forces, get all the ammunition we could, approach several people in positions of influence simultaneously. He was patient, in spite of . . ."

She stopped and stood up abruptly. For a moment, she stood staring at the door, as though uncertain, then she walked into the next room. Patrick followed her, uncomprehending. She was standing by the window.

"They're late," she said. "Dermot and Roberto both said they would ring as soon as they were in a position to report back. I'm worried."

"It's still early," Patrick said. "Only gone eight." But he was worried too. They should have been in touch. There had been an arrangement for them to telephone from the Vatican.

"In the kitchen," he went on, "you said that Roberto was patient in spite of something. Then you broke off."

"Did I?"

"Yes."

She did not answer. With her hands flat against the pane, she rested her cheek on the cold window. Beyond the glass, the sound of traffic was muffled. There was a stillness in the night, a quietness that seemed to have its origin in her, as though she were the calm point in a storm.

"We were lovers once," she said, her voice hushed, her breath clouding the windowpane. "Not like you and me, Patrick. With Roberto, it was . . . quieter. Less happy, often sad. But after so long away from the world, he brought me back to it. He showed me how to live again. That wasn't easy. It took all our energy. There was very little time for love."

She looked out into the night, and for the first time he sensed how lost she was, like a child waking from a dream to find herself in a strange bedroom.

"We'd both had our gods and lost them," she went on, "and we understood that well enough, I think. But he had danced and sung for his god, while I had wept and bled for mine. I had no understanding of his rapture, he mistook my tears for blindness.

"But we made a certain happiness for each other. A sort of balance. Is that the right word? Not like scales, I don't mean that, one weight lying against another. It was more like . . . a tightrope walker, someone who finds balance only by constant movement, who will fall to his death if he remains still for more than a moment. We were like that, always moving, always seeking a new point of equilibrium."

One hand stretched out and brushed the glass, wiping away a film of misted breath like gauze. There were bars across the window, heavy bars designed to keep intruders out. She looked past them as though this apartment had been, not a refuge, but a prison for her.

"Perhaps if we had been more like weights, it would have lasted longer. I don't know. Our balance was too fine, too imperfect, and we lost it in the end. Roberto became too involved in his investigation of the Brotherhood. He let it become his life. But I was just the opposite, you see. It had already been my life, I was trying to put it behind me, to find new ways to live. We might have found a balance there, I can't say. But it was already too late anyway. Roberto's sick. He doesn't have long to live."

FORTY-SIX

As they drove to the Vatican, Assefa tried to pray, but his thoughts were too jumbled to fashion even the simplest of supplications. They hurried through familiar streets grown unfamiliar. Nothing seemed quite real or habitual. Everything had changed subtly: the streets, the shops, the cafes, the people. Rome had become a film set, a mere pastiche of a city, its inhabitants extras in a bad movie. He could not believe that here, somewhere in these streets, there were men and women preparing such a monstrous slaughter.

O'Malley had made several phone calls before setting off. He was leaving nothing to chance. He wanted to speak to the right people, but he had to take great care that what he said was not reported to anyone connected to the Brotherhood, least of all Cardinal Fazzini or any of the other members of the Curia known to be members. Unfortunately, O'Malley knew that this was scarcely the moment to go lobbing accusations against cardinals. Fazzini was closely involved in the preparations for tomorrow's ceremony. To leave the Secretary of State and his department out of discussions about security would be a major breach of etiquette.

The priest hoped he could persuade a small handful of individuals to take personal responsibility for whatever had to be done. Fortunately, he believed he had identified the right people.

Colonel Hans Meyer, the commander of the Swiss Guard, had immediate responsibility for Vatican security. Those of his men not actually carrying out ceremonial duties tomorrow would be carrying Uzis instead of halberds. It was vital for them to be ready to react to an attack from whatever quarter it might be launched. O'Malley was confident that Meyer and his men could be trusted completely. From several sources he had confirmed that the Brotherhood had never been able to infiltrate the Swiss Guard.

True, the old Noble Guard, Palatine Guard, and Papal Gendarmerie had harbored several Brothers in every generation, but they had been abolished by Paul VI in 1970 and, as far as O'Malley had been able to ascertain, had bequeathed no legacy of that corruption to the Swiss. Meyer himself had been born and bred in Lucerne, an area seemingly free of Brotherhood influence. He could be trusted.

Overall responsibility for security lay with Cardinal John Fischer, president of the Vatican's Central Security Office. Fischer was as clean as a whistle. Born in Chicago to German immigrants, he had worked his way up the Catholic hierarchy there under Cardinal John Cody. All they had had in common was their first name. As soon as he was able, Fischer had left Chicago to work for Catholic Relief Services in the Third World: Africa, the Philippines, Mexico. In the early seventies, shortly after Cor Unum had been set up to coordinate Catholic charity work, he had been called to Rome to serve on its board. Once in the Vatican, his considerable abilities as an administrator had led to repeated preferments. His move to Security five years earlier had been seen as a major step toward closer involvement with the papal household.

Finally, O'Malley had left a message for Monsignor Giuseppe Foucauld, the Pope's private secretary. Born in Rome of Italian-French parents, Foucauld was one of the most powerful men in the Vatican. He had the Holy Father's trust, and anything that was destined for the Pope's ear had to pass through his first. O'Malley had still not decided whether or not the Pope should be told of the plot or, for that matter, of the Brotherhood itself. In the long run, he would have to know, of course. But O'Malley was frightened of the consequences of a premature revelation.

A meeting had been set up in the cardinal's office, on the second floor of the Governor's Palace, a long four-story building behind St. Peter's which serves as the city hall of the Vatican State. O'Malley had suggested this venue himself, thinking it better to meet there, away from curious eyes in the Apostolic Palace. The Brotherhood would be on the lookout tonight.

They drove straight through the Arco delle Campane to the left of St. Peter's: the guards on duty at the gate were expecting them. A few moments later, O'Malley parked in front of the Governorato. He took a large bundle of papers from the rear seat and stepped out.

The cardinal was waiting for them in a private reception room behind his office. The building was quiet: all staff except for security personnel had left for the day. A young priest escorted them upstairs, gave them directions, and left discreetly.

Fischer greeted them himself, advancing with an outstretched hand and a warm smile. He was a cheerful-looking man in his early sixties. Over the years, he had put on more weight than was altogether good for him, but he managed to carry it with dignity. His skullcap was perched far to the back of his head, giving him a rather jaunty appearance.

"Father O'Malley? I'm pleased to meet you at last. I've heard a great deal about your work. You may not know it, but we've crossed paths more

than once. Used to have problems with new religions out in Africa—
Kimbanguists, Aladura, all those native churches. Pretty crazy. But the
worst are the new cults getting into the old mission fields. Jehovah's Witnesses, Mormons, Baha'is. Your people used to give us a lot of help." He
shook hands firmly, then turned to Assefa.

"*Tenastilliñ. Indamin adderu.*"

"*Dahina,*" answered Assefa.

"I'm afraid that's about the extent of my Amharic," said the cardinal,
smiling broadly. "I'm sorry, I don't think Father O'Malley mentioned your
name."

"Makonnen. Father Assefa Makonnen."

"I'm pleased to meet you, Father Makonnen. Are you attached to Father
O'Malley's office?"

Assefa shook his head.

"No, Your Eminence, I'm . . ."

"Father Makonnen will explain who he is later," interrupted O'Malley.
"I think it would make more sense that way. There are some things I have
to explain first."

The cardinal raised his eyebrows.

"You sure believe in keeping things mysterious, Father. You weren't too
forthcoming on the phone either."

"No. No, I wasn't. I . . ." O'Malley hesitated. "Your Eminence, have
Colonel Meyer and Monsignor Foucauld got here yet? I'd rather not start
without them."

Fischer glanced at his wrist.

"I'm expecting the colonel any minute now. Monsignor Foucauld sends
his apologies and says he'll be joining us later. He's having dinner with the
Holy Father tonight. They have a few important guests, so he can't really
get away until about ten. Do you mind if we start without him? I have some
very important business to attend to myself tonight."

"Well, it's about that I've come. The . . ."

There was a loud knock on the door. A moment later it opened and a tall
man dressed in the gaudy Renaissance uniform of a Swiss Guard entered
the room. He saluted the cardinal, then the others.

"Hans, come on in."

The cardinal stepped forward, drawing the colonel into the room.

"Hans, this is Father Dermot O'Malley, the director of FRATERNITÀ.
You know? The guys who deal with the Moonies and loonies for us. And
this is Assefa Makonnen. Father Makonnen's some sort of mystery man.
But not for long, I'm assured."

Once the introductions were finished, the American had them draw up
easy chairs round a small table.

"Can I get you something to drink? I've got some great Scotch my brother sent me for New Year. No? Nothing? Well, let me get one for myself. I'll be right back."

"Before we start, Your Eminence," O'Malley broke in, "would you mind if I made a telephone call?"

"Sure, be my guest. There's a phone right over there. Is it an outside line?"

O'Malley nodded.

"You'll have to go through the switchboard. Just give them the number. They'll put you through."

While the cardinal fixed his whiskey, Father O'Malley made his call to Francesca. He explained briefly where he was and promised to ring again before leaving.

Cardinal Fischer came back to his seat, an ice-filled tumbler in hand.

"Who was that, Father?"

"Oh, just a friend who might be anxious about me."

"Anxious? You're not in any trouble, are you?"

"No more than any of us, Your Eminence. But it's trouble I've come about this evening. Serious trouble. I have evidence of a plot against the life of the Holy Father."

The cardinal put down his glass. He looked keenly at O'Malley, then at Assefa.

"I think you'd better tell us all you know, Father."

It took a long time. Now that he had made his knowledge public, O'Malley took care not to throw everything away by rushing. He took Fischer and Meyer step by step through the evidence he had collated, showing them documents to back up each statement. The more bizarre features of the Brotherhood and its history he left till last, saving them until his audience had been well prepared. Finally, with Assefa's help, he outlined what he believed to be the scenario for the morning.

"I have no proof that this is what they intend. Perhaps we have leaped to conclusions. But I'd rather be safe than sorry. It can do no harm to step up security for the audience tomorrow, even to call it off. The Holy Father's life is at risk, I'm certain of it."

The cardinal nodded.

"Yes, Father, I think you're right. You've made a very good case for yourself. Your evidence is extremely convincing." He turned to Colonel Meyer, who was seated on his right. "Do you agree, Colonel?"

Meyer said nothing at first. He picked up some papers from the table and examined them carefully. Finally, he laid them down and looked up.

"Yes," he said. "I can't comment on most of this, it's outside my competence. But you've told me enough to make me very worried indeed. There isn't time to organize fresh security. I'd have to bring in the Carabinieri's antiterrorist unit, the GIS. But they're already up in Venice handling this Migliau business. I'd say we have to look very seriously at calling off tomorrow morning's audience."

"You don't think that's a little alarmist, Colonel?" Cardinal Fischer leaned across the table. "I'm pretty sure Father O'Malley's right about this thing, about this Brotherhood. But surely you have enough men at your disposal to handle any threat they may pose. Your men are well trained and well armed. Now you know the danger, you can seal off the Sala Clementina."

"I'm sorry, Your Eminence, but I'd prefer not to do that. If there is some sort of assault, I may lose men holding it off. Innocent bystanders could be hurt. As a professional soldier, I can't recommend any other course of action: the audience must be called off. But I will need your authority to persuade the Holy Father. Perhaps Monsignor Foucauld could be asked to expect us and to arrange for us to see the Pope at once."

The cardinal seemed to hesitate for a moment.

"Very well. I'll see what I can do."

He picked up the telephone.

"Interno due, per favore."

There was a pause, then a voice came on the line.

"Monsignor Foucauld, please. Tell him this is Cardinal Fischer. Thank you."

Another pause, a longer one this time.

"Hello, is that you, Giuseppe? . . . John Fischer here. I've got Father Dermot O'Malley with me. He spoke with you earlier tonight, asking for a meeting. . . . That's right. . . . Yes, I know. Look, Giuseppe, I've had a long chat with him and Colonel Meyer. There's really nothing to worry about. . . . No, nothing at all. A false alarm. I'm sure His Holiness is tired. There's no need to worry him tonight. Everything can go ahead in the morning as planned. . . . The same to you, Giuseppe. Please give the Holy Father my greetings. I'll be praying that everything goes as planned tomorrow. I'm sure it'll be a great success. *Ciao.*"

Meyer was already on his feet by the time the cardinal replaced the receiver.

"I . . . Your Eminence, what . . . is the meaning of this? We agreed that the Holy Father's life may be in danger. I must protest. Please let me speak to Monsignor Foucauld."

"Please sit down, Colonel. There's no reason to be upset. Everything's under control."

The cardinal reached for a second telephone, a white office model, and dialed a single digit. It rang briefly, then a voice answered. Fischer said, "Could you come up now, please?" and replaced the handset.

No one spoke. Assefa glanced at O'Malley nervously. He could not understand how it was possible for Cardinal Fischer not to believe their story. They had evidence. Assefa had provided full details of events in Dublin. What more could the cardinal want? He glanced at the American.

The cardinal sat impassively, his hands folded calmly in his ample lap. His red-piped soutane was perfectly creased. His shoes were immaculately polished. His rosy cheeks glowed with contentment. He seemed like a large wax doll.

Assefa's eye was drawn by something on the wall, just behind Fischer's head. It was the cardinal's personal coat of arms, painted on a ceramic plate. Assefa had noticed it several times that evening, but now it was as though he saw it properly for the first time.

At the center of the heraldic design, beneath a red cardinal's hat with long, hanging tassels, sat a broad shield. And in the center of the shield a man stood upright in the prow of a small boat, one arm raised high above his head, about to cast a net on the water.

Fischer. Fisher. *Il Pescatore.* The fisherman.

FORTY-SEVEN

The door opened. Two priests stepped into the room and inclined their heads toward the cardinal. They were carrying small submachine guns in what seemed a very professional manner.

"Colonel Meyer," Fischer said, "I regret to inform you that you are being placed under arrest. If you would be so kind as to accompany these gentlemen, they will see you are treated properly."

"Verfluchte Scheisse!" Meyer spluttered and leaped out of his chair. At the door, there was a sound of bolts being drawn back.

"I demand to know what you think you're playing at," the colonel raged. "You have no authority to do this. Who are these men? No one but my Guard is authorized to carry arms here. I don't care if you . . ."

"Take him away." Fischer waved a dismissive hand at Meyer. The priests—if priests they were—stepped forward and grabbed the colonel roughly, each one taking an arm. Before he had time for further protest, he had been bundled through the door. It slammed behind them. There was a sound of footsteps clicking across the marble floor outside, followed by another door slamming, then silence.

Fischer leaned back in his easy chair.

"So," he said, smiling first at O'Malley, then at Makonnen. "What am I going to do with you two?"

"Absolutely nothing at all," the Irishman replied. "And, contrary to expectations, you're going to have Colonel Meyer brought back here. He is going to make his telephone call to Monsignor Foucauld after all."

"Is he indeed? I'm interested to hear that. Perhaps you could tell me why you think that is."

O'Malley gestured toward the table.

"What do you see there, Your Eminence?" There was more than a hint of sarcasm in the way O'Malley used the title. "A list of names, documentary evidence of their connection to an organization called the Brotherhood of the Tomb, documents proving that this Brotherhood exists. As valuable a bundle of papers as ever existed, don't you agree? Now, did you think I'd come here tonight bringing the only copies in existence? Did you imagine I was that trusting?"

He paused and reached for the list of names. He lifted it from the table and waved it in front of Fischer's face.

"Copies of this list, together with Xeroxes of every relevant piece of documentation, have been deposited in the vaults of three major Italian banks. I have prepared letters for the Public Prosecutor, the Minister of Justice, the Prime Minister, and the editors of *Il Tempo, Messaggero,* and the *Giornale d'Italia.* By now, they will all have been delivered by hand by a colleague of mine."

He laid the list back on the table.

"Now," he said, "I want you to listen carefully. If you do not contact each of the individuals I have mentioned by seven o'clock tomorrow morning, they have instructions to open the envelopes. Equally, if any major act of terrorism should occur anywhere in Italy within the next few days, they will open the envelopes. In any event, they will under no circumstances destroy them. Inside, as you will have guessed, they will discover my letter, together with written authorization to open the vaults and extract the documents I have deposited in them.

"Do you understand? You can harm me or not, as you choose. You can go ahead with your plan for tomorrow morning, knowing that it may be preempted. In either case, your Brotherhood is finished. Migliau is on that list. Fazzini. Well, you have seen for yourself. I'm sure you can complete the rest."

He let out a deep sigh.

"It's finished, Your Eminence. It's all over."

Fischer said nothing. He sat watching O'Malley, his eyes unblinking. At the end of a minute, still silent, he got up. He walked slowly into an adjoining room. Another minute passed, then he reappeared. In his arms he was carrying a large pile of papers, all packed in neat brown files and tied with string.

"Are these the papers you mean, Father O'Malley?"

He put the files down on the table. O'Malley stared at them like a man who has just been shown an open grave and told that it is his own. The life seemed to have gone out of him. His body sagged, his head bent, his shoulders seemed bowed beneath an intolerable weight.

There was a knock at the door.

"*Avanti!*" Fischer called.

The door opened and a thin man dressed in the robes of a cardinal stepped into the room.

"Tommaso, please come in," said Fischer, welcoming him. "We were just talking about you."

"Really?" The new arrival raised his eyebrows. "How flattering."

"I don't think you know Father Dermot O'Malley."

"But I've heard so much about him." The stranger held out his hand, waiting for O'Malley to rise and kiss his ring. But the Irishman did not move.

"I see we have forgotten our manners." The cardinal lowered his hand.

"And this," said Fischer, "is Father Makonnen. I think you already know one another."

Assefa said nothing. He knew Fazzini well enough.

"Please, Tommaso, come and have a drink."

"Just a fruit juice for me, please. I've been dining with the Holy Father. My mind should be clear for tomorrow."

"Of course, of course."

Fazzini took a comfortable chair beside Fischer.

"And how was the Holy Father?"

"Fine, fine. He has great hopes for tomorrow, great hopes. Oh, by the way, before I forget. I dropped into my office before coming over. I have the letters you wanted."

He reached inside his soutane and drew out a bundle of about half a dozen thick envelopes. Father O'Malley closed his eyes as though in pain.

"Thank you, Tommaso. I've dealt with Meyer. I think we've taken care of everything." He glanced at his wrist. "Ah, you're just in time for the news bulletin."

He stood and went across to a small television set in the corner. It warmed up in seconds. He switched it to the local channel and returned to his seat.

They did not have to wait long. Half a minute later, a female announcer appeared. The second item was the first public announcement of tomorrow's audience and the conference that would follow it. A photograph of the Pope greeting Presidents MacMaoláin and Mirghani was followed by film of other dignitaries arriving at Fiumicino airport. A professor from Rome's Istituto di Studi Orientali mumbled platitudes about Muslim-Christian relations, only to be outdone by a spokesman from the SNCR, the Secretariat for Non-Christian Religions, who managed to slip in quotations from St. Francis, the Koran, and Hermann Hesse.

Fischer did not switch off after the piece came to an end. He made them sit and watch the rest of the local news: an item about housing in the EUR, another about a by-election, and one on the price of salami. Finally, the announcer shuffled her papers and came to the last item.

"News has just reached us of a road accident in the city involving a fatality. A car with a single driver collided with a heavy lorry in the Via del Corso, not far from the Palazzo Chigi. First reports indicate that the car skidded into the path of the lorry and was crushed on impact. The driver of the car was dead on arrival at San Giovanni Hospital. His name has just been released by the Vigili Urbani. He was Roberto Quadri, a lawyer who worked for a Catholic organization for ex-convicts. The driver of the lorry is reported to be unhurt. There are no further details at this time.

"And that's all for this evening. We'll be on the air again tomorrow at seven with the first news bulletin of the day. There will be a full report on the papal audience and full coverage of the event at ten. Please join us then."

Fischer used a remote-control device to turn the set off. The room filled with an unhurried silence. Dermot O'Malley did not move. Tears ran down his cheeks, but he did not lift a hand to wipe them away.

"What about that other matter, Tommaso? Has it been taken care of as well?"

"Oh, yes—the American and the Contarini girl. I have men on their way there now. It shouldn't take long."

O'Malley looked up. All the gentleness had gone from his face as though it had never been. In its place was a look of blind rage mixed with pain. He threw his head back and roared at the top of his voice, then leaped to his feet, grabbing for Fazzini, toppling the old man from his chair. They fell together, O'Malley on top, his anger overpowering, his hands on the cardinal's neck.

Fischer stood and reached a hand inside his soutane. He took out a small handgun, took two steps toward O'Malley, kicked him off Fazzini, and shot him twice. The big Irishman was thrown backward by the force of the shots. He looked at Fischer with a puzzled expression, raised himself on one elbow, and tried to stand. Fischer fired again, two more shots. O'Malley fell back again, choking. Fischer helped Fazzini back to his chair. When he looked round again, O'Malley was on his knees in a pool of blood, reaching for a chair to pull himself up. The American raised the gun.

"No!" shouted Assefa. The Ethiopian ran for Fischer, grabbing at his wrist. The cardinal swung his arm round, striking him hard across the cheek with the gun barrel. Assefa staggered and fell back against an armchair. O'Malley was on his feet now. With a roar, he made a lunge for Fischer. The American emptied the rest of the magazine, three shots in quick succession. O'Malley collapsed face downward and lay still.

FORTY-EIGHT

She looked away from the window, into the room, but her eyes did not meet Patrick's.

"Three years ago," she said, "he was diagnosed as suffering from AIDS. His doctor told him he had about a year to eighteen months to live. He was shattered at first. For a month or more, he went about like a zombie, as though he'd lost interest in everything and was just waiting to die. And then, quite suddenly, he changed. He'd found out that he could fight it, that a diagnosis of AIDS wasn't a death sentence, whatever his doctors said.

"There were scores of people in the United States who'd lived seven, eight years with the disease. Some of them were completely free of symptoms, living normal lives. What they had in common was a decision not to give in. They meditated, practiced visualization, had acupuncture, herbal remedies—anything that might turn their immune systems round and give them a fighting chance. That sounds incredible. You'd think it should make headlines. But the media aren't interested. They want people to die of AIDS. What use is an epidemic if some of its victims won't lie down?

"It's the same with the doctors. Roberto's already outlived their predictions, but every time he tells them what he's doing, it's as if a wall comes down. They don't want to know about people getting better outside their control."

She sighed.

"The way he's been fighting, by now he should be like some of those people in America, living a normal life again. But any energy he gains, he uses up fighting the Brotherhood. That's what's killing him now, not AIDS. Isn't that stupid?"

She turned back to the window.

"I think of all those people out there, frightened to death of AIDS. They'd come to believe a myth, you see, that medicine could cure them of anything. And then AIDS came along and they were powerless again. But AIDS is just a word, just four letters: they're dying of four letters. They think a virus is killing them, but it isn't. People with healthy immune systems can catch the virus and hardly notice it. It's people who are already tuned in to death who die of AIDS. And our whole society encourages them. Their priests tell them they're sinners and deserve to die. Their doctors say they're incurable. The media treat them like lepers.

"I've already been dead, I know just what it's like to be outside the world. That's how Roberto felt when they first told him he had AIDS, as though he'd been taken to a door and pushed through, never to be let back again.

"That's why we have to destroy Migliau and the Brotherhood if we can. They stand for death, they believe sacrifice is essential to survival, they think there's nothing wrong in shedding innocent blood in search of salvation. Migliau is willing to put any number to death for the sake of the few. It's like the medical profession. They don't want people to die. And yet they'll let thousands die of AIDS sooner than admit they're wrong. 'See,' they say, 'without us you're helpless. Believe in us, give us power, and we'll grant you salvation.'

"Priests are the same. A woman's life is in danger, she needs an abortion—what do they tell her? 'Your child's life is more important than yours, you have to be sacrificed so it can live.' People are starving, they need contraceptives; but the priests tell them God will be angry if they use them.

"That's why Migliau is so dangerous. The world makes a special place for people like him. He'll find scapegoats everywhere: AIDS victims, Muslims, the poor, anyone who doesn't fit into his new order. They'll all become sacrifices, and people will stand around and applaud. 'It's a hygienic measure,' he'll say. 'Wipe out the viruses and health will be yours. Destroy the cancer cells and you'll live forever.' It wouldn't be so bad if it was just a metaphor. But it isn't: he wants real blood on his altar. Tomorrow will be just the beginning if we don't stop him."

She stopped.

"I'm sorry," she said. "This isn't what you wanted to talk about. We . . ."

"Shhhhh."

He raised a hand.

"What is it?"

"I thought I heard something. Is there another way into this apartment?"

She looked round, startled.

"You think . . . ?" She hesitated. "There are just two entrances: the main door from the stairs and the side door to the fire escape."

"Which way is that?" He spoke in a low whisper, drawing her away from the door.

She pointed.

"Along the passage to the left."

"Okay. Go out to the terrace and wait for me there."

She shook her head.

"Thanks, but I'd prefer to stay."

He took her by the shoulders.

"Please, Francesca, don't argue. I know how to handle myself. You haven't been trained."

She raised an eyebrow.

"Oh? And what do you suppose they taught us out there in the desert? How to knit?"

There was a definite sound outside.

"Quickly," she hissed. "Through here!"

She took his hand and pulled him to the kitchen. Hurriedly, she opened the cupboard beneath the sink and drew out a roll of sacking.

"Here!" she said, thrusting it into Patrick's hands. He unrolled it to find a Beretta 92SBF pistol.

"It's loaded," she whispered. "Fifteen rounds." She had already un-packed a second gun for herself.

There was a loud crash as the door of the living room was kicked open. Through the frosted glass door of the kitchen, Patrick could see a human figure move into the room. Patrick reached for the door handle. He was about to turn it when the glass exploded in his face, blown to pieces by a round of machine-gun fire just above his head. He fell back, dropping his gun. The fire from the living room continued, raking the kitchen, smashing plates and glasses, tearing the cupboards to shreds.

Francesca threw herself to the floor on top of Patrick, lifting her gun in two hands. The gunman's head was visible through the hole where the glass had been. She fired quickly, before he changed his angle of fire. Her bullet sliced his cheek.

She rolled for the door, crashing hard against it, twisting sideways behind the wall. A blast of fire raked the floor behind Patrick's legs. Francesca reached behind her, pulling Patrick out of the line of fire into the shelter of the wall. A third burst from the machine gun smashed the door apart and plowed up the floor immediately behind it, where she and Patrick had been seconds before.

There was a pause. Francesca heard the sound of a magazine being withdrawn. She leaped to her feet, aimed through the hole in the door, and fired a succession of shots at the point from which the shooting had come. There was a cry followed by a heavy crash.

Someone shouted from one of the bedrooms.

"Paolo! *Che succede?*"

"Quickly!" Francesca helped Patrick to his feet. Blood was streaming down his face. "Are you all right? Can you see?"

He nodded. "I'm okay. Not . . . badly hurt. Just cut."

"Let's get out of here," she said. His gun was on the floor where he had dropped it. She picked it up and handed it to him.

They were halfway across the living room when a second man appeared in the doorway. He wore a black hood over his face and carried a Steyr AUG assault rifle in a gloved hand. He took in the scene with a single glance and ducked back behind the doorjamb.

Francesca moved to the left behind an armchair, Patrick to the right, throwing a coffee table over for a barricade. The gunman opened fire on Francesca. Heavy-duty 5.56mm bullets tore the top of the chair away in a matter of seconds. She fired back round the side of the chair, but her shots went high, splintering the top of the door frame.

Patrick caught sight of a second man entering the passage from the bedroom beside the fire escape. He fired on him half a second too late. The first man fired a second burst into the chair, forcing Francesca to roll out from behind it, toward the wall. The gunman saw her move and swung his weapon, trying to follow the same arc, but as he did so Patrick fired twice through the thin partition wall. There was a cry and the man toppled into the room.

"Be careful, Francesca! There's a third one in the passage!"

The third man had disappeared. But they knew that, if he was going to fire, he would have to come to the door. They made a run for the wall on either side of the door, flattening themselves against it.

Patrick saw a hand reach round the jamb, caught sight of something flying through the air. Seconds later, there was a blinding flash accompanied by a loud explosion. Patrick staggered back, clutching his hands to his ears, dropping his gun to the floor. Francesca cried out, firing wildly. A second stun grenade followed, knocking her flat against the wall.

Patrick fought against the dizziness, trying to get to his knees. He could not tell which way was up and which down. The room seemed to be pulsating, fluttering, rippling in long, swirling waves. He could not see or hear. He reached out for something to grab hold of. There was a hand, someone had hold of him. And then the hand was gone and he was tumbling like a brick down a well that had no bottom and no top and no sides of the darkest night.

FORTY-NINE

It was the smell that brought him round. That or the heat. His head felt as though someone had filled it with cement and closed the lid with a bang. His first thought was that he was still in the crypt on San Vitale, then he remembered Francesca and Rome and the attack on the apartment.

He groaned and tried to open his eyes. They felt sticky. He reached up a hand and touched them gingerly. His fingers came away wet. The next moment, he was coughing violently and trying to sit up. His lungs were full of smoke, and however hard he tried, he could not find any air. He managed to open his eyes a fraction. Light hit him like a tank meeting plate glass. He blinked rapidly. The smoke was thick and acrid, and it stung.

The room was full of it, heavy black smoke shot with flashes of orange and purple flame. The smell was kerosene. Kerosene and smoke. All around him, the flames were catching hold with alarming rapidity. His legs felt like jelly rolls, and he was certain he was going to die. He fought to keep his eyes open long enough to sort out where he was. Bizarrely, a standard lamp in the corner was still lit, glowing smugly to itself as though all around it were normal. The smoke and flames disoriented him.

Francesca! Where was Francesca? It came to him vividly that he had last seen her on the other side of the room, where she had rolled out of the second gunman's line of fire. How long had passed since the attack?

He tried to call her name, but the second he opened his mouth he started choking on smoke. Groaning, he began to crawl forward in what he prayed was the right direction, keeping his mouth as near to the floor as possible. There was just enough air at floor level to keep him alive. Behind him, he could hear the sound of flames licking greedily at fabric and woodwork. His head felt detached from his body, slamming round the room as though held on a length of elastic.

The area between him and the door was a mass of spreading flame. To his right, the only window to the street was fitted with iron bars half an inch thick. The apartment was a death trap.

There was no way out through the kitchen: its only window was ten feet off the floor and just big enough to spit through. There was no way out. Unless . . .

His fingers touched something soft. He pressed harder and the softness moved.

"Fran . . . cesca . . . Is . . . that . . . you?" he coughed.

There was silence, then a hoarse voice came out of the darkness.

"*Sì.* . . . Patrick . . . What happened?"

"Stun grenade. . . . Don't . . . talk. . . . Got to . . . get . . . to kitchen. . . . Make a . . . run . . . for it."

He took her arm and helped her to a kneeling position. They got what air they could into their lungs, then stumbled toward the spot where the kitchen should be. The curtains were blazing now. Some of the furniture had caught fire. Patrick remembered how quickly Styrofoam fires could kill. He prayed the chairs had been stuffed with horsehair.

The kitchen door was useless as a barrier. Patrick staggered to the food cupboard. FRATERNITÀ had been short of funds: instead of a door, the cupboard was curtained. Patrick ripped it from the hooks that held it to the frame.

"Help me . . . fill the . . . sink."

Together, they threw everything out of the sink: dishes, pans, cutlery. Francesca turned on both taps full. In the room outside, something exploded, tight and angry, like a tiny bomb.

At first Patrick thought the curtain was not going to take up the water. It was dusty and covered with grease on the side that had been turned toward a thousand meals prepared with olive oil. It was like trying to soak a waterproof. Water splashed everywhere, drenching them, forming a puddle on the floor and the broken plates. They pummeled the cloth, swearing aloud at it in English and Italian, willing it to soak up enough water. The smoke was growing denser now. Acrid and poisonous. There wasn't much time. And they still did not know what the passage to the front door was going to be like.

It seemed to take centuries, but at last the curtain was as wet as it was ever going to be. They lifted it dripping from the sink and struggled to disentangle it. Patrick's head felt like a builder's yard; he wasn't sure his legs would take him more than a few feet.

Lifting a large spaghetti pan from the floor, he filled it again and again with water from the tap, pouring it over Francesca, then himself, dowsing them until their clothes and skin were sopping wet.

Holding the water-heavy curtain ready to throw over their heads, they turned for the doorway.

The flames were in perfect mastery now, rising, falling, spiraling in a terrible ballet of light and darkness.

They threw the curtain over their heads and stumbled blind into the living room. Francesca felt her breath sucked away, felt the heat wrap itself about her, seeking her flesh. Her head was throbbing, her heart pounded in her chest like a nightmare trying to break free of sleep.

It was madness, what they were attempting, but there was no choice. They had to go into the heart of the fire if they were to escape from it. "Run!" cried Patrick, taking her arm. They staggered forward, heading in a straight line for where the door ought to be.

Something caught Francesca's foot. She pitched forward into the flames, pulling Patrick with her, rolling as she fell, tangling in the curtain. She had fallen across the body of the man she had shot.

Patrick felt his lungs fill with smoke. His skin felt as though it were about to catch fire. Steam rose in clouds as flames licked the curtain. He pulled Francesca to her knees, urging her forward to the door. He drew the front of the curtain back from his face. A wave of smoke billowed into his mouth and eyes, choking and blinding him. Where in Christ's name was the door?

With an effort they moved forward again, keeping as low as possible to find what little air lay trapped beneath the roiling smoke. Patrick knew they could have no more than seconds before they succumbed. Seconds, and the door as good as miles away, out of sight, out of reach in the blinding darkness.

Suddenly, they were there. Whoever had set the room on fire had closed the door behind him. It was a mass of flame. Patrick raised his foot and kicked hard, splintering the frame. The door caved in and fell outward into the passage.

Behind them, the room erupted with incredible ferocity as the glass in the windows exploded, letting a rush of oxygen inside.

The passage was an inferno. Its walls were wood paneling, not plaster, and all down its length flames tore like beasts at one another, leaping and snarling.

No time to hesitate. No choice. Just the flames and a last dash for life. "Run!" he gasped. They staggered out into hell. The curtain caught fire, they were ablaze, blind fish swimming in agony through a sea of flame.

The front door had been left open. That was the source of the oxygen feeding the flames. They staggered through, out to the landing, their arms flailing wildly to throw off the burning curtain. It fell away in fragments. Patrick fell to the floor, coughing, sucking air into his lungs. Looking up, he saw the astonished face of a fireman bending over him.

FIFTY

No one came for Dermot O'Malley's body. Neither Fischer nor Fazzini seemed to care. They sat and talked of personal matters: a niece's first communion, a mutual friend's illness, the difficulty of obtaining good French wine through the Anonna, the Vatican commissary. From time to time, one or the other would cast glances at Assefa, only to return to the discussion a moment later, indifferent to his presence. He sat immobile, dreaming of Abyssinia, where they built churches beneath the earth and dressed in robes of the purest white. Sometimes he thought he wanted to be sick.

About midnight, Fazzini stood up and shook hands with Fischer.

"Thank you for all you've done, John. I'll see someone comes to take that thing away tonight. I think we'd best not see one another again before the conclave. But if there's any serious delay, be sure to call. After tomorrow, it won't matter so much."

"You're certain everything will go as planned at the conclave? If they don't elect Migliau, we'll have all this to do again."

Fazzini shook his head.

"Even if the present Pope died of natural causes, Migliau would still succeed him. After tomorrow, there will be no doubt. Trust me. When he found the tomb again after it had been lost to us for so long, it was a sign. Be sure of it. He will be a great pope. The first of our kind. The first of a new line."

The Secretary of State turned to go.

"Father Makonnen," he said, "I think you are my responsibility. Cardinal Fischer has enough mess to clear up here. I think perhaps you should come with me. You are expected at the ceremony tomorrow morning. You'll need to be dressed rather more appropriately than that."

Numbly, not comprehending, Assefa stood. Fazzini led him to the door. Outside, a priest was standing, armed with a small Uzi. Like a refrain from a song, O'Malley's words came back to him: *"Over one hundred of the Dead have been brought to Italy from Egypt."*

They walked from the Governor's Palace along the Via della Fondamenta, heading for the Apostolic Palace, where the Secretariat of State was situated. The old cardinal went side by side with Assefa, the priest following several paces behind. Assefa wondered if the man would actually fire if he made a break for it. He had noticed a silencer on the gun.

"I'm sorry you've been dragged into all this through no fault of your own, Father," said Fazzini. "You had such a promising career ahead of you. I've looked through your file, you see. For a . . . black man . . . you've done very well.

"I've managed to get things tidied up in Dublin. You left a bit of a mess there, I'm afraid. A pity about Diotavelli. That caused a certain amount of embarrassment. It's all been put down to the IRA, of course. Such a convenience to have an active terrorist group available to take the blame.

"Now, of course, there's no question of your going back there. Or anywhere else, for that matter. You know too much. You've become a liability. Until now, we've been able to give no satisfactory explanation as to your whereabouts. The assumption has been that you were abducted by the IRA, but that story's beginning to wear a little thin. A body would be useful, but getting you to Ireland could prove bothersome after tomorrow. You wouldn't believe what airline and border security is going to be like a week from today."

He paused as they entered the Sentinel Courtyard.

"So," he went on, "the easiest thing seems to be for you to pop up at the audience tomorrow and for you to have a convenient accident. Don't worry, you won't have either the time or the opportunity to make a fuss.

"Cardinal Fischer tells me you came within a whisker of working out just what's going to happen tomorrow. Congratulations. I suppose I'd best fill you in on the fine details, since you'll need to know what's happening. As I say, you'll be in no state to do very much about it."

He paused.

"Well, the order of events is roughly this. After the Holy Father—you will notice I observe the formalities even at this late stage—after the Holy Father has greeted the heads of state and suchlike, they'll bring in the kiddies. He's expected to get down from his throne for this part, so he can mix with the orphans, pat them on the cheek, give them candies, and so on.

"And that's where we go in. They will come in from the piazza and make their way up the stairs to the Sala Clementina. There'll be fifty altogether, all dressed as Islamic freedom fighters, or whatever they call themselves. They all speak Arabic, of course, since they normally live in Egypt. There won't be any misunderstanding. Everyone will take them for Muslim fundamentalists. They will be heavily armed, and they have orders to shoot to kill.''

"They'll never get through," said Assefa, though he hardly believed it himself. "The Swiss Guards will cut them down."

Fazzini laughed quietly.

"How quaint of you, Father. You're thinking of the time they defended the Pope to the death against the soldiers of Charles V. When was that? Fifteen-twenty something? Things have changed. We've already seen to that little detail. Tomorrow, the Swiss Guards on duty at the Apostolic Palace will discover that they have been issued, not with live bullets as is customary on these occasions, but with blanks. Incidentally, you and your friend Father O'Malley did us something of a favor by bringing Colonel Meyer into this. He'll make an excellent scapegoat."

They walked a little farther in silence. From the San Damaso courtyard, they took a lift to the third floor of the Apostolic Palace.

"You'll be spending the night in a room not far from here, Father. Bernardo will give you something to help you sleep. Please try not to make things difficult for him. I'm sure you'll perform excellently in the morning.''

Assefa turned to go. All resistance had been sucked from him. There was no point in fighting odds like these. Before leaving, he turned to Fazzini.

"Why? What's it all for? What will you achieve by any of it?"

The cardinal eyed him. There was a look almost of pity in his gaze. Pity mingled with contempt.

"We will achieve God's purpose. Not as you conceive it, of course. Not as the Pope conceives it. Not as the Hindus and Muslims and Buddhists and all the mixers and appeasers and ecumenicists conceive it.

"Almost two thousand years ago, God gave power to Rome. He let it happen. Let them tear down His Temple, let them scatter His people. And then He took power from them again. This time He gave it to the Arabs. And then the Turks.

"That was His nightmare, you see, God's nightmare. All the prophets dreaming of a new Zion, and He gave them blood and ashes. For their sins. Because they gave Him the blood of doves and kept their children for themselves. And even when the nightmare seemed to have ended, when they thought they had woken up, He tricked them again. He let them think they had the truth, when all He had given them was lies and approximations. Half-truths are worse than falsehoods. Now they gave Him bread and wine instead of blood.

"He let them rule in the name of Christ, when all the time Christ was with us, bleeding them empty. Wars, inquisitions, plagues—they had to pay, you see, they had to match his sacrifice."

He stopped and strode across to the wall. Above the fireplace hung a wooden crucifix. He lifted it from the hook and held it folded in his hands. Then he stooped and tossed it on the flames.

"But now all that will change. They've had their chance. Now it's our turn. We will offer Him the sacrifice he wants."

He turned and looked hard at Assefa.

"Cardinal Migliau has been chosen by God to be His new high priest. There will be a temple again. And an altar. And worthy sacrifice. In a matter of days, there will be a conclave. In a matter of hours, they will burn white smoke. Migliau will be our new Pope."

"Not if God wills otherwise."

"God does not will otherwise. Listen. After tomorrow, there will be such an outcry in the world. There will be calls for a new crusade. Forget Russia and China. Islam will be revealed as the real enemy. And our new Pope will be the first to call for war.

"The day after tomorrow, it will be announced that he is being held hostage by the same terrorists who carried out the massacre in the Vatican. His life will be threatened. Prayers will be said for him in every church and every cathedral. There will be special masses. And during the conclave, the idea will be put forward that he should be elected pope. *In partibus infidelium.* The Vicar of Christ among the heathen. He will be chosen, have no doubt of that. And a few days later, there will be a dramatic rescue. He will return to Rome in triumph. And instead of forgiveness, he will proclaim the Tenth Crusade. Exactly seven hundred years since the last Christian stronghold in the Holy Land fell to the Saracen."

FIFTY-ONE

At first he thought he was in the hospital in Venice again. The same sounds, the same colors, a face bending over him. And then he saw the bandages. The fire had not been a dream or a hallucination.

"Where am I?" he pleaded.

"San Giovanni," a voice said. A woman's voice. "L'Ospedale San Giovanni. Next to San Giovanni in Laterano. You're in the emergency department. You were brought here several hours ago after a fire. Please don't worry, you aren't badly hurt. Just some burns. They say it's a miracle you escaped."

"Francesca . . ." He tried to get up, but a firm hand pressed him back onto the bed.

"It's all right. A woman was brought in with you. She'll be fine. Don't worry about a thing. Try to get some sleep."

"What time is it?"

"Don't you worry about the time. Sleep, that's what you need."

"No, you don't understand. It's important. Please, what time is it?"

"It's half past seven."

"Morning? Is it morning?"

"Of course. I told you you were brought here only a few hours ago."

"Where is she? Francesca . . . the woman they brought in with me?"

"You'll see her later. Lunchtime. You can see her at lunchtime."

"No, that'll be too late!" He pushed himself up again. He could see clearly now. He was in a curtained cubicle on a bed surrounded by drip stands and other pieces of emergency equipment. The nurse was on his left, a woman of about forty. She reached out and forced him down again.

"Try not to excite yourself. Your wife is in the next cubicle. You'll both be transferred to a ward later this morning, when the day porters come on duty."

He lay back exhausted. Above him, bright lights stabbed his eyes. Two and a half hours. He had to know what was happening.

"Please," he said. "I have to make a telephone call. It's extremely important."

The nurse hesitated, then nodded.

"All right. I'll have someone bring a wheelchair."

"My legs . . . ?"

"There's nothing wrong with your legs. I just don't want you on your feet tiring yourself. Wait here."

He had to speak with O'Malley. The priest had planned to stay at the Vatican until he was sure everything was safe. But he would have tried ringing again last night, but without an answer. Why hadn't he gone to the apartment? Surely someone there would have sent him on to the hospital. And what about Roberto? He had not even reported back. Patrick felt fear grip him like a cold hand.

An orderly came with a wheelchair and helped Patrick into it.

"Can you take me into the next cubicle, please. My . . . wife is there. I need to speak to her."

"I'm sorry, I was told to take you to the telephone."

"Dammit, I can't make this call without a number. She knows. I've got to speak to her."

"Only if she's awake."

The orderly pulled the curtain of Francesca's cubicle back a few inches. She was propped up in bed, her eyes open.

"All right, you can go in. But only a moment, mind, or I'll be in trouble."

"Patrick!" She pulled herself up.

He took her hand and squeezed it, making her flinch.

"I'm sorry, Patrick, it got burned a little. Still hurts."

"Sorry."

"What are you doing in a wheelchair? You aren't . . . ?"

"No, I could walk if I wanted. Hospital regulations. Listen, Francesca, it's half past seven. If Dermot hasn't succeeded in persuading this cardinal about the plot, it'll be too late to stop it."

"I've been thinking about that too. I only woke up half an hour ago. They told me you were still sleeping, that you shouldn't be disturbed. Dermot should have been sent here. Or Roberto. I'm worried, Patrick. I think something's happened."

"I want to telephone the Vatican, speak to the man they went to see. The cardinal. What was his name?"

She thought for a moment.

"He's an American. That's why Dermot trusts him. He had a German name, I think. I know—his name is Fischer, Cardinal Fischer."

"Does he spell that the English way or . . ." Patrick gripped the edge of the chair.

"What's wrong, Patrick? Is there . . . ?"

"Oh, Jesus. We didn't tell O'Malley. The Fisherman. Assefa won't have realized, English isn't his native language."

She took his hand, disregarding the pain.

"What is it, Patrick? What's the matter?"

He told her. She shut her eyes, closing out the pain.

"We can't be sure. Perhaps it's a coincidence."

He shook his head.

"We can't take that risk. What about Roberto? If O'Malley hasn't rung, they'll be opening those letters now. Can we reach Roberto? His apartment? His office? Do you have the numbers?"

She recited them from memory.

He called the orderly and had him wheel him into the corridor, where the public telephones were situated. The orderly found him a handful of *gettoni* and left him alone while he called.

There was no reply from Roberto's apartment. He tried his office number. Just as he was about to give up there as well, a man's voice answered.

"Pronto."

"Pronto. I'd like to speak to Roberto Quadri, please."

"Who is this?"

"A friend. It's urgent I speak to him. Do you know where he is?"

"I'm sorry, Signor Quadri was killed last night. A car crash on the Via del Corso. I'm very sorry. He was taken to the San Giovanni Hospital. I'm sure they can give you more details there."

Patrick put the phone down. He sat staring at the receiver for a moment, then stood up. The orderly rushed over.

"Signore, I don't think . . ."

Patrick pushed him out of the way. He ran back to the cubicle where Francesca was waiting for him.

"Hurry up," he said. "Find some clothes. We've got to get out of here. We've got to stop this thing ourselves."

The nurse who had been with Patrick earlier came running up, followed by a man dressed in a white coat.

"What's the meaning of this? I told you to stay in bed! What do you mean . . . ?"

Patrick shoved her aside and walked up to the doctor. He was young, probably just qualified, and looked as though he had had a busy night.

"Please don't argue," Patrick said. "This woman and I are checking out of here. I'm taking complete responsibility, do you understand?"

"But you can't . . ."

"It's an emergency, do you understand? I don't have time to argue."

He ran into his own cubicle and opened the bedside cupboard. His clothes were there, looking very much the worse for wear. They had been burned and soaked and covered in a variety of unpleasant-looking stains. He ripped off the gown he had been wearing and pulled on his shirt and trousers.

"Please, *signore*, you're in no condition to leave!" The nurse was determined to assert her authority.

"*Vaffanculo!*" snapped Patrick.

He pulled his shoes on and hurried back to Francesca's cubicle. She looked as bad as he did. He wondered how far they would get before the police hauled them in.

"Before we go," he said, "I have something to tell you."

"About Roberto?"

He nodded.

"You'd better sit down," he said.

They found a cab at the hospital entrance, at the top of the Via dei Quattro Coronati. The driver did a double-take when he saw them, but shrugged his shoulders. Some strange sights walk down the steps of hospitals.

Francesca told him to go straight to the Via della Rotonda near the Pantheon, where Roberto's apartment was located. She had taken the news of his death curiously well. Perhaps an abrupt exit had seemed better to her than the lingering death he had been facing for so long. Any tears she might shed could wait for later.

Behind a brick near the front entrance, she found a key that let them into the building and another to the apartment itself. Roberto had always kept it there in case he locked himself out.

Someone had got there before them. The place had been ripped apart. In Quadri's study, papers lay strewn over everything. Filing cabinets lay open, their contents gutted. Empty box files had been heaped up in one corner. The Brotherhood was making certain no loose ends remained untied.

Francesca dashed out of the study to the kitchen. Patrick followed her. Broken plates and empty jars littered the floor. She picked her way through them to the sink and put her hand inside the cupboard underneath. Taped to the roof of the cupboard, as in her own apartment, were two Berettas. Without a word, she handed one to Patrick.

"What now?" he asked.

She looked at him, then down at herself.

"We can't stay in these clothes," she said. "We have to get into the

Vatican, and I hardly think the Swiss Guards will let anybody in looking like us."

There were some of her own clothes still hanging at the back of Roberto's wardrobe. While she changed into them, Patrick took a shirt and suit to the bathroom. By the time they had finished, they still looked distinctly odd, but they might just make it past a suspicious sentry.

"What about transport?"

"The van is still parked in the Via Grotta Pinta. It's just a short walk from here."

"And when we get there?"

"We find Fischer. Or Fazzini. And we put a gun at their heads. What have you got to suggest?"

He shrugged.

"Nothing, I guess. If we had time . . ."

"Yes?"

"I'd look for Migliau. You say he's the head of the Brotherhood. That means he must be behind this whole operation today. And that means he must be in Rome. It wouldn't make sense for him to be in Venice."

"He has a lot of subordinates."

"In that case, why disappear at all?"

She frowned.

"Yes. You've got a point. But, as you say, we don't have time."

In his mind's eye he saw the television screen and the faces of dead children.

"No," he said. "We don't have time. But if you knew he was in Rome, where would you look?"

She shrugged.

"Anywhere. No special place. The Seven live in Jerusalem now. The Dead are in Egypt."

"Dermot said they had brought in one hundred of the Dead. Where would they stay?"

"In different houses, hotels even."

"But they'd have to come together at some point for briefings. There'd have to be a central point."

She thought.

"It's just possible that . . ."

"Yes?"

"Centuries ago, very early in their history, the Brotherhood had members in Rome. Not many, a few hundred at the most. But they had separate catacombs from the other Christians, where they buried their own dead. During the Decian persecutions, they met down there."

"What were they called? Did they have a name?"

"I don't think so. No, I'm wrong, they *did* have a name. I remember now. I was taken there once as a child. I must have been ten or eleven. They frightened me and I wouldn't stay inside. My father called them the Catacombe di Pasqua. The Easter Catacombs."

Patrick stared at her.

"Are you sure?"

She nodded.

"Then that's it," he said. There was a note of triumph in his voice. For the first time he thought he was one step ahead of his enemy. "That's where Migliau is. Not the Easter Catacombs, Francesca. The Passover Catacombs."

FIFTY-TWO

They fought through a growing crush of early morning traffic, forcing the van between cars and buses, breaking every rule of driving, even the Italian variety. Francesca drove south, past the Colosseum and down onto the Viale delle Terme di Caracalla. The catacombs, like so many others, were situated on the Via Appia Antica, the old Appian Way that had once taken Roman armies as far as Brindisi.

After the Porta San Sebastiano, where the Appian Way began, most of the traffic was heading into the city, and they were able to make some headway. The narrow road led them through open country, flanked on either side by the ruined tombs of the Roman upper classes.

Patrick felt a wave of desolation pass through him. The old tombs, for all their pomposity, were as broken and pitiful as the bones that lay in them. He thought of Brother Antonio dreading the resurrection lest a legless man dispossess him of part of himself. A joke, perhaps, yet one rooted in our longing for completeness. But crack open the tombs and what do you find? *Pulvis cinis et nihil.* He looked at Francesca. She had been buried and had returned—in body, he thought, not in spirit. Her old self had been left moldering in the tomb.

They turned off just after the Catacombs of Praetextatus, onto the Via Appia Pignatelli.

"The old Jewish catacombs are just over there on the right," she said, pointing. "The Brotherhood built theirs near them. If anyone stumbled across them, they were meant to think they were just more Jewish tombs and leave them alone."

They stopped about half a mile along, near a small farmhouse.

"The catacombs are beneath that farm," she said. "The people who own it are members of the Brotherhood. We may have to force our way in."

The door was opened by a tall man of about thirty-five dressed in a check shirt and muddy cords. He scowled at them and made ready to slam the door in their faces.

"*Che cacchio desidera?* What the shit do you want?"

"My name's Maria Contarini. I have an urgent message for Cardinal Migliau from the Seven."

He frowned and looked from her to Patrick.

"Migliau? The Seven? What are you talking about?"

For a moment, Patrick's heart sank. They had guessed wrong. Then another man stepped out of the shadows behind the first. He was younger and dressed in tight-fitting black clothes.

"What do they want, Carlo?"

"Says her name's Contarini. Says she's got a message from the Seven. For Migliau."

The younger man stepped into the light. He was suntanned and muscular-looking.

"Who are you?" he asked. He seemed edgy.

"I told your friend. Maria Contarini. With a message for Cardinal Migliau. A personal message. You're to take me to see him."

"Contarini? From Venice?"

"Yes. Listen, I don't have much time . . ."

"We've been looking for someone of your name. Francesca? Is that it? Francesca Contarini. You look . . ."

He froze as she took the Beretta from inside her coat and aimed it at his forehead. Patrick took her lead, drawing his own gun before Carlo could make a move.

"Easy now," Francesca said. "Come out here and put your hands on the wall, high as you can reach. You too, come on."

They got the two men outside and spread them against the wall. Patrick frisked the younger man and found a Browning Hi-Power in a shoulder holster. Carlo was unarmed.

"How many inside?" Francesca asked.

"Go to hell," said the young man.

"Who are you?" she asked. "How long have you been dead?"

"Not as long as you'll be."

"Don't count on it." She turned to Patrick. "Let's get them inside and tied up. Keep them covered while I check the house."

She slipped round the door, crouching low, her gun at the ready. The house was silent. No one challenged her. The place was little more than a one-story wooden shack with half a dozen rooms. It took Francesca less than a minute to confirm that the coast was clear.

"It's okay," she shouted. "Bring them in."

While she took her turn watching their prisoners, Patrick found rope in an outhouse. They tied the two men back to back on the floor in what looked like an extraordinarily uncomfortable position.

"They teach you to tie like that in Egypt?" Patrick asked.

Francesca nodded.

"Along with the knitting," she answered.

The entrance to the catacombs was in the outhouse. A small trapdoor opened onto a flight of wooden steps. Beside it, half a dozen kerosene lamps hung on hooks. There was a box of matches to hand. They each took a lamp and lit it.

Francesca hung back at the top of the steps.

"What's wrong?" asked Patrick.

She shivered.

"I told you, I couldn't face this place when I was a child. The bodies are still down there, you know. Or what's left of them. Thousands of loculi, a mile or more of passages. And only what light you can carry with you."

"Sounds like a nice place to take little girls for a day out. Would you like me to go first?"

She nodded.

"Funny though, isn't it?" She smiled. "Here I am, the ghost, frightened of a few musty old tombs, while you slip in without a care."

"What makes you think I'm not scared shitless?"

"Are you?"

"No. Of course not. I do this sort of thing every weekend for kicks."

"That's all right, then."

Holding the lamp in one hand, he swung his legs over the edge onto the ladder and began to climb down. Francesca waited until his head was clear, then followed him gingerly.

The ladder ended about forty feet down. Patrick stepped off, turning the knob on the side of the lamp to increase the illumination. He found himself in a broad paved area that led to a low, monumental doorway. The walls and edges of the doorway itself were painted with rows of symbolic motifs: vines, bowls of wine, lotus and acanthus leaves, peacocks, doves, and angels with gentle, faded wings.

Francesca joined him, adding her light to his.

"Do you have any idea of the layout of this place?" he asked.

She shook her head.

"Not a very clear one. It's on several levels. They're divided into passages with niches for the dead. I remember some larger tombs as well, and some side chapels. My father told me the large tombs contained the sarcophagi of martyrs or members of the Seven and the Pillars who'd died in Rome."

Patrick took his gun out.

"I'll leave the ghosts to you," he said.
She did not smile in reply.

They met their first ghosts moments later, as they passed through the doorway. The narrow passage swelled to form a small antechamber where mourners had held the funeral *agape*. Its stucco walls were covered from floor to ceiling with paintings, small portraits, each about ten inches square. The style was that of Roman Egypt, the faces replicas of those painted on mummy cases of the period—honest, lifelike representations of men and women who had lived and breathed some eighteen centuries ago.

Everywhere Patrick and Francesca looked, their eyes met the steady gaze of the dead. There were family groups marked out by a border of lilies or laurel, couples side by side, fathers, mothers, lovers—all serious and composed in death. Francesca shuddered and took hold of Patrick's arm.

"I'd forgotten this," she whispered. "They're so alive, they seem to be accusing us. Or waiting for us to join them."

"If we don't find Migliau soon, they won't have long to wait. Come on, through here."

Cobwebs hung at intervals like tattered flags in a dark cathedral. Patrick felt them brush his face as he moved along the first narrow passages, hemmed in by row upon row of marble slabs. Some of the slabs had fallen away, revealing pathetic heaps of cloth and bone.

At its end, the passage opened out again, becoming a mortuary chapel. A simple altar stood by one wall, flanked by twin sarcophagi. Above it, angels hovered, wingless in God. The face of Christ looked down, bearded, large-eyed, a man on the verge of godhood, his hands outstretched to receive his sacrifice. Patrick shuddered.

There was a sound of feet climbing steps a few yards away. A light appeared, then a voice called out.

"Paolo? *Che cosa stai facendo?*"

Patrick put down his lamp and pulled Francesca back against the wall of the chapel. The light wavered, then started in their direction. A man came into view, carrying a lamp like theirs. Patrick grabbed for him, taking him off balance and completely by surprise. He tried to cry out, but Patrick had already thrust an arm hard against his mouth, choking off his scream. The man's lamp dropped to the ground, splintering and bursting into flames. Francesca hurried forward and stamped them out.

With an easy movement, Patrick brought the gun to the stranger's head and hissed in his ear.

"One sound out of you and you really are dead. *Capito?*"

The man grunted and made what seemed like a nodding motion. Francesca frisked him, taking his gun.

"Okay, listen," Patrick whispered. "We've come for Migliau, I want you to take us to him. Understand?"

The man struggled, trying to break free. Patrick tightened his grip.

"Which way? Down the stairs?"

The man jerked his head. Patrick turned him and pushed him toward the opening out of which he had come. At the top of the stairs, he released his grip and took his lamp from Francesca.

"Go down one step at a time," he told the man. "I'll be right behind you."

The prisoner seemed about to protest, then thought better of it. One by one, he descended the flight of stone steps. Patrick followed him closely.

Ten steps from the bottom, the man jumped. He landed awkwardly, stumbled, and got to his feet.

"*Aiuto!*" he shouted in a loud voice. "Astolfo! Alberto! *Correte qui presto!*"

Patrick shot him as he started to run, pitching him back against a funerary slab. Followed closely by Francesca, he rushed to the bottom of the stairs. They had no choice. They had to go on. Migliau must be here. Patrick glanced at his watch. It was nearly nine o'clock. Just over an hour to go.

"Patrick, quickly—change into his clothes! They don't know who fired. The acoustics are bad, they may not be able to distinguish one voice from another. Hurry!"

Patrick shouted, "It's all right! I've got him," then hurried to do as Francesca had suggested. He ripped off Roberto's suit and pulled on the trousers of the dead man. He heard footsteps running farther along the passage, then voices.

"Nico? *Che succede?* Was that you? Who were you firing at?"

"An intruder. It's okay, I got him." Patrick's voice was muffled and distorted among the tombs.

Lights appeared, still some distance from them.

"Hurry, Patrick! Don't bother with the shoes."

Just in time, Patrick pulled the man's sweater over his head. He moved behind Francesca, holding his gun at her head.

There were three men, all holding lamps and guns.

"What's up, Nico? The cardinal's frightened. Who's this woman?"

"Now," Patrick whispered.

They moved apart, Francesca to the left, Patrick to the right, opening fire as they did so, round after round. Their opponents did not stand a chance.

Running now, they raced along the passage, Francesca in front, Patrick trailing, hampered without shoes. Suddenly, they turned a bend in the corridor. There was a blaze of light. Lamps flickered. A fire burned brightly in a metal brazier. Flames twinkled on mosaics of gold and silver. In a high dome, their reflections coruscated like exotic fish in a sea of bronze.

At the center of the room, dressed in black edged with red, an old man sat in a high-backed chair. His clothes were soaked with blood and his hands were crimson. In his right hand, he held a long, thin-bladed knife.

FIFTY-THREE

Migliau gave up the knife without a struggle. He seemed drugged, witless. Behind him, on a stone altar like the one Patrick and Assefa had found on San Vitale, the gutted body of a naked child lay on a film of fresh blood.

Francesca found a sheet on a low bed close by, on which the cardinal had evidently been sleeping. She covered the child and took him down from the altar.

"I loved him," whispered Migliau. Patrick bent to hear him. The cracked lips parted, whispering. "He was my son. They said it was necessary, that I should have a son. For today, to be my sacrifice. He was to be the balance. The payment for Christ's Vicar."

He looked down at the white-swathed bundle Francesca laid on the ground.

"They brought a woman for me," he said. "Seven years ago. She was white, so very white, and frightened of me. She should not have been frightened, I would not have harmed her. Her flesh was pale, not like the dreams of women I used to have. No more dreams now, no more. She stayed with me until a child was certain, then they took her away. I had started to desire her by then. But I do not dream of her.

"I called the boy Giovanni, after John the Zealot. They kept him in a house near the Patriarchal Palace, where I could visit him every month. They never let me see his mother. I don't know what happened to her."

He paused, contemplating a memory.

"All the time I knew his destiny, but I still loved him. That was part of the reckoning, they said, part of the balance. Without love, there could be no sacrifice, no sacrifice that had any meaning."

He looked at them, one after the other.

"I shall soon be Pope," he said, his voice still a whisper. "He is my guarantee, because I loved him. But I shall have no love. No love for God, no love for mankind. There will be nothing now but sacrifice. There will be balance upon balance until every drop is paid for."

Patrick took the old man by the arm and raised him to his feet.

"It's time to go," he said. He felt nothing, not even contempt.

"But there hasn't been time for a conclave yet."

"There will be no conclave." Was that true? If they didn't make it in time, the Church would need to find a new pope.

"What about the child?" Francesca asked.

"You take Migliau," he said. "I'll carry the boy."

It was a race against time now. The worst of the rush-hour traffic had cleared, giving them half a chance. Cars and pedestrians cleared out of their path. Once in the city, Francesca took a circuitous route through side streets, avoiding the main thoroughfares that she knew would still be heavily jammed. It was almost ten when they reached the Vittorio Emanuele bridge and eased themselves into the line crossing the river.

They drove straight across St. Peter's Square, stopping at the bronze doors that formed the main entrance to the Vatican. Within seconds, they were surrounded by Swiss Guards posted there as extra security for the ceremony inside. They formed a ring round the van, pointing their Uzis at its doors.

Francesca had already wound down her window.

"Quickly," she said. "I have Cardinal Migliau in the back. There's no time to explain. We have to take him to the audience."

A thickset sergeant strode across.

"Out!" he ordered, waving his gun at her.

"For God's sake," she said, "look in the back. It's Migliau. He has people planning an attack on the Pope."

"Cover her," the sergeant commanded two of his men. "You, you, come with me."

They went round to the back. A guard turned the handle and pulled the door open. Inside, Patrick sat beside Migliau. On the floor, the dead boy lay wrapped in his sheet.

"Was zum Teufel . . . ?"

Patrick raised his hands in the air and slid out. Two guards grabbed him and threw him against the side of the van. One frisked him, taking his gun.

The sergeant looked carefully at Migliau.

"Are you able to move?" he said. He thought the blood was the cardinal's own, that he had been wounded.

Migliau moved like a man in a dream. Slowly, he crawled to the door, where he was helped down by a guard. The sergeant scrutinized him more carefully.

"Mein Gott," the man whispered. There had been photographs of Migliau all over their barracks during the past week.

"He isn't hurt," said Patrick. "That isn't his blood. If you look beneath that sheet, you'll see where the blood came from."

A guard stepped into the van and drew back part of the sheet. A moment later, he was outside, throwing up.

"What the hell's all this about?" demanded the sergeant, grabbing Patrick roughly. He was still dressed in the trousers and sweater he had put on in the catacombs.

"Listen to me very carefully," said Patrick. "There won't be time to repeat this. Cardinal Migliau is responsible for . . . what your man saw inside. There's no time for explanations. You'll just have to take my word. People working for him plan to launch an attack during this morning's audience. They intend to kill the Pope and the children who will be with him."

He could see the confusion in the sergeant's eyes.

"If you don't believe me," Patrick insisted, "the Pope will be dead. And a lot of innocent children. Do you want that on your conscience?"

"What do you want us to do?"

"Take us to the reception. It's the only way. Please believe me, we're talking in terms of minutes. I don't know exactly when the attack will start or where it will come from. You'd better call up reinforcements. Bring in the Italian security services. But for God's sake hurry."

The sergeant was an intelligent man. He had already been disturbed that morning when Colonel Meyer's disappearance was reported. If this man and woman were involved in some attack, it was implausible that they would turn up like this, giving advance warning. He pulled a handset from his pocket and flicked a button.

"Captain Luft? This is Sergeant Genscher at the doors. We have an emergency. I'd like you here at once."

A curt voice replied. Genscher replaced his handset. Turning to Migliau, he took him by the shoulders.

"Your Eminence, is this true? What this man is telling me—is it the truth?"

Migliau stared at him as though unable to understand. Finally, he began to speak in a slurred voice.

"The truth? I am the truth. That is my destiny. They are about to proclaim me pope. There will be white smoke, and then it will be time for blood. I loved him—that's what is hard to understand."

Genscher shook his head. For the first time in his career, he felt genuinely frightened.

Seconds later, a man wearing a captain's uniform came running through the doors. He paused briefly to take in the scene. Genscher ran up to him.

They talked briefly, then Captain Luft came across to where Patrick and Francesca were standing together at the back of the van.

"Is this true? Is there a plot?"

"For God's sake," Francesca retorted, "we don't have time for evidence. Just tell your men to be ready and get some reinforcements quickly. You can have all the investigations you want afterward."

Luft did not argue. He turned to Genscher.

"Do as she says. Tell Hofmann and Wegener to bring their men here straight away. Contact Carabinieri HQ and tell Colonel Salvi I need help right away."

Genscher saluted and left.

"You," the captain said, addressing Patrick and Francesca, "come with me."

"Captain," Francesca implored, "there isn't time. You have to stop the audience. Get the Pope and everyone else out."

"I can't do that. The audience has already started. I don't have the authority to stop it."

"Who has authority?"

"Colonel Meyer, but he's missing. But even he would need authorization from Cardinal Fischer."

Francesca closed her eyes.

"Cardinal Fischer's mixed up in this. We have to take Migliau to the Holy Father. We have to shock them into evacuating the Sala Clementina. Please, Captain. There are lives at stake."

Luft looked from them to Migliau and back again. Genscher had told him he thought Migliau was mad. Mad and evil? Or maddened by being taken hostage?

"Very well," he said. "I'll take responsibility. God help you if you're lying." He turned to the guards still waiting by the van. "You men come with me. We're going to interrupt a papal audience."

FIFTY-FOUR

Patrick carried the child while Luft escorted Cardinal Migliau. In the Corridore del Bernini they caught a brief glimpse of the imposing Regia staircase before turning right onto the Scala Pia. Guards lined the staircase, saluting as the captain passed, yet betraying bewilderment on their faces.

At the top of the staircase, Luft hesitated before the doors of the Sala Clementina.

"This is your last chance," he said. "Once I open this door, there's no going back."

"If we don't go in," pleaded Patrick, holding the child out to the captain, "this will only be the first of many. We have no choice." He drew the sheet away, exposing the naked child.

Luft straightened himself and opened the door.

Red and black painted pillars rose majestically to a curved, frescoed ceiling on which the figures of Justice and Religion upheld a universe of order and love. In a painted sky, angels and cherubim circled in a cosmic dance. Light and harmony, the world unchanging, archetypes in a heaven of incorruptible delight.

On the floor, a different harmony, vanity seeking grace, jewels and precious cloths conferring an unworldly dignity on the merely mortal. Cardinals in red silk, bishops in robes of magenta, priests in black, and above them all, at the end of the room, seated on a chair of gold, the Pope in white.

Cardinal Migliau took a faltering step into the room. No one noticed him at first. Then a diplomat near the doors caught sight of him. Patrick followed, carrying the dead child in his arms. A deathly hush began at the back of the room where they passed and conveyed itself to the very end. Men and women parted to let the mad procession pass. No one tried to stop them, no one spoke a word.

Migliau held himself erect now, as though entry to this room had granted him new strength. He walked unaided past rows of staring faces, never looking to either right or left until at last he came to the foot of the papal chair, raised on a low dais above the crowd.

"Come down," Migliau said in a voice that was scarcely more than whisper. Those who had hung back to let him pass now crowded forward to hear him speak.

"Come down," he repeated. "That is my throne. Those are my robes. I depose you in the name of Christ."

The Pope did not respond at first. He could not understand what was happening. Migliau he recognized, but who were these others with him? And who was the dead child being carried behind the cardinal?

Captain Luft stepped forward.

"Your Holiness, I must apologize for this interruption. There's no time to explain. We must evacuate the chamber. There is reason to believe that some sort of attack is planned."

The Pope stood, horror on his face.

"I do not understand. Where is Colonel Meyer? Where is Cardinal Fischer? Do they know about this?"

"There is no time, Your Holiness. We have to clear the room. I have ordered the bronze doors closed. We need to get everyone as far away from the Sala Clementina as possible, into the *appartamenti*. Please trust me."

The Pope hesitated a moment longer, then raised his hand.

"Please," he called. "There is no need for panic. I have just been told that, for our security, the Swiss Guard wishes us to move to the apartments behind this room. I want you to follow their advice as quietly and speedily as possible."

At that moment, there was a movement in the crowd. A figure detached itself from the group of cardinals standing near the Pope. Cardinal Fazzini ran forward and threw himself in front of Migliau, taking his hand and raising it to his lips. Then a second cardinal and a third stepped forward and knelt in front of Migliau. They were followed by an archbishop and four bishops.

Patrick laid down the child's body. Looking round, he caught sight of the group of orphans who had been waiting to meet the Pope. They were wide-eyed, many of them openly weeping, while a handful of visibly distressed nuns bustled round them trying to restore order.

On the other side, a collection of priests stood in shocked silence. Patrick glanced at them. At the front stood Assefa.

"Assefa!" Patrick ran forward.

The Ethiopian did not respond. Patrick noticed that the priests on either side of him were holding him by the elbows, as though to prevent him falling. As he came up to his friend, one of them pushed him roughly away.

Patrick hit the man hard, knocking him back. He staggered, then rallied and came for Patrick. Dodging the priest's first blow, Patrick threw himself on him. There were shouts and screams as people struggled to get out of their path.

"Patrick!" Francesca's voice cut through the din. "He's got a gun! The other one."

Patrick twisted round to see the second priest aiming at him. There was nothing he could do. As he watched, Assefa swung his arm down, striking the priest's hand. Two more priests rushed forward and grabbed the first man as he too pulled a pistol.

At that moment, there was the sound of an explosion from below. Less than a second later, another followed it, then a third. They were breaching the bronze doors. Someone screamed. There was a burst of frightened voices.

Patrick ran to Assefa. The Ethiopian had collapsed. Patrick saw at once that he had been heavily drugged.

"Assefa, are you all right? What about O'Malley? What happened to him?"

Assefa struggled to form words.

"O' . . . Malley . . . dead. . . . Fischer . . . Il Pescatore. . . . Patrick, listen. . . . The guards . . . all bullets . . . blanks. . . . No good. . . ."

Patrick stood.

"Francesca, get the pistol from that other priest. I'll take this one. I've got to warn the captain that his men are armed with blanks."

Suddenly, there was a sound of shooting. Burst after burst of machine-gun fire echoed faintly from below. There were shouts from outside as Swiss Guards ran to defend the stairs.

"Captain," Patrick cried, running to where Luft stood by the doors into the *appartamenti*. He grabbed the captain's arm.

"Your men have been armed with blank bullets."

"What?"

"I don't know how. Can you try your gun?"

Luft said nothing. He walked across the room, unslinging his Uzi, and aimed it at the wall. He fired a short burst. The gun rattled, but the wall remained unharmed. When he turned to face the room again, Luft's cheeks had lost all color.

"I have a pistol," said Patrick. "So has Francesca. One of your men has the guns Sergeant Grenscher took from us at the doors. That gives us four."

"Four handguns against how many assault rifles? There'll be a massacre out there."

"Get your men to organize a barricade at the main doors!" said Patrick.

The captain nodded and gave the orders. In spite of everything, he was successfully keeping his head. A group of priests ran to give his men a hand.

A handful of prelates had gathered in a ring about the Pope and was making its way toward the rear doors, leading into the suite of rooms behind. Others were helping the orphans through. In the space in front of the papal dais, another ring of clerics had formed, taking turns to kiss Migliau's hand.

At the main door, heavy shooting was already in progress. Patrick found Francesca.

"Help me," he said.

They ran back to where Migliau stood surrounded by his followers. Patrick dashed into the middle of the circle and grabbed the old man. A cardinal tried to pull him off, but Patrick knocked him down. Francesca covered Patrick while he dragged Migliau out of the ring. At the far end of the room, the doors were riddled with bursts of heavy gunfire. Two Swiss Guards and a handful of priests were trying to hold the barricade.

They hauled Migliau into the center of the room, now deserted by fleeing diplomats and Vatican officials. The door buckled, then blew inward. The men holding it were thrown back.

Through the opening, black-garbed figures burst into the room. They were bearded and round their foreheads wore bands inscribed with Arabic. As they entered the room, they spread out, firing indiscriminately.

Patrick bent and fired at the first man, taking him in the chest. He died with a look of horrified surprise on his face. Francesca shot the man behind him. The others turned, preparing to open fire.

Patrick stood with a gun at Migliau's head.

"Don't come any closer!" he shouted.

The attackers hesitated, recognizing Migliau.

For the first time, Migliau smiled.

"It's all right," he said, his voice almost inaudible in the uproar. "Let him kill me. My son is dead. Let me join him. Let me be the supreme sacrifice. It will be all right."

He raised his hand and made the sign of the cross. Patrick began to drag him back, slowly, the gun pressed at his temple, back toward the rear of the room. More attackers joined the first group, all dressed the same, all bearing headbands proclaiming their love of martyrdom. As they entered the room, they too paused, uncertain what to do next. This had not been planned for. It should have been simple.

Francesca appeared beside Patrick. She had gone for Fazzini, and now she held him as a second hostage.

"You don't have to be afraid," wheezed Migliau, smiling at the gunmen in front of him. "Think how the Seven put him in the tomb. They were not afraid to make that sacrifice. You should not be afraid. You are doing God's will."

The leader of the attack force seemed to make up his mind. He had been trained to obedience. He raised his rifle and fired a single shot, crisp, perfect, like a sacrificial knife cutting through flesh. A fountain of blood rose from Migliau's head, bright as gold. The sacrifice was done. The veil of the Temple had been torn from top to bottom. And the saints would rise up out of their graves.

The next second, the man who had shot Migliau was thrown backward by a hail of bullets. More shots followed, coordinated from both sides of the room. From the doors of the side chambers, men in Carabinieri combat uniform moved in to finish off the remaining attackers. They were not firing blanks.

FIFTY-FIVE

He watched as Brother Antonio scraped the last cement from his trowel. The tablet was in place as it had been before. Francesca's name, her date of birth, her date of death. The old man rose painfully to his feet.

"It's done," he said.

Patrick nodded. It was done. Her ghost had been laid to rest at last. A ray of sunlight rested on her name. There were no flowers, no photograph.

He stepped out of the tomb into the March sunshine. It would be Easter before long. There would be white flowers in the churches. Priests would preach of death and resurrection. "I am the Resurrection and the Life," they would proclaim. In Rome, the Pope in his sick bed would issue an appeal for peace. And the nations would turn deaf ears as always.

He walked away from the tomb, through a long avenue of cypresses, past the long dead and the newly dead, in a straight line, down toward the sea. Across a swell of sun-salted water, Venice shone in the distance, lovely, pinnacled, redeemed out of sea and mud.

She was waiting for him, watching a small boat drift with the tide. She was not as he remembered her. There was gray in her hair and her eyes had seen things he could not imagine. He took her hand, and they stood for a long time without speaking, watching the waves. He had buried the past. Let them think she was dead.

"It's over," he said. "You're free."

She nodded. The shore seemed to stretch away forever.

"There will still be ghosts," she said.

He looked into her eyes, then brought her face close to his own and kissed her gently. She was not a ghost, he thought. He would not let her return to shadows.

She smiled and returned his kiss. But as she did so, she caught sight, far behind him, of the tomb where she had been reburied.

She remembered dim lights in a modern theatre, actors in ancient Irish dress, magical words she could scarcely understand. And Deirdre speaking to her lover before their death:

I know nothing but this body, nothing
But that old vehement, bewildering kiss.

She had known then that they would become lovers. But not how it
would end. Now that night was nothing but a memory, Deirdre's words
nothing but a half-remembered sound. She glanced at the tomb, at the
weeds choking its stone.

He was wrong. It was not over. When the time came, she would explain.
They would have a little time together: a year, two years perhaps. She took
his hand and turned to look at the sea again. For all its loveliness, Venice
was sinking beneath relentless waves. She held his hand more tightly. A
year, two years. What did it matter? Nobody has forever, after all.

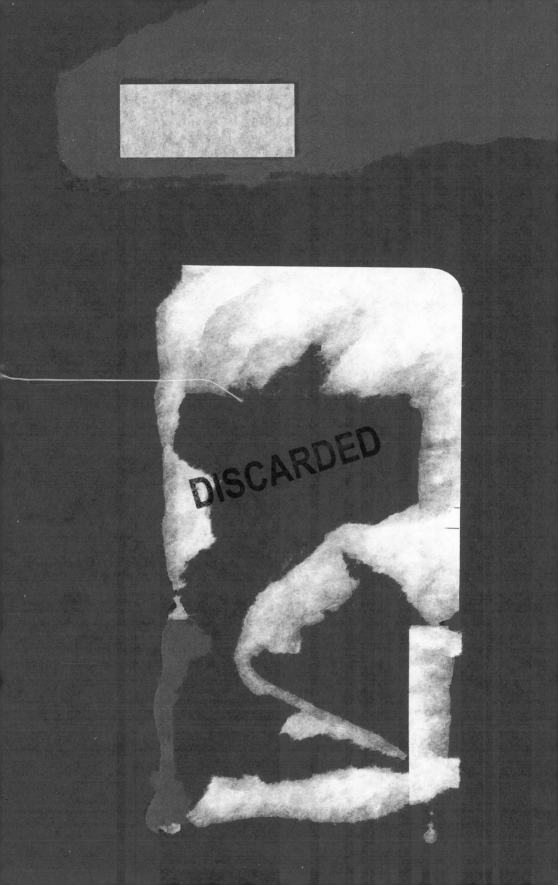